BESTSELLING AUTHOR
THE EXTINCTION S

AUGMENTED

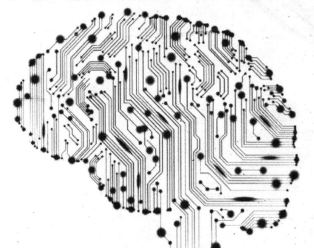

JAMES D.
PRESCOTT

ISBN: 978-1-926456-32-4

Books by James D. Prescott

The Genesis Conspiracy

Extinction Code
Extinction Countdown
Extinction Crisis

New Release!
Augmented

Dedication

A special thanks goes out to Ethan Siegel, theoretical astrophysicist, professor and science writer, for his help scrubbing any glaring scientific errors from the manuscripts. Any that remain are mine and mine alone. As well, a thank you to E. Paul Zehr, professor of neuroscience and futurist, for your terrific help navigating the dizzying future of neural implants. Much gratitude to Lisa Weinberg and the rest of the beta team for keeping me on my toes. Finally, to you, dear reader, who make all of this possible.

"Just because you're paranoid doesn't mean they aren't after you."
— Joseph Heller, *Catch-22*

Chapter 1

Pacific Ocean
Ten years from now…

Dr. Nicholay Panov nudged the joystick, engaging the sub's thrusters to keep her leveled. He'd been descending through the murky depths of the Pacific for nearly an hour. His eagerness to reach the bottom was strong, verging on overwhelming. At least then they would know once and for all if Ben Fisher was crazy or whether there really was something strange down here.

An oceanographer with nearly fifty years of experience, Nic knew every trip to the bottom had a habit of revealing something we hadn't known before. And it was just as true today as it had been in Robert Ballard's day. Back in the 70's, Ballard—famous for locating the wreck of the *Titanic*—had discovered the existence of hydrothermal vents. Ostensibly they were little more than chimneys spewing out a rich cocktail of toxic chemicals. Impressive as that was, it hadn't been the most interesting part. What had fascinated Ballard and company had less to do with the vent itself and more to do with the abundance of life the vent happened to be sustaining. In addition to shaping oceanography for decades, the discovery also gave scientists in far-off fields a new appreciation for the resiliency of life. If it could thrive at crushing depths once thought to be inhospitable, what then might be possible in the oceans of Europa or Enceladus?

"Nic, you're fifteen hundred meters from the bottom."

"Roger that," he replied, checking his gauges.

This was the second descent they'd made in as many days. The first had been via an autonomous underwater vehicle (AUV) named Betsy, but she had suffered some mechanical malfunctions that had forced them to abort. And yet, as the wise old sages liked to say, with every failure came opportunity. The handful of grainy images the AUV had brought back had offered a tantalizing hint that something was down there. The other scientists on board were far less convinced. Ramon and Alfred, in particular, believed the darkened shape was nothing more than a trick of light and shadow, a point Nic had been forced to concede as a possibility. The lack of echo return by Betsy's sophisticated radar systems only strengthened the opposition's resolve. They had scanned the ocean floor every which way and had seen nothing.

But all of this was on Ben Fisher's dime, a reality that helped in some small way to take the edge off whenever Nic caught himself worrying they might be barking up the wrong tree. Faced with the unknown, hadn't Nic really been more interested in subverting his own expectations? A kind of buttress against the massive whopper of a disappointment that was surely on its way. That being said, if this was anything close to what Nic believed it was, then he was about to give Robert Ballard and his crew of superstars a real run for their money.

The sub began to shudder and Nic steadied himself as the claustrophobic vehicle listed from side to side. Several minutes passed before a call came down from the *Archipelago*.

"Hey, Nic, it's Alfred. We're seeing a rather large commotion on the water surface up here. It almost looks like the ocean is boiling. Are you seeing anything on your end?"

"Boiling?" Nic shot back in an almost accusing tone. "Nothing here." His hands touched the sub's cold metal sides as he leaned forward, peering out the tiny porthole before him. And that was when he saw it: a massive disturbance in the water around him.

Then, without a hint of warning, the sub's nose jerked forward, seeming to fall through empty space. Nic felt his insides rise up into his throat as though he were in the front seat of a roller coaster. The force of the sudden drop snapped the umbilical connecting it to the *Archipelago* mothership and in turn severed the sub's power. The vehicle continued falling nose first before its abrupt impact back into the water. The force threw Nic forward, shattering his cheekbone as the side of his face struck the porthole.

Wounded and pitched at a forty-five-degree angle, the sub continued its descent. But the sudden, baffling drop had done more than just batter and bruise them. The severing of the umbilical meant Nic had to rely on the backup batteries. Sitting in near darkness, his lower lip pouring blood, Nic watched as a hairline fracture along the porthole began to spread.

"Please, God, no, not like this." Growing up as a young man in Communist Bulgaria, religion had been seriously frowned upon. And yet, down here, all alone in the growing gloom, he saw no harm in appealing to a greater power, however slim the chances of its existence might be.

Then, all at once, the logical part of his brain came back online, neurons firing in a desperate attempt to save his hide from certain death. But any solution required some understanding of what had gotten him into this mess in the first place. Falling through empty space when you were nearly six thousand meters beneath the ocean's surface didn't make a lick of sense. That much was clear. More inexplicable still was the glowing blue light that was fast approaching.

He watched it, transfixed, until he realized the crack he'd seen earlier now ran the full length of the porthole window.

"Alfred," Nic said, struggling against his agonizing injury. "Do you read me?"

The radio came back with a hiss of static.

Sinking to the bottom of the Pacific with no power, Nic was truly on his own.

The strange light drew closer.

When his final thoughts came, they were for his daughter, Sienna. And for the crew of the *Archipelago*. Had they made it to safety?

The hope had barely had time to crystallize in Nic's mind when the porthole gave way, exposing him to the full force of nearly six thousand atmospheres.

Chapter 2

...And in other news, an international search for an oceanographer and his crew last seen in the Pacific Ocean has been called off. Nicholay Panov and his research vessel, Archipelago, *disappeared nearly a week ago.*

The search continues, however, for Elizabeth Howard, a reporter with the Seattle Times, *missing since last week. Surveillance footage shows her leaving the* Times' *headquarters late Monday evening. Friends and family grew suspicious the following day when Elizabeth failed to show up for work.*

Now over to the East Coast where Miami's mayor, Juan Castro, refutes allegations that his city is lost, despite two of the surrounding three counties sitting under several feet of water. Fears of rising sea levels are once again pushing residents of New Orleans further inland. Hundreds of families have already been evacuated as part of the government's massive relocation effort, one that is expected to continue well into the next decade.

Water is also at the heart of a problem facing the west, where record-level drought has reduced the once mighty Rio Grande to a trickle and threatens to leave millions without viable drinking water.

Across the country, air quality dipped into the danger zone once again as the National Weather Service advised folks to stay indoors, and if you're going to venture out, be sure to wear a government-certified breather.

And finally, tonight, some good news. Neural-Sync, the world's leader in neural enhancement technologies, has reported record profits for the fourth quarter of last year. COO and spokeswoman Lori Fisher issued a brief statement earlier today saying the future has never looked brighter.

Chapter 3

He came awake with the taste of blood in his mouth. He peeled open his eyes, a gargantuan effort in and of itself, feeling like a man who had emerged from a long, restless sleep, only to find himself in a strange place he didn't recognize.

Where the hell am I?

The back of his throat made a loud clicking sound as he labored to swallow, his lips wet with a warm, sour liquid.

And why am I bleeding?

The room he found himself in was immense. The embers of late afternoon sun bled in via a bank of ten-foot-high windows along the far wall. To his left, a row of bookcases stretched up to a second story, the top shelves visible through a glass floor. Close by was a large u-shaped couch, cluttered with a pile of throw pillows.

This was someone's home. A nice home. A modern, insanely expensive home. The kind generally inhabited by bankers and tech giants.

But why does everything look so big?

That was when he realized he was lying on the floor, face down, his arms and legs splayed out like the victim of a crazed Aztec priest, awaiting a ceremonial sacrifice.

In a single motion, he pulled himself into a ball, every muscle in his body screaming in pain. But nothing his tender muscles had to say right now compared to the blazing siren of agony pulsing from the back of his neck.

He rose to his knees, instinctively reaching a hand toward the source of blinding agony only to spot the twelve-inch knife clotted with blood still clenched in his right hand—a hand which appeared to have been dipped up to the wrist in red paint and set to dry in a hot patch of sun. He let out a tiny cry and flung the knife as though it were a coiled snake about to strike him, sending it skittering across the hardwood floor, its momentum halted by the leg of a nearby dining room chair.

Stricken through with terror, Ben's eyes shot back to the couch. Even in the dying light, it was clear he had been wrong about exactly *what* he had seen there. It wasn't merely a heap of dirty throw pillows. A woman was sitting amongst them, her head tilted back at a distinctly unnatural angle. The bony fingers of a cold, skeletal hand curled around his pounding heart. Then he saw the deep red gash that ran from one side of her neck to the other and all at once two things became perfectly obvious: First, whoever this woman was, she was no longer living; and second—well, that one had to do with the bloody knife he had thrown across the room. The one coated with the same blood now smeared all over his hands.

Chapter 4

He sprang to his feet.

This was only a dream. He chanted the words over and over, slapping himself across the face, praying he might wake up in his bed, a disturbing novel tented over his chest. But that pounding ache at the back of his neck was telling him otherwise. This was no dream. Dreams featured plenty of horrors and sometimes things that went bump in the night. Rarely did they include pain. Not like this.

He went over to the woman and pressed the back of his hand against her cheek. She was cold, her flesh the consistency of hard clay. She was wearing what had once been a matching white hoodie and sweatpants. A deep red stain now ran down the front of it. But even in her current state, he could see at one time she'd been beautiful.

"A-all right," he stammered. "Enough messing around. It's time to wake up. Wake up…" He'd been about to shout his own name, in a commanding, pep-talky sort of way. Instead, he stopped short.

He wheeled around, scanning the expensive open living space, feeling a nearly overwhelming surge of nausea.

"What's my name?" He rubbed his blood-encrusted hands down the length of the dark blue suit he was wearing. "Okay, cut the crap, this isn't funny anymore," he shouted at the room, empty except for the echo of his own voice and the dead woman on the couch. "The hell's my damn name?"

Instinctively, his hands began patting his pockets. A second later he found the phone. Out it came, his fingers shaking violently as he struggled to unlock the device. It wanted to scan his fingerprints. "Oh, come on, you piece of crap." He pressed down harder and was denied once again. Yes, of course, it didn't recognize him. He licked his index finger, ignoring the metallic taste of blood, and rubbed it against his thigh before trying again. This time the phone unlocked.

He went into the settings and sitting right there at the top of the page was the name Ben Fisher. He repeated it several times, trying it on the way someone might try on a new shirt. "Ben Fisher...Ben Fisher."

Something about it felt wrong, but what did that mean in a moment like this when nothing felt quite right? Quickly, he went into his pictures. He didn't need to flip very far to find what he was looking for. A picture of a beautiful woman smiling back at him. He swiped again, and this time she was laughing, dressed in nothing but a bathrobe, her hair tied up with a towel, trying to block the photographer—him?—from taking an unflattering picture.

Ben—if that was his name—staggered back to the couch, his legs stiff with pain and fear. He reached out and placed the image on the screen next to the dead woman's face and gasped.

They were the same and seeing that suddenly filled him with an overwhelming sense of grief for a woman he couldn't remember. But pictures didn't lie. And neither did the blood on his hands. He held out his trembling fingers and stared at each of them. Were these the hands of a wife killer? Except he wasn't wearing a ring. And neither was she. So that meant this wasn't his wife, not that that changed the murder equation. Perhaps she was his girlfriend. And did that mean this fancy house belonged to him? Or was it hers? Of course, none of that mattered, not compared to the biggest question of all. What exactly had happened here?

Up near the ceiling, a glint caught his eye. For the first time since he had snapped awake into this living nightmare, he was filled with something resembling hope. The house had a surveillance system, which meant, good or bad, his questions would soon be answered.

Chapter 5

The thought of calling the cops had occurred to Ben. No doubt about it. Hell, how could anyone wake up to a nightmare like this without the notion even crossing their mind? A guilty person, that was who. But he also knew any cop who arrived to find a dead woman and an amnesiac with the victim's blood all over his hands wasn't likely to let him off with a slap on the wrist. He wasn't O.J., after all; he was regular ol' Ben Fisher, whoever the heck that was. By the looks of things, a guy who had money. But even high-powered attorneys had their limits. Besides, something deep inside the marrow of his bones told him he was innocent.

Ben hurried from the living room and down a long hallway, opening every door he could find. Normally these kinds of surveillance systems had a DVR recorder stashed in a closet somewhere. The key was finding the machine and seeing what it had to say. If the playback confirmed his guilt, Ben would turn himself in and be left to grapple with what he had done until the day he died. But if he hadn't done it…

He was in the middle of searching a broom closet when a faint, almost rhythmic noise caught his ear. His muscles tightened in recognition. Those were police sirens. He ran to the front door and found it already ajar. Behind him, a grand staircase ascended from the entrance to the second floor. Gripped by a surge of adrenaline, Ben sprinted up to the landing, taking three and sometimes four risers at a time, a feat that surprised even him. He continued his frantic search, arriving at last upon a room with a comfy-looking king-sized bed, at the foot of which sat a large wicker trunk.

Picture frames on the night tables displayed images of him and the dead woman. To his left was an impressive walk-in closet lined with dresses and shoes. Next to that was a walk-in bathroom, easily the size of a small apartment. But it was the closet on the other side of the room that caught his eye. The door leading into it had been kicked in. Ben pushed his way inside, snapping on the light, distinctly aware that time was quickly running out.

A disheartened sigh escaped his lips. The space on the shelf where a DVR recorder had once sat was empty. Not only that, but the wires protruding from the wall had been cut. Had he cut them in order to destroy any proof of his crime? If so, why would he have kicked in the door? He fished out a small set of keys from his pocket and saw that one of them fit the locking mechanism, still attached to the door's damaged frame.

But there wasn't time right now to dwell on the meaning of any of this. He needed to get moving fast. Ben's gaze dropped to the set of keys in his hand, from which dangled the starter for an Alfa Romeo. A surge of optimism began coursing through his veins, nudging his adrenaline-induced fear momentarily to the side. It was looking more and more certain, at least to him, that he hadn't killed anyone. The missing recorder and the open front door were proof enough of that. More to the point, he needed to find out who was responsible for this heinous crime or risk spending the rest of his life in prison.

Outside, the wail of police sirens was growing louder and Ben decided it was time to go.

Chapter 6

Ben followed the Romeo's built-in GPS, which routed him along Highway 99 and into the industrial district. The GPS in his car didn't only indicate the street his house was on, but also the city in which he lived: Seattle, Washington. It was a rare day here without rain. That was the strange thing about amnesia, Ben was beginning to learn. He might not remember who he was, but somehow, he still had access to the deep-seated part of his brain that retained useless memories of weather patterns, mostly highlights of never-ending rain.

That was where the industrial district came in. Relatively secluded, it would provide a haven while he tried to sort out the best way to extricate himself from this colossal and tragic mess. While some might consider it the seedier part of the city, the industrial district was separated from the trendier West Seattle neighborhood by the Duwamish River, the water acting as a natural barrier between the tougher neighborhoods to the east and the laid-back residential area to the west.

He turned onto South Idaho, flanked on each side by a collection of small warehouses and fulfillment centers. He pulled up next to a company called Tellco. Material Handling Solutions. The irony wasn't lost on him.

Solutions of one kind or another were precisely what he needed right now.

Ben killed the engine and undid his seatbelt. Wincing, he ran the pads of his fingers along the two raised bumps at the back of his neck. The flesh there felt mottled and singed, as though someone had taken a cattle prod to the patch of bare skin beneath his skull.

Next, he patted himself down more thoroughly, looking for anything in his pockets that might help jog his memory or shed some light on his current predicament. His fingers encountered a sharp object in the inner right pocket of his suit jacket. Reaching in, he removed a money clip containing a driver's license alongside miscellaneous bank and credit cards, all snuggled between six crisp one-hundred-dollar bills. The license bore his name, Ben Fisher, along with a picture. His eyes flicked between the face on the license and the one looking back at him from the rearview mirror. They were the same. Handsome in a Nordic sort of way, with pronounced cheekbones, a full set of lips and short-cropped blond hair with dark blue eyes. Only, the face on the license looked calm, self-assured, while the man staring back at him had a pair of deer-in-headlights-looking eyes and sallow skin. Put another way, he looked like a man who'd been through a wringer.

Below his name was his DOB. But even before he had time to crunch the numbers, a four and a zero flashed on a big dark screen inside his mind. And it was right: Ben was forty years old. He scanned further down still and saw his height listed as six feet one and his weight recorded as a hundred and ninety-five pounds. He seemed to be in good shape for his age, except for a pair of early-stage love handles he could feel pushing against the sides of his shirt.

He leaned forward and began searching through the center console, looking for something he could use to clean the blood off his hands. He popped the glove compartment and found a pack of sealed wipes, hastily scrubbing the cold cloth between his fingers and over the rest of his hands. Next, he checked his face carefully for blood spatter and found none, which only reinforced his growing conviction that he was an innocent man. God, at least he hoped he was. With that amount of blood, it was hard to believe, were he indeed responsible, that the rest of him wouldn't have been covered in it.

Before long, his mind began to turn to other questions. Who was the dead woman? What was her name? His phone might be able to help, at least for now. Soon enough, the cops would be using it to track his whereabouts as they began to close in on him. But until then, he intended to learn as much about his situation as he could. He yanked the phone from his pocket and went straight to his text messages. The name 'Amanda Lippeatt' was second from the top. He scrolled through their most recent conversation.

Ben: Happy anniversary, my love.

Amanda: Aww, you remembered. I was starting to wonder.

Ben: I made reservations for Canlis at eight. Hope that's okay.

Amanda: Can't wait! Enjoying a glass of Côte de Nuits before I get dressed.

Ben: On my way home now. Save some for me. See you soon.

He sat staring at the words for several minutes. Those were hardly the words of two people who hated one another. Scrolling back further into the past, it soon became clear the two of them rarely fought, certainly no more than any other couple, and nothing that would even begin to account for what had happened.

17

Ben went to his email. In what appeared to be his main account, benfisherceo@neural-sync.com, there were nearly a thousand unread emails.

He stared at the email address. "Okay, so I'm the CEO and presumably the owner of a company called Neural-Sync," he said to no one in particular. "Hi, I'm Ben from Neural-Sync." He repeated the greeting a handful of times, hopeful it might shake loose memories of a life he couldn't recall.

Most of the emails seemed to deal with customer acquisition rates, lowering costs and projected earnings. Which left him wondering, what exactly was Neural-Sync selling?

He scrolled down. One of his emails was from someone named Lori Fisher, the company's COO. Were they related? A sister or a cousin, perhaps? Ben pulled up his phone contacts, scrolling until he found her name and dialed. It barely rang twice before a female voice answered.

"Ben, is that you?" She sounded firm, but caring. Her voice had the rough quality that came with a lifetime of smoking and maybe a little more, but something told him she hated cigarettes, hadn't touched one in her life.

Was that a misplaced slice of his life coming back to him? He couldn't say for certain.

"Is this Lori Fisher?"

"Sure it is." Confusion registered in her voice at once. "Ben, is everything all right?"

"How exactly do we know each other?" he asked, cutting right to the chase.

A moment of uneasy silence followed. "Ben, is this another one of your crazy jokes? Because if it is…"

"It's not a joke," he said rapidly and then paused, struggling with just how much to say. "I just need you to answer the question. How is it that we know one another?"

"You're my brother."

Ben nodded, feeling for the first time as though he had planted his feet on something resembling firm ground.

"What's with all the questions? You're starting to worry me." She hesitated near the end, although it was becoming apparent she was starting to doubt her brother's sanity. "Are you in some kind of trouble? Do you need help? Should I call the police?"

"No," Ben shouted forcefully before disconnecting. That came out way too harsh. Nevertheless, there was no need to call the cops. Not when they were already at his house, figuring out ways to pin a murder on him.

What he needed, really needed, was to get his hands on that recorder. If the video showed him committing an unspeakable act… well, he already knew what that would mean. But if it showed anything else, then it might give him a fighting chance at clearing his name and finding the real perpetrator, all in one fell swoop.

His sister—weird as that was to say about someone he didn't remember—had already demonstrated how eager she was to involve the police, perhaps even reveal his location. Her intentions might be perfectly altruistic, but it wasn't a chance he could take right now. He needed to find someone else, someone who was willing to help, rather than doing what they deemed might be in his best interests.

Ben scrolled down the contacts on his phone. Most of the names were women. He picked one at random, a woman named Catherine Hindel, and dialed.

"Really?" an angry voice answered.

"Catherine?"

19

"You've got a hell of a lot of nerve calling me after what you did."

The blood drained from Ben's face. She couldn't possibly know, could she? "Nerve?" he asked.

"Do you think you can just treat people like trash and get away with it?"

"I don't understand."

She scoffed. "No shit, you don't understand. What sick part of you thinks that a text message is the mature way to end a relationship?"

"Relationship?"

"Why did you even call? You wanna rub it in my face, don't you? For your sake, Mr. Benjamin Fisher, I hope to God you aren't trying to get something going again between us. You're lucky I didn't spill the beans to Amanda."

Ben stared off at an eighteen-wheeler backing into a nearby loading dock, feeling confused and sick to his stomach. The sun had just disappeared, casting long shadows along the nearly deserted street. "L-listen," he stammered. "I must have the wrong number." And hung up. Had he really been unfaithful to Amanda with this woman? Perhaps there was an innocent explanation. Sometimes people got the wrong impression, didn't they? One person's platonic dinner was another person's hot date.

So far, this wasn't going the way he had hoped. He tried another number in his contact list. This one belonged to a 'Lindsey Martin'.

The person who answered sounded calm and rational. Ben allowed himself a moment of hopefulness she was someone who could help.

"Lindsey?"

"Ben?"

"Yeah, listen, I know this is going to sound strange, but how do we know each other?"

A pause. Lindsay's voice tightened. "Uh, what do you mean?"

"There are gaps in my memory. Big gaps. I know, it sounds weird, but if you could indulge me…"

The laughter that erupted from Lindsay was deep and heartfelt. "Why not. Sure, I'll play along. Who knows, maybe this is part of some twelve-step program you're doing. Making amends to those you've harmed, right? *You* want to be indulged. That's cute. Well, we dated briefly about six months ago. You told me you loved me and wanted to spend the rest of your life with me. And like an idiot, I believed you until I found out you were also dating another woman named Kathleen. Not to mention your live-in girlfriend Amanda, but I already knew about her. Things were sort of on the rocks. That's how you put it. So I shouldn't have been entirely surprised, but yeah, one day you just stopped calling. You want to know what kind of person you are, is that it? How about a handsome, wildly successful man with a ton of potential to be a really good, if not decent, human being?"

"Potential? I sound like a grade-A douche."

Lindsay snickered. "Your words, not mine. But I won't quibble with their accuracy."

"You mentioned that Amanda and I were on the rocks…"

"Maybe you were, maybe you weren't," Lindsay shot back. "Hard to know now what was true and what wasn't."

"Have we spoken since then, you and I?"

She sighed. "No. Well, not unless you count the weird-ass text you sent me."

21

"What text?"

"Yeah, it was a couple days ago. Hey, what is all this, Ben?"

"Believe me, I wish I knew. Something bad happened and I'm trying to get to the bottom of it."

"Are you having some kind of mental breakdown? Is that what's going on?" For the first time, Lindsay almost sounded worried.

"I'm not sure. Do I have a history of mental health issues?" he asked her, unable to overcome the bizarre sensation that came with talking about himself as though he were a stranger.

"None that I was aware of. At least, nothing you admitted to."

"Fair enough. Okay, thank you."

"Anything else?"

"Only that I'm sorry. I know at this point it doesn't mean much." He drew in a deep breath and let it simmer in his lungs for a moment. "I know it's hard to understand. In fact, I don't think I get it myself, but I'm only starting to learn who Ben Fisher was. And at first blush, I can't say I like what I see."

"Good luck, Ben," she said, sounding as though she thought he was going to need it, and then hung up.

Staring down at his phone, Ben recalled something Lindsay had said—that two days ago he had sent her a strange text message. He went back to his own texts and scrolled down until he found their last conversation. He stared at the message he had written to her, wondering what it meant. Just three simple words, but with an infinite number of meanings:

Take it out!!!

What was the "it" he had been talking about?

It sounded sexual. Without a doubt, that was probably how she had interpreted it as well.

Just then his phone began vibrating as it played the theme from *2001: A Space Odyssey.*

How did he know that?

The name on the screen read Sienna Panov. He hesitated, justifiably gun-shy, before he answered.

"This is Ben."

"For the sweet love of God, I finally got a hold of you."

Ben felt a lump settle in his throat. He wasn't sure if he could take a fresh shellacking from yet another former girlfriend. "Please tell me we never dated." The dread in his voice was unmistakable.

"I beg your pardon, Mr. Fisher?"

"Oh, never mind," he replied, a sense of relief washing over him. "Listen, Mrs. Panov…"

"Call me Sienna."

"Fine. Sienna. I don't know what this is about, but this is really not a good time…"

"Hold on, don't hang up!" she pleaded. "I've been trying to reach you for well over a week. It's about my father."

"Your father?"

"Nicholay Panov. The oceanographer. You hired his team to investigate deep-sea thermal vents in the Pacific. You can't have forgotten. You paid the oceanographic institute nearly five million—"

A knock came at Ben's window. He glanced over and a heavy-set, middle-aged man sporting a beer baby glared back at him. "Buddy, you gotta move your car."

Ben held up a finger to indicate he'd only be another minute. His head was spinning. "Five million?"

"Yes." She paused, suddenly unsure. "It was you and I who sorted out the details. Surely you're aware the research ship he was on, the *Archipelago,* and her crew disappeared without a trace. The U.S. Navy claims they searched for days, but I have reason to believe they did no such thing. There's something they're hiding, I'm certain of it. Something terrible happened and they're trying to sweep it under the rug."

Ben shook his head. "I don't know what you're talking about, honestly, I don't." The chances she was going to believe him were nil, but truer words had never been spoken.

Another knock from the pregnant man outside. "Hey, asshole, move your car this minute or I'll move it for you." The guy was less than an inch from the driver's side window, his hot breath forming a ring of expanding fog on the glass. Ben nodded and started the car.

"My father's missing and I need your help finding out what happened to him. Every door I find keeps getting slammed in my face."

"Listen…" he began to say.

"The only reason he was out there was because you were the one who hired him. Mr. Fisher, and at this point, you're my last hope…"

"Sienna, this is really not a good—"

"I won't take no for an answer and that's final."

Ben couldn't help but smile at her persistence. He also recognized an opportunity. "Fine, I'll help you, but there's something I need in exchange."

Now it was her turn to stammer. Ben sensed at once how his insistence on a *quid quo pro* might have come across.

"For heaven's sake, I didn't mean it that way. Listen, I'll explain in person. Where can we meet?"

"How about the Square Knot Diner?"

Ben punched it into his GPS. "Fine. I'll meet you there."

He was about to slide the Alfa Romeo into drive when the car door flew open and a pair of rough hands closed around his left wrist and the back of his neck.

Ben let out an involuntary yelp of pain as he was dragged from the car, the engine still idling, and thrown face first onto the ground. For a moment, he had a flashback of being at his house, looking up to see his girlfriend's dead body. That initial burst of sensory images was drowned out by the stabbing pain behind his ears. He felt his arms being twisted behind his back and a pair of cold metal bracelets closing around his wrists. He cocked his head enough to see a burly-looking cop digging his knee into the small of Ben's back. The cop wore mirror shades, even though the sun was nowhere in sight.

"Ease up, Officer," Ben said. "You trying to break my neck?"

The cop eyed the marks on the back of Ben's neck. "Oh, you're one of those."

"One of what?"

"A booster," the cop replied.

"A booster?" Ben repeated, completely lost. "Am I under arrest?"

"You were asked to move your vehicle—"

"And that's grounds for arrest?"

The cop stood him up and pushed him against the side of the car. "We got a report from a Tellco employee that after he asked you to move it you threatened to kill him."

Ben's face blanched. He turned to see the guy with the beer belly standing nearby, wearing a shit-eating grin.

"Shoulda left when I told you the first time, buddy," he shouted from several feet away.

"Well, he's obviously lying," Ben said. The handcuffs were already starting to cut off his circulation.

The officer spun him around. He had an impressively large head. "I'm gonna need your license and registration."

"It's on the passenger seat. The registration is probably in the glove compartment."

"Watch him for me, will you?" the cop told Baby Belly, who was happy to oblige. He came up and wrapped his meaty fingers around Ben's wrist.

The cop ducked into the car and popped the glove compartment.

"Ticket me if you have to, but I have somewhere to be."

The cop emerged holding a semi-automatic pistol between two fingers. "You got a license for this?" he asked, one eyebrow arched.

Ben remembered the money clip. There was no gun license in sight. "I don't know. Maybe it's in there."

"Then I'm afraid you're gonna have to call your friend from jail to reschedule that meeting."

"Yeah, you don't understand," Ben started to tell them, his annoyance quickly escalating from fear to panic. He began stepping away from the car and now Baby Belly, a man who outweighed him by at least forty pounds, was struggling to hold him in place. The cop jumped in to help and reached for his Taser.

The sight sent a surge of adrenaline flooding into Ben's system. The muscles in his arms, legs and chest grew taut. His teeth clamped shut. Baby Belly swung a massive punch into Ben's midsection. It was a blow that would have sunk an average person and should have floored him, but the blow landed with barely an ounce of pain. With a sudden jerk, Ben pulled his wrists apart. A metallic ping sounded as the handcuff chain snapped and pieces fell to the ground. He directed his first shot toward the cop and the Taser he was raising to fire at him. A single strike to the man's oversized head sent him careening backward, pinwheeling as he fell, knocking his skull against the concrete. The cop lay without moving.

Ben spun toward Baby Belly, a man who was far more accustomed to doling out the beatings, rather than receiving. The fat man's eyes flared with a sense of unknown fear. He turned to run, but Ben wasn't done with him just yet. He grabbed a handful of his sweaty shirt and yanked the back of his head into his closed fist. Baby Belly's legs crumpled, sending him sprawling onto the ground in a giant heap.

For what felt like an eternity, Ben stood rooted in place, staring down at the impossible. The silver handcuff bracelets were still around his wrists, along with the remains of the chain. It now jangled like a wind chime whenever he moved. Nearby were two men who could have easily subdued him but, instead, were laid out on the ground. Ben Fisher's day was getting worse by the minute.

He ran to the unconscious cop and fished around until he found his keys. Undoing the bracelets, he let them fall to the ground. After that, he collected his pistol, got back in his car and sped away.

Chapter 7

Sienna Panov had no sooner hung up from her conversation with Ben Fisher than her nose caught the distinct odor of something burning.

"Oh, crap!"

Her pug, Buddy, covered his face.

She tossed down her phone and ran into the kitchen. Tendrils of smoke billowed up from the oven. A pair of oven mitts sat on the counter. She grabbed them with one hand and opened the oven door with the other. Smoke billowed out, triggering the alarm and an ear-bursting squeal. With all the grace of a newborn calf, she reached into the oven and pulled out a tray of jet-black muffins. Dejected, she plopped the tray on the countertop and dashed for the alarm, waving at it frantically before it succeeded in deafening her.

After popping open a few nearby windows, Sienna returned to the kitchen and blew a few strands of her long dark hair out of her face as she surveyed her handiwork.

Buddy stared at her.

"I know what you're thinking," she told him. "'You may be a good scientist, maybe even a great one, but you couldn't bake a muffin if your life depended on it.'"

This was her third attempt in as many days and each had proven more disastrous than the last. Over the last few decades, women had been put in the rather unusual position of needing to master two completely different sets of skills. On the one hand, the right to get a job and excel in whatever profession they chose. That was easy enough given the fact that women were just as intelligent and capable as men. And that wasn't only the opinion of female university professors. It was a fact born out of cold, hard science. But, on the other, despite what some once described as 'liberation', many women were expected to work a full-time job *and still* cook, clean and keep house.

As far as the burnt muffins were concerned, in her own defense, the conversation with Ben had made her lose track of time. There was no getting around the obvious, in her mind. The man didn't seem like himself and she wasn't sure if he was experiencing some sort of psychotic break or if the pressure of running a billion-dollar company had started to take its toll.

Of course, there could be another, darker, explanation for his sudden change. It was possible that Ben Fisher had something to do with the fate that had befallen her father, the infamous oceanographer, Nicholay Panov.

While her gut argued vociferously against the likelihood of that being true, her mind, a sharp and at times over-analytical instrument, wasn't nearly so quick to rule out the possibility.

Ben's role aside, there was no denying that her father's devotion to environmental science and the overall health of the planet had been her motivation to follow in his footsteps. Her work in glaciology was focused on the relationship between volcanic activity and

29

the Earth's changing temperature over long periods of time. More often than not, this fixation on understanding the link between the two brought her to the Arctic and the Antarctic, two of the most inhospitable places on the planet. There, she would drill down through the ice sheet in order to extract cores tens of meters in length. Written within tiny bubbles of air trapped for thousands of years was a treasure trove of data on the history of the planet's ever-changing climate.

Where she and her father differed had been his fascination with water in general, oceans in particular. He referred to them as the lungs of the planet, since they helped to absorb CO_2 and regulate the Earth's biosphere. But more than that, they alone allowed the existence of all living things on the planet, including humanity. As an oceanographer of nearly fifty years, his own area of interest had been focused on the growing acidification of our oceans. In pursuit of that, Nic, as he was known to his friends, had spent his life trying to sort out the many factors associated with this growing trend toward destabilization and what it meant, both short- and long-term, for the planet. Recently, the focus of his work had slowly begun to shift toward what could be done to reverse the trend.

The environmental movement's biggest coup had come a little less than ten years ago when strict new regulations on carbon fuel emissions had been imposed around the globe. At last the planet had come together to save our only home. She couldn't help recalling the joy on her father's weathered face as he wept at the news. With realism in mind, the goal for the first decade had been to see CO_2 levels stabilize in an attempt to calm the Earth's climate and slow its warming effects.

So it hadn't been hard to fathom the depth of her father's surprise and consternation when ten years on, the newest readings had shown something rather unexpected. Despite a fifty percent reduction in CO_2 emissions over the last decade, the levels of CO_2 and methane in the atmosphere were now five times what they had been. Frankly, it simply didn't make any sense.

Even if human activity had continued during the last ten years as it had for the last two hundred, no one would've expected this kind of result. To say 'baffling' was an understatement. It had been downright shocking. Which was why he had run the numbers again and again, returning to the field on countless expeditions, collecting new sets of data to crunch. Regardless of how he approached it, the results remained the same.

But Nicholay's devotion to the scientific method had also left him vulnerable to underestimating the political dimension of the climate debate. When word of his initial findings had gotten out, environmental extremists had denounced him as a quack. The planet was marching inexorably away from fossil fuels and into an era of renewable energy. The battle in the public sphere had already been waged and won. And yet here was this little-known oceanographer with the audacity to suggest that despite humanity's best efforts, greenhouse gases in the atmosphere were actually increasing. As a sign of this disturbing trend, the pollution masks commonly seen worn by individuals in Asian countries had begun to make their appearance in America. As things worsened, those who could afford them wore full oxygen masks whenever setting foot outside, a movement made even more infamous as a result of being showcased on the fashion catwalks of New York, Paris and Milan.

Given the state of play, it wasn't at all surprising when a minority of ultra-extremists had latched onto her father's work and hailed it as proof we needed to do more to free ourselves from our old polluting technologies. But others harbored the undeniably rational fear that if Nicholay's findings were accepted as fact, it could lead to a rollback of a decade of progressive environmental policies. Good scientists weren't in the habit of weighing how popular their findings would be. They made measurements and reported the facts as accurately as they knew how.

As it turned out, the main chink in her father's armor also happened to be the one question he hadn't yet been able to answer.

Namely, why was it happening?

It was one thing to show folks the data and say, "Trust this." It was something else to offer them a clear and compelling explanation of why it was happening. This was common knowledge to any trial lawyer worth their salt. You could lay out plenty of evidence for a heinous crime, but in the end, juries wanted to know why.

Those who accepted Nicholay's findings were left to ask themselves, how could it be that after the world had finally smartened up, the problem of climate change had gotten so much worse? That was the final part of the mystery her father had eagerly been trying to settle when he'd agreed to do a little side work for Ben Fisher, one of the greatest and most reclusive tech magnates of the twenty-first century.

Perhaps on account of that last point, Sienna had been rather surprised when she had received a call from Ben himself. She was the one who helped organize her father's expeditions. What made the call so astounding was Ben's reputation as a man rarely seen and even more rarely heard. Since Neural-Sync's inception, the COO, Ben's sister, Lori Fisher, had been the face of the company.

The final message she'd received from her father was now nine days old, his words still etched in her mind. He had sent her an email via satellite claiming to be on the verge of an incredible discovery. Cautious by nature, he'd refused to say anything else until he'd completed yet another submersible dive, scheduled for the following day.

For days she had searched her mind for an explanation. Had a rogue wave sunk his research ship, dooming him along with his entire crew? Certainly, it remained a possibility she couldn't deny. Although it still failed to explain why the Navy had lied to her about conducting a search when they had gone nowhere near the area the *Archipelago* had last been spotted. How did she know this? One of Nicholay's colleagues, a Dr. Lisowski onboard the NOAA ship *David Starr Jordan*, had been in the area. Following the disappearance of the *Archipelago*, her crew and Nicholay, Lisowski had been busy doing what the U.S. Navy had claimed yet, clearly, refused to do.

After nothing had been heard from her father or any of his crew for over a week, it was easy in times like this for one's mind to conjure up the worst possible scenario. In her heart, she still held out hope that the *Archipelago* had pulled into port somewhere and simply neglected to get in touch. Such a scenario was hard, if not impossible, to believe but not when compared to the alternative. Not simply because of her mother's recent passing, nor the fact that her father's death would make her an only child, an orphan.

There was also another purely emotional reason she wanted him to be alive. If her father truly had been lost at sea, along with the great discovery he had made, a large chunk of Sienna's sorrow would come from knowing his body would never be recovered. Anyone who doubted the power of a gravestone only needed to speak with the parents of a missing child to see the denial of grief in action. There came a time when knowing, regardless how terrible the news, had to be preferable to living in limbo.

Buddy barked, dislodging Sienna from her thoughts.

Sienna grabbed her phone, checked the time and swore. Ben would be at the Square Knot Diner in a few minutes. She had to leave immediately if she was going to be there on time. She hoped for Ben's sake he hadn't been lying when he'd told her he would help. Playing nice wasn't her strong suit, a characteristic which had not proven very productive on the dating scene, but sure had a funny habit of producing results in every other realm of her life.

Chapter 8

It was dark by the time Ben pulled into the alley and killed the motor. He wasn't sure how long it would be before the cops would come looking for him. He only hoped the officer hadn't had a chance to lay eyes on Ben's driver's license before Ben had decked him.

Ben had no sooner slammed the door when he spotted a tall, thin man staring at him from the street. The man was holding up his phone as though he were filming or taking a picture and Ben's pulse began to quicken. Was his face already being plastered all over the news?

Looking over his shoulder, Ben saw the alley was empty except for a small mountain of garbage bags twenty feet away. When he returned his attention to the man, he saw him moving purposefully in Ben's direction, first at a brisk walk and then, as Ben himself began to move, the man burst into a staggered run.

"Don't you do it, you son of a bitch," the skinny man shouted as he barreled toward him.

Ben braced himself for another attack and watched in surprise as the man ran past him holding an outstretched cell phone. He got to the mountain of garbage bags, clicked a button on his phone and began pumping his fist in the air like he'd just scored the winning touchdown in the Super Bowl.

"Yes, baby, yes! That's how it's done!"

The skinny man strolled back in his direction, his face plastered with a look of triumph.

"Are you feeling okay?" Ben asked.

"Feeling okay? You just missed a 1k Neuro credit, buddy. Sucks to be you, but I saw it first."

"I don't have the foggiest idea what you're talking about," Ben replied.

"That's what they all say." The skinny man snickered before he stopped and stared at Ben. "Hey, aren't you that guy?"

Now Ben's pulse really was racing. He forced a crooked smile and winked. "That's what they all say."

Seconds later, Ben entered the Square Knot Diner. Nestled next to the on-ramp to Interstate 5, the place was situated in a two-story brick building constructed sometime around the turn of the last century. The sight he encountered there left him wondering whether he had somehow left Seattle altogether and taken a giant step back into the glory days of small-town America.

A tiny bell over the door rang as he entered. A lunch counter sat to one side, flanked by black high-backed stools, most of which were filled with a mixture of construction workers, tourists and hipsters. On the other side was a row of booths, most of them occupied by twos and threes. Except for one near the back which held an attractive dark-haired woman with a set of flashing green eyes. She stood when she saw him come in.

"Mr. Fisher?" She held out her hand. "Sienna Panov. I wasn't sure you were gonna show."

They eased into the booth and Ben pushed the menu aside. The last remnants of adrenaline were only now beginning to flush from his system. Besides, eating was the last thing on his mind. "Call me Ben."

"All right, Ben it is." The smile on her face couldn't hide the deep sense of anxiety roiling just beneath the surface.

"Sorry I'm late," he explained. "I got held up."

"That makes two of us," she replied, reaching back to tie her shoulder-length, raven-black hair into a ponytail.

"If you don't mind me saying, you don't sound like the person I pictured over the phone."

Her eyebrows did a little dance. "You can thank my parents for that."

"Where were they from? South America?"

Sienna let out an involuntary spasm of laughter. "Wrong continent. They were from Bulgaria. Escaped the USSR in the 1980s and came to America. Antiquated as the term might sound, they were Gypsies, which probably explains my complexion. My people have something of a bad reputation in Europe, some of it deserved, some of it not. You see, most people hear Gypsy and think crystal balls, but most don't have the foggiest idea where we came from."

Ben was intrigued. "Okay, I'll bite."

"My people migrated to Europe from India around the seventh century. As the story goes, back then, the locals thought we'd come from Egypt because of our dark skin and took to calling us Gypsies." Sienna stared down at her menu before looking back up at him with those dazzling green eyes. For a brief moment, she resembled that haunting and world-famous *National*

Geographic picture of the Afghan woman. "I wasn't kidding about what I said over the phone, by the way."

The TV on the wall opposite him was playing twenty-four-hour cable news. The sound was muted, but Ben could see the picture of a young woman with short brown hair and sharp features. She appeared to be in her late twenties. The caption below read: *Reporter Elizabeth Howard still missing.*

The visual stirred a feeling of recognition from deep within him. Did he know this woman?

"You seem distracted," Sienna observed, muffling the annoyance in her voice.

Ben twisted in his seat, glancing back toward the plate-glass window that looked onto the street and into the alley where his car was parked. He described the skinny man's antics, wondering if a local asylum had recently swung open its doors and released all its patients.

"You really *have* lost your memory, haven't you?" she said, obviously under the misguided assumption he'd been using a line on her this whole time.

A waitress showed up just then, late fifties and about as pleasant as could be expected under the circumstances. "So, what'll it be?"

"I'll start with the coffee," Sienna said, motioning to Ben.

"What about you, sugar?"

"How about a glass of whiskey?"

The waitress scowled.

"Never mind. Just give me a coffee."

"How do you like it?"

Ben paused. He wasn't sure.

"Tough question, huh?"

He smiled weakly. "You'd be surprised."

"I'll bring milk, cream and sugar and let you work out the rest. Anything to eat?"

"Maybe give us another minute or two," Sienna suggested, holding up the menu.

The waitress sauntered off.

Sienna folded her arms, resting her elbows on the table. "How little do you remember?" Her initial skepticism appeared to be slackening.

He straightened in his seat. "Not much at all," he professed. "I know my name is Ben Fisher—at least, I pieced that out after looking at my ID. I know I have a lot of money. I also seem to have a rather unusual definition of the word 'monogamy.' Oh, and I'm the CEO of a company called Neuro-Sync, whatever the hell that is."

"Neural-Sync," Sienna corrected him, shaking her head and letting out a tiny laugh. "Oh, goodness, where do I begin? Your company has probably done more to change the world as we know it than any that's come before. That guy running down the alley with his phone, we have you to thank for that."

"Me?" Ben asked, leaning forward, his eyes filled with astonishment.

"About eight years ago, Neural-Sync came out with a revolutionary new brain implant, designed to augment human capabilities. But this wasn't just top-secret super-soldier stuff. Part of your mission statement was that you wanted a world where superhumans were the norm, not the exception. It also doesn't hurt that Neural-Sync more or less has a monopoly on the market."

Ben couldn't help thinking about his confrontation with Baby Belly and that cop. Was the power he had felt surging through his muscles somehow connected to what she was saying? His fingers returned to the back of his neck and the tender pain he still felt there.

"Of course, you have one," she told him. "I mean, it would seem kinda weird if you didn't. Millions of people do. Those things are everywhere and for reasons that are totally your own, you'd rather live the life of a reclusive playboy than take credit for your invention. It feels weird being the one to tell you this, but what you created was so far ahead of its time that no one's been able to duplicate it. Some say it's the metal alloy the implant's made of. And the size. Yours can fit on the end of a ballpoint pen. Your nearest competitor is still struggling with devices the size of a wedding ring case with wires that look like something out of a 1970s dystopian sci-fi movie. Not to mention the hole those poor folks need drilled through their skulls to insert the thing in the first place."

Ben sat listening, dimly aware that his jaw was hanging open in awe. "I did this?" He couldn't help but wonder once again whether he was dreaming.

"Have you noticed how nobody in this diner even recognizes you?" Sienna remarked.

Ben glanced around, observing people going about their business. If Elon Musk walked in, the place would go crazy. "I hadn't considered it."

Sienna sighed, removed her phone from her pocket and began searching for something online. Seconds later she held up the device to Ben, showing him what she had found. It was the cover of *Time* magazine and on it was an African-American woman. She was tall and slim, but not overly attractive. Despite that, she had an air about her that was both kind and determined. The caption next to her read: *Lori Fisher, changing the world one brain at a time.*

40

"That's my sister?" Ben looked down at the skin on his arms, trying to make sense of what he was seeing.

"You were both adopted," Sienna explained, laughing. "Listen, I don't have time to go through your whole family history. You know why *I'm* here. I need to know what you want in return for helping me."

The image of the dead woman on the couch was threatening to return and Ben did what he could to press it back into some safe place where it wouldn't torment him. He leaned forward. "Listen, Sienna. Within the next day or so, you're gonna see stuff about me on the news. I need you to know right up front that none of it is true. Somebody very close to me was murdered and whoever did it is trying to frame me."

Sienna recoiled, folding her arms tightly over her chest. She didn't need to speak for Ben to know exactly what she was thinking. Was she sitting across from a murderer?

"There may be a way I can prove my innocence," he insisted. "My house is rigged with cameras and when I went to find the recorder, I saw that someone had ripped it out from the wall."

"Yeah, but where's the recorder now?"

He shook his head with more than a touch of despair.

Sienna's face brightened. "Well, maybe a copy was stored in the security company's cloud?"

"God, I hope so." Suddenly, a searing pain wracked the back of Ben's head, as though an icepick had perforated his skull and been driven directly into his brain. His hands went to the source as his face twisted with agony.

Across from him, Sienna reached out with concern. "You're not having some kind of stroke, are you? You want me to call an ambulance?" She began to dial when Ben reached out and stopped her. Already the pain was beginning to subside. Stars danced before his eyes.

"Have you considered that somebody might have done something to your implant?" she asked him.

Ben shook his head, flinching from the pain of even that slight movement.

"I know someone who might be able to help. But if I do this, then it's your turn to keep your end of the bargain."

Just then the waitress returned with two coffees in white mugs.

"Actually, we're going to need those to go," Sienna said as she held out her bank bracelet and let the waitress tap her own to collect the fee.

Ben was already at the door, peering across the street and into the alley. Two cops were standing by his Alfa Romeo. "How did you get here?" he asked her.

"I drove."

"Good, we'll take your car then."

Chapter 9

M tapped his earphones, pausing a soundtrack from the Golden Age of cinema he'd been listening to, and glared at the woman in the recliner. A cloth had been pulled tightly over her face, making it hard for her to breathe. She was trying to speak, but all he could think about was Morricone and *Once Upon a Time in the West*. Now *there* was an artist the likes of which the world might never see again.

Like Morricone, M was a different kind of artist. Except his music sheet was people, his symphony their screams and pleas for mercy. He tilted the plastic pitcher hovering several feet above her head. A thick stream of water walked across her features and over her mouth. The woman coughed and sputtered. M continued watching until she cried out for him to stop.

"I have an important question for you," he told her. "If, that is, you feel ready to start being truthful?"

The woman mumbled from beneath the tightly bound cloth. It sounded to him like a yes.

"By the way, do you prefer Elizabeth or Liz? Or Mrs. Howard?"

More mumbling.

"Yes, you're quite right, I didn't ask about your

preferred gender pronouns, did I? How incredibly insensitive of me."

A dozen feet away, a laptop sat on a dirty milk carton, streaming images from the local news. *The Search Continues for Missing Reporter* read the headline plastered along the bottom of the screen. He stroked Elizabeth Howard's wet hair. "They're still looking for you. This doesn't need to continue, you know. All this nonsense can stop as soon as you tell me what you did with the documents Ben Fisher sent you."

M couldn't make out exactly what she said after that, but he waterboarded her some more anyway.

'M' wasn't his real name, of course. In his line of work real names were a big no-no. But he supposed there was no harm in divulging what it stood for. Magician. It was definitely cute, maybe a little too cute. The problem was, the names that stuck were rarely the ones we give ourselves. He had a knack for making problems disappear. So there you had it.

M went to the laptop, to see if his work had reached a national audience yet. Grabbing Elizabeth hadn't been terribly difficult. He had contacted her at the paper, pretending to be a disgruntled executive from Neural-Sync, a whistleblower with the kind of dirt that could corroborate whatever was in the dossier Mr. Fisher, in his infinite foolishness, had decided to turn over to her. In journalism, two sources were always better than one. For their meeting, he'd made sure to pick an expensive hotel with a room facing the water.

Rule One: When setting a location to meet with strangers, never choose to do so in a hotel room. But rules and good judgment could be subverted. It happened every time you were in a hurry and crossed against a red light. Risk versus reward. And in Elizabeth's case, the reward had been too good to miss out on. Oops.

M scrolled up and down the feed from the major cable news websites and frowned.

Removing her from the room without the act being caught on camera had been merely a question of suitcase size. Injecting her with barbital beforehand had also been a big part of the illusion. These days, you couldn't very well go strolling through the lobby of any respectable hotel with shrieks emanating from your luggage.

A noise behind him made him turn. He caught the sound of tiny footfalls disappearing into the distance. His attention flicked to the chair. It was empty.

Like a wild animal, M sprang to his feet, adrenaline flooding every muscle fiber in his body. He glanced at a scalpel on a nearby table, but knew he wasn't going to need it.

He could hear her faint screams up ahead, informing M that she'd entered the house of mirrors. In her disorientation, she had likely assumed he'd brought her to a warehouse in some shady part of Seattle. But she was wrong, and Elizabeth wouldn't be the first to discover Happy Funland. At least that was the name he gave the now defunct and rotting amusement park he called his 'office'.

No doubt, Elizabeth was certain she was running through some sicko's version of a nightmare and that all she needed to do was find her way outside, and to safety.

M came to the house of mirrors and scanned the area. Some of the glass was broken, littering the ground, transforming it into a minefield of shards. A shaft of light from where part of the ceiling had collapsed revealed a trail of fresh blood. He grinned.

Dress it up however you wanted, when all was said

and done, human beings were innately hunters. But sometimes, like today, they were also prey.

M took off in hot pursuit when something struck him square in the chest, the impact knocking his legs out from under him. He landed on a pile of soft wood, torn up and covered with moss from the seeping rain.

A heartbeat later, a lead pipe flashed before his eyes as Elizabeth swung it down at his head. M rolled out of the way, his vision still blossoming with starbursts.

"You sick son of a bitch," Elizabeth shouted and came at him again, striking him in the head.

M fell backward in a heap and Elizabeth took off running. His head was swimming. And yet in spite of his disorientation, he could still hear her outside, yelling for help. It didn't seem to matter that she was forty-five minutes from the city, secluded in a place that had been long forgotten. Thankfully for M, there was no one around to hear her scream, unless you counted the mice and the deer that had taken up residence in the decaying buildings.

M rose to his feet and realized suddenly that things had gone quiet. Quickly, he hurried past the broken mirror and outside. Tall grass swayed amongst the abandoned rides and dilapidated carnival games. In three quick moves, he was up on the roof of a nearby building, scanning in every direction. Soon he spotted her to the south, running through a field and toward a nearby clutch of red cedar trees. M hopped down and gave chase. The implant didn't only feed his muscles with incredible strength when he needed it. The device also helped regulate the amount of oxygen in his muscles and numbed the pain from injury and discomfort from lactic acid burn. He felt bad for her. She had guts, but she hadn't been enhanced and therefore didn't stand a chance. Which brought him to Rule Two: Know when you're outmatched.

M's phone began to ring, just in time for Rule Three: Never discuss your business over the phone in a way that might someday be used against you.

He took off at a full run, already closing the distance between predator and prey.

No one in his line of work answered with, "M the hitman, how can I help you?"

M tapped his earpiece and accepted the call, answering as he always did.

"Dave's Pizza…"

Chapter 10

Lori Fisher's office at Neural-Sync was a study in contradictions, very much like the woman who inhabited it. High ceilings and white walls, hung with expensive and rather incomprehensible modern art, all at eye level. Most of it was the pretentious kind of crap a kid could make if you gave them plenty of paint and a spray gun. The furniture was a hodge-podge of antiques, except for the desk, which was made of fine crystal and cost a fortune. For her part, Lori was dressed modestly, in an earth-toned pant suit and just enough make-up to keep from looking like she'd just sprung out of bed. As if that weren't enough, she was also a black woman, operating in what some still argued was a man's world. Few, if any, in the company liked her, many probably didn't think she belonged. She was only COO because she happened to share the same foster parents as her brother, Ben Fisher. A good chunk of Lori's forty-five years on this earth had been spent letting people make her feel like she didn't belong. That she wasn't good enough. But those days were long gone.

"Sandy, increase the temperature by five degrees."

"Yes, Ms. Fisher," Sandy's disembodied voice replied. She sounded almost human. "Will there be anything else?"

"Has anyone called?" Lori was thinking about Ben. Had been all day.

"I'm afraid not. Benjamin has still not come in today. Would you like me to reach out to him?"

Lori started to bite at the nail on her left hand and stopped the moment she noticed. She set her hand back down on the crystal desk, relishing the cool surface. "Not just yet."

"Understood."

She returned to her work, hopeful the repetition and monotony would pull her focus away from the knots of tension eating away at her. It had been hours since Ben had called, speaking to her in a rambling, enigmatic way, and when word came that the police were at his house, her stress had breached levels she'd rarely experienced—not even while managing Neural-Sync's global operations 24/7.

Her cell phone rang and Lori scooped it up in a blur of speed. She paused as she read the name on display. John Smith, Director of Research and Development.

John Smith wasn't really his name and he didn't work for Neural-Sync either.

Lori grinned at the phone. "What took you so long?"

"I'm guessing you've heard." His voice was deep, soothing, but she also knew that was how he got people to lower their guard.

"Is that supposed to be some kind of joke?"

A soft chuckle. "Your brother is threatening to drop a whole lot of scandal at the company's feet and you know who's responsible for that."

She hated this man, hated him down to his rotten core, but he was right. As CEO of one of the largest and most powerful corporations in the world, Ben's little dilemma would be blood in the water for an army of reporters, ravenous for a story on the man who hated any kind of publicity. He wasn't only threatening the future of Neural-Sync, this little problem had the power to unravel the tentative reality regular people clung to. The sorts of stories that got them out of bed and into a dangerous world in order to be productive, so that they could wake up in the morning and start the process all over again.

"You still there?" he asked, the inflection in his voice betraying early notes of his notorious impatience.

"There might be a way to make this go away," she said. "Have you called the chief of police?"

"No, because that would be sloppy and runs the grave risk of making things worse. Don't get the peasants involved. We need a high-level solution here. Keep it in-house."

She nodded. Not because she agreed with his assessment, but because she understood precisely what he wanted her to do. And in the half-second it took to contemplate the man's implied request, Lori knew she was going to disobey him, and not for the first time today.

"I got this," she told him.

"I hope so. I don't need to remind you that COOs are unmade all the time."

"You just did," she said and hung up.

Lori drew in a deep breath.

"I detect an elevation in your heart rate, Ms. Fisher," Sandy's melodic voice said from everywhere and nowhere. "I can lower the temperature in the room if you would like."

"Not the temperature," Lori said, rubbing the corners of her eyes. "Just the lights. Say, half of what they are now. Hmm, a little more, please. That's good."

She went to her phone again and scrolled through her contacts until she found the name she was looking for.

"Dave's Pizza," the voice said, slightly out of breath. "Is this for pickup or delivery?"

"This a bad time?"

"No, the cat got out. But I'll get her back."

"It's regarding Ben Fisher."

A pause.

She had used his name. That was a no-no.

"Would you like the usual then? Medium all-dressed and a Coke?"

"No, just follow him. Make sure he's okay."

"Understood. Thirty minutes or less, that's our motto," M replied in a sing-song voice.

Lori hung up, and then called out to Sandy.

"Yes, Ms. Fisher."

"If John Smith from Research and Development calls again, tell him I've stepped out, will you?"

"Of course. If he should call would you like me to take a message?"

Lori laced her fingers and cracked three knuckles, relishing the release. "Don't bother, Sandy. I already know what he's going to say."

Chapter 11

Knut Rafnkell's computer repair center on the edge of South Park, Seattle, was surprisingly spacious and tidy for a shop situated above a strip joint. But this South Park had little to nothing in common with the twisted humor of its cartoon namesake. Unlike the fictional town, the Seattle version boasted a crime rate nearly two hundred times the national average. It certainly explained the bars on the second-story windows and the door buzzer, normally reserved for jewelers' shops and loan sharks.

Knut was a bear of a man. He had an imposing presence and a keen distaste for bullshit. Although his name and appearance were all Icelandic, most everything else about the man was thoroughly American. He was also wearing a monocle, which he flipped down over his eye. Even from where Ben was standing, he could see bits of data rushing by on the tiny screen. Perhaps even stranger was the fact that Ben was able to read and understand what he was seeing, even though it flickered by at high speed and backwards. Knut was scrolling through Ben's background online.

"When you said you were bringing Ben Fisher—*the* Ben Fisher—I was sure you'd taken a stray hit off a hobo's crack pipe," Knut said, his wide features forming into an irresistible grin.

Sienna returned the gesture.

"How exactly do you two know each other?" Ben asked, eyeing the glass display cases loaded with all manner of tech: VR digital eyewear, holographic projectors, encryption and decryption keys. The dizzying effects of what had felt like a small-scale aneurism in the diner still hadn't quite cleared away. It was a good thing he had opted not to drive.

Sienna slapped the big man's shoulder. "Knut here wrote me an algorithm designed to measure the levels of methane and CO_2 in Antarctic ice cores."

"What can I say?" Knut said, blushing. "I'm a sucker for a beautiful woman." He flipped up the monocle, looking like Groucho Marx in *A Day at the Races*. "So, what can I do for the great Ben Fisher?"

Ben's expression grew serious. "Someone I care about was murdered and I think the killer might have been captured digitally by my home security system."

Knut nodded. "Why not just view the DVR data? That's your main collection point."

"He tried that," Sienna piped in. "But whoever broke in ran off with it."

"So you want me to access the security system's cloud, is that it?" Knut said, rubbing his meaty hands together.

Ben nodded. "Bingo."

"Bingo's for old ladies," Knut said, and led them past a dark curtain and into a back room.

They watched as the big guy settled into his seat before three monitors. With the grace of an accomplished surgeon, Knut cracked his knuckles and lowered his monocle.

"Surveillance company name?"

"Irongate."

"Address?"

Ben gave him that too.

"Password?"

Ben swallowed hard.

"You see, that's part of the reason we're here," Sienna began to explain. "He doesn't remember."

Knut leaned back in his chair and let out an explosive burst of laughter. "You run one of the biggest tech companies in the world and you forgot your password. Oh, that's rich." He cackled in his chair for nearly a full minute before settling down. Wiping the tears from his eyes, he said, "Ah, thank you, you have no idea how much I needed that."

"Glad I could be of service," Ben replied, trying to keep his composure.

"You see, it's not that simple," Sienna tried to explain. "Ben's suffering from amnesia."

"I woke up in a pool of blood," he jumped in. "Feeling like someone had cracked my skull open."

Knut turned in his direction. "Maybe you did crack your skull. You ever think about heading to the hospital and getting that checked out? My aunt died of a blood clot. Dropped right in front of me, foaming at the mouth. Not a pretty sight, my friend, let me assure you."

Ben waved a dismissive hand in the air. "Yeah, well, right now hospitals are out of the question."

"Suit yourself, friend, but hauling your corpse to the curb after your brain goes pop will cost extra."

"Duly noted," Ben said. He wanted desperately to rub at what felt like a molten needle poking at the back of his neck, but didn't want to give Knut the pleasure of thinking he was right.

Knut's fingers, large as they were, danced over the keyboard with surprising grace. "All right, babies and ladies, now we are getting somewhere. It always amazes me how the biggest security firms have the weakest firewalls." Knut double-clicked on a file that launched a video program. The screen filled with ten tiny color videos from Ben's home surveillance, each of them set with the time and date, stamped in the upper right-hand corner.

Ben looked on, an uneasy out-of-body feeling creeping into his bones. He caught movement in one tiny video and saw it was from earlier that day. Was that Amanda? She moved soundlessly through the kitchen, wearing a pair of white sweatpants and a matching hoodie. She opened the fridge, poured herself a glass of wine and then closed it with her hip. All three of them stared with muted horror and fascination. It was like watching footage of the *Titanic* moments before it met the iceberg.

Amanda was busy sipping her wine, her feet curled beneath her, when a figure in a long coat and wide-brimmed hat entered the frame from the bottom. Amanda sat up at once, startled, clutching a hand to her chest. They spoke for less than thirty seconds before the man in the trench coat lunged at her. He reached into one of his pockets and came out with a shiny object. The two of them struggled briefly, Amanda kicking him off of her. She nearly got away, but he threw himself onto the couch, pinning her in place. Thankfully, the gruesome details were too difficult to make out, but when the man stood, Amanda was already dead. The killer sat her upright, trying and failing repeatedly to keep her head from lolling to one side.

A second later, he spun, apparently reacting to a

noise. He ran from behind the couch and hid behind a nearby bookshelf. That was when Ben entered the living room, sorting through mail, not really paying attention to the room around him. Just as he seemed to notice something was terribly wrong, the killer approached him from behind. But it wasn't the knife Ben got, or even a blow to the head. The killer pulled out what looked like a stun gun and jammed it into the back of his neck. Ben's body convulsed before collapsing to the ground.

"Get a copy of that," Ben said, his mouth dry, tears rolling down his cheeks. He couldn't remember a thing about Amanda and yet the tragedy of what he had just seen was almost too much to bear. Sienna stood next to him, frozen stiff, her hands balled into tight fists, covering her mouth. Even Knut was speechless.

"Knut?"

"Huh?" the big man said, still somewhere else. "Oh, yeah." He returned to the keyboard and began clattering away. "Hey, that's weird."

"What is?"

"It's not letting me transfer the file."

"What's blocking it?" Sienna asked.

"I'm getting an error message." He displayed it for the others to see. It read: *The File You Requested No Longer Exists*.

Ben moved in next to him. "Sure it does. We just watched it." He reached out to mash some buttons.

"Hold on, Cañonero," Knut shot back. "This is my recital and I'm the only one who plays this instrument."

"What's going on?" Sienna asked, still perturbed.

Knut stopped long enough to eye them both. "It looks like a hacker far better than me got in there and deleted the file."

"Better than you?" Ben said, clearly distraught. This

56

was the single piece of evidence he needed to clear his name and the only clue as to who killed Amanda.

"Believe me when I tell you there aren't very many."

"But why would someone go out of their way to commit murder and then erase all evidence of my innocence?" Ben asked heatedly.

Knut was perfectly willing to bite. "Well, for starters, you're the CEO of a huge corporation that's revolutionized the world. It shouldn't surprise you to learn that not everyone's happy with the new direction you've sent us in."

Sienna grabbed at the end of her ponytail and pressed it against her upper lip, a habit she often did when contemplating difficult problems. "They didn't kill you," she observed. "Even when they had every opportunity."

"What do you suppose that means?" Knut asked.

Ben pondered the question. "You said yourself the neural implant I created has changed the world, and not entirely for the better. Perhaps someone out there thinks a quick death would be too good for a person like me. Perhaps they believe I need to suffer."

"But who's sick enough to do such a thing?" Sienna asked. Her opinion of humanity in general was, at best, a dim one, but even she was at a loss to explain such a seemingly Machiavellian plan.

Ben's gaze settled on the two of them. "Seems to me the only way to find that answer is to understand this thing I invented and what exactly it's done to the world."

Chapter 12

The workshop section of Knut's business was situated at the back of the store, out of the way of prying eyes. And it was just as well, because mere words were inadequate to describe the level of disorder Ben and Sienna encountered there. Every available workspace was spilling over with logic boards and computer components. Some were in boxes, others not. There hardly seemed to be any rhyme or reason to the mayhem. At least Ben didn't think so. Knut, on the other hand, seemed to know his way around the heaps of cyber-crap like an old man in a junkyard. He flicked on a computer monitor and clicked a few buttons until he came to the Neural-Sync website. Knut then brought his phone to the back of his own neck. A series of pictures appeared on the monitor. Knut with a petite Asian woman standing before the Eiffel Tower. Then another image took its place, this one of Knut, the same woman and a little girl sitting around a Christmas tree, their faces beaming. He stared at the images and as he did, a wheel on the monitor began spinning.

Authentication Confirmed.

Knut's profile came up.

"What the heck just happened?" Ben asked, amazed

and perplexed in equal measure.

"The system works by scanning your brainwaves in relation to specific stimuli," Sienna explained.

Ben's eyebrows rose. "Your brainwaves act as a sort of password. Is that what you're saying?"

"Precisely," Knut replied. "You upload images that have a particular meaning for you. You use the app to scan the waves the images generate in your brain and then voilà, you're good to go."

"That way no one can break into whatever Neural-Sync's got sitting in your brain." Ben couldn't help but feel like he'd fallen asleep and woken up in the future.

Knut nodded. "It's the strongest encryption I know of, short of quantum encryption, but we're still not there just yet."

"Is that yours?" Ben asked, pointing at an image of a brain on the monitor.

"That's her," he replied proudly. Four pulsating blue dots were visible in various parts of Knut's brain. "But my NED's only a second-generation. You bastards keep releasing a new, upgraded version every year. No one can keep up."

"NED?"

Sienna took this one. "It stands for Neural Enhancement Device. It's inserted via the bloodstream and then breaks into three smaller devices, settling in distinct parts of the brain."

"Parts?" Ben's head was starting to swim.

"Of course," Knut chimed in. "Our brain isn't a one-stop shop. Think of a shopping mall. Sure, it might be one big structure, but it's comprised of individual stores that provide a variety of goods and services. You wouldn't head into a lingerie shop looking for the newest iPad." Knut's belly started gyrating as he struggled to stifle a fresh burst of laughter.

Sienna took over. "The areas of human functionality that NEDs improve are intelligence, memory, athleticism and equilibrium."

As far as Ben was concerned, the first three were fairly straightforward. And the third, athleticism, probably explained how he'd been able to dispatch those two guys who greatly outweighed him. It was the final one that threw him for a loop. "What's equilibrium do?"

"That one's about mood and happiness," she explained. "It usually gets boosted for folks with PTSD or depression or any form of mental health-related issue. In fact, it was the main reason you started your company, to help vets suffering from the after-effects of combat. Everything else, well, that came later."

"What's a boost?" Ben asked, unable to keep from feeling weird that strangers were explaining to him what must have been his life's work, and his greatest accomplishment.

"This is where I have to take issue with Neural-Sync," Knut said, not an ounce of humor left on his Icelandic features. "This isn't a fire-and-forget kind of implant. You don't simply get it installed and you're good. Boosting any one category costs Neuros. Think of them like tokens that enable you to buy boosts that you can put into any category you want. Feel your memory could use some improving? Then dump the points you bought in there. Not so worried about remembering your grocery list by heart? Think you're a bit of a doofus? Then throw your points into intellect and make yourself smarter. Everyone's got a different strategy. Some prefer to put all their eggs in one basket while others spread their points around like it's Easter."

"So there must be a ton of laid-back athletic geniuses

with photographic memories running around," Ben wondered out loud, his mind reeling with the possibilities. He noticed a programming book on the shelf and began flipping through the pages. Despite the rapidity of his movements, Ben could feel dense packets of information seeping into his mind.

Sienna watched him, her green eyes sparkling, not entirely sure what to think. "Thank goodness there aren't. To your credit, the cost of each boost doubles with every one you buy."

"Damn right," Knut added, frowning. "The first costs ten bucks, the second twenty, the third forty and it keeps going like that until it hits a hundred million a boost."

"A hundred million for a single point of intelligence or athleticism," Ben said, astonished. "That sounds insane. Who would spend that much?"

Sienna shook her head. "You'd be surprised. But buying boosts isn't the only way to get an upgrade. Neural-Sync's placed what they call Neuro tokens of varying denominations all over the world. You can only see them through the app, which looks like the camera screen, but with Neuro token icons overlaid onto the real world. Collect enough Neuros and you can trade them in for a boost. Or sell them," Sienna said, a distinct note of disapproval in her voice.

"Sell them to who?"

"There's a trading platform on Neural-Sync's website," Knut said, pulling it up. "A sort of auction house where you can put the Neuros you've collected up for sale for people to bid on."

"So that guy who nearly knocked me down in the alley," Ben said, a dark light coming on behind his eyes. "He was rushing to collect a Neuro."

"Yeah, and judging by his eagerness, it was probably a big one. We call them prospectors," Sienna explained. "For many, collecting the random Neuros that spawn all over is something of a gold rush. In only a few years, your invention has completely reshaped our society. Even more, I would argue, than the internet. And just like the internet's inventor, no one really knows a thing about you."

Ben raised his hand. "That includes me."

Knut returned to his Neural-Sync profile page and a cartoon image of his brain with the four blinking blue lights.

"Is there a way to see how many points you have?" Ben asked.

"Sure," Knut obliged. "Some folks get a bit touchy about revealing their spread, but I'm not ashamed." He pressed a plus icon on the screen, expanding a new area.

Intelligence (2)
Memory (2)
Athleticism (0)
Equilibrium (6)

"I dropped about eleven big ones," Knut told them. "A grand for the implant and the procedure. That was the cheap part. Then another ten grand for ten boosts. While the first one was only ten bucks, the tenth cost a little over five thousand."

Ben shook his head. "I can't imagine other companies aren't getting in on this. Neural-Sync can't be the only one."

Knut scoffed. "You're kidding, right? Neural-Sync's got the market completely cornered and its customers by the short and curlies. In fact, your nearest competitor, a company called Hear 4 You, produces a device called a cochlear implant that plugs directly into the brain, allowing deaf people to hear. The product works just fine. The problem is, the device is the size of a bus compared to the NED. Imagine having something the size of two cigarette packs with wires burrowed through your skull and into your brain. NED's a thousand times smaller, requires no invasive surgery and does infinitely more. In a nutshell, it's light years ahead of anything else on the market."

"You're saying nobody's tried to knock us off?" Ben asked with no small amount of skepticism.

"Sure they have," Sienna said. "They just haven't had much success. Part of the NED's edge comes from the unusual metallic alloy. The old Ben could probably have explained how it works, but it seems to merge perfectly with the human body without causing any kind of immune response."

Ben's gaze returned to the screen where Knut's stats were still being displayed. "I see you put nothing in athleticism and nearly everything in equilibrium."

Knut flexed one of his giant biceps and smiled. "I was blessed in the gun department. It might surprise you to learn this, but I've suffered from depression, especially after my wife and daughter…" The big man grinned as a tear rolled down his cheek.

Ben laid a hand on his shoulder. Even though he had nothing but the vaguest sense of Amanda's presence in his life, he knew something about what Knut was going through. He turned to Sienna. "What about you?"

She rubbed the back of her neck self-consciously. "I'm a hundred percent *au naturel*. I think the world's already messed up enough as it is without super-sizing people's abilities and egos."

"Ego?" he wondered out loud.

"Oh, heck yeah," she replied without missing a beat. "I mean, in the 60's and 70's when you met a guy he would probably ask for your astrological sign. Ten years ago, your Instagram page. Today the first thing he wants to know are your stats. Too many points in intelligence and he'll assume you're an idiot or too driven. It's a lose-lose situation."

"Let me assure you," Knut said, folding the considerable girth of his arms over his chest. "It's no bloody picnic on the other side. A woman hears you only have ten boosts, you probably won't hear back from her. There's a law that's been passed that employers aren't allowed to ask, but they still do."

"How many boosts can you have?" Ben asked.

"As many as you can afford," Knut shot back. "Guys like me normally have ten or so. Yuppies, around fifteen. Even rich folks start tapping out around eighteen. That's why those damn Neuro tokens are so popular. I know a guy who got twenty boosts without spending a cent. He won the implant from some online promotion and for the next five years he spent nearly every waking minute going up and down the West Coast harvesting Neuros." Knut's gaze settled on Ben. "I'll bet a rich guy like you would probably have at least twenty-five boosts. That's about—" Knut's brows creased from the calculation.

"Two hundred sixty-seven million, seven hundred seventy-two thousand, one hundred and fifty dollars," Ben let out in a single breath.

Knut and Sienna stared at him.

"Not including tax," Ben added.

"You're some kind of savant, aren't you?" Knut said, crunching the numbers with his calculator and seeing that Ben was right.

"I don't know," Ben replied. "The number just appeared in my head, fully formed. I don't remember adding anything together."

"All right, Mr. Fisher," Knut said, waving him forward with one hand, his cell phone in the other. "Let's see what's going on in that brain of yours."

Knut signed out of his own profile and held his phone to the back of Ben's neck. A second later appeared an image of a youthful-looking Ben dressed in torn clothes, his face covered in dirt. Then came another. He was older here, standing proudly next to a man at least thirty years his senior. This time, Ben's clothes were clean, and he was holding an acceptance letter from MIT. The images stirred something deep within him. Somehow, he knew the man wasn't his biological father, but he loved him dearly.

A greeting appeared.

Welcome back, Mr. Fisher.

That was when he realized not one of the pictures was of Amanda.

Up came an avatar of Ben's brain along with four areas glowing blue. Below that were his stats.

Intelligence (53)
Memory (-1)
Athleticism (75)
Equilibrium (41)

"Holy shit!" Knut shouted.

Sienna's eyes went wide. "That's not possible. It would cost hundreds of billions, maybe even trillions of dollars."

"Not if you owned the company," Knut said, shaking his head.

"I'm not so sure about that," Sienna replied. "Check his stats from the last time he signed in."

"Okay, this is from two days ago." Knut punched a few keys.

Intelligence (15)
Memory (15)
Athleticism (15)
Equilibrium (15)

"Wait a minute, this doesn't make any sense," Knut said, backtracking to make sure he hadn't made a mistake. "No one can boost that fast without dying."

A cold fear suddenly gripped Ben's heart. "Dying?"

"You can't add more than ten boosts to any given category at a time," Sienna told him. "Any more and the brain suffers serious trauma and bleeds out. Your company ran experiments on rats and monkeys until they figured out the acceptable limits."

"Go back to the current spread," Ben asked him. When Knut did, Ben pointed to his memory stat. "Any reason why that one's reading minus one?"

Both Knut and Sienna shook their heads and leaned in for a closer look.

"No clue," Knut admitted. "I've never seen anything like it before."

"It might explain the amnesia you're experiencing," Sienna suggested as she rubbed the palms of her hands along her thighs, a nervous habit she had since childhood.

Ben's mind returned to the throbbing pain at the back of his neck and the burst he'd received there from the stun gun. "Do you suppose my NED could have been damaged during the attack? A good stun gun can

66

generate a six-hundred-thousand-volt shock. The right strength at the right location might have knocked something loose."

Sienna's features softened. "I'm not sure, Ben. I imagine only a doctor who's familiar with the implant could tell you with any certainty."

Just then Ben's phone began to vibrate in his pocket. He pulled it out and saw it was his sister, Lori. For a moment he considered letting it go to voicemail before he got an idea.

"Lori."

"Ben, why aren't you answering your phone? The cops are at your house. They called the office looking for you. They won't tell me what's going on. Are you in some sort of trouble?"

Ben turned his back. "Someone broke into my house and killed Amanda." In any normal human being this would have been a nearly impossible sentence to get out without choking back tears. Ben suspected there was a whole river of sorrow being held back by the smallest of dams. Perhaps once his memories began returning, so too would his sense of loss and devastation. For now, all he felt was fear over the danger of his present situation and a bitter determination to come out the other end of this a free, and cleared, man.

Lori did the weeping for him. "Oh, Ben, you can't be serious." There was a pause as she struggled to collect herself. "You need to speak with the police or they'll think you had something to do with it."

"I have people helping me."

"What people?"

"Listen, Lori. There's something I need you to do for me. Does Neural-Sync have any military contracts with the US Navy?"

"Um, yes, of course we do, but w—"

"Good, I need you to get hold of our liaison over at the Pentagon and gather anything and everything you can find on a ship called the *Archipelago*."

"I don't understand."

Sienna watched him intently, her face a picture of hope and appreciation.

"Just do it, please. Repeat the name of the ship for me."

Lori's voice was steady and in control. "The *Archipelago*. I don't know what this is all about, but just be careful."

Ben told her he would and hung up.

Knut snatched Ben's phone from his hand. "I wish you'd told me earlier that the cops were on your tail."

Ben splayed his feet. "Why, you thinking of turning me in?"

The staccato of laughter emanating from Knut startled Ben. "Hell no. For a guy with a jacked-up IQ, you sure miss the obvious stuff." He plugged the phone into the computer and opened a program called Tracer Kill. "They can track you using your phone, so I'm rerouting the signal. That way, anyone checking your movements will think you're in Thailand. Ko Samui, to be exact. A beautiful island. It's where I met my wife." Knut's attention wandered for a moment, before returning to the task at hand. "I can't do anything about the content of your text messages or what you say in phone calls, but keep up the ruse that you're in Asia and it may buy you a few days."

Knut handed him back his phone. Ben was about to return it to his pocket when he heard it beep. A reminder popped up for tomorrow.

12pm meeting with Granger at the Purple Cafe and Wine

Bar (VI).

He read it out loud.

"Does VI mean the number six or something else?" Sienna asked.

Ben thought about it briefly and then said, "I think it means 'very important'."

"But who's this Granger person and what is the meeting supposed to be about?"

"I haven't got the foggiest idea," Ben said.

"Tell me you're not going to go meet him."

Ben didn't reply, but then again, he didn't need to.

Chapter 13

Sienna set fresh sheets and a comforter on the couch's armrest.

"I really appreciate you letting me stay here for the night," Ben said, meaning every word of it. Her pug, Buddy, sat next to Ben, wagging what passed for a tail and licking at his fingers whenever Ben tried to pet him.

"I think he likes you," Sienna said, grinning.

"Are you surprised?" Ben replied with a raised eyebrow.

"To be honest, I am. Buddy's a misanthrope, just like me."

Ben gave her a wink. "Really? You, I can see, but Buddy? He sure looks like a people person to me."

Sienna sat down next to the bedding she'd brought. "It's not something I like to advertise, especially given my line of work. Some people think just because you're a glaciologist that some part of you must love humanity, but the truth is, I don't. Not because of how they treat the planet like a garbage dump. It has more to do with disappointment, I suppose."

"I'm not sure I follow," Ben said, his brow furrowing.

Sienna folded her arms over her chest, squeezing together a part of her anatomy that might've sent the old Ben into a hormonal tailspin. He was beginning to learn that appreciating beauty was one thing and acknowledging little more than one's physical form, was another altogether.

"Humans have been living in communities and cities for thousands of years," Sienna began, "and we still can't seem to figure out how to get along with one another. We're like a big dysfunctional family that can't stand to sit next to one another at Thanksgiving dinner, let alone resolve a squabble peacefully. I mean, spin a globe and press your finger down on any part of it and you're likely to find a place where tribes of one kind or another are clawing at each other's throats. Heck, in some cases they have been for years, maybe even millennia. Israel and Palestine, Serbs and Croats, Tutsis and Hutus. People said after World War II and the Holocaust that genocide would never happen again, that the world wouldn't allow it. And yet it continues to this very day." Her eyes flashed with an intense mix of passion and sadness. "Believe me, I'm not getting on a soapbox. I'm only trying to say, this is who we are as a species. It seems to me that our moments of caring and compassion tend to be the exception, not the rule."

"That's quite a worldview you have there," Ben said, feeling the pain at the back of his head slowly returning. "Call me naïve, but I think, in the end, those great qualities you mentioned are the ones that will win out. Maybe that's why I started Neural-Sync. A great equalizing force in the world. I mean, think about it. You can take an ordinary flub off the street and augment them into a virtual god."

"God is dead," Sienna said sarcastically. "Isn't that what Nietzsche taught us?"

Ben smiled. "Maybe, but now we have new gods." They grew quiet for a moment, contemplating how two people could see the world so differently. Ben cleared his throat. "Anyway, I just wanted to thank you for sticking by me even though we hardly know one another."

"If I hadn't seen the video where your girlfriend…" Her voice trailed off. "What I mean to say is that I wouldn't know what to think. But it's clear to me now that you're an innocent man and that someone is out to make the world believe otherwise." Sienna's eyes fell. "Besides, I still expect you to uphold your end of the bargain."

"Just remember, as far as the cops are concerned, you may be harboring a dangerous fugitive."

"You don't look very dangerous to me," Sienna said. "And if I'm wrong, I've always got Buddy here to put you back in your place."

On cue, Buddy let out a whimper and licked Ben's hand.

Sienna retreated to her room after that, leaving Ben to untangle the mess of thoughts clouding his head. The stun gun to the back of his neck might have wildly improved his intelligence and physical prowess, among other qualities, but it had also robbed him of his memory, perhaps the most valuable asset any of us own.

Buddy was still sitting on the couch watching him eagerly as Ben picked up his phone and began scrolling through the hundreds of emails he had noticed earlier. He got about halfway down the page before he noticed one from Sienna's father, Nicholay Panov. There was no text present, only a grainy image of what looked like the opening of a hydrothermal vent. They formed near volcanically active areas along the ocean floor. Sea water circulated through superheated rocks and was ejected in a jet of dark, mineral-rich fluid. It was once believed that all non-microbial life required energy from the sun to live, a notion that had quickly evaporated when scientists discovered a vast array of biological life surrounding the vents. Ben stared at the image, wondering what it could mean, uncertain if it was worth pulling Sienna out of bed. He returned to his email and forwarded the image to his sister Lori.

From: benfisherceo@neuralsync.com
To: lorifishercoo@neuralsync.com
Subject: Greetings from Ko Samui!

Lori,
Could you forward this on to the Neural-Sync Navy liaison? I need anything they can give us on Nicholay Panov and the disappearance of the *Archipelago*.

Love,
Ben

With the message sent, the wise thing would have been to go straight to bed. Buddy was already there, curled up between his legs, snoring like a champ. Ben smiled and instead typed his name into Google. The top three search results were titled: 'The CEO you've probably never heard of. Who is Ben Fisher and where did he come from?' 'Ladies' man Ben Fisher, Neural-Sync's enigmatic CEO.' 'How Neural-Sync's brash young CEO is set to change the world.'

Ben shook his head and clicked on the image tab. Most of the pictures were of the company's logo. Even more were of Lori, which wasn't a big surprise given she'd been the face of the corporation since its inception. Three rows down, images of Ben with different women began to appear. Had he been with Amanda when all of this was happening? There was something surreal about looking at a version of yourself you couldn't recall existed. In a way he couldn't quite explain, his past behavior looked like more than a rich kid enjoying his newfound wealth. It almost felt compulsive. And yet here he was, sleeping in a beautiful woman's apartment and the thought of jumping into bed with her seemed somehow distant and secondary. Definitely a different version of the Ben than the one outlined by the press and archived cloud banks of Google.

Apart from making his NED go haywire, could the attack also have rewired some part of his brain? He typed the question in and did a search. Up popped the case of a man in Dayton, Ohio who became a virtuoso piano player after he took a bad beating to the head. Ben guessed anything was possible and he doubted he'd be able to connect all the dots tonight, regardless of his enhanced intelligence.

Ben switched out the light and gave Buddy a final pat in the dark, thinking about what he'd seen about himself on the internet, wishing he could somehow forget.

Chapter 14

Site 17
Xinjiang, China

Dr. Bo Zhou removed his mask and stared in awe at the readout from the ground-penetrating radar. As the lead scientist in charge of the Site 17 dig and the only fully certified dual-trained paleontologist and archaeologist, it was his job to know what they were seeing.

Next to him stood Karen Hobbs, a British anthropologist with more than thirty years of excellent field work under her belt. The two had birthdays separated by six months and just as many years, Zhou being the senior of the two. She was lean, with long angular features and skin the color of fresh almonds. The latter was mostly from years spent outside on dig sites, much like this one in Xinjiang.

And yet, in all of Zhou's five and a half decades on this earth, he had never seen a readout like this. Karen looked no less stumped. They had come here in search of Genghis Khan's tomb. His sudden and unexpected death in 1227 had shaken the world and much of the massive empire he had created over the course of his reign. Past expeditions had looked by the Orion River in

Mongolia with little to show for the effort. The move to a series of promising sites in China had been billed as a widening of the net, so to speak. Which was why Site 17 had shown so much promise. Drone surveys from five hundred feet up had indicated a structure of some kind had stood here long ago. How long, they wouldn't know until they investigated further.

But now the peaks and valleys of shadow on the radar readout were forcing them to rethink many of their previous assumptions. The reason was rather simple. First of all, Genghis' tomb was expected to have a circumference of about fifty meters. The structure they'd just discovered was ten times as big and much deeper. Moreover, the square shape and dimensions reminded Zhou of the Yonaguni Monument, a stone structure of unknown origin previously discovered off Japan's southern coast. It featured steps, passageways and numerous raised platforms. Each side was tapered, giving the impression of depth and height.

Zhou glanced at Karen and grunted. "I would ask what you think it is, but I can see by the look on your face you're just as confused as I am." Karen wasn't the only one whose complexion had been battered by the sun. Zhou's short powerful arms looked like fried dumplings, crispy brown on one side and pale on the other. His face was round and jovial, which only served to mask his rather legendary temper.

"Reminds me of an Aztec or Mayan temple, don't you think?" Karen said, turning the image, the way one might turn a photograph of something vaguely human.

"Message the crew," Zhou said. "And tell them to start digging." He began to walk away.

"Where are you going?" Karen asked, always the busybody.

"To talk to the Stickler," he answered without turning around.

This time it was Karen's turn to grunt.

•••

The Stickler Zhou had been referring to was Li Xiu Ying. She was what some called the government minder, a representative of the Chinese Communist Party. Her stated role was to ensure Yanks like Zhou and Brits like Karen didn't make off with any valuable Chinese artifacts or damage important historical sites. But her real job was to spy on the operation and report back on any find which might work to contradict or undermine the current Communist view of China's past.

Not surprisingly, Li displayed little sense of humor. A petite woman in her early thirties, she was suspicious, implacably rigid and an overall pain in the ass. It didn't help the woman hated to talk about herself, something that had surprised the American-born Zhou, but also something he had come to understand about the Chinese character in general. There were ears everywhere, one of the unsettling realities of living in a police state. The illusion of freedom was ubiquitous—business owners in Bentleys, travelling abroad and living the life—but the slightest misstep, the wrong word uttered, turning your back on your country's attempts to turn you into a spy... If you were unfortunate enough to find yourself going against the state, you were SOL, as the kids liked to say.

He found her in his air-conditioned trailer going through his things.

"Excuse me," Zhou said, feigning shock and outrage.

She stopped what she was doing—"Section three, subset eleven of the articles governing heritage sites clearly states all findings are subject to oversight"—but only because she couldn't do more than one thing at a time. She resumed her search.

"You're probably looking for this," Zhou said, waving the radar printout in the air. "I've already emailed you a copy."

"Your email was received and has been forwarded to my superiors," she recited in a broken, robotic version of a language that sounded something like English, but with all of the soul sucked out of it. "Of course, they will want to know what it is you found."

"The crew is digging as we speak." While on the surface this interaction appeared rather benign, Zhou recognized it was anything but. Whatever they had found, he could tell by the depth and size that it was far older than anyone appreciated just yet. There were really two things Li wanted to know. First, was it Genghis' tomb? And second, would it be a find bigger in cultural magnitude than the discovery of the tomb of Qin Shi Huang, China's first emperor? This was the tricky part and an old hand like Zhou knew he had to tread carefully. Because once it became clear the structure— assuming it was one—was not thousands of years old, but maybe even millions, the government would swoop in and bury it in so much red tape, it might never see the light of day. So he had to rely on perhaps the most ancient form of human communication. He had to lie.

"Judging by our initial findings, we have not found Genghis' final resting place. More than likely it's a run-of-the-mill temple, perhaps dating to the third century BC." Zhou screwed up his face in an Oscar-winning look of disappointment. "Sorry to disappoint you. But of course, we'll dig it up anyway. No doubt the National Museum will have plenty of new vases to fill its shelves." As he watched her eyes glaze over, his heart rejoiced. A find as mundane as Zhou described held little promise of a promotion or accolades.

Li started past him and stopped. "Should you find anything of interest, be sure to report it to me at once. Is that understood?"

Zhou raised his three middle fingers and grinned. "Scout's honor."

Chapter 15

Ben Fisher entered the Purple Cafe and Wine Bar and was struck at once by the wine tower rising up before him. An eye-catcher if ever he'd seen one, the tower's shelves were stacked with more than a thousand bottles and featured two spiral staircases that led to the ceiling fifty feet above their heads. The place was an alcoholic's dream come true, he thought as he scanned the many faces having lunch around him. Nearly half of them had masks hanging over the back of their seats. A handful wore the cloth types, dipping them down to sip a glass of wine or take a bite of food.

But breathable air wasn't foremost on his mind. He was looking for Granger, the man he was supposed to meet here at noon. Or at least someone who fit the mental image Ben had created in his mind. Two other sets of stairs led to a mezzanine with more tables. Below that, a set of swinging doors opened onto the kitchen, offering a brief glimpse now and then of the flurry of activity going on behind the scenes as businessmen and women waited impatiently for their meals.

The maître d' approached, a white towel slung over his forearm.

"Table for one?"

Ben shook his head. "I'm here to meet someone."

The man went to a leather-bound book and began flipping through pages. "Their name?"

"Granger."

The maître d' scanned the list and drew a blank expression. "We have no one here by that name."

"You mind if I look around a bit?"

"Be my guest."

Ben stalked the lower dining room floor, swinging his gaze from table to table, paying particular attention to anyone sitting alone. Granger could very well be a female, but something inside told him he was male and older. Could that be a sign Ben's memories were starting to return? He pushed on, finishing the main floor and taking the stairs to the second. An older gentleman wearing an oxygen mask sat at a table that overlooked the restaurant. The placid expression on his face changed to one of surprise when he caught Ben's eye.

"Granger?" Ben wondered out loud.

The man rose from his seat and approached, placing a firm hand on Ben's elbow, his eyes scanning him up and down. Although he looked like he could be in his early eighties, he seemed surprisingly agile and alert. He lifted his mask and hacked up a lung.

"Damn forest fires," he muttered. "The air's getting harder to breathe now that those sons of bitches are burning year-round."

Ben wasn't sure how to respond to that, so he kept quiet.

"I didn't expect you to make it," Granger continued. There was a rough, gravelly quality to his voice. How much of that came with age and how much with the questionable state of the air outside was anyone's guess. He motioned for Ben to sit.

81

"You've seen the news, I take it?"

Granger nodded. "It's just terrible," he said, the compassion on his face unmistakable. "As I understand it, the police only want to ask you a few questions. I'm sure it wouldn't hurt to do as they ask."

"I didn't do it, you know."

Granger's eyes never wavered. "I believe you. But something about you feels different. Would you believe, when I saw you come up those stairs, I got the distinct impression you didn't recognize me? Maybe you've just had a lot on your mind."

"Well, let's just say that my memory isn't what it used to be," Ben began to explain. "Listen, I need to understand how we know each other and what the purpose was for our meeting today."

"You're not kidding, are you? Well, that's simple enough," Granger replied. "At least in part. I'm on Neural-Sync's board of directors and probably one of the few allies you have left. Over the last few months, the board's become a den of vipers, eager for any excuse to strip you of your responsibilities." Granger's head tilted. "How much of the last week do you remember?"

"Try 'how much of my entire life do I remember?' and the answer's nothing," Ben replied truthfully. There was no longer any point attempting to put a funny spin on the stark reality facing him. "All I know is that someone killed Amanda and wants me out of the way."

Granger's mask fogged as he listened intently. "Do you have proof of this?"

"The security system captured the murder."

"You watched it?"

"I did. Saw the person ambush me when I arrived home."

"And they let you live?" The lilt in Granger's voice

was filled with surprise.

"Which is why I'm more and more certain the intent was to frame me. Whoever did this ran off with the recorder. My phone is all I have left, so when I saw we were scheduled to have an important meeting, I was hoping you could tell me what it was about."

Granger shrugged his narrow shoulders. "You were the one who asked to meet. You told me you had something vitally important to tell me. You used the words 'earth-shattering,' which surprised me since you're not the kind prone to hyperbole."

"Earth-shattering," Ben repeated dreamily. "Maybe someone didn't want us having this conversation."

Ben's phone made a sound, notifying him a new text message had just come in.

The old man nodded. "That's entirely possible, but don't you think there could be a more prosaic explanation? I mean, you're talking about what sounds like a conspiracy."

"Crazy talk, I know. I've been racking my brain and can't seem to find one."

Granger smiled weakly, his yellow teeth barely visible through the transparent plastic oxygen mask. Another beep. This one caught Granger's ear. "Someone's trying to get your attention."

"It can wait," Ben said. "Listen, was there anything else unusual I mentioned to you? Anything at all that stands out?"

"Hmm, you did bring up someone named Tang."

"Tang?"

Granger started coughing again. "No, Lang. My apologies. Dr. Lang. Although I can't say who the man is or how he might be involved."

A third beep and this time Ben pulled out his phone

to shut it off. His thumb was hovering over the power button when he saw the words on his screen.

Don't trust him.

Ben felt cold fingers walking up his spine.

"Everything all right?" Granger asked.

Ben's eyes found the old man's face and the look of concern he was wearing. The text had come in without a name, so it was impossible to tell if it was someone attempting to help or confuse him.

"No, it's nothing," he replied, beads of sweat gathering on his forehead.

"Are you sure? You don't look so well."

"I need to know more about Dr. Lang and why I might have brought him up."

Granger's shoulders rose. "I wish there was more I could tell you, Ben. I'm not a lawyer, but it may be in your best interest to speak with the authorities. Clear your name. A cloud like this hanging over you is bad for everyone, including Neural-Sync."

A commotion downstairs drew Ben's attention away from the plea Granger was making. Four men in dark suits were pushing aside the maître d' and heading this way, each of them staring directly at him as they broke into a run. Ben rose to his feet, his heart now beating a furious racket in his chest.

"Ben, what is it?"

The men in dark suits split into two groups, each of them taking one of the two stairways that led to the second floor. The one in the lead was rippling with muscle, his friends not far behind. "Mr. Fisher, stay where you are."

If there had been any doubt in his mind they were coming for him, that doubt was now gone. He spun around. He was trapped. The men reached the second level right as Ben grabbed the railing and flung himself over. He fell through the air, distinctly aware he was about to drop twenty feet and break both his legs. The ground came up fast. The balls of his feet were the first to land. Without any conscious thought, his legs bent and he lowered himself into a roll, landing upright, bumping into a waiter with a tray full of dishes. The waiter fell back, scrambling without luck to rebalance the weight. The dishes fell with a deafening clatter. Ben stood for a second, still in disbelief he'd made it down in one piece.

The men hung over the railing, pointing at him. Three of them ran for the stairs, while the fourth attempted to duplicate his move. He landed a split second later and Ben grimaced at the sound of breaking bones. The man writhed in agony as Ben headed toward the entrance. Two others were there, waiting for him. Fear was surging through him as he skidded to a stop and backtracked toward the kitchen. He kicked open the swinging door. Intense heat and the aroma of cooking meats struck him at once. Ben pushed his way past line cooks in dirty aprons and prep staff.

A quick glance revealed two of his pursuers hot on his trail, pushing their way into the kitchen. Frantic workers pointed, directing the men toward him. There had to be a back door somewhere around here. He found a long corridor off the kitchen and followed it. A handful of open doors lined the right side of the wall, a quick glance inside the first revealing nothing more than a desk filled with receipts and an ashtray with a burning cigarette. This must be the office area, he thought, spotting a metal door with a push bar in the distance. *Get outside.* His mind repeated the words like a mantra. All he needed to do was get himself outside.

A straight arm emerged from one of the open doorways, striking him in the neck and knocking him to the ground. Ben held his throat, struggling for air. A thin man stepped into the corridor, his right hand still balled into a fist, his left holding a syringe. "Do you believe in magic?" he asked, plunging the tip into Ben's thigh. But before he had a chance to pump its contents into his bloodstream, Ben leaned back and drove the heel of his boot directly into the thin man's face. His features twisted with shock and surprise and, ultimately, with pain. His body lifted off the ground several feet before landing flat on his back, his head bouncing off the tile floor.

Ben removed the syringe and noticed for the first time the man's face and hands were covered in scratches. He was moaning, rocking side to side. Ben stuck him with the syringe and emptied the contents. Almost at once, he was tackled from behind by one of the men in dark suits. They both sailed over the thin man's prone form, crashing to the ground.

The guy on top of him was strong, his muscles bunched up like taut cords pressing into Ben's back. He was trying to keep Ben pinned down until reinforcements arrived. Ben snapped his head straight back and into the bodybuilder's nose. He heard the man growl and tighten his grip.

"Stay down, asshole," the man rasped into his ear.

A set of footfalls was fast approaching.

Ben pressed his elbows apart, breaking the man's grip. He then slid a knee under him and used it as leverage to stand, the assailant still on his back. Bodybuilder moved to grab him in a rear choke hold and Ben grabbed one of his arms with both his hands and twisted it. Bodybuilder howled with pain, his massive arm now turned unnaturally behind his back. That was when Ben spotted his friend charging down the corridor. He waited until the man was less than five feet away before he flung the bodybuilder forward, knocking the two men's heads together. It was only enough to daze them, but that was all Ben needed. He turned on his heels and ran for the exit.

The restaurant back door led into an alley. The moment Ben appeared the lights from a dark SUV parked by a dumpster came on. He heard the electric motor give a loud whine as the driver hit the accelerator and turned the wheel toward him. There was nowhere to go except for a nearby street, some thirty feet away. Without any hesitation he took off running, the car quickly closing the distance.

He wasn't going to make it. The ladder from the fire escape dangled fifteen feet in the air. Certainly out of reach, but in less than a second he was about to become roadkill. Ben leapt into the air with all of his might, his arms and legs pinwheeling. One thought exploded across the canvas of his mind in bold, bright red letters—*You're not gonna make it*. The fingers of his right hand closed around the bottom rung and his legs swung out in front of him. Below, the car sped by, slamming on its brakes. With relative ease, Ben hurried up the ladder and from there up the stairs to the roof of the building. He quickly noticed he could hop from one building to the next by jumping the five-foot gaps between them. He did so a dozen times until he felt like he was far enough away from his pursuers that he could safely head back down to street level.

Fresh rain clouds had rolled in since he arrived at the restaurant and they were mixed now with the ever-present smog he could feel burning his lungs. This was

87

probably why there were so few people on the streets. For years, terrible air quality had been the norm in large Chinese cities. But never in America, not like this.

His phone began to ring just as Ben was climbing into a nearby self-driving cab. He looked down and saw Amanda's name and picture appear.

"Who is this?"

"That's one hell of a way to talk to your girlfriend."

The voice belonged to a male and Ben repeated the question, this time more forcefully.

"This is Detective Hernandez. We've been calling, Mr. Fisher, and you haven't been picking up."

"I didn't do it," Ben shot back, in answer to the unspoken accusation dripping from Hernandez's every word.

"Do what?" Now the detective was playing dumb.

"Someone's trying to pin the murder on me and I didn't do it. I've seen the video from the attack and it clearly shows someone was in my house. I came home from work and found her dead."

Hernandez cleared his throat. "So, you *were* there?"

"Yes, but she was already gone."

"Funny, you don't sound very choked up. If I came home to find someone I loved slaughtered on my living room couch, I'd be a mess."

"Yeah, well, we all deal in different ways."

"Regarding that video you mentioned, the DVR player was gone when we arrived. You have anything to do with that?"

"Of course not. I'm looking for it myself. It's the one thing that can clear me."

"That's something we can both agree on," Detective Hernandez said with more than a touch of irony. "But here's the thing. The footage from that day was also erased from the cloud. Rather convenient, don't you think?"

Ben drew in a sharp breath. "No, not if your goal is to erase all evidence of my innocence."

"Or your guilt."

"Am I under arrest?"

"Not yet, we just have a few questions."

"So that wasn't your men at the restaurant earlier?"

"Restaurant? I don't follow."

"Never mind."

"Look, the sooner you talk to us, the sooner we can sort this out. Where are you right now?"

"Ko Samui."

"Pardon me?"

"Thailand. It's beautiful here. The air's a bit cleaner and the people are great. I highly recommend it. I gotta go, but I'll be in touch."

He hung up right as Hernandez was about to object.

Ben was paying the cab with the banking bracelet he'd borrowed from Sienna when an email came through. This time it was Lori. The Navy contact she had reached out to was willing to talk, but only in person and only to the next of kin. That didn't bode well for Nicholay's chances of still being alive. Ben considered whether he should tell Sienna. After just getting ambushed, there was no telling what kind of trap she might be walking into. For the time being, at least, Ben had bigger fish to fry. Namely, figuring out who this Dr. Lang was Granger had told him about. And more importantly, whether the old man could even be trusted.

Chapter 16

...And more now from Mumbai, where a serious outbreak of tuberculosis is being blamed for the deaths of tens of thousands of the city's inhabitants. According to Eva Campos, the head of the WHO, the pathogen's rapid spread is a perfect storm of antibiotic-resistant bacteria and the knock-on effects of worsening drought in the area.

In an ironic twist, security services in China are accusing the United States of stealing technology secrets and are vowing to ramp up retaliation.

And finally, back home where enigmatic billionaire and founder of Neural-Sync, Benjamin Fisher, is being sought in the stabbing death of his live-in girlfriend, Amanda Lippeatt. Police are saying the investigation is still in its early stages and that Mr. Fisher is not a suspect, but merely a person of interest. They encourage him to meet with police. According to authorities, he has not been seen since the murder.

Chapter 17

Sienna pulled into the University of Washington's parking lot at about the same time Ben was sitting down for lunch with Granger at the wine bar. She switched off the motor and sat for a moment, taking in the beautiful scene before her. UW's open courtyard was lined with cherry blossom trees in full bloom, walled in on either side by collegiate Gothic-style buildings. If any American university belonged on a postcard, this was definitely a top contender.

She got out and went to the trunk to retrieve the eight-thousand-pound backpack that was probably responsible for the pinched nerve that had been bothering her of late. Sienna had no sooner grabbed what she needed when a white plumbing van pulled up perpendicular to her car. The van's sliding door popped open and two men in ski masks grabbed her and pulled her inside. Half a second later, the vehicle's tires screeched as it tore away at high speed.

Inside, rough hands held her in place as the vehicle navigated out of the parking lot. She began to scream, thrashing about to fight her way free.

"Hold still," a stern male voice said as he held his gloved hand over her mouth.

Sienna bit down with all her might.

The man swore and wrenched his hand free, waving it about in pain. Something fell out of his other hand and thudded onto the carpet at her feet. She reached down and picked it up. It was a stun gun. She went for the sliding door, but blocking her way was another person in a ski mask. Behind the wheel, a long-haired male in baggy clothes was busily engaged in making their escape. The one facing her raised an expandable baton.

In response, Sienna leveled the stun gun, pressing the button and showing her assailants the bluish electric arc. She swiveled left and right, anticipating an attack from both sides.

"Don't make us have to hurt you," said the man with the baton.

Sienna thought about the stun gun in her hand. Did these people have something to do with the murder of Ben's girlfriend?

The man threatened her again. But the *he* part wasn't quite right. This man's voice was far too soft and feminine.

"Jesus!" the one next to her shouted. "She practically took my finger off."

"Stop whining, Birch," the high-voiced man scolded him. "You still got nine others."

Sienna used her free hand to brace herself in the rocking van, her stun gun never wavering. "What do you people want from me?"

"To help you," the woman replied.

Sienna scoffed. "Sure, by kidnapping me in broad daylight? You won't even show me your faces."

"We need to make sure we can trust you first."

Sienna shook her head. "Well, you can't, so let me out and I'll pretend like none of this ever happened."

"You're trying to find out what happened to your father, aren't you?"

Sienna paused. "Why? Do you know something?"

"We might, but first you need to stand down."

The guy with the bleeding finger crawled past her and slinked over to the person with the baton.

"I'm not letting go of my weapon, if that's what you're asking," Sienna insisted. "How about you stay where you are and tell me what you know."

The one with the baton laid down her weapon and removed her ski mask. Sienna was surprised to see it was a woman with dark red hair. She was attractive in a sort of earthy way. "I'm Willow," she said, her hands in front of her, palms out. She nodded to the person Sienna had bitten. "This here's Birch and…"

"Let me guess," Sienna cut in. "The driver's name is Oak."

Willow smiled. "Those aren't our real names—"

"Yeah, no kidding."

"—but they'll do for now."

"Who are you people?" Sienna demanded. "And are you aware that kidnapping is a serious felony?"

"We aren't terrorists, if that's what you're wondering."

"Then what are you?"

"Let's just say we're interested in getting to the truth." Willow turned to the driver. "Pull over here, will you?" Then, reaching onto the passenger seat, she retrieved a laptop. "I don't need to be the one to tell you the kind of shitstorm your father's research has set off."

"No, you don't. And it certainly felt to him like every tree-hugger in the world came out to tear him a new one. That's what happens when you tell the truth. Some people love you, but most end up hating you as bad as

93

they've hated anything in their lives."

"Then there are those who try to silence you," Willow said.

Sienna's mind rewound to one of the most painful moments in her father's life. After snippets of his work had been leaked to the media, thousands of threatening emails and public ridicule had quickly flooded her father's life, tsunami-style. And that was the problem with leaks. At worst, the information leaked was incomplete and out of context; at best, well, there *was* no 'best'. How could anyone have been expected to read what he wrote with an open mind when he himself had yet to fully unpack the data and consider what it was telling him? Instead, self-proclaimed social justice warriors and internet trolls had descended en masse, focused on poking holes in phantom conclusions he'd yet to even postulate. Seemingly overnight every politician, pundit and spin doctor had weighed in, tailoring their weaponized words in support of one corporate agenda or another, all motivated by the pursuit of increasing personal wealth. Damned be the facts or her father's reputation... But as Willow's words rang in Sienna's head, it was clear she meant more than that.

"Are you saying someone did something to him?"

Willow's eyes dropped to the laptop, where she had a video ready to play. A frozen landscape came into focus, the frame filled with steep, snowy cliffs. Nearby, loose chunks of ice bobbed in the roiling seas as the camera was lowered into the water. Bubbles whizzed by on either side, signaling the descent of an underwater rover on its way to explore the depths of the Arctic or Antarctic Ocean. Which one it was, Sienna couldn't be sure.

The rover's trip down felt like it would take forever.

The whole time Sienna's head was hammering a sick beat in her chest as she wondered what it might show her when it got to the bottom. Eventually, a white shape emerged from the silty gloom. What might have passed for the bow of a ship was like nothing she had seen before. Over the years, her father had shown her countless images of sunken ships—the *Titanic* resting at the bottom of the Atlantic, the *Bismarck*, the USS *Hornet*, to name but a few. Each of them had one startling fact in common. Despite the often brutal damage inflicted on them, they were easily recognizable.

Her fingers still clenched around the stun gun, Sienna leaned in for a closer look. It was hard to imagine ever witnessing a more mangled wreck. The steel hull was rippled, like water after a pebble is tossed into a still pond. Other parts were twisted and bent almost beyond recognition. Slowly, the submersible repositioned and the name of the ship became visible. She knew precisely what she was about to see, but all the fortifying in the world couldn't have lessened the sting.

The letters were stretched and warped, like the ship itself, but the word was just clear enough to make out. *Archipelago.*

The submersible swung around, revealing the disturbing fate that had befallen the ship and her crew. The hull had been crushed from some unspeakable pressure. Sienna stared in disbelief, wondering whether the ship's final resting place had been deep enough to explain the damage she was seeing.

"What the hell happened?" she asked, barely aware she was speaking.

"Keep watching," Willow told her.

The submersible swung around what passed for the stern, following a trail of debris. Ahead, a much smaller yellow ball came into visual range and suddenly Sienna felt her entire body twitch in protest. She knew what the yellow ball was. It was the submarine her father had used during his deep exploratory dives. This was what he used to study the deep-sea vents as well as the underwater volcanoes that littered the ocean floor. Slowly it came closer, Sienna's anxiety spiking as it did. She knew as the submersible drew even with the wreck she might spot her father's corpse, crushed in the distorted remnants of his favorite sub. She struggled to close her eyes and yet at the same time she couldn't look away. Was this really the way she wanted to remember him?

"Please stop," she said, not caring that her words came out sounding weak and pleading. No child deserved to see a parent they loved in such an undignified situation. "I don't know where you got this, but it can't be the *Archipelago*."

"Why is that?" Willow asked, befuddled by the strength of Sienna's insistence.

"It's simple. The footage you showed me is filled with ice floes. But my father's ship sank somewhere in the Pacific."

"Apparently not," Willow replied.

Sienna struggled to make sense of what they were telling her. What would he have been doing near Antarctica? "All I want to know is whether or not Nicholay's body is in there." She was referring to the yellow sub, crushed nearly beyond recognition.

Willow's eyes skittered away briefly before returning to Sienna's gaze. She nodded. "I'm afraid so."

"The Navy said they searched for days and couldn't find him," Sienna said, growing anger in her voice.

"They said a lot of things that have been untrue," Willow replied. "But I think you already knew that."

Sienna didn't bother responding. She had too many questions of her own. It was hard enough holding back the tidal wave of anger and sorrow threatening to overwhelm her. She clenched her teeth and did her best to compose herself. "Where did you get this?"

"Let's just say we found it on Naval Intelligence servers."

"You hacked government servers?"

Willow frowned, deep lines forming along her brow. "Well, none of us expected them to just hand it over. We may not be the most sophisticated group, but we know not to bother wasting time with freedom of information requests. The point is, someone high up didn't want your father's research getting out. At first, we wondered whether an extremist group could be behind the *Archipelago*'s disappearance. The kind of militant environmental organization that would make Greenpeace look about as lethal as a Girl Scout troop."

"With names like Willow, Oak and Birch," Sienna said, "and the whole kidnapping routine, I was starting to think you were the extremists."

Willow shook her head. "Oh, no. We're the good guys."

Sienna smiled. "Yeah, that's what the extremists say too. 'We're good. The other guys, they're the evil ones.'"

"We weren't convinced you would show up if we invited you all nice and polite-like," Willow said, a hand on her hip and her lips pulled to one side in a sneer. "The point is, unless environmentalists have really upped their game in the last few years, there's no way they could have done that to your father's research vessel."

"That doesn't leave a lot of options," Sienna said, the stun gun now resting by her side. "You think the US Navy destroyed my father's ship and killed his crew in

97

order to shut him up, then moved the wreckage to hide what they did? Is that what you're suggesting?"

Willow shrugged. "That's one theory. But we shouldn't assume our navy alone is capable of something like this. There's a big wide world out there. Let your imagination run wild. You might be surprised what you discover."

Sienna scoffed. "Now you really are starting to sound like a hippie." Nevertheless, she let her mind grow quiet and did exactly what Willow suggested. It didn't take long for other options to emerge. "Are we talking Russia?"

"You're lukewarm," Willow replied.

"North Korea?"

"Think bigger."

"China?"

"It's a theory at least."

"If that's true," Sienna said, taking the idea and running with it, "why? I mean, I get my father's research was wildly unpopular. But in the last decade, much of the world had already embraced a move to greener technologies. You would think the old guard responsible for the bulk of the greenhouse emissions would have welcomed his findings."

"Maybe," Willow said. "But you're forgetting one thing. There's a new old guard in town, one that may be willing to defend their turf with even greater ferocity than their predecessors."

It was a good point and one Sienna hadn't considered. There was something particularly ironic about the whole idea. An industry built on responsible stewardship of the planet, silencing the voice of someone trying to bring light to the fact that we might be in more trouble than we thought.

"At this point," Willow continued, "all we can say for sure is that something is going on and I worry that it's much bigger than your father or any of his findings. He might have uncovered the tip of a much bigger iceberg. And clearly, there are forces whose sole purpose is to keep as much of that iceberg hidden as they can."

Sienna shook her head in disbelief. There was more to the tragedy at hand than her father's death. He hadn't been alone on the Archipelago. "What about the crew?" she reminded them. "I should reach out and notify their families."

"I wouldn't do that just yet," Willow advised. "Although there's something you should know. Something we'd been intending to tell you all along. Apparently, not every member of the crew was lost. William Schroder was thrown on to an ice floe during the explosion and was rescued close to death by a passing geological survey ship."

That was an astonishing and hopeful bit of news. It meant that a member of the crew had survived. With any luck, this Schroder might be able to explain what had happened to the Archipelago. And maybe, just maybe help find those responsible for murdering her father and the crew that had served him so faithfully. "Where can I find this guy?" she asked.

Willow shrugged. "We're looking into it, believe me. Seems he's disappeared."

Sienna curled a lock of her hair around her finger. "When you find out where he is, let me know. I'd like to be the one to ask him some questions. I'm not sure kidnapping is the best approach."

Chapter 18

Site 17
Xinjiang, China

The dig area was so vast, Bo Zhou used a golf cart with specialized wheels to get around. The rain, which had fallen all through the night, was slowing down the process of removing thousands of metric tons of soil from the enigmatic structure below.

Zhou was driving along the edge of the hole already carved out by the eight China-made excavators when he felt his back tires get stuck in the mud. He turned the wheel and hit the accelerator, not managing to do much apart from spray a fan of mud behind him. He swore, feeling that old frustration boiling up to the surface. He called it his dragon. Whenever the world threw up a silly, time-consuming obstacle, he felt the dragon emerge from its lair to breathe fire over everything.

"Come on, you worthless piece of crap, get moving."

He switched the cart into reverse and attempted to backtrack. The temper was a genetic gift he had received from his grandmother. Both of Zhou's parents were loving, mild-mannered and, above all else, practical. They had fled China in the 70's during the Cultural

Revolution, opting to settle in America and pursue a dream shared by most of the desperate and destitute who came knocking. In short order they had started two businesses, both of which were typical, a touch cliché. The first was a small Chinese food kiosk in the food court of a local Wisconsin mall. That was the business his mother ran. His father ran a corner store conveniently situated below the family apartment.

Zhou was an only child, although not for lack of effort on his parents' part. China hadn't officially enacted the one-child policy until after his parents were already gone. His mother had longed for another little one and it was no secret she wanted that little one to be a daughter.

But it was not meant to be. The gods had decreed Zhou would be an only child. And not surprisingly, Zhou's parents had poured their hearts and souls into providing him the greatest opportunities possible. As his father told him, "I'm running a shop so that you won't need to."

When Zhou's years in high school had proved he was brighter than many of the other kids, his parents had been thrilled. It was clear from a young age his father envisioned him going into medicine, computer programming or perhaps architecture. His mother, on the other hand, dreamt Zhou might one day join an Olympic team and bring home a gold medal. And they had their reasons. Each of those provided a large measure of bragging rights coupled with the prospect of a comfortable yearly salary. That was as long as a gold medal could be parlayed into lucrative endorsements. Either way, Zhou had been hardly surprised by the looks of horror he'd received upon informing them he had been accepted into Yale's anthropology department.

His father's head had shaken back and forth in disbelief while his mother had put her face in her hands and began fits of gentle sobbing.

You would have thought they had just heard news that the world was coming to a rather sudden and dramatic end. The betrayal his mother felt had been so great she had refused to speak to him for a month. And even after his penance was done, her communications were limited to two- to three-word sentences.

Realizing his parents' acceptance was not forthcoming, Zhou had set off to make the most out of his passion for ancient peoples and the societies they'd lived in. Further study in the field of archeology helped to supplement his background in anthropology.

In 2008, when he joined a team investigating a cave in Siberia, everything had changed. Zhou and his partner from the Russian Academy of Sciences had found the finger bone from a previously unknown hominid. Like the Neanderthal, this was a cousin on the human family tree that had gone extinct tens of thousands of years ago. They named it Denisovans after the seventeenth-century Russian hermit who'd lived in the cave. Acclaim and awards soon came flooding in. Not surprisingly, his mother's favorite accolade came from the Archaeological Institute of America, who awarded Zhou and his partners each a gold medal for distinguished archeological achievement. In one of the weird twists of fate that life was often filled with, he supposed, in the end, his mother had gotten her gold medal wish after all.

Zhou had just about worked himself out of the mud when Karen appeared next to him.

"I think you should have walked," she said, eyeing his half-buried tires.

Zhou conceded. Try as he might, the situation with the golf cart was not going to end well. He stepped out and set the hard hat atop his head as he and Karen headed to the command post on foot.

"How was your meeting with Li yesterday?" she asked, a slight hesitation in her voice.

Zhou shrugged. "About as well as could be expected. I told her we were digging up a two-thousand-year-old temple. In China those are about as common as ponds filled with giant carp."

"I should tell you, some of the additional readings came in this morning," she began, biting her bottom lip, a clear sign she had found something that either worried or frightened her.

"Go on," Zhou said, trying to play it cool.

"As you ordered, we dug a vertical shaft fifty feet down, so that the bottom lined up with the base of the structure. We then examined the soil there and came up with a date."

He stopped and looked at her. "It's older than we thought, isn't it?"

Karen nodded, her teeth clamping down even more on that poor lower lip.

"Give me a number."

"The structure appears to be somewhere in the neighborhood of thirty million years old."

Zhou felt his eyebrows do a little dance. "Is that it?"

"Not even close."

Zhou crossed his arms. He'd known the site was different, but he was beginning to worry about just how different it was.

"I was going over the shape of the structure last night and fed the data into a program that created this 3D model." She pulled up the image on her phone and held it up for Zhou to see. While from the top down it appeared to be square, from the side, one could see spindles of thread jutting out from each corner, at the end of which sat a double-sided hook.

"What am I looking at?" he wondered out loud.

"They appear to be pylons leading to some type of anchoring system."

Zhou grunted. Engineers today often used similar methods when reinforcing a wall, such as in the case of the Freedom Tower in New York City. Although, if this were true, the images Karen was showing him seemed to take that idea so much further. "Why would whoever built this feel the need to anchor it so thoroughly? Looks like overkill to me."

"Who's to say what was going on thirty million years ago? Maybe they were worried about asteroids and earthquakes."

Zhou nodded, not believing a word of it. A theory was emerging in his mind, had been since he had crossed paths with that very first radar reading. A theory, he worried, that might push the current understanding of reality just a little too far. "Is there anything else?" he asked, not entirely certain he wanted to hear the answer.

"That shaft we dug ended near the south-west anchor, so we were able to send down one of the robot drones and retrieve a sample." She held up a small plastic container.

Zhou took the case and lifted the lid. Inside was a shiny silver substance he couldn't immediately identify. The shape was distorted, probably from the tools the robot had been forced to employ in its effort to free the sample. He plucked it up and used the sleeve of his shirt to rub the edges. Overhead the sun was poking out from behind a low bank of clouds. He watched in amazement as the sun's rays glinted off the edges. From here it almost looked as though it were shimmering. Thirty million years in the ground and what appeared to be metal looked brand new. But the alloy, whatever it was made of, didn't only twinkle. It radiated the entire spectrum of visible colors.

"Send this to the Institute of Metallurgy and tell Tatiana we need to know what this is ASAP."

"But Dr. Barulina is in St Petersburg," Karen replied, concerned. "If Li finds out she won't be happy."

"I'll risk her disappointment. Send it to Tatiana. She's the best."

Chapter 19

M arrived at Elizabeth Howard's apartment door and planted his feet. Yellow police tape blocked the entrance with a large X. Carefully, he peeled back the upper and lower ends on the left-hand side and removed his lockpick gun. He inserted it into the opening and held the trigger until he heard the lock pop. Once inside, M reattached the tape and closed the door. Out came the rubber medical gloves, which he put on as he surveyed the layout.

Faint light streamed in through a pair of sheer white curtains hanging in the living room. He had to admit, Elizabeth hadn't only been feisty—she had also been something of a clean freak. *House & Home* magazines sat on the coffee table, still fanned out for optimal viewing. The dining room table looked as though it had never seen a plate or glass of wine in its life. Even the kitchen sink was spotless. Say what you would, this was the home of a tidy person. And that suggested the documents Ben Fisher had handed her ought to be around here, perhaps hidden with the same thoughtfulness she applied to keeping the place clean. M could say that with some confidence because he had already checked her desk at the *Seattle Times* the very night she'd gone missing. M had gained access posing as a member of the cleaning crew, but had failed to turn up anything useful.

He was also growing increasingly confident that what Ben had given her was not a stack of incriminating documents. Maybe twenty or thirty years ago they might have been. But zeroes and ones were far lighter to carry and easier to broadcast. That meant he was looking for a laptop and more likely a USB.

On a whim, M went into her bedroom and peeled open the top drawer of her dresser. He eyed the contents with a faint smile. Each sock was matched with its twin and set in rows according to color. Not only tidy but highly organized, maybe even a touch OCD. Continuity and repetition was the mantra of the obsessive-compulsive and that was good because it made her predictable.

M's mother had often used a whipping rod to instill important life lessons in him. The first was that violence is an insult to yourself and your creator. The second was to always defend the weak against the tyranny of the strong and the third was that the ends justified the means.

The inherent contradiction in those first two pearls of wisdom, especially given they were doled out via corporal punishment, had never dawned on his mother. Contradictions aside, M considered himself a pacifist, and often told casual acquaintances the dim view he held of violence was a byproduct of his strict upbringing.

In those times when he found himself defending the strong and oppressing the weak, he would find justification for his actions by telling himself he'd simply fallen off the pacifist wagon. It was in such moments that he realized choosing the moral way tended to be a lot like choosing what to wear in the morning. The rules you followed depended greatly on the circumstances. But 'rules' might be the wrong word. Morality was a suggestion and suggestions could be followed or discarded depending on the situation. His mother had had no problem breaking her first and second rule in pursuit of the third.

And unlike Elizabeth Howard and her adherence to a rigid set of values, M recognized his talent for operating in the gray zone as his greatest asset. It made him nimble and, more importantly, unpredictable.

A medium-sized plant by the window drew his attention and M went to examine it. The edges of the clay pot showed streaks of dry earth, as though someone who couldn't stand a mess had taken a cloth and wiped it down. M poked a finger into the thirsty soil. He wiggled the digit an inch to the right and repeated the move. On the third try, the nail of his index finger struck something hard. He reached in with his whole hand now and came out with a clump of dirt. Working it through his fingers the way someone might work a pair of Chinese Baoding balls, M realized he'd literally just hit pay dirt. In this case, it was a USB wrapped in two layers of cling film. Smiling, he slipped it into his pocket and headed for the door.

He was in the process of closing it behind him and replacing the edges of the tape when he felt a presence. M turned, one hand inside his jacket, his fingers around the grip of the pistol he kept there.

A young boy, no older than nine or ten, eyed him with a childish mix of suspicion and innocence.

From M's point of view, the kid was a witness and leaving witnesses behind went against perhaps his most important rule, Rule Four: Always be invisible.

He took three steps toward the kid and stopped. The child looked up at him, a smudge of dirt streaking one cheek. He was skinny, maybe even malnourished.

"You wanna see a magic trick?" M asked, the edges of his mouth tweaked into something resembling a smile.

"What kinda trick?" the boy asked, suddenly disarmed of any suspicion. His curiosity had gotten the better of him, as it tended to whenever a child was promised a treat.

M removed the rubber glove from his right hand with a snap, reached behind the boy's ear, and produced a crumpled hundred-dollar bill.

"Oh, wow!" the kid said, holding it at both ends.

"There's a lot more in there," M told him. "Do your homework and listen to your mom and maybe someday I'll be back to fish them out for you."

M turned and left, the boy still rooted in place with a mystified look plastered on his face. Reaching the entrance, M headed back into the smoggy air, all the while thinking about rules and how what made us human wasn't the ones we followed, but the rules we decided to break.

Chapter 20

A cursory search on the internet for anything on Doctor Gerald Lang had led Ben to the Washington Health Research Institute and the Department of Neurology. By any measure, the building itself was modern and situated right in the heart of downtown Seattle.

Ben got out of the cab and cut through the gathering haze as he made his way inside. A directory of suites by a bank of elevators indicated the neurological research department was on the eighth floor.

That was good enough for him. When the elevator doors opened on eight, they revealed an older woman in formal wear sitting behind a desk.

She peered up from behind a pair of horn-rimmed glasses. A string of white plastic beads ran from one temple tip to the other. "May I help you?"

"I'm here to see Dr. Lang," Ben said, hopeful the words would prove just as powerful as 'open sesame'.

The woman's tired eyes hung on him for a moment before returning to her computer monitor. "I'm afraid Dr. Lang isn't available."

"That's not possible," Ben protested. "We have a meeting scheduled five minutes ago." The lie rolled easily enough off his tongue, he thought.

"I'm sorry, sir. I see no such meeting in our system. Besides, Dr. Lang isn't even on the premises."

The expression on Ben's face softened. "Oh, silly me. Gerald probably wanted me to meet him at home. You don't happen to have his address, do you? Save me some time."

Her features squished up in confusion. "That's strange, we got an email from Gerald yesterday saying he was heading to the lake house—" She stopped herself short, realizing she might have said too much.

Ben winked. "Don't worry, it'll be our little secret."

She smiled weakly as he headed back to the elevator.

Once again in the lobby, Ben made a general search for Gerald Lang, pulling up anything he could find. A number of images came up. Scrolling through them, he spotted what he thought was a familiar-looking man in his mid-fifties, wearing a doctor's smock. The man had milky-white skin with a few scraps of hair clinging to the top of his scalp and what might be described as a baby face. It was only further on down the page that Ben located a picture of the good doctor sitting on a dock by a lake at dawn. That led him to a social media page about six years old.

The caption read: *Just what the doctor ordered.* Next to the image were a number of comments extolling the good doctor in his inordinate luck. Moving down, Ben found what he'd been looking for.

Betty Foster: "Heavenly! Where is this?"

Dr. Gerald Lang: "Boyle Lake."

Ben clicked his fingers in mid-air with an audible snap. "Gotcha!"

Another search during the cab ride over helped to identify Lang's not-so-modest lake house: a beautiful two-story post-and-beam Craftsman-style job with a gabled front entrance and twin front doors. Ben got out of the cab and ordered the machine to wait there.

He approached the front door and rang the bell. He stood waiting for several minutes with no answer, but the sedan in the driveway made it difficult to believe no one was home. He didn't want to throw a rock through a window, that was hardly any way of introducing himself, but he would if they left him no choice.

"Dr. Lang," he called through the door. "I need to speak with you. It's very important."

Peering past the lightly frosted glass that framed the double-door entrance, Ben could see the vague outline of a figure. Whoever they were, they seemed to be holding something. From here it resembled a rifle.

"I've called the cops," a male voice said from inside. "I'm perfectly within my rights to blow your head off if you don't leave my property at once."

"I didn't come all this way to hurt you," Ben pleaded. He felt reasonably confident he could break in and disarm the man without much difficulty. The question would then become, how willing would he be to talk after such a move?

The voice from inside came again. This time it was closer. As in, right on the other side of the door. "Ben? Is that you?" A man's astonished face appeared in the window before it disappeared. The lock on the front door clicked open before the door followed suit, revealing the haggard face of a terrified-looking man, his deathly white complexion only broken by the dark circles ringing his eyes. He was a mere shadow of the relaxed figure Ben had found in that photo on the lakeside dock.

Ben stepped inside and Dr. Lang slammed the door shut behind him. He was holding a scoped AR-15. For a second, it seemed as though he was about to set it down when he stopped. "You came alone, right?"

"I have an auto-cab waiting outside, but otherwise it's just me." Ben was still reeling from the familiarity of the man's face and the fact that he appeared to know Ben by name.

"I heard about your wife on the news," Dr. Lang began, heading from the foyer into a high-ceilinged living room comfortably furnished with couches and armchairs. At the far end was a large stone fireplace. Above it hung an antique musket.

"Amanda," Ben said, battling the lingering sorrow he felt for the death of a woman he couldn't quite remember. "We weren't married."

"Still," Dr. Lang said, shouldering the AR. "Can I get you anything to drink? How about your favorite?"

"My favorite?" Ben said, simultaneously intrigued and worried. Granger had been the one to mention Dr. Lang by name and Ben still had his doubts about the old coot, no matter how harmless he looked. Suspicions aside, the rifle in Lang's possession wasn't doing anything to settle his nerves. "Enlighten me."

"Bourbon on the rocks."

Ben smiled and raised a hand. "Hey, you only live once."

The two men went into the kitchen where Lang set down two glasses, plopped in a few ice cubes along with about an inch of Stagg bourbon. They clinked glasses and drank.

Ben's eyes sharpened as the heat rolled down his throat and into his belly. "You're right, that is good."

The smile on Lang's face wavered. He leveled the rifle. "Who the hell are you?"

113

Raising both hands, Ben said: "Wait a minute. You said yourself you know who I am."

"Do I? Ben Fisher doesn't drink. Hasn't touched a drop in years."

Ben lowered his hands and placed them on the countertop. "Enough messing around. I think it's time I came clean." He motioned to the couches nearby.

"You think? How about I give you five seconds to start talking before my finger starts squeezing this trigger."

Ben sighed and proceeded to explain everything that had happened to him, at least, everything he could remember.

"The two of us met up four days ago," Dr. Lang said. "Are you telling me you don't remember any of that?"

"Unfortunately, the stun gun must have wiped it all away," Ben told him. "It just doesn't make sense that I can't remember anything about my life and yet I can remember a ton of strange and useless things."

Lang smiled warmly. "Yes, that's the difference between declarative and procedural memory. The first refers to past events. The other is long-term memory connected with the ability to perform certain tasks. General amnesia is the loss of declarative memories."

Ben's shoulders sagged. "The way you put it makes it sound pretty permanent."

"Sometimes it is," Dr. Lang said, truthfully. "Sometimes it isn't. And you're saying a stun gun to the back of your neck did this?"

He nodded. "Yeah, but that's not all it did."

Dr. Lang's brow furrowed. "What do you mean?"

"The neural enhancement device I have sitting inside my skull. When I got shocked, it seems some areas got

114

boosted to extraordinary levels, levels that might have killed a normal person. I can do incredible things now. Things I couldn't have dreamt of. The flip side is that I woke up with no memory of anything that happened before the attack."

"What sorts of incredible things are you referring to?"

In a blur of movement, Ben snatched the AR from Lang's hands and field-stripped it in seconds.

Lang's gaze shifted from his now empty hands to the components laid out neatly on his kitchen counter. "Wow, you weren't kidding."

"Obviously, if I was in the market to hurt you, I would have done it already," Ben told him. Hopefully now the old guy would ease up a little. "These abilities have already gotten me out of a bind or two," he admitted. "Kept me from being killed, really. But wouldn't you know, not remembering a stitch about who you are is a different kind of death, one I wouldn't wish on anyone." Ben swallowed and his throat made a clicking sound. "I'm curious about something you said earlier. About us meeting up four days ago. I need to know what we spoke about."

Lang led Ben into the living room. "This time I think we should grab a seat." They settled into plush leather chairs opposite one another just as a dark-haired woman and a ten-year-old girl appeared from another part of the house.

"Give us a minute, will you, honey?" Lang asked, grinning and trying hard to mean it.

"You have a family?" Ben said, turning in his chair, a look of concern furrowing his fine features.

"I'm doing what I can to keep them safe. Although if any of this is going to make sense, it's best that I start at

115

the beginning. Over the last eight years I've run several studies examining the neurological effects of NEDs on the human brain," Dr. Lang explained. "For reasons I frankly never really understood, the FDA abandoned their long-standing policies on comprehensive analysis and immediately greenlit Neural-Sync's use of implants within the general public. Sure, your research wing implanted the devices in rhesus monkeys and a few pigs, but human brains are a vastly different affair. As I told you when I came to meet you in your office four days ago, the opportunities for improving lives with NEDs are no doubt beyond our ability to grasp. Giving the gift of sight. Allowing a deaf child to hear his mother's voice for the first time. Leveling out the destructive impulses of folks with depression or soldiers with PTSD. None of that should be downplayed or underestimated.

"True as these things are, none of it addresses what has clearly become the implant's largest market—everyday people interested in augmenting some aspect of their lives, whether that be boosting physical or intellectual prowess, improving memory recall, emotional health or resilience to pain. The potential for making the world a better place was extraordinary and I would like to believe at least a part of that had something to do with the FDA's decision to close its eyes to the possibility of medical complications."

"I couldn't agree more," Ben said, rubbing the back of his neck. "It's opened up a new phase in human evolution. Strange as it sounds, even though I invented the bloody thing, I still don't understand what it can do, nor how it works."

Dr. Lang clasped the palms of his hands together. "If I'm going to be honest, the bloody thing, as you call it, is a marvel of medical engineering. I mean, for starters think about the NED's size. You could balance it on the tip of a ballpoint pen. Inserting it doesn't require invasive surgery with drills burrowing holes in your skull."

"It's injected into the bloodstream," Ben said, no less amazed than when he'd heard it the first time from Knut.

"That's right, and it travels through the roadmap of veins along the spine and into the brain. Once there, it separates into three sections where navigation markers guide each part to key locations. First to the hippocampus, the part of the brain responsible for memory as well as neurogenesis and neuroplasticity."

"Neurogenesis," Ben said, his focus turning to the lake behind the cottage. "One section of the NED comes to rest in the hippocampus where it stimulates the birth of new neurons."

"That's right."

Ben drew in a deep breath. He wasn't sure if he was remembering or whether his heightened intelligence was helping him deduce the nature of the terms. "And neuroplasticity is the brain's ability to rewire itself to form new synaptic connections."

"Precisely," Dr. Lang said, impressed. "The more someone trades in Neuro tokens to boost their intelligence, the more brain cells and connections will be made. Imagine your mind never suffering the ravages of old age. Imagine becoming sharper at ninety than you were at thirty.

"The second section of the NED comes to rest in the hypothalamus, a spot just above both the pituitary gland and the brain stem. From here, control can be exerted over the release of CRH, corticotropin-releasing hormone, a hormone responsible for triggering adrenaline. Those stories you often read about in the news, where a young mother is able to lift the weight of a car in order to save her trapped child, that's pure adrenaline at work.

"And as with intelligence, the greater that category has been boosted, the greater the release of CRH and ultimately adrenaline. One added benefit of its location is in its ability to help manage pain, since the signals that run up the spinal cord pass through the thalamus on its way to the cerebral cortex.

"Last but certainly not least, we come to the temporal lobe, the part of the brain that deals with the wide range of human emotions. By applying varying patterns of electrical stimulation anxiety can be reduced and feelings of happiness increased."

"You mentioned the implant's size earlier," Ben said, trying to wrap his mind around such a tiny device doing so much.

Dr. Lang went on his phone and pulled up an image of Neural-Sync's closest competitor. It was a similar image Knut had showed him. "Neural-Sync is way, and I mean way, ahead of anything else on the market right now. But here's the bit that truly blew me away, an aspect that hardly gets any coverage in the media: the power supply. Remember that image of Neural-Sync's competitor?"

Ben nodded. The picture Knut had shown him was still burned into his brain.

"Well, that sucker comes with a battery pack that needs to be plugged in every so often and recharged. With the NED, nanogenerators piggybacking off each detachable section use the patient's own blood flow to generate eight hundred microwatts of power. Without a shred of doubt, you've managed to create a truly revolutionary device."

Ben crossed his arms and felt the muscles in his face tighten. "I'm sensing a major 'but' coming."

"The consequences of power boosting are no secret."

"Power boosting?"

"It was a problem that happened shortly after release of the device," Lang said. "Boosting any one category more than ten points within a month could lead to aneurisms. Shortly thereafter, Neural-Sync instituted limits on how many boosts could be applied within a given period."

"And your study?" Ben asked. "What did you find?"

"After eight years of meticulous analysis, we found that anywhere from two to five percent of all of those implanted had suffered a series of mysterious, debilitating and often fatal side effects. Now, any optimist might find a five percent fatality rate a completely acceptable number given all the benefits a NED can provide, but keep in mind, it won't be long before nearly everyone in the Western world and, soon enough, the entire planet will be outfitted with one."

Five percent of billions was a frightening number of fatalities to consider. "That's close to four hundred million deaths," Ben mumbled through lips that were starting to feel numb and lifeless. "In fact, it's more than the populations of the United States and Canada combined." Ben shook his head in an effort to chase away the growing feeling of dread. "You mentioned symptoms. What are they?"

Dr. Lang folded his hands over his lap, the edges of his mouth turned down. "There are three. They always begin and end the same way and once they start, to date, cannot be stopped. The first is acute memory loss, followed by the second, generalized numbness. The third and final stage is complete muscular immobility. Once there, the patient is usually hours or days away from ceasing any autonomous respiratory activity."

"You mean they stop breathing," Ben whispered.

Dr. Lang nodded. "The only other time we've seen a similar range of symptoms are from patients who go in for an operation and never wake up."

"Any clue what's causing it?"

"No," Dr. Lang replied in the infuriatingly honest way that doctors tend to. "Although we suspect it may have something to do with the unusual metal alloy that makes up the NED's outer shell." He produced another video online showing a magnified version of the device being subjected to various forms of light.

"It's shimmering," Ben observed, mesmerized.

"Yes, it's real pretty, but there's no telling how this metallic compound might be poisoning our bodies."

Ben drew a blank. "But wouldn't autopsies on the implanted deceased reveal scar tissue around the device? Or some other sign the body was being affected in some adverse way?"

"That's part of the mystery," Dr. Lang admitted. "Most of the old-school metal implants require patients to receive special doses of antibiotic to prevent the body from rejecting them. Acute inflammatory response is the most common side effect, often resulting in the formation of cysts and fibrosis. And even in the cases where they take, such as microchips inserted into a biological specimen, the device quickly finds itself surrounded by a layer of scar tissue, impeding its effectiveness. Neural-Sync's NED, on the other hand, isn't only bio-friendly, the outer shell meshes seamlessly via nerve proprioceptors that connect it neurologically to the surrounding tissue. As far as the body is concerned, it's been there all along."

Amazed as he was, Ben's mind couldn't help returning to the three symptoms Dr. Lang had discussed and the inevitable fate they led to. "Could my memory loss be that first stage you mentioned?" He braced himself for the answer.

"I'm sorry to say, it looks that way," Dr. Lang said, confirming Ben's worst fears. "At some point you'll start to hear a ringing in your ears, then numbness in your extremities and eventually you'll lapse into a deep slumber from which you'll never wake up. It's possible that the shock you received during the attack set the process in motion."

"How long do I have?" There was a surreal quality to asking such a question.

"That's hard to say. Hours, maybe days." The features on Dr. Lang's surprisingly youthful face settled into something resembling sadness. "A better, more immediate question is, who would kill to prevent this information from getting out?"

"You mean like someone from within the company?" Ben wondered.

Dr. Lang shrugged. "I'm not sure. Soon after you and I first discussed the results of my research, I began to notice a dark SUV following me around. You had warned me at the time to be careful, but I failed to heed your concern. It was only after I heard about Amanda's… death… well, I realized how arrogant and foolish I'd been and spirited my family out of the city and to the lake house at once."

Ben got up and went to the plate-glass window overlooking the lake. The water was much higher than the photo he'd seen online, the one from six years earlier.

But while his eyes were busy with the ever-changing landscape, his mind was running through the possibility someone at Neural-Sync was behind this. "If it is someone at my company, the list of suspects isn't that long."

"Your sister Lori," Dr. Lang offered, shrugging apologetically when Ben spun around. "I'd hate for it to be true, but you can't deny she may have some motivation. After all, blood is thicker than water." That last part came out with more than a hint of irony.

"What do you know about Granger?" Ben asked, scratching the stubble forming on his chin.

"While the inner workings of Neural-Sync don't really fall into my area of expertise, I do remember you telling me that Granger was the newest member on the board and the one you got along with the least."

Ben recalled the mysterious text message he had received during his meeting with Granger.

Don't trust him, it had read.

Granger had told him he was Ben's only real ally on the board, that the rest of the members were itching to remove him as CEO. Perhaps the accusation of murder was all the justification they needed. Or perhaps Dr. Lang's suggestion Lori had a role in all this also had some merit. Even with an implant boosting his brain power, sorting out who he could trust wasn't proving any easier.

"There's another possibility," Ben suggested. "Maybe the real culprit is one of Neural-Sync's clients."

Dr. Lang seemed to mull over the idea. "Apart from the general public, the US military is probably your largest customer."

"And maybe they're worried the bad publicity I was about to bring down on my own company would put too much at risk."

Lang stood and walked over to him, his mouth tweaked to one side in doubt. "I'm ashamed to say NEDs would continue to sell even if the fatality rate was as high as ten percent or even more. Under normal circumstances, I'd advise you to follow the money. However, this is one of the rare instances where the money would continue to flow freely regardless of how dangerous the device proved to be. For proof, all you need do is look at the fatality and disfigurement rates with plastic surgery. Risks are the things that happen to someone else."

"So what do you suggest then?" Ben was at a loss.

Dr. Lang met Ben's gaze and held it. "Follow the metal. Find out where Neural-Sync is getting that exotic alloy. My Spidey senses tell me you might have pulled a Zuckerberg and 'borrowed' a cutting-edge technology that didn't belong to you."

The implication of Lang's comment was rather serious. "You mean, someone may be trying to get even?"

"It's difficult to say," Lang admitted, crossing his arms. The man looked tired, like all he wanted to do was close his eyes and never open them again. "At least until we know more."

Ben's focus was back on the lake. "You should take your family and hide."

Dr. Lang wore a bewildered look. "That's why we came up to the cottage."

"You need to hide better. Your social media profile's already given you away. The people who are out to keep these secrets hidden, they're deadly serious."

Ben waited another minute or two for the words to sink in. Then he thanked the doctor, wished him luck and left.

Chapter 21

Ben was in the taxi, heading back to Seattle, his mind still grappling with everything Dr. Lang had just told him. Foremost among those bits and pieces was the harm NEDs risked causing to millions of people worldwide. Had that been the secret Ben had uncovered, the reason he'd been framed and nearly killed?

The possibilities were still swirling when he noticed a black SUV pull up alongside him. The tinted windows made it hard to see who was inside, but it looked out of place on backcountry roads, such as the one he was on. Moreover, it was driving against oncoming traffic. The passenger window rolled down and a man in dark clothing leveled a H&K submachine gun out the window and opened fire.

Ben felt a bullet tear open his shoulder as he dove for cover. He clutched the wound, blood squeezing out between his fingers. Meanwhile, the self-driving taxi kept going as though nothing were out of the ordinary.

Ben rolled into the front seat and disengaged the autopilot.

"Warning. Please return to your seat. Warning."

"Yeah, sue me," he barked, snapping the seatbelt on and flooring it. The taxi's engine screamed in protest as the acceleration kicked in, leaving the SUV several meters behind them.

But the SUV would not so easily be denied. Ben heard a growl behind him as the large vehicle thundered down the country road in pursuit.

The man in the front passenger seat leaned out, firing wildly at him.

Bullets thudded into the taxi's trunk and back window, shattering it.

More shots riddled the front windshield, spidering lines in the glass, obscuring his vision.

Next the SUV came alongside him again, the passenger preparing to finish what he started. Ben spotted the move and jerked the wheel. The two vehicles collided, but his was the smaller of the two. This was a battle he was losing, and fast.

Ahead was a sharp curve and he slowed just long enough to take the turn. On the way out, he accelerated. The quality of his tactical driving surprised even him. But would it be enough?

The SUV was only a few meters behind, but instead of firing at him, the guy with the H&K shot up his back left tire. It exploded and Ben clung to the wheel to avoid losing control. The SUV dropped back and swung to the right, aiming for his other back tire. Ben turned the wheel to cut off the angle, but he wasn't fast enough and out it went too.

"Attention, tire pressure dangerously low. Please return the vehicle for maintenance! Attention!"

Now he was only driving on two front tires and the car didn't want him to forget it. His speed was slowing, down now from nearly a hundred to seventy-five. Another turn was coming up ahead and Ben wasn't sure he would make this one. He tapped the brake and that was when the SUV pulled a pit maneuver—they drew their left bumper along his right back bumper and then turned enough to spin him out.

The taxi fishtailed before ending up in the ditch. The SUV also lost control, careening into a row of shrubs. Ben shook his head, groggy from the impact and the wound to his shoulder. The taxi was straddling a three-foot depression. On either side of the road was a line of Douglas fir trees extending as far as the eye could see. Across the gravel road and slightly ahead of him was the SUV. Already, the two men inside were climbing out and heading his way.

Staying low, Ben moved to the passenger side, opened the door and slipped out. But instead of running into the forest where he would probably be gunned down, he slithered on his belly, into the space between the depression and the underside of the taxi. The heat coming off the electric motor was intense, so too was the odor of overheating batteries.

The men approached the vehicle from either side. Ben was facing the driver's side where the guy with the H&K was standing, fumbling for the door handle. Reaching out, Ben grabbed hold of his ankles and yanked him off his feet. The man flew back, tumbling like a freshly chopped tree. His submachine gun fired off a burst of rounds as he hit the ground. Ben rolled out, stripped the weapon out of the stunned man's hands and put three rounds in his chest. On the other side of the depression, he could see the SUV driver's legs and he cut across them with another burst. Down the driver went, screaming.

Ben stood and walked carefully around the back of the broken taxi. He found the driver, lying in the ditch, a pistol in his hand.

"Drop it," Ben told him, the pain from his own wound a distant memory. His NED was taking care of that, along with the strength he'd used to yank the other gunman to the ground with such ease.

The driver's hand was shaking.

"Set the gun down and we can talk," Ben assured him.

But the driver wasn't in the mood for a chat. He brought the barrel up to his right temple and fired.

Chapter 22

The activists in the white van were kind enough to drop Sienna back at her car before peeling away. She watched Willow and the others leave the university campus with rather mixed emotions. On the one hand, she had just been kidnapped and held against her will, an act that opened a whole slew of fresh concerns. If a bunch of tech-savvy tree-huggers could locate and abduct her, then what was stopping some government agency with infinitely better training? In the time it took to bat an eye, the illusion of relative safety she had enjoyed for most of her life had effectively been shattered. No doubt her father's death had been the first sign of distortion in that particular mirage, but his life had been lost deep in the Pacific Ocean, a far cry from the hazy streets of Seattle.

And hazy was right. She opened her front seat and grabbed the mask she kept in the glove compartment. For years the West had seen pictures of critically polluted cities in countries like Bangladesh, India and China, to name but a few. Today that distant vision was becoming a reality here at home. The days when parents would yell at their children to play outside and get some fresh air were long gone. But it was the speed with which the transition was taking place—that was what Sienna and the few others willing to acknowledge the changes around them had found so puzzling.

It all took on new meaning when one plotted CO_2 and methane levels on a simple graph. On the Y axis was the parts per million measurement. The X axis displayed time. When you traced the line backward into the past, you quickly saw the current levels of either gas hadn't been this high in the atmosphere since the Pliocene, a period five million years ago when North America was populated with giant carnivorous birds and truly bizarre-looking elephants named gomphotheres.

And yet, when that same graph was spread over the last three hundred years, something very interesting became apparent. The presence of warming gases in the atmosphere clearly began to rise with the onset of the Industrial Revolution. No shocker there since for the first time, man-made factories were pumping tons of carbon into the air. But when you looked at the middle half of the twentieth century, well, that was when the changes became really startling. More precisely, from the mid 1940's onward, the points on the graph could be seen spiking at an incredible rate.

Again, we had just fought a world war and American industry was heading into its golden age. Not to mention the Earth's population was beginning to climb. But even when you ran the numbers, and she had many times, something wasn't adding up. There was an unknown factor at play, one that appeared to be tipping the scale towards a warmer planet. Did human activity play a role? No doubt about it. Could other natural processes also be at play to account for not only the massive spike, but also the continued rise even after humans had finally smartened up? It was the basis of her father's life's work, a thesis equally unpopular on both sides of the political aisle. To the left, it sounded like climate change denial. To the right, it sounded like an admittance of guilt. The middle road held the answer. Sienna felt it in her bones, the way she could feel the ground beneath her feet and the tinge of toxic air scratching at her lungs. Politics aside, she couldn't help but wonder what she might find along that middle road, the space somewhere between human activity and natural processes. And more importantly, she wondered whether it would leave humanity with any hope for survival.

Sienna was still gathering her things, preparing to head to her lab at the university when a large black SUV pulled up alongside her. Suddenly her heart leapt up into her throat.

Oh, God, not again!

She clutched her backpack and turned to run.

"Sienna," a familiar voice called out through the open passenger side window.

She stopped and turned. "Ben?" It was dim inside the vehicle, but even from here she could see he was in distress.

Sienna approached, gave one last look just to be sure and then got in.

"I was about to tell you I'd just had a hell of a morning," she began. "But something tells me yours was far worse."

"I think I have an idea why this is happening," he told her. Sienna looked down and saw his light blue dress shirt was soaking wet and was covered in blood.

"Oh, my God, what happened?"

"It's complicated," he replied.

"And this SUV," she said. "Is that complicated too? There are twigs and branches wedged into the front grate." She then popped the glove compartment and pulled out a pistol.

Ben eyed the weapon in her hand. "Hey, be careful with that. Unless you know how to use one."

Sienna dropped the clip into her free hand and racked the slide, ejecting the round from the chamber. "Not everyone around here hates guns," she said, smirking. "The question is, do you?"

"Let's just say I keep surprising myself."

She studied him, noticing Ben seemed to be favoring his left shoulder.

"You're hurt," she said, her concern growing.

He waved her away. "It's nothing. Just a scratch."

"Right. Stop pretending you're indestructible and pull over." She pointed to a free spot along the side of the road.

He complied and sighed as he slid the car into park, but kept the engine running. "We don't have time for this."

Ben's left shoulder was covered in blood. There was a tear where something had torn his shirt. "Would you just hold still," she scolded him. "You're not gonna do either of us any good if you bleed to death." He winced as she held his shoulder in place for a better look. "Yeah, whatever it was grazed you, but this is gonna need some stitches. I've got a first-aid kit at home."

"That's not a good idea." He told her about meeting Dr. Lang and the ambush that had led to his injuries. "He says the two of us had met a few days before Amanda was killed. That data he had collected on the safety of the implants showed a link to premature death."

She eyed him with a growing sense of fear. "You think someone was trying to suppress the information?"

"It's possible," Ben admitted, dabbing his shoulder with the pads of his fingers and seeing that the bleeding had stopped. "And I know what you're thinking."

"You do?" she asked, her mind in precisely the spot he had guessed.

"Of course. You're wondering if the people who attacked Amanda, Dr. Lang and your father are somehow connected."

"It isn't a wild leap to suppose they are. I just had my own little incident."

Ben's brow furrowed.

"A group of activist hackers gave me a ride in their van. They had Navy salvage video of my father's ship sitting at the bottom of the Weddell Sea off the coast of Antarctica."

"Antarctica? How can that be? I thought he was in the Pacific."

Sienna grimaced. "I don't know either. None of this is making a whole lot of sense."

Ben's lips drew a thin line across his face. It was apparent he wasn't only perplexed, nor was he merely sad for her loss. He couldn't help but blame himself for putting her father in danger to begin with. "So, he's gone?"

She nodded and then turned away.

"Did they say how it sank?"

"That's the thing," Sienna said, rubbing her hands together, suddenly feeling chilled. "It was hard to tell. The ship looked like a giant had reached down and crushed it into a ball. It's a miracle anyone survived."

Ben's eyes grew wide. "Someone lived through that?"

"William Schroder. A crane operator. Picked up by a geologic survey ship that was in the area. Willow and her people are working to track him down."

133

"Willow?"

She smiled. "Don't ask. They're some sort of environmental group. If we can find this guy, there's a chance he might be able to tell if the Navy sank their ship."

"Who says our Navy were the ones behind this?" Ben said, letting his words dangle out there in the open.

"Nothing, really. I suppose it could be anyone."

"Which leads me to a point I was going to make earlier. The men who attacked me were black ops. Boosted and deadly. But sending out a hit squad is a far cry from ordering a Navy ship to open fire on a civilian research vessel. It's much harder to keep something like that a secret."

"Unless our country wasn't behind it at all," Sienna postulated.

"The men who attacked me were not foreign agents. They were Americans. I'm certain of it."

"Well, Willow seemed pretty confident the Chinese were the ones who sank the *Archipelago*."

Hearing that seemed to resonate with Ben.

"What is it?"

"Just something Dr. Lang said. He was talking about the NED and how he believed it was experimental technology we might have stolen from the Russians or the Chinese."

"That makes two independent sources pointing in the same direction. What else did he have to say?"

"Only that he believes the key lies in identifying the implant's unusual metal alloy. If we can figure out who made it…"

"Or who it was stolen from," Sienna said, finishing the thought, "it should point to the people who framed you for murder and who killed my father."

Just then Sienna's phone beeped.

"Anything useful?" Ben asked, trying to keep his eyes on the road.

"Looks like Willow's already come through. We got an address for William Schroder."

"Where to?" Ben asked.

"Take Highway 5 south," she told him. Sienna found a duffle bag in the back seat. She rooted through it and came out with a lightweight black jacket. "You'll need to wear this to hide the blood on your shirt. I'll see if there's some gauze in here too for your shoulder."

"Got any other details on our destination?" Ben asked. "Is this guy in witness protection or something?"

"No, he's a patient at Western State Psychiatric Hospital."

Chapter 23

They drove for close to an hour before the hospital came into view. Built sometime in the mid-nineteenth century, Western State Psychiatric pre-dated the Civil War and looked every bit its age. It wasn't so much a single building but a collection of them, assembled on a sprawling patch of land.

Ben parked and followed Sienna through the front entrance. A woman in a nurse's uniform sat behind a glass partition.

"We're here to see William Schroder," Ben informed her, brimming with self-assurance. People who worked behind desks were practically trained to smell who did and didn't belong. It was also her job to block as many unwanted visitors as possible.

"Are you next of kin?" the receptionist asked.

"He's my brother," Sienna told the woman. "Our father died in the same accident that sent him here."

The receptionist's brows knit together. "I'm sorry to hear that." She slid a clipboard through the partition in the glass. "Print your name next to the X and sign below that."

Sienna did so, signing Sienna Schroder instead of Panov.

"Same for you, sir," the nurse said.

Ben took the pen and signed Ben Smith.

"Thank you, Mr. Smith. The two of you can head down the hall on your left. The elevator will bring you to the fourth floor. You should find Mr. Schroder in the recreation room."

They did as she said, stepping out onto the fourth floor. "That's a good sign," Ben observed.

"That she believed us?"

"No, that William's hanging out in the rec room. With any luck he'll be lucid enough to fill us in on what he saw."

Another nurse greeted them at the doorway. Behind her, sun streamed in through a string of high windows. Tables, maybe fifteen in all, were evenly spaced throughout the large room.

"We're here to see William Schroder," Sienna told her.

The nurse nodded and pointed to a man sitting at a table in the corner. For some reason, Ben expected to see people wandering around in their pajamas. Instead many of them were wearing regular clothes.

They approached William. He had a rugged build, with powerful-looking arms and a wide jaw. For the most part, he appeared comfortable in the jeans and white t-shirt he was wearing, except for the fact that his hands were pressed up against the sides of his head, blocking his ears.

This was another discovery that surprised Ben. It wasn't easy asking someone questions when they couldn't hear you. They sat down opposite him. William traced their movements with his eyes. What was more, his hands were heavily bandaged and so were his feet. This wasn't looking very hopeful, although it certainly

137

brought home the traumatic nature of what he might have gone through.

"Hi, William," Sienna said, introducing herself and Ben. "We'd like to ask you a few questions. Would that be all right?"

He peeled his bandaged hands away from his ears and placed his palms on the table. "I'm not crazy, you know."

Ben nodded. "We know."

"Good." William winced and covered his ears again.

"We wanted to ask you about what happened," Ben began.

"You mean on the…" The man's weathered features tightened. "The, uh…"

"*Archipelago*?" Sienna chimed in, clearly pained by the man's struggle.

"Yeah, that's the one," he said, staring up at the ceiling. "I didn't forget, you know."

"I'm sure you didn't," Ben offered, suddenly concerned for a whole new reason.

"Anyway, you're too late. I already told the others everything I know."

"Others?" Sienna said, surprised.

"The cops. Least they said they were cops. Asked me a bunch of questions and then left." William's eyes were squinted shut.

"Are you still in pain from what happened?" Sienna asked him.

"You mean from my hands?" he asked, raising them in the air. "You probably can't tell, but frostbite took a few of my fingers and toes. The pain was so bad the doctors put one of those, uh…" He struggled to find the word. "You know, one of those things they put in your head, to help numb the agony."

138

Ben leaned forward. "They implanted you with a NED?"

"Sure, if that's what you call it. They jacked it up too. They call it something with a b. The word starts with a b."

"Boosting," Ben said.

"Exactly. Now I can't feel a thing." He whacked his hands on the table with a loud boom as though to prove his point.

Sienna jumped, startled.

Ben spun to see the nurse eyeing them.

"That's good to hear, William," Ben said.

"Yeah, it ain't my body that hurts anymore, it's my mind. That high-pitched whine. Sounds like a dentist's drill. Do you hear it too?"

Ben swallowed. "I can't say that I do. Does it ever go away?"

William shook his head. "Hell no. And at night, it gets way worse. Sometimes it's like a… like one of those things they use to fix a piano."

"A tuning fork." This time it was Sienna who jumped in.

"Right on," William said, jabbing one of his inflated and mummified hands at her. "And other times it sounds like waves crashing against a cliff."

Ben and Sienna exchanged a worried look. An acute and perhaps even chronic form of tinnitus was what William was describing. Hadn't Dr. Lang also mentioned something about a subset of patients using NEDs who experienced symptoms that were eerily similar?

"I know you already spoke to the other investigators," Ben said, folding his arms along the table's edge. "But is there anything else you can tell us about the events on the *Archipelago*?"

William's eyes fell to his lap. His lips began to do a little dance, as though he were poking at a loose piece of food with his tongue. "I don't remember all that much. And maybe that's a good thing. Dr. P… um…"

Sienna leaned in. "Panov."

"Yeah, Dr. Panov was in the sub near the bottom. I was on the crane, ready and waiting for his signal to ascend. My job was to hook the sub and hoist it back onto the… uh, the… the *Archipelago*."

"Then what happened?"

William's gaze drifted to the ceiling. "Pretty much the next thing I remember was the light and waking up on a chunk of ice. The ship was gone and I was all alone. I thought I was gonna die."

"Wait," Sienna said. "What light are you talking about?"

"Huh?" William asked.

Now it was Ben's turn. "You said you saw a light before coming to on an ice floe. What kind of light did you see?"

"A blue light."

"And where did you see the blue light?" Sienna asked. "Was it all around you?"

"No," William said, shaking his head. For a moment, the cloudy film over his eyes seemed to clear. "We lost contact with Dr. Panov and a few seconds later the sea started to glow, as if there was a bright blue sun down beneath us, rising up at us from the depths. Then the sea just opened up and swallowed the ship." He closed his eyes and clutched the sides of his head. "That's all I can remember," he shouted, drawing nearly every gaze in the room. "Don't make me go there again," he pleaded. "Please, I'm begging you, don't make me."

The nurse came over. "I'm sorry, but I'm going to have to ask you both to leave."

Sienna stood and began to apologize. Ben stood too and leaned over the table. "What were you doing near Antarctica?"

William stopped shouting, looking up at him now.

"The *Archipelago*, William. It was found off the coast of Antarctica. Why did Dr. Panov stray so far from where you were supposed to be in the Pacific?"

William shook his head. "I don't know. We weren't anywhere near the Antarctic when it happened. We were in the Pacific."

Chapter 24

Most of the trip back to Seattle was spent processing the conversation they'd just had with William Schroder. The challenge was reconciling the man's story with any semblance of reality.

Ben had caught the flicker of pain wash over her as William had described losing contact with her father's sub.

"It's hard to imagine what he must have gone through in those final moments," she said, staring out the window at the billboards along the interstate as they whizzed by one after another. "It's hard to explain, but somehow, hearing about it was so much harder than looking at the pictures of the mangled wreckage on the ocean floor. Made it feel more real, more frightening. It also made me angry at him and angry at you."

"At me?" Ben asked, although he knew perfectly well what was coming.

"Of course. He was a seventy-five-year-old man suffering from hypertension and type one diabetes. He should never have been out there, had already told me he'd sailed his last expedition. Then Mr. Ben Fisher comes along offering him more money than he'd earned over the course of his entire career. How could you have expected him to turn down something like that?"

"I don't remember what I was thinking," Ben said, wondering whether any answer he gave would only dig him a deeper hole. "But I suppose I thought it was important enough that he do it."

"I know you didn't hold a gun to his head or anything. He could never sit still. Some invisible thing seemed to be chasing him his entire life and he always made sure to be one step ahead of it."

"Some people aren't suited for retirement. They're born. They work. Then one day they slump over their desk and die."

She nodded. "Yeah, well, in our case, his work brought him away from the people who loved him the most. When my mom found out she had Alzheimer's, a part of me hoped he'd scale back his workload and finally spend some time at home. As you know, he did the exact opposite. I should have seen it coming. He loved oceanography. There's no denying that. But his fear of facing himself, of facing the pain and the quiet… that pretty much guaranteed he would always be little more than a figment of our imagination. The guy who showed up for a few weeks a year."

"You did have a few good years after your mother passed," Ben said, eager to find the positive in any bad situation.

She nodded. "I suppose that's partly why I'm so pissed off. I was only starting to get to know him in the way children do when they become adults themselves."

Ben struggled to relate, overcome with a feeling of frustration over an itch he couldn't scratch. "At least you have a past to be frustrated over. Everything I know about my history comes from the internet. Can you imagine how messed up that is? I lived with a woman who's now dead and I can't even mourn her. I have adoptive parents I know nothing about and a sister I don't remember who feels more like a work colleague than a family member. Then there are pictures of people I've never met before on my NED security sign-in protocol. The second their image pops up, my brain recognizes them and signs me in, but to my conscious mind, they're complete strangers. I haven't even gotten to the people who are after me, after us, and why they want us out of the way so badly."

Sienna was looking at him, tears behind her eyes. She was scratching the top of her head in an attempt to stop from showing any kind of weakness. "When you put it that way, I realize I've been ignorant and self-focused. It isn't your fault my father went on that final expedition. I wanted you to be guilty of forcing him into it, but I was just scared to face the truth that he didn't want to be with my mom and I."

"Your father had his own reasons and I would wager they had more to do with him than they had with anyone else."

They encountered traffic on the outskirts of Seattle proper. As the car slowed, Ben's mind returned to their conversation with William Schroder. "I've been thinking about that blue light Schroder mentioned and what it might have been."

Sienna shook her head with disdain. "He said the ship sank in the Pacific, but it's clear now that wasn't the case. Hard to put too much stock in anything he said. He was in a psychiatric hospital after all."

"You would be too," Ben shot back, "if you tried to convince people you'd seen something incredible. All I know is it raises a number of disturbing questions."

"The biggest one is, why did we waste our time talking to him? Call me a cynic, but I don't really believe much of what he said."

"That's a little categorical, don't you think?"

"If a man told you he was in one ocean, saw a light approaching from beneath his boat and woke up in an entirely different ocean, wouldn't you call him crazy?"

Ben gripped the steering wheel as the car slowed to a crawl. The traffic here was bumper to bumper. "I might have before I heard about the crumpled state the *Archipelago* was in when the Navy found it. That guy might be crazy, sure. But what if he's not? What if he's simply describing something he doesn't understand? How would a radar operator in the 80's have reacted to a stealth jet?"

"They wouldn't have," Sienna said, smiling. "The darn thing wouldn't have showed up on the radar screen."

"That's right. And if someone were to tell them they saw an aircraft fly through the area, they'd be left to wonder what it was you were smoking."

"So what are you saying?"

"It's starting to look like your father might have stumbled onto some kind of weapon he wasn't meant to see."

"Under the ocean?"

Ben nodded. "Maybe it's some kind of experimental, next-generation sub being tested by the military. Whatever's going on, Neural-Sync knows about it and at some point, so did I."

"A secret worth killing for," Sienna said, almost to herself.

"Is there any other kind?"

It had become abundantly clear over the last twenty-four hours that the people chasing them would not stop until the job was done. Twice now, armed men had attempted to apprehend him and twice now he'd managed to evade them. For her part, the ease with which Sienna's abductors had been able to locate and grab her was just as alarming.

Fortunately, at this point, there was little evidence that the environmentalist hackers and the black ops types were in cahoots. In other words, it didn't appear that the men who were after him were also after her. At least not yet. Nevertheless, going forward, neither of them should return home. For Ben that was even more true, especially given that right now, Detective Hernandez and the Seattle Police Department wanted nothing more than to sit him down for a lengthy interview.

The thought reminded Ben of the Eagles' song—the one about Hotel California and how you were free to check in, but you could never leave. He couldn't help but be amazed when you considered how concrete details about his past continued to elude him and yet the lyrics to a song from the 1970s had remained firmly stitched in place. What had Dr. Lang called it? Procedural memory? Augmented or not, the mind was truly an amazing organ.

Soon enough, the traffic cleared and they sped into the city. Ben parked the SUV a block from Sienna's apartment, killed the motor and hopped out. His mind circled back to the risk of returning to Sienna's apartment. The problem was that she was now the sole remaining custodian of her father's research. After his ship had disappeared, she had visited the family home in Bellview and grabbed his laptop as well as boxes of data from his previous expeditions. Her sense of duty was

146

clearly strong and went far and above finding the people who'd murdered him and his crew.

The front door to her building came into view just as Ben caught sight of a commotion up ahead. Car horns blared at two men in the middle of the street. They were locked in an epic fistfight, blocking the road as they tussled, jumping up on car hoods and swinging madly at one another. A crowd quickly gathered, cheering them on. It seemed people couldn't keep from watching a good fight and these two dingbats were putting on one hell of a show. One of them, a chunky guy with beefy arms and a hipster-looking fedora pressed down to his ears, was battling a thirty-year-old guy wielding a skateboard. The hipster rolled and dodged each time the skater guy swung the board at his head. He was agile for someone who had probably never seen the inside of a gym. That was when Ben realized he was probably augmented. But he was still relatively slow and lumbering, which meant he'd gotten the implant, but he just hadn't either been able to afford or done much toward boosting his fitness skills.

"Any idea what's going on?" Ben asked a teenager with a heavy backpack who was filming the brouhaha.

The kid pulled his mask away and answered without taking his eyes off the battle. "The inevitable. A black Neuro spawned on the sidewalk and those two dudes both went for it."

"A black what?"

"A Neuro, man," he said, exasperated, as though Ben had been teleported here from the other side of the planet, which in some respects wasn't too far off the mark. "It's worth like a hundred grand."

"You mean dollars?"

The kid turned and sneered at him. "Dollars? No, credits." A deep line appeared in the kid's forehead. On the street behind him the two men tumbled to the ground in a flurry of flying fists and loud grunts. "Wait a sec. Do I know you?"

Ben took an involuntary step backward. He was suddenly aware Sienna wasn't with him.

"Aren't you that guy?" The kid lifted his phone to film Ben. "The guy from the news. The one who killed his wife. Holy shit. Hey, everyone…" The kid looked around with frantic excitement, but no one was listening. All eyes were glued on the hipster, now hatless. He had the skater man pinned to the ground and was rummaging through his pockets. Out came his vanquished foe's cell phone, which he held aloft in triumph before flinging it to the ground where it shattered.

By the time the kid with the backpack swung back around, Ben was already gone.

•••

"What happened to you?" Sienna asked. She was holding the apartment building's front door ajar and waving him inside.

"To be honest, I'm not entirely sure. I just can't shake this feeling that I've single-handedly made the world into a far crappier place," he said, closing the door behind them.

Leading him to the elevator bank, she stopped and smiled. "You know the old saying. The road to hell is paved with good intentions."

"Yeah, you aren't kidding."

"Well, for what it's worth, if it wasn't you, it would have been someone else."

"I've made millions off of people's addiction to self-improvement."

148

"Probably billions, actually," Sienna said, matter-of-factly. "And they do call NEDs the new plastic surgery."

"They do?" Ben said, struggling to swallow down the bile that had risen into his mouth.

They got in and pressed the button for the sixth floor.

"Oh, sure. I mean back in the day, if you were getting pushed around, you might go to the gym. If you weren't very smart, you'd hit the books. If you were pissed off at your father for never being around..." She stopped short and Ben couldn't help detecting a heavy thread of emotion tickling the back of her throat. "Well, you'd see a shrink. Now, all you need is enough to get the implant and the free time to stalk the streets for Neuros. Ben Fisher, the first CEO to suffer a crisis of conscience." Sienna paused before her apartment door, the key poised before the lock. "In all seriousness, maybe you just couldn't take it anymore and threatened to bring down the whole crooked house of cards."

He snickered. She was being kind and he appreciated that. Something must have happened to make Ben turn on the company he had created. Dr. Lang believed it could have something to do with the health threat the implant posed. That might certainly have been part of his calculation, but he knew something far bigger was at play.

They entered her apartment. Nothing appeared to be disturbed. The place was still a mess, just as Ben had found it the first time he arrived. Something else was off and it took him a minute to figure it out.

"Wait a sec, where's Buddy?"

"He's staying with his dad."

Ben shook his head in confusion. "You mean your ex?"

A rosy hue crept up Sienna's neck and into her cheeks. "We've been broken up for about six months, but we still share custody."

Laughing, Ben said: "Is that what they call it nowadays? Does he pay doggy support?"

She crossed her arms. "As a matter of fact, he does. Are you done ridiculing me in my own house?"

"Forgive me," he said sincerely. "I was only teasing. My bad." He reached out with his left hand in a peace offering and winced.

"Okay, that's it. Go in the bathroom, sit down and take off your shirt. I'll get the needle and thread."

"We really don't have to—"

She raised an index finger to her lips. "Shush now. I don't wanna hear another word. I may live in a pigsty and bake like a crack addict, but I won't let a guest bleed openly under my roof."

Ben laughed and began to comply.

"I also won't let you keep running around in that ratty old suit."

He looked himself up and down. "Something tells me it was probably very expensive."

"Yeah, well, now it looks like you pulled it out of a Dumpster. I'm bringing you some stuff the boyfriend left behind. He's been nagging me to bring it to him and I just can't be bothered. That's why things didn't work. He was raised with Mommy and Daddy wrapped around his little finger. Growing up, no sooner had his underwear hit the floor than she'd wash them. Same with every meal. Made him whatever he wanted. Not me. My father was always away from home on some adventure and my mom was gone touring with the Seattle Symphony. She was a classical pianist, one of the best in the country, until the onset of early Alzheimer's slowly began to erode her mind." Sienna bit her lip while her fingers toyed with a length of her hair. "Her music, that was the last thing to go. She couldn't use the toilet by herself, but she could still play. Once that went, any light that was left in her was largely extinguished."

"Was that why you took pity on me?" Ben asked, shrugging out of his shirt and laying the tattered remains over the edge of the bathtub.

"I don't know," she said, pondering the question. "I agreed to help for my own selfish reasons. I needed the truth."

She disappeared and returned a moment later carrying a pair of jeans, a cotton t-shirt and a black hoodie.

"I'm afraid this was all I could find," she said, handing him the clothes.

"It'll have to do."

Sienna washed her hands and dipped the needle in rubbing alcohol. "This may hurt a bit," she warned him as she began sewing his wound shut.

Ben's expression remained stoic. "I wanted you to know that I've had someone reach out to the Navy about your dad."

"Who?"

"Lori Fisher."

"You mean your sister."

Ben grinned. "Yeah, it's just strange to say the words when you don't feel them."

"It just takes time," she encouraged him, poking the needle into his shoulder and pulling it out on the other side of his wound.

Not this time. Not for me, he wanted to say, but stayed quiet. That was what Dr. Lang had made clear enough. Ben was the lucky recipient of the poetic justice award.

'Guy develops a dangerous product only to have it ultimately destroy him.' In time, the numbness would slowly creep in. Some time after that he would fall asleep and then stop breathing altogether. Assuming he didn't get killed by a spec ops team first.

"Hey, what's that?" Sienna asked, studying his forearm.

Ben looked down, rotated his left forearm and grunted. A string of thirteen numbers was etched in blue pen and ran from the crook in his arm all the way to his wrist. Some of them were smeared, but he could still make them out.

4043191165708

"Is that someone's phone number?"

"No idea," Ben replied, staring down at it, just as surprised as she was. His shock grew when he saw another set of digits on his other arm.

350278 1110222 2100

"Any idea what they mean?" she asked, leaning in to put the finishing touches on her sewing job.

"Not yet. They could mean anything. A phone number with an extension. A passport number. Who the hell knows." Ben felt like his head was about to explode. He was still staring down at the numbers when Sienna's phone buzzed from her back pocket. She stared down at it.

"You gonna answer that?" he asked.

"I'm not so sure I should." She held it up to show him.

Instead of an incoming name or phone number, only the word 'Blocked' appeared.

"Who knows, maybe it's the person who's behind all of this."

She drew in a deep breath and answered.

152

"Hello?" Her features froze in an act of intense concentration. "Yes, this is she."

Ben could hear a man's voice on the other end, but nothing more. Seconds later she hung up without saying another word.

"Tell me it wasn't Chad demanding his clothes back."

She looked at him with a mix of excitement and concern. "No."

Ben stood, worried they might have to leave at once.

"It was a man and he didn't give me his name. He said he was from the Navy and that he had something important to tell me about my father, but that we couldn't talk over the phone."

"Did you agree to meet?"

"I didn't get a chance to agree or disagree. He rattled off an address. 400 Broad Street. Told me to be there in fifteen minutes. Said if I was late or brought anyone along, he would know it and disappear along with the information he had."

"There's a pretty good chance it's a trap," Ben said, silently weighing their options.

"That could be," she admitted. "He said Lori Fisher had contacted him."

Ben nodded, rubbing his hands together. So his sister had come through after all. Still, the person on the other end of that call could have nefarious intentions. Unfortunately, there was only one way to find out.

Chapter 25

Lori Fisher and M sat tucked away in a darkened booth at the New Coconut Grove. The place was a throwback to the popular nightclub from the 30's and 40's, right down to the palm trees and the Eastern decor. Nearby, patrons chatted at tables draped with white linen while a full brass band played Glenn Miller's *In the Mood*.

"I shouldn't be drinking this," Lori said, staring down at her martini as she struggled to make small talk. She was still wearing her trademark pantsuit, which made perfect sense as she'd come directly from work.

M was across from her, pulling on a Diet Coke from a red paper straw. "Tell me you're not pregnant."

Lori let out an almost involuntary spasm of laughter. "Only if you believe in immaculate conception. No, that boat sailed for me long ago."

"Because of your age?"

With anyone else, she might have been insulted, but M had an almost childish quality to him. It was one of the things that set him apart from the other sociopaths she'd worked with. He had a heart and he was intelligent. That didn't mean he was some sort of babe in the woods, except where it concerned social etiquette. If a woman said she felt fat, M would be sure to agree if that was what he believed. Or perhaps he didn't care. Either way, the result was the same.

He repeated the question when she didn't answer right away. This was supposed to be about business, but was quickly turning into questions about her love life or lack thereof.

"Some men find a powerful woman intimidating," she answered. "Let's just say my success in the professional sphere has shrunk the pool of viable suitors. But if you must know, the reason I shouldn't drink is because I'm running a marathon next month. The event is in Denver. The elevation should mean I won't need a mask."

M's eyes moved up and down the visible part of her body. "You do seem fairly fit."

Fairly? "Everyone has their poison. Mine just happens to be running."

"At least you have a shot at winning now."

She looked at him, puzzled. "What's that supposed to mean?"

M shrugged. "Well, those Kenyan folks did a fine job cleaning up on nearly every race for years. Had something to do with the high altitude of the region they train in as well the prevalence of running in their culture. Nowadays, any jackass with enough money can grab one of your fancy implants and boost his fitness to godly levels. Kinda hard to lose when your body can perform at twenty times the normal rate."

Lori crossed her arms. "I'll have you know, I'm not implanted."

M's eyebrows both shot up in unison. He sipped his Diet Coke.

"And furthermore, yes, there are some people who rely on boosts, but do you know what happens to them?"

M shook his head. "Yeah, they win."

"Often they do, but shortly afterward, the poor bastards drop dead from exhaustion. A neural implant may boost existing abilities, but it doesn't turn you into Superman. You know how many idiots have sold their homes in order to get augmented? Doesn't matter how much adrenaline flows through your system or how many new brain cells are generated. You punch a brick wall just right and every bone in your hand is gonna shatter."

M sipped again. "The truth is, you people have ruined just about every professional sport on earth, not to mention the Olympics."

"Nonsense," she argued, her voice taking on a more serious edge. "If anything, I'd suggest we've radically improved mental and physical competitions."

"Don't be so defensive. I'm simply saying that *Jeopardy* hasn't been the same since every contestant comes sporting a photographic memory and jacked-up intelligence." He became quiet. "Perhaps I've gone too far."

"No, I want to hear it," Lori said, lying.

M swallowed, not catching her sarcasm. "Well, you've also created an arms race among children."

"BS," she shot back. "There are laws against implanting kids."

M snickered with a touch of humor and condescension. "There are all kinds of laws on the books, but you certainly won't be shocked to hear most of them don't do a darn thing. Do you really think poor families aren't saving up for the chance to get one of their kids implanted? Course there isn't enough for all of them, so they pick the one with the most potential and send them to a back-alley doctor. A hundred years ago, those were places where young women went to get abortions. Today, scared kids are having black- and in some cases white-market tech installed. There's an arms race going on, and you and your brother are the next Alfred Nobel."

Nobel, known today for prizes in the fields of peace, literature and science, had once been known as 'the merchant of death' for his most infamous invention: dynamite. Horrified, he'd set out to change the moniker by bequeathing the bulk of his estate to a foundation in his name.

Certainly, these were arguments Lori had heard before, but never to her face and never rattled off with such cold precision.

Across from her, the look on M's face betrayed his growing realization he might have gone too far in his critique. Friendly banter aside, when all was said and done, Lori Fisher was his employer and could even be dangerous if you managed to get on her bad side.

"What about Ben?" Lori said, as though raising his name proved her point. "There was a time when even he was a regular mortal."

M took another sip. "Fisher?"

She nodded, stirring her martini with a small plastic sword.

"He was born to a prostitute who returned to her pimp and was murdered two weeks later."

"I see you've done your homework." Lori was impressed.

"His father was one of her customers, a soldier from a local army base, I believe," M went on. "He was raised by a neighbor. An older man who recognized the kid was bright, had an aptitude for technology. Helped him get into MIT, I believe."

"That's my point," Lori said. As someone who rarely drank, a few sips in and she could already feel it. "He did all of this before NEDs were a sparkle in anyone's eye."

"I see what you mean. And yet the question remains. How would a mere mortal Ben Fisher fare in today's ultra-competitive environment, against kids and adults who were armed to the teeth with all the boosts money could buy?"

Lori stiffened. Even her voice became a notch tighter. "Fine, you've made your point. Now drop it." She swallowed and straightened her jacket. "I take it you were successful in your quest." She was talking about the Elizabeth Howard affair.

M leaned back and nodded. "She had it hidden in a plant." He reached into a pocket and handed her the thumb drive.

She took it, studied it with dispassion and then placed it on the table in front of her. "I'm trusting you didn't view its contents or make a copy." Her eyes narrowed ever so slightly.

"I assumed it was encrypted," he replied. "But if you're willing to fill me in, I promise not to tell anyone."

"I'm afraid not. If any word of this got out…" She drew in a sharp, ragged breath. "Well, I can't imagine what would happen."

"You don't think the general public could handle the truth. Is that what you're saying?"

Lori was taking a sip and nearly choked on her drink. "Not this truth. Finding out the last five or six decades have been a lie, that's not something the average Joe on the street is likely to handle well."

"Seems to me folks are pretty distracted as it is, hunting this magic neural currency you've got popping up all over the place."

Lori's full lips were drawn into a thin line. "I sense another critique coming."

M shook his head and sipped at his Coke and kept quiet.

"It's important you understand you're working for the good guys here. We've created a world as free of war and suffering as it's ever been. And if we play our cards right, things will continue to improve at an exponential rate. The Chairman of the Joint Chiefs is confident we're close to reaching a breakthrough on fusion power. But I think he's wrong. I think the next advance will be in the field of gravity. It's something we experience all the time and yet it's the one force we know so little about."

"You're talking about anti-gravity," M clarified.

Lori's eyes lit up. "Not only that. I'm talking about interstellar space flight. And if enough boosted brainiacs put their heads together, perhaps even a way of saving our home before it's too late."

•••

Following his meeting with Lori, M headed back to his car, located in the underground parking structure. The thick concrete meant summoning a pickup was not possible. Besides, he figured a little exercise couldn't hurt.

He was still trying to make sense of Lori's speech about working for the good guys as well as her enigmatic comments about a series of potential scientific breakthroughs. He reached his vehicle and slid into the back seat. He normally kept all four seats pointing forward, even when the car was in autonomous mode. But sitting down M could see that wasn't the case. The seats were all facing one another and the one diagonally opposite him was currently occupied.

The barrel of M's pistol was locked onto the center of the intruder's chest. M let the gun fall into his lap when he saw who it was. "That's a damn good way of getting yourself shot."

Granger kept the mask on, his breath wheezing in and out. His legs were spread wide open. Women called it manspreading and it seemed to M the higher the age, the wider the spread. The fabric of Granger's right pant leg was about halfway up his shin, exposing a long black sock and a series of soft blinking lights above it. He had always heard the old man wasn't all human, but now he was beginning to understand exactly what that meant.

"She's too soft," Granger said, his voice muffled, but easy enough to make out.

He was talking about Lori. M had enough sense to put two and two together. "How do you figure?"

Granger reached into his pocket and pulled out a digital recorder. When he pressed play, Lori's voice filled the empty space between them. "The Chairman of the Joint Chiefs is confident we're close to reaching a breakthrough on fusion power."

"Is nothing private anymore?"

Granger shook his head. "Lori had her orders and instead she chose to take matters into her own hands. She's got a soft spot for Ben..."

"That can happen between siblings."

Granger's wheezing spate of laughter sounded more like a scoff. "Lori was right about one thing. What's at stake here is bigger than any one man or woman. What was made can be unmade. And I intend to unmake Ben Fisher, and maybe Lori too unless she steps back in line. Did you do what I asked?"

M nodded. "Yes, I filled a new USB with Neural-Sync financial documents and passed it off as the one I took from the reporter's apartment."

Granger reached out a hand clad in a black leather glove. His fingers twitched. "Let's have it then."

M felt himself hesitate before complying. He handed over the real USB he'd retrieved from the reporter's apartment. Granger gripped it between his thumb and his forefinger. He stared intently at M as the leather of his gloved hand whined. A second later, the USB was crushed between his fingers.

"You work for me now. We're no longer interested in retrieving Ben Fisher. I'm afraid it's too late for that now."

"I see," M said, growing more and more certain he knew what was coming next.

Granger's hand disappeared and came back with what looked like a credit card.

"What is this?"

"A gift. Mainly because I know what happened the last time you met face to face with Ben Fisher and you've still got the shiner to prove it." He was talking about M's failed attempt to grab him at the Purple Cafe. "You're getting augmented, but this time it's on us. Call it an early birthday present."

The features on M's face tightened painfully. "Boosted," he said, waving the card. "I'm grateful, don't get me wrong, but there are dangers if we go too far. I read about a young man last year who boosted so much at one time, his eyeballs burst. I'm not kidding. Blew right out of their sockets."

"Don't worry," Granger assured him. "Olivia will see that you're taken care of."

M nodded. That was exactly what worried him.

Chapter 26

Site 17
Xinjiang, China

Back at the dig site, Zhou was busy overseeing progress on the excavation. As soon as the structure's roof was exposed, he and a team had descended to see if they could identify the material used in its construction.

A second group, headed by Karen, was positioned at the southwest corner, digging straight down to the foundation. Additional passes with the ground-penetrating radar had revealed a handful of suggestive features in that area. It was hard to say what they were, but given the building's overall simplicity and symmetry, it offered a series of targets they couldn't pass up.

One of Zhou's newest team members to arrive was Devon, a late twenty-something with long hair he often tied up in a man bun. He was a few meters away, analyzing the roof.

"Any luck so far?" Zhou asked him. The kid might look like a barista at Starbucks, but he was one of the best structural engineers they could find.

"It looks a heck of a lot like run-of-the-mill concrete," Devon replied, rising to his feet and using a forearm to wipe a generous amount of sweat from his brow. "But without the brittleness and low tensile strength."

"I don't have to tell you, this has been sitting here a very long time," Zhou replied, unimpressed.

The kid came toward him. Swinging from his neck was a magnifying loupe. How quaint that in this day and age, some people still preferred a little old-world tech.

"Not only ancient," Devon admitted, "but also suffering from the elements for thousands of years as it was slowly buried. Given that, it's absolutely incredible how well it's held up. Oh, there is something I want you to see."

Zhou approached and followed Devon back down to the strange concrete-like surface.

"Go ahead and have a look through my magnifying glass at this spot right here," Devon suggested, indicating an area with his index finger.

Zhou went along, hoping the kid would get to the point, and quick. Squinting with the sun at his back, Zhou caught a flash of multicolored light. "Huh."

"You saw it, didn't you?" Devon was beaming.

"Is that what I think it is?"

Nodding, Devon replied: "The same exotic alloy you sent off to get tested. It's everywhere you look, ground up and sprinkled in as a super-powerful binder agent. We do this nowadays with steel dust, but it's nowhere near as strong as this."

Zhou looked down at his feet, but it was not the fancy concrete he was contemplating. He was wondering what, if anything, lay inside.

"Get the MIMO," he told one of his grad students, who ran off at once.

The MIMO was a phased array radar system capable of peering through concrete walls, and with any luck, the very ones beneath the heels of his boots. The principle behind the device was simple enough. You fired S-band radio waves against the target. Like traditional radar, the device read the return signal. In this case, however, ninety-nine point nine nine seven five percent of the signal never penetrated the surface you were attempting to see through. But the point zero zero two five percent that did make it was amplified, providing a wealth of information.

The grad student returned minutes later driving a pickup truck. Several others helped him unload the device, which looked like a cross between a lawnmower and a double-wide winter push shovel. A large set of wheels helped it navigate over the uneven terrain leading from the truck to the center of the structure's roof. The other impressive aspect of the device was that it was automated. The grad student entered the size of the designated search grid and let the machine do the rest. Slowly, it rolled forward, silently performing its job. Zhou only wished some of the students he'd brought with him from Yale were as conscientious.

MIMO's other benefit was that data received was transmitted at once to any tablets logged onto the system.

The group assembled around the screen Zhou was now holding as an image slowly began to populate.

Devon cleared a frog out of his throat. "Um, Dr. Zhou, if I could ask you something while we're waiting?"

"Yes," Zhou replied, the even tone of his voice hiding the deep anxiety he was feeling.

"I understand from speaking with Karen that you've been hesitant to make a statement about the site. But I was sort of hoping that you might. I mean, there's already a number of conclusions we can draw from what we've discovered so far."

"Such as?" Zhou asked, allowing the Socratic philosopher in him to take over. He often avoided pontificating, preferring instead to let the student tease the knowledge out themselves. And it often worked when he wasn't feeling impatient or hot-tempered, which seemed to be most of the time.

"Well," Devon said, swallowing again, only now with a mouth that had become significantly dryer. "The geologic time scale suggests this place was built around thirty million years ago, which in itself is a rather shocking discovery, given *Homo sapiens* are the only species we know of who had a similar level of technology. Neanderthals and Denisovans built tools and perhaps even makeshift shelters, but for the most part, they lived in caves and maintained a rudimentary form of technology for the entire duration of their time on Earth. Whoever these people were…"

One of Zhou's eyebrows rose, a sign Devon was traveling into uncharted and potentially hazardous territory.

"Okay, maybe not people as we know them. But they couldn't have been us."

"That is true," Zhou acknowledged, patting dust off his pant leg. "Which leaves us with three important questions. Who were they? Where did they come from? And where did they go?"

"Come from?" Devon asked.

Zhou's eyes rose to the sky where puffy white clouds stood out against a powder-blue sky.

"Oh," Devon said, suddenly uncomfortable with the professor's rather remarkable insinuation.

165

"Or not," Zhou replied. "Either the entire history of the planet needs to be rewritten, or there's another explanation. I won't pretend to know what that is, which is why I've opted to keep quiet. I'm confident the answers will present themselves before long." Zhou glanced down and saw MIMO was nearly done. Then the sound of voices nearby caught his attention. He looked up and swore under his breath. Li was heading this way, intent on seeing for herself the progress they were making.

"Dr. Zhou, I was intensely disappointed you missed our last status report."

"I was occupied," Zhou said, his chin down and eyes raised to half whites.

The image was coming in and Zhou wanted nothing more than for her to leave and let them do their job in peace. The others, including Li, shuffled behind Zhou and studied the ever-sharpening image on the screen.

"Hollow space," a female grad student said, a hand covering her mouth.

"Are those tunnels?" Devon whispered to no one in particular.

"More like corridors," Zhou said. He could see them crisscrossing the whole area they had scanned, like the roads in the core of a city. But it was the largest room in the center of the image that caught his eye. MIMO had showed the rooms and corridors within the structure were empty, not unlike many of the tombs in Ancient Egypt looted by thieves millennia ago. From here, however, the largest chamber in the center of the image looked different from the others. Zhou zoomed in and the picture became painfully pixelated. He pulled out slightly and let his eyes focus. A single, rectangular object in the room gave off a particularly strong signature.

Zhou was in the middle of contemplating what that might be when the radio attached to his belt roared to life, making him jump.

"Zhou, it's Karen, do you read me?"

His hand went involuntarily to his heart to make sure it was still beating. "Go ahead."

"The excavators have reached the foundation on the south side and there's something here you should see. Two things, actually."

A weird mix of impatience and fear raced up the back of his neck. "Spit it out."

A cackle of laughter from the other end. "I had a feeling that was coming. We've found a metal plaque which appears to have markings of some kind."

"And the other thing?"

"Below the plaque is an opening into the structure."

Chapter 27

At night, the Seattle Space Needle resembled a giant burning brazier, her silhouette framed against the twinkling lights of the bustling city. She had been built as a centerpiece for the 1962 World's Fair. Over the decades that followed, she had come to symbolize the city itself in much the same way that the Golden Gate Bridge symbolized San Francisco or the Empire State Building did New York.

The Naval officer had told Sienna he would be on the Needle's observation deck, facing south and wearing an orange ballcap. Given that Mariners and Sea Hawks fans generally wore blue and sometimes green caps, he had a much better chance of standing out.

The plan was simple enough. Sienna would head up first and spot him without making contact. Ben would follow soon after and hover out of sight, but close enough to react if things went bad.

It didn't take a genius to see the plan had plenty of room to go bad. For starters, his gut had a serious objection to the location for the meeting. An elevator ride and over eight hundred steps stood against the prospects of making a clean getaway should they find themselves in trouble. Even upon entering the Purple

Cafe Ben had been careful to check for possible exits. In this case, the number of escape routes was severely limited.

For her part, Sienna hadn't wanted to hear anything about Ben's many misgivings. She was on an almost suicidal mission to find out everything she could about her father's death. He also knew Lori had been the one to help establish contact with this man, whoever he was. Ultimately, he would have to play along for now, but if they arrived and that strange feeling in the bottom of his gut hadn't gone away, Ben had no compunction about aborting the meeting altogether.

He waited in line for the elevators, surrounded by tourists on all sides. Sienna was several feet ahead of him. When it was her turn to climb on board, they exchanged a nervous look before the elevator doors closed.

It was less than a minute later when an attendant with a walkie-talkie came to stand before the steel elevator doors and plopped down a sign. *Maximum capacity reached. Next elevator in twenty minutes.* The grumbles started almost immediately.

"You've got to be shitting me," said a guy standing next to him, wearing sandals and white shin socks. Two kids and the guy's wife were dressed the same way.

"Boyd, not in front of the children."

The little boy sighed. "Don't worry, Mom, I know all the curse words," he said enthusiastically.

Ben pushed past them and out of the line. He couldn't afford to wait around. By now Sienna was already up on the observation deck and so was whoever they'd come here to meet.

•••

169

Sienna hadn't been up here in years. They must have renovated sometime in the last little while because the place looked modern, in a minimalist sort of way. Recessed lighting bathed the area in a warm, futuristic glow. A promenade outside featured a glass floor, designed for the sole intention of allowing brazen young men to scare the crap out of their girlfriends. Anyone with a fear of heights as acute as Sienna's would struggle just to be up this high, let alone tempt fate by standing on a few sheets of glass hundreds of feet in the air. She would sooner smack her thumb with a hammer.

These errant thoughts continued to jostle through the nervous circuitry in her brain, as another part of her mind scanned the people around her. The place wasn't very well lit for seeing faces. Not that that was much of a surprise. The circular viewing area she was standing in had been purposefully made to force the eye beyond the glass partition toward the twinkling city below. It was quite a sight, but not the one she had come to see.

The man on the phone had told her he would be looking south, she reminded herself as she pushed through the dense throngs of visitors. They seemed to be heading in every direction at once.

The top of an orange ballcap poked up above the sea of bobbing heads. Slowly, deliberately, she moved in that direction. The man they had come here to meet was less than fifteen feet away now. The same one who had promised to shed some light on the darkened mystery of what had befallen the *Archipelago* and those aboard her.

Sienna drew close enough to get a better look. The man with the orange cap stood facing out the window, seemingly enthralled with the nighttime vista below. She moved next to him and stared in the same direction.

170

"It's beautiful, isn't it?" she said. "All those lights. The hundreds of thousands of people."

The man looked over and grinned politely. He was somewhere in his early fifties. Mostly fit except for a little something extra around the midsection. His loose jeans and white sweater draped over his shoulders screamed tourist. He'd overdone it a little, but overall it was pretty convincing.

"I've lived here all my life and never bothered to see it for myself," the man said.

"That's the way of the world," she offered, hoping they might dispense with the small talk and move on to the business that mattered. That roaring fire of impatience always burning within was threatening to engulf her.

"You from around here?"

Sienna grit her teeth. "Let's just cut to the chase, shall we? What do you have for me?"

The man's eyes grew wide. "Have for you?"

"Believe me, you don't want to waste my time." There was a dangerous edge to her voice and Sienna watched with a certain amount of pleasure as a palpable thread of fear settled over his face. His lips retreated between his teeth as he stepped away, watching her cautiously from the corner of his eyes. Sienna's own gaze narrowed in confusion.

She caught the sound of laughter on her other side and snapped her head in that direction. A thin guy stood next to her wearing a powder-blue windbreaker. His dark hair was slicked back over his scalp.

"I could have sat here watching that all day," he said through a crooked grin. Like the man himself, his lips were thin and parted on one side, revealing teeth stained by years of smoking filterless cigarettes. "Gotta say, I didn't think you'd come. I hung back for a bit, watching you."

"To ensure I came alone."

He nodded, his long, pointed nose moving up and down like a conductor's baton. "You're not the only one sticking your neck out, Sienna. It seems we have some mutual friends who take offence when the American people are being lied to."

"Do you have a name?" she asked. "Something I can call you."

"How about Ralph?"

"I had a cat named Ralph. Okay then, Ralph, what do you say we get down to it? Tell me what it is you know."

That smile again. "Is that the way you think it works? If so, you haven't been in this business very long. I set the meeting, so I set the terms."

Sienna felt her arms cross over her chest. "All right, I'm listening."

"Talking is what I want you to do. A little bird tells me you and Mr. Fisher are working together. I want to know what your objectives are and what you've discovered so far."

Sienna straightened. "You already know why I'm here. What you're really asking for is information on Ben. I don't think it's a surprise that he's a suspect in Amanda's murder."

"Did he do it?"

She shook her head adamantly. "No, but the proof has disappeared and he's trying to get it back. He's also trying to find out who set him up."

Ralph's chin scrunched up in a look of doubt. "Some have said he's one of the smartest people on the planet. And you're saying he hasn't got a clue."

"Well, he's having memory problems. He seems to think it has something to do with his company."

That last bit seemed to pique Ralph's interest.

"Now it's your turn," she told him.

"Fair enough. What sank the *Archipelago* in the Weddell Sea wasn't any kind of conventional weapon. The kind of damage visible couldn't have been caused by a missile or a torpedo. I could show you pictures, but—"

"I've seen them. His ship looked like a beer can after a house party. We spoke to William Schroder, the crane operator who was admitted to the psychiatric unit at Western State Psychiatric Hospital. He told us a ball of blue light attacked the ship."

Ralph nodded. "Our best guess was that they were using some sort of energy weapon."

"What does that mean?"

"A Holy Grail for the arms industry, for one. Let's just say whoever can harness and direct the laws of nature is bound to have an enormous tactical and political advantage on the world stage. And the usefulness of such a technology goes far beyond killing. Among other things, one could also use it to manipulate the weather."

Sienna's mind spun from the possibilities. She thought of the depressing nightly newscasts droning on and on about flooding in the East and drought in the West. The folks along the Rio Grande sure could use some rain right about now. If technology existed that could make that happen, it would feel to the folks in that area like a real no-brainer.

"But here's the thing," the man continued. "At this point, it appears we're dealing with a technology stolen from either the Russians or the Chinese."

"That makes sense," Sienna acknowledged. "Ben met with a doctor who suggested the technology in Neural-Sync's NEDs was stolen."

Now it was Ralph's turn to look surprised. "No doubt from the same source. It appears the Chinese are way farther ahead of us than we gave them credit for."

"America, playing technological catch-up with China," Sienna said with noticeable chagrin. "I always knew the day would come, but—"

"Just not so soon," he said completing the thought. "None of us did. You can thank Operation THOTH for helping to even out the playing field."

"Thoth?"

"Egyptian god of technology. Our intelligence sources tell us it's a top-secret project designed to steal cutting-edge foreign technology, reverse-engineer it and then put it to work within American corporations. There's an agent who goes by the code name Mirage. We suspect her real name is Michelle Mackay, or something similar. She's top-tier and has likely been behind the operation since its inception. You find Mirage and you'll find your father's killer." Ralph let that sink in for a bit.

"We also have a date and a time of great importance," Ralph told her. "Exactly eight days from now at nine pm. We don't know what will happen or where it will take place. All we can say for sure is that whatever it is, it won't be good."

Sienna swallowed hard. That was precisely what they didn't need. In a matter of days from now, something terrible, maybe even cataclysmic would take place. She knew one thing for sure. Every single moment between now and then would be vital.

Then Ralph said, "There's something else you should see." He held up his phone, which displayed a picture of

174

Ben meeting with a woman in a lab coat, her unusual posture the result of a rare condition that twisted her spine. "This is Dr. Tatiana Barulina, from the University of St. Petersburg. She is a world-renowned metallurgist, an expert in amorphous metals and cutting-edge alloys. It appears Mr. Fisher was quite a busy man in the days leading up to his girlfriend's murder."

"What are you suggesting?" Sienna said, afraid of where Ralph might be going with this.

He laughed. "Not what you think. There was something that Ben got tangled up in. Something with far-reaching enough implications that a group of powerful people thought it necessary to silence him. The world of intelligence is filled with secrets. But something tells me this one's bigger than all the rest. Good luck." Ralph gave her a half bow before turning and disappearing into the crowd.

Sienna started after him, only to be stopped by a hand closing around her arm. She turned to find Ben. Sweat was streaming down his forehead. He looked like he had taken the stairs.

"Did he show?" he asked, catching his breath.

She nodded. There was a lot to fill him in on and not much time to do it.

Chapter 28

After the meeting with Ralph, Ben and Sienna returned to Knut's.

Ben sat at a table, surrounded by bits of salvaged computer junk, trying to make sense of the jumble of numbers he had found etched on his forearms. The first set, *4043191165708*, was by far the toughest. He had tried treating it like a phone number, a password, a cypher and everything else he could imagine, and yet every alley he had turned down led nowhere.

The other set of numbers was a different story.
350278 1110222 2100

The main clue had come from Sienna's meeting with Ralph.

"I don't think they mean a damn thing," Sienna said, her frustration getting the best of her.

Staring at the string, Ben suddenly saw something. "Didn't you say that Ralph warned you something very bad was doing to happen eight days from now?"

She stopped pacing and moved up next to where he was sitting. "Yeah, in eight days at exactly nine in the evening."

"And what's nine pm when converted to the twenty-four hour clock?"

"Twenty-one hundred," she replied.

He pointed to the last four digits.

"Okay, that could work. But what about the rest of it?"

"They're GPS coordinates. If you place decimal points after the number five and after the third number one, you get this: 35.0278 111.0222."

"Great, but where does it lead?"

Ben typed it into the map feature on his phone. The answer came back almost immediately. "The Barringer Crater in Arizona."

They both stared at the picture of a massive crater, the result of a meteor strike in Arizona fifty thousand years ago.

"What's there?" she asked. "Besides a giant hole."

Ben shrugged. "No clue. But I'm guessing we'll find out in eight days' time."

Just then Knut appeared, both of his hands full. He raised one at a time. "All right, your disguises are ready."

The pieces of their disguise Ben saw dangling from Knut's hands told him one thing: This was going to be rough.

•••

A few minutes later, Sienna and Ben were standing in front of a mirror.

Sienna covered her mouth with both hands, stifling a belly laugh at Ben's expense. "Oh, you look absolutely ridiculous."

The mustache and glasses Ben was wearing definitely aged him, but it was the padded suit and the built-in belly that really brought the disguise together.

"You don't look so hot yourself," Ben pointed out.

Sienna looked in the mirror and frowned, holding out the frumpy jeans she had been given, along with a blonde wig.

Armed with Tatiana's name and position, Ben had searched his phone for any sign the two had contacted one another. He soon found an email exchange dated three days before the attack in which he had asked Tatiana if she would be willing to analyze something for him. She had said yes, but made clear she didn't use telephones and that he was lucky she had even checked her desperately overflowing and outdated AOL account. If Ben needed any clearer sign he wasn't going to get Tatiana on the phone, that was it. Thus began Knut's hunt for appropriate disguises and fake passports.

"Over here," Knut said impatiently, motioning to a white background. They were getting new passport photos taken, the kind that would allow them to fly to Russia and back without getting snagged by the authorities.

Knut snapped their pictures. "You think air quality in Seattle is bad, just wait until you get to Eastern Europe. If you find yourselves starting to get short of breath, use these." He handed each of them one of the best masks on the market. "And don't worry, you'll fit in just fine. Anyone with plans to see fifty wears one on the streets and sometimes in the house."

"How do you know all this?" Sienna asked, impressed.

Knut blushed. "Every moment I'm not helping people like you, I've got my nose buried in a book."

"You're a rare breed," Ben said.

"Maybe, but I still wish I could read anywhere near as fast as you."

Ben smiled. "If you have a stun gun handy, I can try jacking your NED."

"Appreciate the offer," Knut said, smirking as he transferred the images onto his laptop. "I enjoy my life as a mere mortal."

An hour later, with new passports and plane tickets to St. Petersburg in hand, Ben and Sienna headed for the airport.

•••

The flight was crowded and uncomfortable, but largely went without incident. Ben had gone through every magazine on the plane and all before the plane had even left the ground.

He had picked up a book in the airport on learning Russian and proceeded to flip through its pages. After ten minutes, he turned to Sienna who was sitting next to him. "Ty khorosho vyglyadish' v etikh dzhinsakh."

She glanced at him with a look of amazement. "Not bad. What did you say?"

"I said you look good in those jeans." He laughed and she joined in.

Ben asked the flight attendant for a newspaper. In it, he read about how the general public's transition from driving to fully autonomous vehicles had been easy enough. The relative freshness of the technology hadn't stopped many drivers from letting go of the steering wheel. In other words, the road to ubiquitous faith in algorithms shuttling us safely from point A to B had been a surprisingly short one. There had been many deaths along the way, but ultimately, the roads had become safer. The same transition had been going on in the aviation industry and for far longer, although it was still difficult for Ben to wrap his head around the reality that in just the last few years pilots too had become obsolete.

Slowly but surely, computer code had assumed more and more of the heavy lifting. With millions of flights every year, the system got more than its fair share of real-world practice. Not only that, but apart from the odd mishap—often covered extensively by the twenty-four-hour news outlets—overall, it seemed to perform quite admirably.

Self-driving cars were no different and there were currently thousands of dead passengers every year to prove the point. And yet, dangers notwithstanding, the general public had adapted to the new reality as though it had been there all along. Not only could people order their cars to come pick them up, some enterprising individuals even hired their vehicles out to act as couriers and taxi cabs while at work. Far from emptying the streets, large stretches of asphalt were often clogged with driverless cars, moonlighting as couriers and taxis. A quote from the article said that for every problem you solved, two new ones were created. It was a maxim that could apply as much to advances in technology as it could to life in general.

Even in his own readings and observations, Ben had also noted the elasticity with which humans adapted to certain kinds of change. The introduction of Neural-Sync and their revolutionary NEDs was a prime example. Ten years ago, the thought of sticking something inside your brain to boost cognition, strength and help regulate your temperament would have seemed unfathomable, perhaps even Orwellian. Today, it was not only commonplace, it was practically mandatory. For many, it offered an ability to join the gilded ranks of society. Those unable to afford the prohibitive cost or without the time required to hunt down newly spawned Neuros, well, the technology only served to widen that disparity.

Looking back on a life he didn't remember, Ben couldn't imagine, when all of this started, that had been the outcome he'd had in mind. But nothing about hopes or outcomes changed people's eagerness to augment themselves in any way they could. Years before, no one could have foreseen how quickly we would adapt to the birth of quantum computing and nanotechnology. Far from sounding like something out of a Hollywood movie, they were terms that nowadays would hardly raise an eyebrow.

Clearly, the human ability to adapt was one of our greatest strengths, arguably one of the reasons our species had survived the ravages of time and all the challenges that entailed. A testament to that was the call to arms to stop treating the planet like a college fraternity house and begin an era of responsible stewardship.

Put that way, it was hard to argue against. And to that end, the most developed countries in the world had taken the lead and made great strides in cutting down the amount of CO_2 being released into the atmosphere. As Sienna was quick to point out, the world had celebrated. Then Nicholay Panov had come along and ruined everything, like that annoying bouncer who flipped on the ugly lights before the last song was done.

But that adaptability also cut both ways. Ben considered the masks people wore. New businesses were always cropping up. Better masks. Masks with lightweight oxygen tanks. Masks painted to appear beautiful or scary. Humans were adapting all right. But were they willing to face reality? They had tackled climate change head on and the problem had only grown worse.

Were the hydrothermal vents Nicholay had found somehow to blame, or was something else going on?

Chapter 29

Neural-Sync headquarters was a modest forty-story high-rise on 5th and Columbia. Covered in glass, what it lacked in height, it more than made up for with depth. What the public didn't know was that the building descended fifteen stories beneath street level. It had been an engineering nightmare, but it had proven useful as an area for the company's extensive R&D department. It was also where M was heading. Or, more accurately, where Granger had sent him to get boosted.

As promised, a young woman in a teal business skirt and blazer named Olivia greeted him at the building's front entrance and led him into a service elevator.

"Mr. Granger has asked that we take extra-special care of you," she said, flashing him a rather convincing smile. She didn't look a day over twenty-five.

She was probably fresh out of school, working here as an intern, which was really a polite way of saying she was working for free.

"I'm sure he did," M replied.

She cleared her throat, the elevator descending with no noticeable sense of movement. "I have you down here as Mr. M. Do you mind if I ask what it stands for?"

"Magician," he told her curtly. "A nickname my friends gave me when I was young." That was a lie, of course, but it wasn't like he was going to share the true source of his moniker with an intern. Hearing it was liable to send her packing and then Granger would blame him for frightening the poor girl. Instead, he tucked a hand inside the inner pocket of his leather jacket. "Wanna see a trick?"

She grinned awkwardly. There was a sexual connotation to the question. One M hadn't intended, but one she had taken nevertheless.

Just then, the elevator doors opened into a corridor humming with activity. A man and a woman in soft white biosuits passed before them heading down an intersecting hallway. Glass partitions divided labs where groups of scientists busied themselves.

"What are they all working on?" M asked.

The girl smiled again. "The future."

She led him into a brightly lit glass room. It seemed no one here believed in privacy. M had boosted before, on three different occasions actually. And each time he'd gone to a Neural-Sync outlet and had the work done there. Technically speaking, the process was fairly straightforward. They synced you into the system, pulled up your NED profile, deposited any new Neuros from gift cards into your account and away you went. As far as M was concerned, all of this seemed a little overkill.

The room was sparsely furnished. In the center sat a white leather dentist's chair. Hovering over the chair was an LED light on a retractable arm. The sight reminded him of Elizabeth Howard and the regret he felt over her attempted escape. He wanted to believe that if she hadn't done that, he might have kept her locked away until the countdown was over. Once the arrival and meetings were behind them, Lori, Granger and a whole swath of the THOTH personnel would be far more relaxed. At least, they would be far less on edge.

On the wall near the entrance was a first-aid kit. A six-inch drain sat at the foot of the chair.

"I take it this is where they perform the lobotomies?" he asked, half joking.

"At one time," Olivia replied. "But that was before I joined the organization. Would you mind grabbing a seat?"

To his surprise, he noticed she was wearing a white lab coat now. The back of his knees struck the leather chair. He stumbled into it, smacking his scalp against the headrest. He repositioned, the motion filling his ears with the whine of leather.

"You're just full of surprises, aren't you?"

She grinned. "Did you take me for Mr. Granger's executive assistant? I can't tell you how often that happens."

"Yeah, something like that."

Olivia approached and looped the arm straps around his wrists and tightened them. Afterward, she did the same to his ankles.

"This is beginning to feel kinky," M said, distinctly aware that an alarm bell was going off inside his head, but feeling powerless to do anything about it. He had come here under his own strength and no little girl was going to scare him off.

Olivia watched him, her bright eyes flashing some sense she knew precisely what he was going through. "Don't be afraid, Mr. M. The restraints are only a precaution."

"Afraid? Who's afraid? Not me."

Olivia might be many things, but in this case, she was gracious enough not to contradict him.

"Great, now just relax." She held up a tablet and lined up the blinking circles with his eyes. "You've done this before."

He had. M stared into the circles until the image morphed into a picture of his mother setting down a giant chocolate birthday cake with six candles poking out the top. Seeing it filled him with longing and deep sadness. Far too quickly, the image was gone and another took its place. This time he was in the driveway, wearing a police uniform, leaning against his squad car, beaming with a pride born from a paucity of opportunity and a truckload of hard work. The sense of accomplishment was still lingering when the final image appeared. This time it was a baby, swaddled in a blue blanket, sleeping peacefully. M forced himself to look. Ordered his eyes to stop from slamming shut. He knew the identification process would fail if he gave in to the impulse. That the torture of happier times and lives that might have been would begin all over again.

A soft female voice spoke from the table: "Identification confirmed."

M watched his stats roll up on the screen.

Intelligence (8)
Memory (6)
Athleticism (5)
Equilibrium (3)

"The old man has a real beef with equilibrium," M said. "When he looks at all this, do me a favor and remind him those points were already there."

She regarded him with a strange expression before nodding. "Of course. What exactly would you like to boost today?"

"Depends, what's on this thing?"

Olivia took his card and scanned it. "Two hundred."

"Dollars?" M said and laughed. He'd known Granger was a cheapass, but this was something else.

"No, Mr. M, two hundred boosts. Now where would you like them?"

His eyes flared as though he'd just been told his spleen and liver had swapped places. "I knew it. That son of a bitch is trying to kill me. You heard what they say, boosting more than ten units at a time can make your brain run out your ears."

"We've been working to solve that problem."

"Yeah, well, call me back when you do." M struggled against the restraints.

"Mr. Granger was concerned you might not agree once you discovered the danger involved." Olivia brought out a needle from her pocket, flipped off the cap and plunged it into the side of his neck.

"You bitc…" he started to say as he felt the world starting to slow to a crawl.

"Mr. Granger also left me with strict instructions that all of these units were to be put in a single category."

By the time Olivia began to apply the changes to M's NED, his head was slumped over, a thin trail of drool running down his chin.

•••

He came awake to a bolt of blinding pain searing a spot just behind his eyes. He howled in agony and a frightened Olivia dropped the tablet, where it struck the hard floor and shattered. All he wanted to do was grasp the sides of his throbbing head. A second later, his hands

187

were there, trying to press away the pain. Two stout men in blue security uniforms rushed in and skidded to a stop when they saw the crazed look plastered on M's face.

Fragments of torn memories were rushing through his tortured mind. He couldn't think straight, needed to get up and walk off this terrible feeling. The slight bit of resistance at his legs was easily overcome as he snapped the leather restraints. M staggered to his feet.

"Easy, buddy," one of the guards said, slowly removing his expandable baton, his other hand stretched out before him. They looked like two men trying to negotiate with a wild animal. But all M wanted to do was get out of here.

Little by little, the blinding pain in his head was already beginning to subside. But these two jokers were blocking the door. The corridors beyond led to the elevator and the elevator led to freedom. M started forward, struggling against the vibrations coursing through every muscle in his body.

"We need you to sit down, Mr. M," the other guard said in a voice that betrayed his deep fear.

M sensed the fear, could even smell some strange part of it. The animalistic center of his brain had a newfound clarity, but his intellect felt as though an opaque film had been pulled over his thinking process. Where the world and the things in it had once appeared sharp and clear, now they were dull and hazy.

He headed for the door, almost oblivious to the guards' presence. Had he forgotten about them, or was he ignoring them the way one might ignore a pair of pesky moths flying around your face?

When M got too close, the guard's baton went into the air and started to come down. M caught it on its downward arc and shifted its trajectory toward the guard with the shaky voice next to him. The hard metal end struck the man on the back of the head. M raised the guard's arm and lowered it again, looking like a man adjusting a pair of life-sized action figures.

Shaky dropped to the floor and stayed there while the other man tried to break free from M's iron grasp. The guard let the baton fall from his hand as he tugged wildly against what felt like a bear trap closed around his wrist. In a blur of motion, M flung the man behind him, where he crunched into the glass partition. A red smear appeared as he slid to the floor.

Cleared of obstructions, M went through the doors and into the corridor. Men and women in lab coats who had gathered to watch the encounter scattered in terror. M wasn't interested in hurting anyone. But those two men had attacked him first and he'd had no other choice but to defend himself the way he'd been taught from an early age. His mother was a pacifist and she had instilled him with a respect for the sanctity of life and the importance of preserving it at all costs.

He got no further than ten paces into the corridor when he felt the muscles in his body begin to tire. His breaths were becoming deeper and at the same time devoid of the oxygen levels his cells were crying out for. M braced himself against the wall, feeling the energy slowly drain from his limbs. Raising a hand, he watched it tremble violently. It took a moment for him to realize what was happening. The boost had effectively dismantled the internal inhibitors that helped ensure the release of only safe amounts of adrenaline into his body. As a result, his system had been rocked by a massive hit of adrenaline, an amount far in excess of what the body normally allowed, even under the most extreme situations.

189

The woman returned and stood a few feet away. He knew her name started with an O, he just couldn't recall it at the moment. Ophelia? Or was it Oprah? A weak grin lit his face with the absurdity.

"What have you done to me?" he asked her, his breath slowly returning.

"Don't worry, the fatigue you're feeling will pass. And each time your NED maximizes your output of strength and endurance, you will recover faster."

M nodded at news he found only mildly encouraging. But none of that had changed the fact that there were gaps in his memory. He asked her as much.

Empathy washed over her features. "I'm afraid there are always some unforeseen consequences when excessive boosting is at play. Memory loss is one of them."

Sapped of rage, M felt an overwhelming sadness begin to envelop him. An image of his mother's face appeared before him. She looked concerned, but also a touch disappointed. He was on the ground and no son of hers ever let himself get knocked down for good. *Up on your feet,* that look said. And he did as it said, pushing against the glass wall, until the world was once again underfoot.

A text came through just then and with some effort, M reached into his pocket and plucked out his phone. It was a message from Granger and there was an attachment. A plane ticket.

Surveillance footage shows they're heading to St. Petersburg. Two of my top security personnel will meet you at the airport. Remember, pack lightly. I'm counting on you to fix this.

M lowered the phone and watched his mother's ghostly-stern features slowly dissipate from view. She had contracted to the size of a postage stamp by the time he became dimly aware he could no longer remember her name.

Chapter 30

Site 17
Xinjiang, China

Zhou was still unsure whether his invitation to dinner would go unanswered when he heard the knock at his trailer door.

The crew was busy working to clear the passageway they'd found into the structure. Near the base, countless millennia of mud and grime had formed an almost impenetrable barrier that needed to be chipped away little by little without causing damage. In the eighteenth and nineteenth centuries, archaeology had been a different beast entirely. Schliemann's excavation of Troy had consisted of gouging a deep trench through the middle of the site. Today, the goal was less about treasure hunting and more about understanding and preserving humanity's past. The age of the discovery put Zhou in a thoroughly unprecedented situation. A thought, both exciting and unsettling, had been hovering about him since the structure's discovery. If not human, whose past was he about to discover?

Zhou opened the door to find Li, still dressed in her formal work clothes. She was holding a cactus.

"It is customary not to show up empty-handed," she said, offering him the plant. For a moment, he thought he caught the glimmer of a smile on her lips, but couldn't be sure.

"That's very kind of you," Zhou acknowledged, stepping aside to let her in. "It won't surprise you to learn I'm normally terrible with plants. Cacti are the only thing I have a chance of keeping alive."

He led her a few paces away to the trailer's kitchenette. The table nearby was set for two. On the counter were takeout containers from a local restaurant. "I took the liberty of ordering us food. Cooking in a dollhouse like this would be thoroughly unpleasant and, given my skills, perhaps even dangerous."

Zhou definitely got a smile from that one as Li settled into her seat.

"Something to drink?"

She waved a hand. "Oh, I shouldn't."

"One glass won't hurt," he said, approaching with the Chinese version of a French white wine. "Chow Mein and a drink. You deserve a break after all your hard work."

Li looked decidedly uncomfortable as Zhou served them both and sat down. "I invited you to dinner for a very simple reason," Zhou began to explain. "It's important that we learn to get along. Not only the two of us as individuals, but the two of us as citizens of vastly different countries."

The muscles in her face grew tense.

Zhou cleared his throat. "Believe me, this isn't about comparing and contrasting systems. I don't involve myself in politics, not when there's a job to be done." He raised his glass. "To continued cooperation."

Li clinked his glass and both of them drank. They began to eat. Zhou studied her delicate hands, articulating her chopsticks with expert precision. Years spent alternating his own cultural habits with a knife and fork had suddenly exposed his own inadequacies. But when Zhou had said he had a job to do, Li might not have realized that this dinner was a big part of that. It was only a question of time before she caught on to the significance of the find, a recognition she would report and by doing so set into motion a terrible chain of events. Although Zhou was not a hundred percent certain what each of those steps might look like, he was confident the end result would mean the closure of Site 17. Hence the dinner and hence his attempts to garner a friendship. After all, it was a lot harder to rat out a friend than an adversary.

Over the course of the meal, Zhou told her about his childhood, growing up in the US with Chinese parents and the challenges of straddling two radically different cultures. They were on the beginning of their third glass of wine when he asked about her.

Her cheeks, already flushed from the alcohol, grew a shade deeper. Zhou couldn't tell if she was embarrassed to talk about herself, or fearful as many Chinese were that somewhere, someone might be listening in—a fear Americans were largely oblivious to. His eyes shifted to the ring on her wedding finger.

"Tell me about your husband," he said instead, hoping to direct the conversation into more comfortable territory.

"There is not much to tell," she said. "Huan runs a dried goods business he inherited from his parents. They are elderly and live with us."

Zhou nodded. "And what of *your* parents?"

194

Li's eyes glazed over as she shook her head. "They are gone."

"I'm sorry to hear that," he said, meaning every word.

"That is life," she replied stoically, setting her glass down, spinning the stem in a slow circle. "My mother and father were artists who chose to flout the rules. Such behavior can only be met by punishment commensurate with the crime."

"Your respect for the rules, is that why you decided to work for the government?"

She stopped spinning the glass as her eyes narrowed. "My respect for the rules tells me I shouldn't be here with you, discussing such things."

Zhou grunted, realizing what might have seemed back home like a friendly chat felt to Li like an interrogation. "If I overstepped—"

Li straightened in her chair. "For both of our sakes, Dr. Zhou, it is important that we forgo the pleasantries and speak plainly. I know why you invited me here."

"You do?"

"You tried hard to shield me from the facts of your discovery, but there is an expression from the last great war. 'Loose lips sink ships.' And I am here to tell you your ship was sunk long ago."

Zhou leaned back, his voice deepening. "I see."

"Without a doubt, what you have uncovered is the greatest find in human history."

The compliment was thoroughly appreciated and certainly true, but Zhou knew this wasn't going in a good direction. Not for him and certainly not for the find.

"Lying to a government official is punishable by imprisonment and even death," she informed him, her voice devoid of any hint of emotion. Her fine, youthful features stood out in stark contrast to the weight of her pronouncement. "Protocol also requires me to inform my superiors about the nature of the discovery. I am quite confident they would view the secrets hidden within the structure as representing quite a boon to Chinese innovation."

"No doubt," Zhou conceded, suddenly feeling more naked and vulnerable than he ever had before.

She folded her hands. "I am, however, willing to keep your little secret, for a price."

Zhou felt a jolt run through every fiber of his body. Here was the one they'd nicknamed the Stickler not only bending the rules, but tossing them out the window altogether. Corruption at its finest. "Listen, I'm an archaeologist, not a millionaire. You know that, don't you?"

"It isn't your money I want."

Zhou's demeanor became decidedly uncomfortable. "What is it you're after then?"

Li lifted her hands off the table and then folded them over her chest. "I told you earlier that my husband owns and operates a dried goods business. What I neglected to mention was that the local prefect's son has recently opened a competing enterprise. And now the father has seen fit to launch an investigation into my husband's business practices."

Zhou nodded, a twinkle of recognition in his eye. "In America, that's called clearing out the competition."

"Maybe, but that does not make it right. Like me, Huan has always followed the rules. But we are powerless to stop his inevitable prosecution. If Huan is arrested, they will confiscate our life savings, destroying any hopes our daughter has at a successful life." There were tears in Li's eyes. "I cannot let that happen."

196

"Unless he sells his business."

Li nodded, the look of frustration on her face intensifying. "He already has a buyer. But if the prefect rules against him beforehand, he will be able to claim it on behalf of the state and hand it to his son to manage. This is how things are done in China."

"I see. So what exactly do you want me to do?"

"Leaving China is not the hard part," she explained. "However, taking your money with you is nearly impossible."

"You need me to smuggle your life savings out of the country and keep it safe until you arrive in America?"

"Help get our money there, yes. But you must also take us along too."

●●●

Not long after, Zhou went down to the dig site to clear his mind. Technicians in rubber suits were using water pressure hoses to cut through the solidified mass blocking the entrance.

"Feels like it's taking forever," a voice behind him observed.

Zhou grunted. It was Karen and she stood with her hands on her hips, staring up at the plaque.

"I'm starting to wonder if that's sediment or some kind of decayed doorway they're cutting through."

Another inaudible sound from Zhou.

"I don't know, what do you think it even means?" she wondered.

Zhou half turned. He was deep in thought. "Huh?"

She pointed at the strange symbols carved into the metal plaque over the archway. "It's made from the same alloy we've seen all over the site."

Zhou regarded the plaque, his manner distant, distracted.

197

"Any thoughts on what it says?" Karen tried again.

"'Ye who enter here, beware,'" he said, wryly. "Who knows."

"You seem extra grumpy tonight." They had that kind of relationship. They were colleagues, sure, but they could also call each other out when need be. At least most of the time. "Is there something on your mind?"

"I had dinner with Li," he replied, deciding to leave out the gory details.

"Really? The ice queen eats?" Karen laughed.

"She's not as icy as she looks."

She tilted her head. "Oh, crap. Tell me you didn't."

Zhou smiled. "Are you insane?"

"I don't know, I'm just putting two and two together."

He shrugged. "I thought I could thaw that cold heart of hers. Figured if we sat down and got to know one another, she might like us and not be in such a rush to report the magnitude of what we found here."

Karen was shaking her head. "Let me guess, she saw right through you and ran to tell on us the minute your little soirée was over."

"Not quite." He explained how Li was blackmailing them.

Karen stood there a moment in stunned silence.

Zhou glanced over. "That was my reaction too. It's hard enough dealing with this, but now we're risking the prospect of prison on both ends."

"Let me get this straight. If you deny her, she could report us and send in the authorities to shut us down. And if you agree, you could get caught and sent to a reeducation camp or worse."

"The technical term for our little dilemma is far too vulgar to say out loud."

198

Karen grinned. "Effed if you do, effed if you don't."

"Thank you for protecting my virgin ears," Zhou said, squeezing out a smile. "But to answer your question, I'm not sure what I'm going to do. Stall as long as possible, I suppose." His gaze shifted back to the stone tablet. "Tell me we have people working on this."

Karen nodded. "Of course. Just don't expect anything too soon. After all, it took years to figure out Egyptian hieroglyphs and we had a cheat sheet."

She was referring to the Rosetta Stone, a tablet that contained text in ancient Egyptian hieroglyphics, Greek and Demotic. Discovered by Napoleonic scientists while the French ruler was on military campaign in Egypt, the full translation took another twenty-three years to be completed.

Devon ran up to them a moment later, panting for breath.

"What is it now?" Zhou asked, already on edge.

"We just got some of the thermal readings back," he told them, handing him a tablet.

Zhou and Karen studied the mostly navy-blue image. In the center was the pixelated trace of an orange blob. "What am I looking at?" he asked, sounding cross, but fighting the tingle dancing up the back of his scalp.

"It's a heat source," Devon replied. "And it's coming from inside the structure."

Chapter 31

St. Petersburg, Russia

The trip from St. Petersburg's Pulkovo Airport to the Institute of Metallurgy was like driving through a guided tour of history. The city had been the capital of Imperial Russia from the seventeenth century until the Revolution, when the capital was transferred to Moscow. They drove first through Palace Square, a sprawling space centered on the Alexander column built to commemorate Russia's victory over Napoleonic France. Bicycles around here were plentiful, the riders' breathing gear adorned in artistic and creative ways.

"There's so much history here," Sienna said, fogging the taxi's window as she stared outside in wonder.

Ben agreed, but couldn't shake the gnawing desire to rip the fake mustache off his lip. With a flick of his wrist, he gave into temptation and sighed with relief.

Sienna turned and grinned.

"I just needed a break," he said, admitting guilt. "I've been dreaming about doing that since Knut first glued it on."

She suddenly seemed far away.

"You're thinking about what the Navy contact told you back in Seattle, aren't you?"

"Doubt. I suppose that's the best way to sum up what I'm feeling right now."

Ben stared at her. "Do you think he was lying?"

"That's hard to say. I mean, short of strapping him to a lie detector, that isn't anything we can ever know for certain. Every avenue we've gone down has only reinforced my belief that you and my father got caught in the middle of something big. Ralph even said as much. And now I'm involved too."

Ben nodded, watching with interest the way her nervous hands wrestled with one another. "So what is it that you're doubting?"

"Us," she said, looking up at him, ashamed. "Whatever this secret is, it's obviously big enough that someone hasn't thought twice about killing to keep it quiet. I suspect by the time this is done, my father and your girlfriend will not be the only innocent victims."

It sounded to Ben as though Sienna were wavering, maybe even wondering if they should give up. He crossed his arms, perhaps a nervous tic of his own. "And what if doing nothing makes things a whole hell of a lot worse? You said yourself it's obvious the secret these people are hiding is big enough to kill for. How many have to die before it becomes worth exposing what they've done? Or worse yet, what they plan to do?"

"I'm not worried about dying," she shot back, her normally soft, pink lips drawn into a thin line. "My doubts are purely numerical."

"Ah," he said, grasping her point. "It's only you and I against a potentially huge apparatus."

She nodded. "Something like that."

"Well, I agree. But rather than a weakness, have you considered that right now that may very well be our main asset?"

Her eyes shone. It was a point that hadn't occurred to her.

"Large organizations are slow to react and suffer from an often-crippling ailment: overconfidence. Here's the thing though. In six days from now, something major is going to go down. What that is, we don't yet know. What is becoming clear, however, is that the impending event is somehow connected to Neural-Sync as well as whatever your father found beneath the ocean."

Shortly after that, they arrived at the Institute of Metallurgy, a modern-looking white structure, ten stories high and surrounded by greenery. Ben and Sienna followed a winding stone path to the front door. It was a great opportunity for Ben to practice his Russian. He asked around for Dr. Tatiana Barulina and was directed by a well-meaning woman to the east wing of the tenth floor.

They arrived before her office and knocked more than once with no response.

A deep feeling of concern began creeping into Ben's bones. If she wasn't here, it would take time to track her. Time they didn't have.

"Maybe she's not in today," Ben speculated, watching a female technician in a lab coat as they passed by. He waved down the next one to cross their path, a young fresh-faced man wearing a pair of Crocs beneath his smock. "We're looking for Dr. Tatiana Barulina," Ben said in passable Russian.

The young man smiled. "Good luck," he said and stalked away.

Ben frowned. "The hell was that supposed to mean?"

"Your Russian is even better now than it was on the plane," Sienna said, impressed.

"Thank my NED, it's done most of the work."

She shook her head. "I want what you have."

Ben smiled, unable to keep from thinking of his own internal life clock clicking rapidly down to zero. "Uh, yeah, believe me when I say you don't."

"So what should we do then?" Sienna asked. "Do you think she's here or should we try to find out where she lives? We didn't exactly announce we were coming. For all we know she's at home with the flu."

They heard a man's voice call out from behind them. Both Ben and Sienna turned at once to find a rather small figure, one hand perched on his hip, grimacing.

Ben was thrown off. The person before him looked female, but was dressed like a man with a short business-friendly haircut. A curled spine had her hunched forward. He hesitated. "We're, um, looking for—"

"Okay, out with it, stretch," the person snapped in fluent English.

Ben grinned painfully. "You speak English?"

"No, you're imagining things. Now get out of my way. You're blocking the door."

Ben and Sienna stepped aside. The figure brought up a key chain hanging around their neck and unlocked the door.

"Dr. Barulina?" Ben said, entering after her.

She spun around and poked an angry finger in the air. "Hey, shoes off."

He looked down and saw the doctor was wearing a faded pair of black socks.

They complied.

203

"I'll warn you up front. I don't have time to answer dumb questions," she said. "My colleagues here know me. We don't tell each other how to dress or what to do on our spare time. Do you follow me?"

Ben nodded. "I think so. We've met before, haven't we?"

Dr. Barulina remained silent, her lips squished to one side.

"Do you remember?" he tried again.

"I already told you I don't answer dumb questions," she snapped. "Of course we met. Is that why you came all this way? To test my memory? I can assure you it's a steel trap."

He looked over at Sienna, who seemed to be enjoying every second of this. She nodded at the doctor, as if to say, *Keep going.*

"It's just since we last spoke, something happened to me. I mean there's a huge spread of time I don't remember anymore. That's why I was asking."

"Amnesia," she said, leaning as far back in her chair as her curved spine would allow. "Good, now we're getting somewhere. You were kind enough to bring me a sample. At the time, you asked me to analyze it." She pushed off the desk, crossing her chair over to a shoulder-high wall-mount filled with hundreds of tiny drawers. Each of them had a white label written in pencil. Most of the labels were dog-eared and appeared to have been erased and written over many times. Tatiana grumbled to herself as she hovered over one drawer after another. "All right then, stop hiding from me," she scolded whatever she was looking for. Then not long after—"Ah-hah, come here, my little friend," she said, coaxing out a small plastic case which she deposited on the desk between them. Her fingers were small and about as well worn as the socks on her feet. With careful precision, she unlatched and then opened the lid. Inside was a round piece of silver metal no larger than the ball bearing at the end of a pen.

"This is all I have left," she told them. "When you brought it in, you told me it was used in the manufacture of cerebral implants."

Ben nodded. "Yes, we call them NEDs."

A flash of disapproval. "Call them what you like, but what you brought me was like nothing I'd ever seen before. After our lab ran an analysis, I attempted to contact you over the phone and never got a reply."

"I was busy being framed," he replied wryly.

"To each his own," she replied, unconcerned with his personal business.

"Can you tell us about your findings?" Sienna chimed in.

Dr. Barulina swung her considerable attention toward the glaciologist. "And who might you be?"

"I'm Dr. Panov," Sienna said by way of introducing herself. "I'm helping Mr. Fisher to gather vital information on the unique characteristics of the alloy you tested."

Dr. Barulina let out a deep gale of laughter and Ben noticed for the first time her impressive collection of fillings. "Unique is one way to put it. Another is absolutely extraordinary. And it isn't an alloy. It's pure and took several tests and retests before we could identify what it was with any degree of certainty."

Ben felt his hands grip the sides of his seat. "So, what did you find?"

The corner of Dr. Barulina's mouth rose. "It's metallic hydrogen."

The shock pushed Ben back in his seat. "Hydrogen?"

"That's correct," Barulina replied. "But it requires an extraordinary amount of pressure, often atmospheric. It's what planetary scientists believe sits at the core of the gas giants in our solar system, Jupiter and Saturn. I should tell you, scientists at Harvard claim to have created some using a diamond vice." She cleared her throat with disapproval. "The jury, however, is still out on whether or not their claim can be taken seriously. The process is incredibly difficult, if not impossible. Besides, the sample they pointed to is microscopic. Nothing whatsoever like this. The most amazing part is that it retains its compressed shape even when it's no longer under the enormous pressure required to turn it from a liquid to a solid."

Ben couldn't help thinking about the NEDs and the sheer volume of metallic hydrogen parked out there in people's heads. "Even by conservative estimates, Neural-Sync probably receives a ton of this stuff a year."

Dr. Barulina shrugged. "Not possible. Not by any manufacturing method I'm aware of."

Ben rubbed at his cheek. "But why such an exotic metal?"

"Don't ask me," she snapped. "It's your company, isn't it?"

Harsh as it sounded, the question was indeed a legitimate one. "Seems the more I learn, the less certain I am about that."

Tatiana's features softened. "From the tests we've run to date, metallic hydrogen does have properties that are beneficial from a bio-engineering perspective. For starters, it does not elicit any kind of inflammatory response from the body. It is also incredibly strong and resistant to all forms of corrosion." Dr. Barulina folded both arms and rested them on the edge of her desk, her neck craned to see them. "It's also a terrific conductor and we believe is responsible for the dynamo effect that powers the magnetic fields of both Jupiter and Saturn."

The dynamo theory held that a rotating layer of electrically conducting fluid helped to create and perpetuate a planet's magnetic field.

Sienna cleared her throat and spoke up. "You mentioned earlier that the creation of metallic hydrogen required immense atmospheric pressure. Could hydrostatic pressure create the same result?"

Ben saw where Sienna was going with this and it piqued his curiosity. While atmospheric pressure measured the weight of the atmosphere at sea level, hydrostatic pressure measured the force of a liquid on a given area.

One of Dr. Barulina's eyebrows twitched. "Manufacturing under the ocean?" She shook her head. "I don't see how that's possible."

"That wasn't necessarily what I meant," Sienna replied, eager to clarify. "Could some raw form of metallic hydrogen be present deep beneath the ocean?"

Dr. Barulina looked stumped. "Off the cuff, I want to say no, but I suppose that would be very unscientific of me." Releasing a deep sigh, she said: "I'll have to think about it."

Ben stood, ready to leave. For the moment, they'd learned everything they could. "You'll get back to us with the rest of your findings?"

She nodded and then stopped and swung her chair back to the collection of drawers behind her. "Oh, I nearly forgot. There's something I revealed to you the last time you were here that might be worth showing you again." She swore to herself as she flung open one sample drawer after another. "Believe me, I'm normally far more organized that this."

Ben sank back into his seat as he and Sienna exchanged a smile.

"Bingo!" Dr. Barulina shouted, swinging back around with two new plastic cases. Each of them had words scribbled in Russian. She positioned both cases side by side, opened the lids and then slid them across to Ben and Sienna.

They peered down. Each plastic container contained a silver metallic substance partly encased in a small rock.

Sienna gave a startled little gasp.

"Is that what I think it is?" Ben asked.

"Unprocessed metallic hydrogen," Dr. Barulina replied, a look approaching religious reverence on her face.

The second sample looked something like a NED, but was several times larger. The one Ben had sent her was the shape of a Tic-Tac, but only a fraction of the size. The limited amount of research he'd conducted had shown that under the proper magnification, the seams between each of the three sections of the NED was visible. Zoom in more and things like the unit's serial number and manufacturing date also became visible. But the point was, the NED he'd brought for her to study looked nothing like what they were staring down at now. Had this come from part of Neural-Sync's production facility?

He asked her the question, in response to which Dr. Barulina shook her head. She placed a hand over the container on the left. "This one was sent to me from Joe Knight, a former NASA scientist living in Florida."

"And the other?" Sienna asked, hanging on Dr. Barulina's every word.

Dr. Barulina's fingers toyed with the plastic case. "This other sample came to me from a man named Bo Zhou, an archaeologist at a dig site in China. I'm not one to put words in people's mouths, but it seemed to me he believed it was very old."

"I need to ask you another favor," Ben said, concerned about what the answer might be.

"You should know I'm not such a big fan of favors," she told him. "They have a funny way of multiplying in size and number."

Sienna flashed her best PR smile. "Is there any chance you could give us the contact information for both of these men? Maybe even their addresses. It sure would be helpful if we could talk to them."

As Sienna asked the question, Ben couldn't help thinking about the minutes falling off the countdown. Neither of them knew what would happen when the timer reached zero. What they did know was that they would need to be in Arizona when it happened and not running around the world. The implication was obvious enough. If Dr. Barulina was kind enough to comply, the time constraint meant Ben and Sienna would need to split up and follow both leads at once.

Dr. Barulina turned to the computer on her desk and pulled up files on Joe Knight and Bo Zhou. "This goes against every protocol we have," she grumbled.

"Don't worry," Ben reassured her. "It'll be our little secret."

Chapter 32

It was dark by the time Ben and Sienna got a taxi to the airport. The fake mustache in his pocket, the one that did more to irritate his upper lip than disguise his identity, was gleefully calling his name. He would wait until the last possible moment to put on the 'stache and glasses. That Sienna had it so easy in the get-up department was not lost on Ben. She simply had to wear a blonde wig, a new look that actually worked rather well on her. He would never say it to her face, but it brought out her naturally dark gypsy features and striking green eyes.

"You thinking about what Dr. Barulina told us?" Sienna asked, the self-driving cab changing lanes.

Ben caught his gaze shifting away from Sienna's blonde curls. He clenched his fists and looked away. "How could I not be?" he fibbed.

"If there's any chance low-grade metallic hydrogen could be present in areas along the ocean floor, it might explain what it was my father stumbled onto."

Ben wasn't sure. "If it's so plentiful down there, then why isn't every country scouring the sea bed scooping up truckloads of the stuff?"

"I never said I had all the answers, but it's worth considering."

She was right about that. The real question was how exactly to take full advantage of the contacts Barulina had provided them with.

"Listen, I know what you're really thinking," she said.

"You do?" He asked the question from a place of deep sincerity. How could she know that when the only thought he'd allowed in had something to do with hair?

"And you don't need to worry about me," she continued. "I've always wanted to travel to China and meet up with Dr. Zhou."

He looked at her, a sense of relief settling over him. Maybe she had read his thoughts, or at least the deep lines of concern etched in his face. "We might be safer together," he said, hating the misogynistic way his words might have sounded.

The expression on Sienna's face confirmed his fears. "You don't think I can take care of myself, do you?"

"No, I trust you just fine. We aren't dealing with a group of guys in an alley out to pick your pockets. These guys mean business. We also have to assume they've been boosted, which gives them an unbelievable advantage over a mere…" He hesitated.

"Mortal?" she snapped with disbelief. "Is that what you were about to say? I haven't got one of those implants and I'll bet I could still kick your ass."

Sienna hadn't seen the way things had gone down with the cop in the industrial part of town or on the road near Dr. Lang's lake house. But he let it go. Sometimes it was better to believe you were a badass even when reality suggested otherwise.

"The good news for you is that it's mainly me they want," Ben said, not trying to sound conceited. He rolled up his sleeve and looked again at the smudged numbers on each forearm. It was a constant reminder that sometime within the next six days, a terrible and world-changing event would occur. Although terrible probably depended on which side of the equation you were on.

In the brief amount of time he'd spent looking into Joe Knight—the former NASA employee Dr. Barulina had told them about—he had learned two interesting facts. The first was that Joe hadn't only been a NASA employee, he'd been a backup astronaut, but sadly one who had never made it to the moon. The second offered a little more detail about where he lived. It wasn't merely Florida, beautiful beaches and an ocean to match. Joe resided in the New Everglades, a section of the state that had once been dry land and now required a fan boat to move from point A to point B. Ben was hopeful, for both their sakes, that Zhou and Mr. Knight might finally be able to tie together some of the disparate threads they'd already uncov—

Ben's thoughts were cut short by an incoming call on his cell. He glanced down. It was Lori.

"Greetings from Ko Samui," he answered.

"Ben, cut the crap. I know you're in St. Petersburg and so does Granger."

"So it's confirmed then—he's one of them?"

"One of who?"

"Let's start with the people who have tried to kill me at least twice," Ben said, exasperated. "And by the way things look from here, you're on his side."

Lori's voice was crackling with emotion. "Listen to me, Ben. Granger is not a man to be trifled with. He does want you dead and I've been fighting behind the scenes to stop it from happening, but there's only so much I can do. You need to stop this crusade you're on."

"That bastard killed the woman I loved," Ben shouted. "Then he left me there to take the fall and you're telling me to just drop it. I should never have trusted you."

"I'm on your side," Lori pleaded. "You need to believe me. Granger wasn't going to let you rot in prison. He just needed to make sure you weren't going to stick your nose where it didn't belong."

"Didn't belong? I don't even know what to say to that."

"I'm calling to tell you if you let this go, Granger might go easy on you."

"Can you hear yourself?" Ben said, his temperature spiking. "Granger's a board member, he isn't a god."

"Granger was only elected to the board after you went off the reservation," Lori said, trying to explain, but only digging herself in deeper.

"It's obvious you know more than you're telling me," Ben shot back. "And I suggest you start talking."

Next to him, Sienna could hear just enough of the exchange to look shocked and worried.

Lori was silent for a moment. Then: "You found something that didn't sit well and you tried to ignore it, isn't that right? You tried hard. I could see it on your face every day at work, in meetings. But you couldn't let it go. You told me you needed answers the folks here at Neural-Sync didn't have, or wouldn't give you."

"Answers about what?"

"I'm not sure."

"You're lying."

"No, I'm telling you the truth. Everything here is so compartmentalized. But you see, that was the way you made it. In the days before… before Amanda was killed, you hid a bunch of files."

"Files?" He had no clue what she was talking about.

"Yes, Ben. Files on the things that you found. You said it was too explosive for the world to see, but also too important to remain hidden. You made two copies. One you put on a USB and gave to a reporter named Elizabeth Howard. If you have any interest in saving your life and the life of the woman with you, then you need to remember what you did with that other copy."

Ben squeezed his eyes shut, searching for any hint of a memory that might shed light on what Lori was talking about. "I don't remember," he said, feeling defeated. "The contact you sent our way from the Navy mentioned an agent who goes by the code name Mirage. He believed her real name was Michelle Mackay. Maybe she has the files. Or was that entire meeting designed to throw us off the real trail?"

"I told you I've been trying to help you," Lori repeated.

Just then a high-pitched ringing sounded in his left ear. He wiggled his jaw and rubbed his ear canal with the tip of his index finger, but the sound remained. Ben covered the receiver and spoke to Sienna. "Do you hear that?"

She shook her head. "Hear what?"

He recalled how Dr. Lang had talked about people with NEDs complaining about a ringing sound that progressively grew louder.

"Ben, are you still there?" Lori asked, palpable concern in her voice.

"Barely," he admitted.

214

"Listen, Granger saw video from the Seattle-Tacoma International Airport showing you and Mrs. Panov boarding a plane for St. Petersburg. That was how I knew you were there. It's also where he sent a team to get you."

"I've met some of Granger's teams before," Ben said confidently. "And I wasn't impressed."

"Well, this team is different. They aren't a bunch of meatheads with guns. Like you, they've been… augmented."

"What are they trying to hide, Lori?" Ben demanded.

"There isn't time to explain it all," Lori said, and the way her voice trailed off only confirmed the magnitude of what they were up against. "Find out where you put those files and hand them over to Granger and all this will go away. I promise."

Lori's solution sounded to Ben about as easy as teleporting himself back to Seattle. How could he hand over files he didn't know existed? Moreover, why do such a thing when he must have seen fit to risk the danger of gathering them in the first place?

Outside the taxi, the sound of a large-engine vehicle sounded behind them.

Ben glanced behind him and spotted a pair of mean-looking men staring back at him. The SUV accelerated, slamming into the back of the taxi.

Sienna let out a startled little scream.

The last time this happened it had nearly gone very bad for him.

A narrow alley was coming up on their right, far too tight for a big SUV.

"Take your next right," he barked.

"I don't understand," a pleasant-sounding voice said in Russian. "Please repeat your command."

215

The turn was coming up and the SUV getting ready to knock them off the road.

"Bloody hell," Ben shouted. There wasn't time to repeat the order in Russian. He lurched forward and jerked the wheel hard to the right.

The car chastised him in Russian as the vehicle veered violently enough to raise one set of wheels six inches off the ground.

The alley was narrower than Ben had anticipated, with less than a finger's length of room on either side. A rogue door handle scooped off the left mirror with a loud bang. Behind them, they saw the SUV turn to follow them and slam its brakes just short of wedging its front end inside the tight space. Quickly it backed up and tore forward, intending to circle around and cut them off.

"We can't outrun them," Ben told her. "As soon as we clear this alley, we bail out. Got it?"

She nodded, gripping the overhead handle, her eyes wide and alert.

Emerging into a crowded street, Ben slammed the brakes and both of them leapt out.

As they weaved through crowds of tourists and pedestrians, a quick glance around revealed they were in St. Petersburg's red-light district. Already the character of the people and the shops had morphed dramatically. A nearby sign in pink read 'Pussy Deluxe.' Across the street a tall brunette in black stockings and bra danced in the store window to draw in new customers. Her act appeared to be working, since a crowd of men had already gathered to watch.

"It gets worse," Sienna said. "This is nothing."

Ben shot her a look. "Really, and how would you know?"

"I've heard stories."

"Sure, you have."

She smirked and pulled off her wig, stuffing it into her jacket pocket. "You don't think that I... really? You do, don't you?"

"As Dr. Barulina so eloquently put it, 'Your personal life is not my business.'" Just then Ben spotted two men in black jackets tear around the corner behind them. He took Sienna by the arm and guided her under a sleazy hotel's flashing neon sign.

"What are you doing?" she asked, struggling against him.

"Stop fighting me. I'm trying to get us off the street."

Drunks and homeless people littered the two flights of stairs that led up to the hotel. One of the men was snoring loudly and Ben took Sienna's arm and helped her scramble over him. He grunted and swore in Russian, but remained asleep. The smell here was an awful mix of vodka and urine.

The dimly lit lobby looked like something out of a 1980's documentary on urban decay. Torn-up couches were pressed against the wall on one side of the room. A high wooden desk sat on the other. Manning the desk was a skinny Steve Buscemi lookalike with half as many teeth and twice as much grease in his hair. A small old-fashioned television was poised on the corner of the desk, sucking most of his attention. A yellowed piece of paper taped to the desk read: 'Cash up front. Drunks or drugs—call police,' in both Russian and broken English.

"We need a place to stay," Ben said in Russian.

"Three thousand rubles an hour. You pay now," Toothless Buscemi replied without bothering to peel his eyes away from the screen.

Ben put out his arm so the attendant could scan his wristband.

The man grunted.

"Do you take credit cards?" Sienna asked, fishing around in her pockets.

Ben went back to the darkened stairwell and spotted the men in black jackets enter the building and begin heading up the first flight of stairs. Each of them in turn reached under their coats and came out with SIG MPX compact submachine guns.

Heart hammering in his chest, Ben rushed back to Sienna, who was now busy arguing with the clerk.

Reaching over the counter, he grabbed the clerk's collar in a clenched fist.

"Is there another way out of here?" he asked the terrified man.

Toothless Buscemi aimed a quivering finger toward a long hallway and what looked like the vague outline of a door beyond. They hurried in that direction and started to pull open the door when one of the gunman entered the hotel behind them. He caught sight of them and fired twice. The bullets ricocheted off the door frame next to Ben's head in an explosion of sparks. The rounds kicked up a puff of chalky white powder as they buried themselves into the gyprock on the opposite wall. A second later, Ben and Sienna were through, racing up a flight of stairs, panic clawing at both of their throats.

Ben had hoped this exit would lead them into a back alley where he and Sienna could disappear into the crowds walking down the seedy streets. But these stairs went up and up was bad, very bad. They were getting pushed into a tight corner where they might both be killed.

Chapter 33

Ben and Sienna exited onto the roof. They could hear at least one of the gunmen charging up the stairs after them. He was swearing in Russian. Sienna only knew a handful of words, most of them crass, and this man coming after them was repeating all of them in a kind of sick loop.

"Over here," Ben yelled. He was standing by the edge of the roof, and from here it looked like he was suggesting they jump to their deaths.

Sienna hurried over to see what he was talking about. "Shouldn't we try hitting him with something when he comes through that door?"

Ben pointed and Sienna saw what he'd been trying to show her. The roof on the next building over was at least a twenty-foot jump. That was Olympic athlete level, not something glaciologists did on a regular basis. Any attempt would mean a certain fifty-foot fall to her death.

Ben backed away from the edge as though still contemplating the plan when one of the gunmen, a brawny guy with a crewcut, came bursting through the metal push door and onto the roof.

Time slowed as Crewcut began to raise his SIG. Ben was also on the move, pushing off against the roof's loose gravel with his back leg and charging at their

219

assailant. There was no possible way he could get there in time, but even in that slowed-down version of reality Sienna was currently experiencing, Ben somehow closed the distance in three giant strides.

Ben brought his fist down on the top of Crewcut's weapon, their attacker grimacing with a burst of pain and surprise as the weapon skittered out of his grasp and onto the ground. Then came the flash of a knife. Ben bobbed and weaved, dodging repeated strikes and slashes. At one point, Crewcut tried to thrust the knife into Ben's belly. Spinning around, Ben rolled out of the move and ended up behind Crewcut. He clamped his hand around the wrist holding the knife and brought it down against his raised knee. The sound of snapping bones was drowned out by the cry of agony emanating from Crewcut's mouth.

Sienna ran for the SIG lying on the ground right as Ben took hold of the man's chin and wrenched his neck violently to one side. Crewcut crumpled to the ground, dead.

Just then, a second figure emerged from the stairway and saw Ben standing over Crewcut, looking the other way. Sienna shouted, raised the weapon until the barrel was aiming at the man's chest and pulled the trigger. The SIG kicked back in her hands as three rounds fired out in quick succession. The first passed between his legs. The second struck him in the chest. The third passed through his right eye. He fell back toward a third figure. Compared to the others, this one was far more wiry, and nimbly dodged the falling body of his comrade.

Ben turned just as Wiry stepped onto the roof. His face was marked with broken veins and his eyes were wild and animalistic. With tremendous speed he rolled to the right, avoiding a fresh burst from Sienna's weapon.

He then switched directions and closed in on her, landing a heel in her stomach and knocking her to the ground.

Sienna felt the gun fly out of her hands and go tumbling over the edge of the roof. She tried to raise herself up and felt a burst of pain bloom from her midsection.

Wiry closed the distance and grabbed her by the throat. "Do you want to see a magic trick?" he asked, grinning, his distorted face closer now and even more grotesque.

Sienna wanted to scream for help, but couldn't utter a word, couldn't even breathe. From somewhere on her right, Ben leapt through the air, knocking Wiry off of her. The two figures tumbled horizontally end over end through the air, finally falling and rolling dangerously close to the roof's edge. Ben and Wiry hopped to their feet in unison, squaring off in a hailstorm of flying fists. Both of them were blocking and dodging with dizzying speed. Sienna could see they were tiring, but what was also apparent was that Wiry's strength far exceeded Ben's. Watching them hop from one rooftop obstacle to another was like something out of a parkour exhibition.

At one point, one of Wiry's strikes landed squarely in the middle of Ben's chest, flinging him back against a brick chimney. He grunted and fell face first into a heap.

Wiry then turned his attention back to Sienna. Having recovered from the blow she'd taken earlier, she scrambled toward the staircase and the submachine gun from the second assailant.

Grabbing her by the hair, Wiry lifted her to her feet with the ease of a man lifting a piece of discarded clothing. "My boss wants you both," he told her. "Believe me, it's nothing person—"

A hollow booming sound filled the air as Wiry's head jerked back and his lips parted in a yelp of pain. Ben's fist was buried into the small of Wiry's back. Ben spun him around and then kicked him square in the chest, sending the man tumbling down the stairway behind him.

"We need to go," Ben said, wincing with pain of his own.

Their only option was to make it to the other roof and down to the street through the neighboring building.

"Do you trust me?" he asked, staring at her with his blazing blue eyes.

She nodded, not sure if she wanted to know what was about to happen next.

"Follow my lead," he said, grabbing her by the belt with his right hand. "When I jump, you jump."

She was suddenly overcome in a cold sweat. "Okay," she whispered.

The two of them ran, Sienna trying hard to keep up. The meters from the edge became feet and then inches.

"Now!" Ben shouted.

And Sienna felt them both lift into the air, her right arm pinwheeling, her legs bicycling through empty space. It was both the most terrifying and exhilarating thing she had ever done.

The two of them landed on the neighboring roof and made a half-roll. Scrambling to their feet, they ran for the emergency exit. She glanced back long enough to see Wiry appear on the other roof and catch his hardened gaze as he watched them head for the exit. A moment later, he had disappeared and somehow Sienna knew he wasn't going back down. He was getting ready to jump the gap between the roofs and finish what he had started.

Ben closed the push bar door behind them. There was no lever to enter from the roof, but both of them were sure this wouldn't stop him for long.

Chapter 34

The door leading from the roof had no sooner closed than Sienna was struck by the thumping rhythm of techno music blaring up at them from below. The descent was narrow and dark and Ben held Sienna's hand as they hurried to the relative safety of the streets below. Wiry was coming after them. There was no doubt about it. Already, he might be upstairs, pounding his way through the rooftop access door. Those thoughts were thumping through Sienna's brain to the tempo of the increasingly loud techno beat. They had entered some kind of alternative dance club. A part of her realized that was a good thing, for it meant crowds of people who could mask their movements and aid their escape.

They reached the base of the staircase and turned a corner into a red throbbing light. Writhing within the light was a crowd of people in unusual outfits. Ben and Sienna stepped into the club's main lounge and stopped cold. In a shadowy corner, a man in a black leather suit and mask was sitting on his haunches. Around his neck was a leash held by a woman in dark stockings and an officer's hat. She wielded a riding crop and shouted something muffled by the blaring music before cracking the whip against the man's backside. He scurried to her heel and rubbed his cheek against her thigh. Similar scenes were playing out all around them. A shirtless bartender with clothes pegs clamped around his nipples regarded them, at first confused and then amused by their bewilderment.

It wasn't a big mystery that Ben and Sienna didn't fit in around here. Which was not a good thing. It meant that not only would this place not give them any cover from the man who was after them, Sienna was also starting to wonder if they were about to become part of someone's twisted fantasy.

They were busy shoving their way through the leathery crowd when Wiry appeared. He spotted them too and was pushing toward them. The mass of people continued undulating to a nauseating beat. Sienna felt herself becoming lightheaded. Ahead was the exit and freedom. The assassin was only a few feet behind them now, his arms outstretched trying to grab at them, when a woman in knee-high boots started yelling. He must have bumped into her and now she was raising hell. She struck him with her whip and when he shoved her away, two men in black leather bondage suits leapt onto him, like dogs on a bone. Soon the crowd was surging all around him and all Ben and Sienna could see before they passed through the exit was Wiry's hands trying to claw his way out from a group that was beating on him from all sides.

Moments later, Ben and Sienna reached the safety of the street and melted into the flow of the pedestrian traffic. Never mind that the flow consisted of prostitutes and sex tourists. No matter how offbeat your sexual tastes, there was some way to satisfy that urge here.

Weakened from the combat on the roof, Ben ran his hands through his short, blond hair and saw that they came away smeared with blood. They needed to get off the streets. He took her by the arm and steered her into an alley.

"Where are we going?" she asked, still dazed from everything they had just experienced.

Ben struggled for breath, feeling as though a giant weight was pressing down on his lungs. His muscles were utterly depleted too, each step requiring a monumental effort of will.

One foot in front of the other, Ben. You can do this!

If he was an electric car battery, the red warning lights would all be flashing.

Recharge! Recharge!

"We need to find a taxi," he finally whispered, the world spinning around him. Glancing over at her, Ben smiled weakly. "You're a lot tougher than I thought." He had felt some level of skepticism at her ability to handle herself and was secure enough to admit he had been dead wrong. And he didn't only mean it as a throwaway line. If she hadn't shot the second assailant and distracted the third and tougher one, Ben's dead body might very well be lying on that same rooftop.

A beaming smile filled her face. "That may be the nicest thing anyone's ever said to me."

"I'm sorry to hear that, but don't get all mushy on me now," Ben said in a serious tone. That ringing in his ear was back and stronger than ever. Was it a product of the deafening techno beat they'd just been subjected to or yet another symptom of the excessive boosting he'd undergone? It was hard to say.

225

Up ahead he saw a cross street and a stream of traffic heading in both directions. He lifted his hand to point the way and then proceeded to collapse.

•••

He awoke hours later in a hotel room. Sienna was next to him.

"What the hell happened?" he asked, touching his head. Drawing in a deep breath, he could already feel the pain in his lungs had gone down.

Sienna rolled over. Her eyes were puffy with sleep. He felt bad for waking her up.

"You need to go on a diet," she said, matter-of-factly.

"Huh?"

"After you passed out, I had to get some prostitute to help carry you into a cab." Sienna's eyes flit to the ceiling as though she were trying to remember something. "Prostitute or cross-dresser. I'm not sure which, but they were nice enough to help, so I guess it doesn't really matter."

"We can't stay here," he said, jumping out of bed and realizing for the first time he was in his skivvies. His clothes were laid out on the chair behind him. "Whoa!" His eyes jumped between Sienna and his mostly naked body.

"Don't worry, Romeo. Nothing happened." She got out of bed and put on a shirt and shrugged into her jeans. "I needed to check that nothing was broken."

Ben felt the back of his head and the bandage sitting there. A length of gauze was wrapped around his forehead. He must have had a quizzical look on his face.

"The hotel was nice enough to let me pillage their first-aid kit. I told them you slipped and hit your head."

The expression on Ben's face changed.

226

"What is it?" she asked, now fully dressed.

"I'm not sure anymore that splitting up is such a good idea."

"It's not like we're engaged or anything," she said, grinning.

Ben blushed. She was making him feel like a college kid after his first sexual experience. "For your information, I'm thinking of our safety. The thin guy who attacked us last night. I've seen him before. He's like me."

"Augmented, you mean?"

"Not just augmented, he's beyond that. The way I got boosted by that stun gun, it was a miracle that I wasn't killed. But facing him last night, I felt... " His voice trailed off.

"Outmatched?"

Ben nodded. "Yes. In every way. He came at me before, at the restaurant in Seattle, but he wasn't nearly as powerful then. Whoever's behind this must have super-boosted him." And who else had the capability of doing such a thing but his own company, Neural-Sync? It was merely one more pixel in an image that was growing more obvious by the second.

"You really think we should stick together?" Sienna said, twirling a finger in her curly hair, an act Ben had come to recognize as a sign she was deep in thought.

"We can't risk being separated if he comes at us again," he explained. "I could barely handle him as it was. I'm sorry to say, tough as you are, you simply wouldn't stand a chance."

Not surprisingly, Sienna was not a big fan of hearing that, and Ben not a big fan of telling her, but if they were going to be honest with one another, it was the truth.

227

"Time is our number one adversary, Ben. Didn't you say so yourself?" She was referring to the point in time indicated by the markings on his arm. A moment that was fast approaching. To make matters worse, they were still not fully certain what would happen when that time actually arrived. Was it a clock ticking down until the end of the world? Did it mark the opening of some massive terrorist attack? And what, if any, connection did it have to Neural-Sync and the implants they produced?

At this point, only one thing was relatively certain. Whatever was set to happen when that clock struck zero, it would not be good for anyone but Granger and a handful of others.

"Okay," he relented. "You see Zhou in China and I'll head to the New Everglades."

Chapter 35

Sienna had left the St. Petersburg hotel for the airport an hour ago. Ben was getting ready to do the same when he stepped out of the shower and reached for the towel. He watched his fingers close around the cloth and bring it up to him, and yet he couldn't feel a thing. His entire hand had gone completely numb. He wiggled his digits and then opened and closed his hand repeatedly, but the deadness remained. The thought of a heart attack occurred to him briefly, one he quickly dismissed since the numbness was in his right hand and not rolling up his left arm.

First the tinnitus. Now the numbness in his extremities. As much as he didn't want to face facts, it was obvious his symptoms were catching up with him. The smart thing to do was find a specialist who could remove his NED. But what if the wiry sicko with the broken face showed up again? It would be like a toddler squaring off against a grown man.

Just then his phone rang. Ben set down the towel and checked the caller ID. It read 'unknown'. He hesitated and then answered it anyway.

"Ben, it's Dr. Lang."

Ben felt a sense of relief, not that it hadn't been someone else, but that Dr. Lang was still safe.

"Just the man I wanted to speak to," he said, articulating the numb digits on his right hand.

"I need to talk to you, can we meet?"

Stepping out of the bathroom, Ben said: "You changed your number?"

"I did," he replied, somewhat out of breath. "You told me to hide better, didn't you? I've been doing just that with nothing to pass the time but run low-tech experiments."

"Experiments?" Ben checked the time. His flight was leaving soon. "Listen, meeting right now won't be possible. You'll have to simply tell me over the phone." He out of everyone knew that wasn't ideal. There was no telling who was listening in. But better options were in seriously short supply. He could hear Dr. Lang breathing on the other end of the line. "Go ahead, Doc. Tell me what it is you found."

"The exotic metal in the neural device…" Dr. Lang began.

"Yeah, we've just learned what it is. Metallic hydrogen."

Dr. Land went quiet for a moment and Ben wasn't sure if the man was confused or awestruck. "Yes, of course, that makes perfect sense," he blurted out.

"How's that?"

"The exotic properties of the metal. You must have seen what it does for the gas giants in our solar system."

"You mean the dynamo effect?" Ben asked. "Sure, but what does that have to do with us?"

"It appears the implant performs much the same function in the human body."

"By creating a magnetic field?" Ben asked, taken aback.

"Yes, a biomagnetic version of that. The body produces one naturally, although it's incredibly weak. The implant simply magnifies the electro-magnetic field that already exists."

"For what purpose?"

"That's why I'm calling you. I've detected an unusual signal in the atmosphere. One that occupies a band of the electromagnetic spectrum somewhere between microwaves and radio waves."

"You mean like wifi?"

"Close, but this is far weaker."

"So what does it have to do with the biomagnetic field you mentioned?"

"Everything," Dr. Lang said, breathless. "The NED and the field that it helps to generate in the body enhances the signal, effectively turning everyone who uses the device into a giant receiver."

Ben's concern was rising by the second. "Receiver for what?"

"I'm not certain, but it looks like some sort of signal that's being sent directly to the NED."

"You're not talking mind control, are you?" Ben asked in disbelief.

"No," Dr. Lang replied. "Nothing that straightforward. You see, the NED works as advertised. If an implantee boosts his intelligence, the device will immediately begin promoting the growth of new brain cells via neurogenesis as well as fortifying the connection between cells through neuroplasticity. That's all fine and good. But the device is also getting instructions from the EMF band I mentioned."

"Instructions to do what?"

"The signal appears to be triggering the creation and release of tiny amounts of opiorphin into the system. It's a natural anesthetic the body produces on its own, many times more powerful than morphine, but non-addictive."

"Isn't that simply part of the device's pain management module?"

"It might be, but that falls under equilibrium and the data I had collected on patients with or without boosts in that area still showed signs of opiorphin release."

"I don't understand," Ben said, feeling suddenly dizzy. "Then it sounds like you're saying we're being drugged?"

Dr. Lang sighed. "Not exactly. You see, the amounts are so small, most don't notice them. But it fits perfectly with my earlier findings."

"The five percent of people who were experiencing negative side effects," Ben said, looking down at his hand.

"That's right. A ringing in the ears. The loss of declarative memory, numbness in the extremities and eventually death as the patient simply stops breathing. I didn't understand the connection before, but now I do. It isn't the device that's doing it, so much as the instructions it's being given over the EMF band."

"But I thought this thing was unhackable?"

"There's a very good chance that it is. This seems to be accomplishing its goal in a completely different way. This isn't using ones and zeros to break in the way someone might hack a bank to clear out your life savings. Whoever's doing it is using the body's own biology against it."

He wanted to tell Dr. Lang about the numbness, that his symptoms were getting worse, but didn't see the point. Ben could already hear the recommendation coming at him hard and fast.

Get it out of your head.

Then another thought, this one more troubling. Had that been what he'd meant in the text he had sent an old fling, Lindsey Martin?

Take it out!

But he knew that wasn't possible, not yet.

"Do you think Neural-Sync is behind this?" Ben asked instead.

Dr. Lang thought about it for a moment. "I don't see how they couldn't be involved somehow. But Neural-Sync isn't merely some random company."

"I know," Ben said, feeling the full weight of Dr. Lang's words. "It's my company. Although why would I implant myself if I knew all of this? We're still missing something." A thought occurred to him. "Can you tell where the signal is coming from? Perhaps if we know who's broadcasting it, we'll know who's behind it."

"I'm not sure I can," Dr. Lang admitted. "Although even if we did know, it might not shed any light on their motives. Or what they might hope to accomplish."

"Maybe it's supposed to act as a distraction," Ben surmised.

Dr. Lang was hesitant. "Distraction? How so?"

"Whether or not the opiorphin being fed into our systems is the only thing numbing us, I'm not sure. What I do know is that the device has people going nuts in other ways. I can't tell you how many fools I've seen these last few days chasing Neuro tokens into dark alleys or fighting one another in the streets because one guy got there first. We're losing our minds, numbing ourselves in other ways, mainly to the joys of real life. It certainly didn't start with Neural-Sync and assuming we don't all suffocate in a choking cloud, it won't end with it either. We've been on this path a long time. Clearly, someone noticed and decided to take things to the next

233

level and maybe one beyond that. The real question is, what is all this attempting to keep us from seeing?"

Ben was still thinking about it after he hung up from his conversation with Dr. Lang. An image popped into his head of a mosquito. He had read somewhere about how the ubiquitous little buggers had a numbing agent in their saliva, one they applied to a patch of skin to prevent their victims from feeling a sting. Was that what was happening to a chunk of humanity? And if so, what was being stolen from them?

Ben stared down at his hand and shook it, relieved the numbness hadn't yet travelled past his wrist. The pieces were beginning to fall into place. All at once, a burst of buried memory struck him. He saw himself flipping through pages on a tablet, jotting down the numbers he saw onto both of his forearms. Then came other images, these ones far more fleeting. Images of people's faces to begin with. Then words—THOTH as well as something else. Apollo 18.

It was common knowledge that the Apollo program stopped in 1972 with Apollo 17. So what exactly was he seeing? Ben stood for a moment, scratching his chin, left to wonder just how deep this went.

Chapter 36

Xinjiang, China

The twelve-hour flight from St. Petersburg to Altay Airport in Xinjiang province gave Sienna more than enough time to consider what she hoped to accomplish. It was one of the more remote parts of China. As such, the final leg of the journey was an hour-long taxi ride from the airport to what Dr. Barulina had dubbed Site 17, near the border with Mongolia. Her driver, this time a human rather than a computer, was a local Kazakh named Ali who wore his smile the way some women wore their makeup, which was to say all the time.

The vistas here were truly breathtaking—lush valleys surrounded by mountains that had once been snowcapped but were now as naked as Sienna felt. She was heading to a place she'd never been and hoping for a reception that might shed light on the mysterious connection between the exotic metal Neural-Sync used in its NEDs and the one uncovered on Dr. Zhou's archeological dig.

After travelling for some time, the taxi pulled onto a long dirt road that snaked through a wide valley. Soon the dirt road led to a checkpoint where a skinny guard in loose clothing put a hand out for them to stop. He approached the driver who motioned to Sienna in the back seat. She rolled down the window.

"I'm here to see Dr. Zhou," she explained.

"No visitors," the guard said, waving his hands in the air. This guy was also smiling, which wasn't doing a whole lot to lift Sienna's spirits.

"No, you don't understand. I've travelled very far. I need to see him right away."

The guard pulled the radio off his belt and said something in a Chinese dialect she didn't understand.

"Zhou say no visitor," the guard exclaimed, waving them away.

The taxi driver turned the wheel and began to make a u-turn when Sienna shouted for him to stop. She got out, a move that surprised and perhaps even frightened the guard. He unslung the AK assault rifle he carried over his shoulder and leveled it at her.

"Lady, come," Ali said, grinning wider now, fearful Sienna was about to get herself shot. "Lady, please come now."

Sienna reached into her bag and came out with a small plastic case. It made a rattling sound as she shook her hand. "Get back on the radio and tell Zhou I was sent by Dr. Tatiana Barulina."

The guard looked at her, uncertain.

"Put your gun down," she ordered him, "and send the message."

The barrel of his rifle wavered before the guard obeyed, calling again to Site 17 on his radio.

Several tense moments passed. The boldness and anger that had seized hold of Sienna, much of it the product of a long, cramped flight, was starting to fade. And with that came the cold realization she might have bitten off more than she could chew. She wasn't in Kansas anymore, that was for sure. They could shoot her and dump her body and no one would ever know.

At last the order came back and the guard let them pass. Sienna returned to the taxi and let out a deep sigh. The knot in her belly had been loosened, but not entirely worked free. She had managed one hurdle, but it was only the first of many.

•••

"You're not Dr. Barulina," Zhou said, more than disappointed. He was sitting in a mud-splattered golf cart.

From where Sienna stood, he seemed positively annoyed. His short and powerful physical stature made him stand out among the other Kazakhi workers around him. The visual confused her even more because the man looked Chinese—no surprise there, since they were in China after all—but his accent. He sounded American.

"I never claimed to be Dr. Barulina," she protested. "Something must have gotten lost in translation." Behind him, Sienna could just make out the massive hole they'd dug and the far edge of the slate-grey object resting inside of it.

"You've come a long way," Zhou replied. "Whatever you have to say, please make it quick. We've got a lot of work ahead of us."

Sienna had spent so much time worrying about what she needed to learn from him she had neglected to sort out how to explain why she was there. At least in a way that wouldn't have him calling the cops. Or what passed for a cop around here. She raised her hand and rattled the plastic case. "This tiny sample you sent in to Dr. Barulina's lab. It's the reason I've come."

Zhou's eyes narrowed. "Go on."

"I'm here for an exchange of information. You show me yours"—she wiggled the case again and tilted her head—"and I'll show you mine."

"Tatiana sent you?" he asked with more than a hint of doubt.

"How else do you think I found you?" Sienna said, looking around. "This isn't exactly 5th and Broadway."

Zhou motioned to the empty seat beside him. "All right, get in. I'll give you five minutes."

•••

He brought her to a small cluster of trailers overlooking the dig site. Sienna stepped out of the cart on shaky legs. The view from just beyond the gate hadn't done justice to the sight before her. It looked as though they'd uncovered a massive military bunker. It was square with sloped edges. A white tent had been set up at the building's southwest corner.

They were joined by an American woman in her early thirties with brown hair and an expression that oozed professionalism. Zhou introduced her as Karen. Everyone here seemed to be on edge.

"Let's get on with it," Zhou said. "What is it Dr. Barulina found?"

"You go first," Sienna insisted for obvious reasons. Once the archaeologist had what he wanted, there was nothing stopping him from ejecting her from the premises.

Zhou folded his arms and remained quiet.

"Okay, fine, then I'll start," Sienna said, not seeing a way around the impasse. "While this substance is incredibly unique, it's also used in the manufacture of a neural implant by a company called Neural-Sync."

Zhou's face creased with surprise. "Really?"

"You've heard of them?"

238

"Who hasn't? I think they're one of the worst things that's ever happened to the human race."

Sienna bobbed her head back and forth. "Or one of the best. I suppose it all depends who you ask."

"You work for them." Words that came out of Zhou's mouth as a statement, rather than a question.

Sienna snickered. "Oh, God, no. I'm a glaciologist. I've been working with someone—let's call them an interested party—to find out where this material came from."

"And you think it came from here?"

"At this point, I can't say, but the thought definitely crossed my mind when Dr. Barulina told us both samples were nearly identical."

"Nearly?"

"The way two steel alloys can be very close, but still not exactly the same."

"So where did it come from?" he asked.

She could see Zhou was trying to squeeze her for every last drop.

"Now it's your turn," she insisted.

Zhou complied, no doubt curious to get the final identification he'd been waiting for. He told her about thinking they'd found the tomb of a famous ruler, only to discover it was both older and more advanced than they had anticipated. Zhou also explained that they had uncovered several areas where the strange metal had been molded into anchors. He suggested they might be tiebacks, an engineering method used to reinforce a wall against an external force. Additionally, four large metallic loops had been found, one at each corner. And finally, he told her about the heat signature and the planned mission to explore the interior.

"Any idea what purpose it served?" Sienna said, stunned that such a thing existed, let alone that it had been uncovered.

"We don't know yet," Karen told her. "Perhaps whatever you're about to divulge will give us a hint."

"So you're going inside?" Sienna asked.

"We are," Zhou replied. "And you're not coming with us, if that's what you're asking."

"But you're welcome to watch from the observation trailer," Karen said.

Zhou shot her a disapproving look.

"I called Dr. Barulina," Karen explained. "And they told me she's left for a week-long conference in Naples. So Sienna here's got us by the short and—"

"I get the point," Zhou said, cutting her off.

"It's quite possible whoever's trying to stop our inquiry is after something at this site," Sienna told them.

"The heat source," Karen said, reflexively.

Sienna tilted her head. "Could be."

"So we're in a tight spot," Zhou admitted. "I've told you everything we know. Now it's your turn."

"There's just one more thing I want," Sienna said, holding up an index finger.

"Then you'll tell us?" Zhou's face was glowing red.

"I promise."

"Shoot."

"Let me go in there with you."

"It might not be safe," Karen warned her.

Sienna's shoulders made an involuntary little shrug. "My father was an explorer who died doing what he loved. If I live half the life he did, I'll consider myself a lucky woman."

Zhou nodded. "Fine. But you'll have to sign away any liability."

"Done."

He gave her a look. "Go on then. Spill it."

Sienna handed him the sample he'd sent to Dr. Barulina. "The metal is what's known as metallic hydrogen."

Karen's eyes fluttered. "Metallic what?"

"I know. It's a hard one to wrap your head around. At room temperature hydrogen is a gas. When exposed to extreme cold, say minus four hundred and twenty-five degrees Fahrenheit, it becomes a liquid. But when subjected to extreme pressure, it becomes a metal."

"Wow," was all Zhou could say. She had blown his mind.

Karen set her hands on her hips. "But shouldn't the samples we've uncovered become a gas again once they're exposed to the air?"

"From what I've been able to gather, the simple answer is no. Think of diamonds, themselves created by immense geological pressures. Plucking one out of the ground doesn't suddenly rearrange its atomic structure."

"So where on Earth could such an exotic metal be produced?" Zhou asked.

"That's why I'm here," Sienna told them. "Astrophysicists believe the cores of Jupiter and Saturn are made of both liquid and metallic hydrogen, formed from the unbelievable forces exerted by the gas giant's atmospheric pressure. My colleague and I are also working on a separate, although much less likely theory."

"And what, may I ask, is that?" Zhou said, cocking a single eyebrow.

"Production could be occurring in some of the deepest parts of the world's oceans."

She realized it was a long shot and perhaps not entirely feasible for a variety of reasons, but it was all she and Ben had.

"We're ready," the voice said.

Zhou's radio crackled. "Okay, we'll be right there," he answered and set it back on his belt. "What size are you?" The question was directed toward Sienna.

"I'm a six."

Karen shared a look with Zhou. "That's a small."

He nodded. "Then let's go. You're about to get your wish."

Chapter 37

Florida

The silver sedan Ben rented under an assumed name had been touted as a top-of-the-line model. Not only would it drive itself, navigating the journey via GPS—a rather common feature nowadays—but many of the bells and whistles inside were also voice-activated. The moment he dropped into the driver's seat, the vehicle synced with his phone.

"Welcome to Florida, Mr. Smith," the vehicle greeted him in a soothing female voice. "Your current location still reads Ko Samui, Thailand. Would you like to change that now?"

"Hell, no," Ben snapped, shaking his head. The car was reading the altered signal Knut had used to mask his movements. The last thing he wanted was some over-eager car to blow his cover and signal his whereabouts to the bad guys.

"Just bring me to Archbold, Florida, would you?" he told it.

"Very well," the vehicle replied.

Seconds passed and nothing happened.

"Hey, what's the hold-up?"

"I am waiting for you to fasten your seatbelt, Mr. Smith."

Ben laughed and buckled in. "You're a real smartass, you know that?"

"I am sorry. I do not understand."

"Oh, never mind."

"Thank you for riding with Avis. Press the green button on the display screen to engage conversation mode."

"Conversation mode?"

"Yes, I am versed in a wide range of subjects. Please indicate whether you would prefer a simple chat, a philosophical discussion or a real heart-to-heart."

This was getting weird. "Heart-to-heart?"

"Heart-to-heart selected. Tell me, Mr. Smith. What is your deepest fear?"

"I'm living it, right now," Ben replied.

"You have a great sense of humor. Has anyone ever told you that?"

"There's a red button beside the green one. What does that do?"

"Press the red button to suspend conversation mode."

Ben hit the red button.

"Are you sure?" the car asked, with a touch of sadness.

"I've never been more sure of anything in my entire life."

•••

The hour of silence that followed was rather pleasant. Ben spent most of it replaying the fight in St. Petersburg and the soreness in his back from where his shoulder blades had met that brick chimney. Ben was busy adjusting his seat when the vehicle pulled into a charging station. Perplexed, he checked the battery levels and saw they were more than three-quarters full.

"Hey, why are we stopping?" he asked.

"Recalculating," the car said, in that soft, pleasant voice.

"Are you lost?"

"Please, stand by."

The charging station had a diner attached. A handful of other vehicles were parked nearby, although most of them looked gas-powered. Then he realized this wasn't a charging station at all. It was a gas station. "Okay, don't go anywhere," he ordered the sedan and got out into the blazing Florida sun. Ben felt his eyes squint from the glare and the dense humidity. Mixed with an atmosphere filling every day with more particulates, he found himself struggling to breathe. He returned to the car and grabbed the mask Knut had included in their kit.

With that done, Ben hurried across the asphalt, shimmering from the heat, and into the diner. A bell above the door rang as he entered. A few uninterested stares came his way before returning to their meals. Ben went to the counter and grabbed a seat.

Seconds later, a young woman pushed through the swinging doors and into the dining area. Ben's breath caught in his throat. She was beautiful. He might even go so far as to say she was too attractive to work in a place like this.

"There ya go, Earl," she said, setting the plate down before a scruffy-looking man. She went on and did the same to the other two patrons. It was only after she turned that she saw Ben and headed over.

The waitress blew stray strands of hair out of her face. "Hey there," she greeted him, warmly. Her cheeks were slightly flushed.

Ben felt himself react physically. But not because of her beauty. There was something very familiar about her.

"What can I get you?"

"I'm not here to eat," Ben informed her. He pointed to his car. "I think I'm lost. Or at least my car is lost."

"Oh, that," she said, laughing. The name on the pin said 'Lianne.' "You ain't the first and you sure as heck won't be the last. The maps in those fancy cars haven't been updated yet. Cities and towns have all moved north, on account of the water rising up and all."

"I see. I'm looking for a town called Archbold. It says it's in an area called the New Everglades."

Lianne nodded. "That's 'cause the old Everglades are mostly underwater. Archbold ain't all that far from here. Keep heading along Highway 98. You can't miss it."

He started to thank Lianne when she straightened, throwing him a funny look.

"Everything all right?" he asked.

"Your name isn't Ben by any chance, is it?"

Now it was Ben's turn to feel a flush coming on. "Have we met before?"

"You came in here about a week ago. Yeah, I remember because you were driving a fancy car and dressed in an expensive-looking suit."

"I was?"

"Tall, good-looking blond fella. Yeah, I remember. You were lost then too. Came in here looking for directions."

"You must be thinking of someone else."

Lianne stuck the pencil behind one ear and set her hands on her hips. "Oh, no. Not unless you have a twin brother."

Ben smiled and shook his head.

246

"Yup, I recall you came in asking lots of questions, throwing your money around like a real big shot."

"I did?"

"You even asked me out. Told me you'd fly me up to Seattle."

Ben shook his head. "That doesn't sound like me." Not anymore, but that last bit he kept to himself.

"I told you I didn't date customers and you tipped me a hundred bucks for nothing. I mean, you didn't even eat. You hopped in your car and took off. Fact, now that memory serves, I'm pretty sure you were going to the same place."

For a moment, Ben stood watching, feeling an eerie flood of emotions. He had thought she looked familiar. But he couldn't reconcile the person he was now with the way he had behaved before.

"Thanks again," he said and turned to leave. He was barely out the door when he heard Lianne call out to him.

"Hey, you forgot my tip."

Chapter 38

Ben followed the waitress' directions until it brought him to the end of Highway 98. Apparently, not all that long ago, 98 had turned into Route 27, but that was before the water started rising. Sitting at that junction now was a boathouse and a dock. Parked alongside it were a dozen fan boats. This was the new shoreline.

As he got out of the car and approached, Ben noticed the house itself rested on several rows of wheels, three-quarters of which were under the waterline.

"You got the same look on your face as everyone else who sees her," a gravelly voice said from a few feet away. "Name's Rusty."

The two men shook. The palm of Rusty's hand was rough and calloused. He was a redhead, with pale freckled features. He had a straw cowboy hat, worn with a slight cocky forward tilt. "Water's been moving up a foot or so every year. Once the road disappeared, I got myself a contract to run folks to and from the dry patches. Six boats and six drivers, including myself. We can bring you anywhere within a twenty-mile radius."

"So if there are homes out there," Ben asked, "then I take it the whole area isn't flooded?"

Rusty took off his hat and rubbed the top of his balding head with the meaty part of his forearm. "No, sir. There are a number of lucky homes that happened to be on higher ground. Some walked away, but it might surprise you to learn just how many refused to go. Hell or high water, as they say." He let out a cackle of laughter.

Ben smiled and pointed to where Route 27 once stood. "I'm trying to find Joseph Knight. I understand he lives south along this road… er… waterway. If it were up to my stupid sedan, it might have tried to plow through."

"Technology," Rusty opined. "Can't live with it, can't live without the internet." Another cackle, this time subdued. He eyed Ben up and down. "So, you looking for Old Joe, then."

Ben nodded. "That's right."

"I'm about as close to Joe as he'll let another man get and I think you're best off leaving the old coot alone. Ain't worth the effort to take the abuse that surly man's been known to dish out to strangers."

"Abuse?"

"I've seen him make grown men wet themselves." Rusty used his tongue to fish a piece of stray food from between his front teeth. "That was not a pretty sight."

"I've come a long way," Ben explained. "I'm willing to risk a little abuse."

"Either brave or stupid. I'm not sure which, but I do like your style." He reached into his back pocket and produced a business card—'Rusty's Water Craft Rental' and below that a Florida phone number and links to his Facebook and Instagram page. "Normally it's two hundred a trip, but I'm not so sure you'll make it back in one piece, so let's say one and call it even."

249

"You said you had six boats," Ben said, studying the business card.

Rusty nodded proudly. "That's right."

Ben counted the ones he could see along the dock. "Looks to me like they're all here."

Rusty threw a nervous glance in that direction. "Yeah, well, that's 'cause rush hour ain't here yet."

Ben nodded, not buying it. "I like you, Rusty. So I'll give you fifty bucks."

"Seventy-five," Rusty countered.

"Fifty."

Rusty thought about it for less than five seconds before breaking down and agreeing. Ben knew even at fifty he was getting gouged, but he hadn't been lying when he'd said he liked the guy.

Less than ten minutes later, they were off. The boat itself was a shallow metal platform with a handful of bucket seats, powered by a giant and incredibly noisy fan. The earmuffs Rusty had given him were no match for the beating his hearing was about to take.

Ben was up front, relishing the wind whipping through his hair and pressing the mask into his face. Toward the back of the boat sat Rusty, his back right up against the fan cage. They followed a kind of roadway carved through the swamp grass, cutting sharply left and right as the path shifted. More than once a stray alligator submerged or hurried out of their way.

"You don't wanna fall out here," Rusty shouted over the racket, his generous belly vibrating with laughter. "Won't be much of you left."

Soon they came to a gradient where the land gradually edged out of the water. Rusty increased the speed, and Ben wondered what on earth he was doing. He braced himself as the fan boat reached the edge. But instead of stopping violently, the boat simply pushed over the grassy surface and kept going. He threw an impressed look back at Rusty, who was busting a gut again. No doubt he'd seen Ben's body tense and got a certain thrill out of tormenting folks who weren't from around here.

A moment later, they were back on the water, a process which repeated itself several times as they pushed across terrain that wasn't entirely marsh and wasn't entirely dry.

Through the tall grass, Ben saw that they were approaching a bungalow. The fan boat crested up onto dry land once again and crossed the fifty-meter distance to the house. Like the dock, the bungalow was raised up on what looked like stilts, although the house itself was surrounded by a patch of dry land. To their right the owner of the house had his own dock along with a fishing kayak and a fan boat. On either side of the dry patch on which the house sat were alligator pens. A mangy-looking dog chained between the house and Joe's dock was barking his head off.

An older man with deep lines across his weathered face glared at them, a shotgun lying across his lap. The old man yelled at it to be quiet. The dog let out a few last barks before shutting up.

Rusty killed the engine. Ben removed his earmuffs, certain that every bone in his body had been rattled out of place. He worked the fingers of his hand again, willing more feeling to return and shelving his concern and disappointment when it didn't.

"Joe, I brought you a visitor," Rusty called out from a distance. Judging from his body language, it looked like Joe wasn't the kind of guy you walked up to without first announcing yourself.

"Tell him to go home," Joe shouted, sounding cross, but not nearly as rough around the edges as Rusty did.

"Come on, Joe," Rusty said, fiddling with his earmuffs, picking at the decal on the sides with what remained of his well-bitten fingernails. "The man says he travelled a hell of a long ways to see you. Least you could do is shake his hand and say hello."

"Only if he's interested in shaking the raw end of my shotgun."

Rusty leaned over to Ben. "He's not in a good mood today. Something bothering you today, Joe?" Rusty asked, with genuine concern.

"Maybe there is, what's it to you?"

"Just being a friendly neighbor is all. Oh, that's right, today was Lou-Ellen's birthday." To Ben—"His wife. She died fifteen years ago, right before he came here. Might have had something to do with him showing up in the first place."

"Joe," Ben said. "I understand you used to work for NASA back in the sixties and seventies."

"Maybe I did," Joe replied, gruffly. "I don't see how that's any business of yours."

"I got your name from Dr. Barulina. She says you sent her a sample of some rather unusual metal. I was hoping we might talk about it."

"You're not a reporter, are you?"

"Reporter?" The question caught Ben off guard.

"It's a simple yes or no question," Joe snapped from his porch. He had both hands on the gun now. "Either you are or aren't. There's no in-between."

"No, Joe. I'm not a reporter. I own a company that uses the same kind of metal you sent to Tatiana."

"Ben? Ben Fisher?" the old man said.

Ben nodded. "Yeah, we've already met, haven't we?"

"We sure have," Joe said, tucking the shotgun under his arm and heading over. He shook Ben's hand. "Thanks, Rusty, I'll take it from here."

Rusty's eyes were wide.

The two men headed back toward the house.

"Hardly anyone's come by since you were here last week," Joe said, opening the screen door and ushering Ben inside. "You'll have to forgive the mess."

Ben turned to Rusty before he entered and made a phone gesture with his thumb and pinky. "I'll call when I'm done for that pick-up."

Rusty stood rooted in place, wearing the face of a man who had just watched someone pet a lion without getting eaten. "You got my number?"

Ben reached into his pocket, produced Rusty's business card and waved it in the air. Rusty gave him a thumbs up and Ben turned and stepped into the place Joe called home.

As he did, visions from Ben's most recent flashback kept playing through his head. The one about Apollo 18. A mission kept out of the history books. Which only begged a far more pressing question. Why?

Chapter 39

Site 17
Xinjiang, China

The addition of Sienna meant that the six-person team tasked with entering the structure now numbered seven. Each of them was dressed in a neoprene suit and breather unit. They resembled a bunch of divers in search of an ocean. A high-frequency radio was built into the face masks, the same kind used by groups exploring caves. The oxygen levels inside were normal, at least what passed for normal these days. Which was to say, Zhou's order that they be enclosed in special suits had more to do with preventing any contamination of the interior than any risks it might pose to the crew.

Li would observe the operation from the control room as John Bleck, the excavation's lead technician, guided them through the maze of corridors. HD cameras fitted next to LED lights on their helmets would provide John's team with a set of eyes inside the structure.

Zhou and the others checked and rechecked everyone's equipment. One by one they gave the thumbs up.

Sienna was the last to give the go-ahead, her heart clomping through her chest and up into her ears, where she could feel her pulse pressing defiantly against the sides of her mask. *Get me out of here,* was what it said. She took a moment to steel herself before following the others inside.

Ahead of her, lights from the team's helmets bobbed and crisscrossed one another as they examined their surroundings. They were heading down what looked like a long-darkened corridor. Like the others, Sienna scanned up the concrete walls to the ceiling. The surface looked polished and free of erosion. While that was startling in and of itself, she couldn't help being surprised at the lack of lighting. In fact, apart from the building as a monument to an advanced form of engineering, there was no other visible sign of technology.

The interior was completely dry, their footfalls kicking up clouds of dust. It reminded her of footage her father would bring back from the ocean floor and the way the sediment billowed around the sub whenever it got too close to the bottom.

They came to the first intersection and split into two groups. Zhou pointed to her, Devon and Karen. Together they continued on while the others turned left.

Soon they came to a metal door embossed with an image. The door itself didn't look like it had been made from metallic hydrogen. It appeared to be a super-durable variety of steel. But the door's resistance to rust or wear was not what drew the bulk of their attention. The steel door, or what they had assumed was steel, was burgundy, stained with some sort of metallic paint. Standing out against the reddish color was the white outline of a tall object that looked like a torch.

"Are you seeing this?" Karen asked, speaking to the control room.

"We're getting it," John replied. "But we haven't the foggiest idea what it is."

Zhou stood, breathing heavily as he stared at the image.

Approaching, Sienna went to run her gloved finger along its edges when he gently took her hand.

"Don't touch," Zhou said. "Not until we know what we're dealing with here."

•••

The wonder Zhou was experiencing was like nothing he had ever felt before. In many ways it was a universe unto itself. The site went farther back than any self-respecting archaeologist would ever be allowed to go, a limit enshrined within the very definition of his discipline. Archeology studied the remnants left behind by past human culture, a time scale that stretched no further than about ten thousand years into the past. The rest belonged to the paleoanthropologists and the other nerds who studied the natural world. So to be standing in the corridor of a place that was both incredibly old and yet shockingly modern—well, there were hardly words that could do justice to such a perplexing feeling.

"It looks like a building," Karen said, still studying the image on the door.

"I know this is going to sound crazy," Sienna added. "But it sort of reminds me of the Seattle Space Needle."

Zhou's first reaction was to laugh at the comparison. Partly because she was right, but partly at the absurdity of comparing two things that couldn't possibly be related. His eyes delicately traced their way down the white lines, the way a man's hand might trace the curve in a woman's back. When he got all the way to the base, he noticed something.

"Wait a minute. One. Two. Three. Four."

"What is it?" Karen asked.

Devon and Sienna too came forward to see what Zhou had just found.

"What is it?" John asked, from control.

"I'm not sure," Zhou said, his voice distant. "Look at the bottom part of the image. It's only two-dimensional, but you can still see two large rings and what look like cables running up to a central pillar."

"You're right," Sienna said. "Just like the roof of the structure. I could see them from outside. But what do you think it means? Was this some sort of pre-human skyscraper?"

Zhou's gaze moved back to the top of the structure and to what he had assumed were tiny flecks of white paint around the disc area. But he saw now those dots weren't sloppy workmanship. They were craft of some kind and they were flying. And it hit him then, a blow to the gut that nearly brought him to his knees. No, this hadn't been the base of some tall building. It had been the anchor for a…

"Giant space elevator," Sienna exclaimed, her mind blazing a path down the same improbable trail.

Chapter 40

Joe Knight's New Everglades home was not so much a cluttered mess as it was a treasure trove, packed with paraphernalia from his days with the U.S. Air Force and later with NASA. The layout was open-concept. A couple of ratty old couches sat in one corner along with a well-worn recliner. A bookcase nearby featured what Ben guessed was every novel by Tom Clancy and a few by the many others who'd followed in his footsteps. The place was fairly dim, an effect only enhanced by the abundance of wood furniture. Not surprisingly, the smell of pine was strong, almost cloying. The odor made sense when Ben spotted the old tree-shaped air fresheners hanging around the room.

Joe must have noticed Ben's nose wrinkle. The old man smiled knowingly. "I got a sensitivity to certain kinds of smell. Anything burnt drives me up the wall. A pot stays too long on the stove or a burnt piece of toast does something to my brain. Sends me into a rage."

"For a minute, I wondered whether you were trying to hide a body," Ben said, trying not to sound serious, but failing miserably.

"Oh, I got plenty of those. Mostly in the closet and under the bed where they belong."

"Joe, I should tell you up front. I had an accident recently. Knocked big parts of my memory out. It's part of why I'm here. To retrace my steps and get a handle on what we might have spoken about last week."

The old man stood halfway in the kitchen. "I see. Nothing too serious, I hope."

"Nah," Ben lied.

"Thirsty?"

Ben wavered.

"Well, if you want something to drink, it'll have to be coffee."

A liquor cabinet by the living room had a padlock on it.

"You worried about thieves?"

"Only thief who comes out here is one who's ready to meet his maker. No, let's just say when my wife died I remarried that liquor cabinet. Went from one blurred haze straight into another. Found my vice later in life, but I sure made up for lost time. Anyway, as they say, once an alchy, always an alchy."

"Why not just toss the bottles, remove the temptation?"

"I could do that," Joe admitted. "But there wouldn't be any challenge in it. You see, this way, I gotta make a choice every morning to keep the world clear and in working order."

Ben nodded. It made a certain kind of sense given he was on something of a wagon himself. He'd only recently begun the slow process of uncovering his own vices, an admittedly odd exercise that felt like snooping into the life of a stranger. Only the stranger was him. And the main vice he'd discovered, namely living the life of a rich, soulless playboy, had turned out to be far less glamorous than one might have thought. A point brought home to

259

bear after the attack when his calls for help were rather justifiably received with a healthy dose of cursing, followed by an empty line. "Yeah, a coffee would be great."

Joe was busy in the kitchen while Ben glanced around. A picture of Joe next to Neil Armstrong at Rogers Dry Lake in California caught his eye. Behind them was an X-15, an experimental aircraft from the 1960s. At the time it had set speed records for manned flight after reaching Mach 6.70—a record only broken a decade earlier—and had been the first plane to touch the edge of space. On the table below it was the same white pilot's helmet from the photograph.

"Feels a bit like a museum, doesn't it?" Joe said, handing Ben a steaming mug.

Ben took it and thanked him. "You could charge an admission fee."

"I'd consider it, if I didn't hate people so much." He watched Ben pause in mid sip. "That's right. It isn't Starbucks, it's instant. But it grows on you. I promise, by your third cup you'll be begging me for more." Joe tilted his own mug back and let out a sigh of appreciation.

"Tatiana mentioned you were a NASA scientist," Ben said. "She never told me you were a test pilot."

Joe's sharp eyes flashed with a subtle recognition of Ben's amnesia. "I was Neil's backup on the X-15 project."

"Backup? I didn't know there was such a thing."

"A rather grim business," Joe explained. "Nothing like being an understudy for some Broadway play. No, in my case, the only reason I would get called up is if Neil had gone out on a test run and hadn't come back."

260

"I see. I just assumed you were working in a NASA lab and decided to bring your work home with you." He was referring to the sample in Tatiana's possession.

"I did keep a few souvenirs from my time with the space program. But I wasn't a scientist. Like Neil, I was an aeronautical engineer turned flier. Some say our type made the best pilots because we understood everything about the craft there was to know." Joe's expression hardened. "Guys like Chuck Yeager and a few other hotheads without degrees thought we flew too mechanically. Anyway, I played backup from the X series flights right into Apollo. Maybe that's just a polite way of saying I mostly stayed on the ground, not a very nice place to be when you're itching to get up off the ground any way you can. And as for the sample I sent that Russian lady, for your information, I wasn't the guy who snuck it out of some lab. I was the one who brought it home."

"Brought it home?"

Joe nodded, taking another drink. "You got me blabbing on about myself again. What I want to know is how you lost that memory of yours."

Ben's eyes traced back to the picture of Joe and Neil Armstrong. "The short version is, someone broke into my home, killed my girlfriend and left me face down in a puddle of blood to take the rap."

Right away, Ben noticed a dramatic change in the old man's face. That low simmering anger always lurking beneath the surface now bore marked hints of sadness. This was a new piece of information. Something that had happened after Ben's last visit. "You know a thing or two about loss, don't you?" Ben said.

Joe's eyes glazed over. "Did you know Lou-Ellen smoked since she was fourteen years old? No, of course not. How could you? Well, she never could break free from those infernal things no matter how many times she promised she would stop. One night, fifteen years ago, before the water had come up like it is now, she told me she was taking the truck to the store to get more cigarettes. She always bought three packs, that was her pattern, and would rush out as soon as two of the three were done. But this time she'd gotten distracted by something or other and didn't realize before she smoked her last one. Now I'm not sure if you've ever lived with a smoker, young man, but let me say from experience, you have not known a more foul temper until you're locked in a small space when that pack goes empty. It probably won't surprise you to hear we got into a fight. Rushing out at nine at night, well, I told her she could just as easily go the following morning, but of course she wasn't having any of that and drove off cussing like a banshee. I felt truly sorry for the fella at the store who had to serve her." Joe grew quiet.

"Something tells me she never got there," Ben said somberly.

Joe shook his head, the deep lines in his chin starting to quiver. The old man was fighting it. Ben wondered whether he'd ever told anyone the full story of what had happened.

"A high-school math teacher on a bender went through a stop light and plowed right into her. Doctor said she died right there on the spot, but I'm not sure about that. Two troopers showed up to tell me. We drove together after to see her and I'll never forget the frozen look of anger on her battered face. They cleaned her up as best they could, but I could still recognize it. No one knows when or how things will end. To go out pissed off just doesn't seem right."

Ben put a hand on the man's shoulder. "Back during the Civil War, Stonewall Jackson lay dying after suffering a mortal wound during the battle of Chancellorsville. His last words were, 'Let us cross over the river, and rest under the shade of the trees.'"

Joe squeezed his eyes shut. "That's the way it ought to be. A peaceful transition. If she had to go, that's how I would have wanted it to happen."

Slowly, Joe began to pull himself together. He let out a deep sigh. "Another coffee?"

Ben smiled. "Why not? You were right. It's kinda growing on me."

"I knew it would." He went to the kitchen. "You never finished telling me how you ended up here."

Ben drew in a deep breath. "It's something of a long story." Over several minutes, he laid it out as best he could from the initial memory loss to discovering he was the CEO of a company that specialized in neural implants. He also told Joe about the people who were after him and that he thought it had something to do with Neural-Sync. Finally he told him about that flash of memory where he'd seen the words 'Apollo 18.'

Joe came back with the fresh coffee and set a mug down before Ben. "I was afraid that's why you'd come back. After you left the first time, I spent a long while wondering whether or not I should have ever opened my mouth about it."

"It's vitally important that you do, Joe," Ben urged him. "I believe millions, maybe even billions of lives may be on the line."

"Well, there's no way to understand it unless I start again from the very beginning. You see, during Apollo 17, I was Commander Cernan's backup. Like I said earlier, always the bridesmaid, never the bride. I was at the Mission Control Center in Houston. Eugene Cernan was the commander. Ronald Evans was the command module pilot and Harrison Schmitt was a geologist and lunar pilot. That was the three-man crew.

"Like the earlier Apollo missions, these boys were tasked with studying the lunar surface. On the third day, the capsule was passing around the far side of the moon when something weird happened. You see, at that time, radio signals couldn't reach Earth from over there, so we didn't hear a peep out of them during the entire fifty-five-minute transition. Not until they reemerged…"

•••

(Apollo 17 Unredacted NASA Transcript)

(Inaudible jumble of angry voices)
CAPCOM: Cernan, everything okay up there?
(Arguing continues unabated)
CAPCOM: Fellas, give us a status update. All systems here are in the green. You should be beginning to prep for touchdown at Taurus-Littrow in approximately one-zero minutes.
(Agitated voices begin to settle)
CAPCOM: Status update.
Cernan: Houston, this is Eugene. We were just having a spirited discussion.
CAPCOM: Roger, I can see that. Keep your heads on straight, gentlemen. You'll only get one shot at that landing.
Cernan: Roger that. Everything here is under control.
Evans: Uh, Houston…
CAPCOM: Yes, Ron. What is it?
Cernan: It's nothing, Houston.
Schmitt: Eugene, let him speak, dammit.

CAPCOM: Gentlemen, whatever problem you're having, I suggest you sort it right away. Ron, if you have something to say, spit it out, but make it quick.

Evans: Roger that, Houston. It's just that when we looped around the far side... well, we saw something and we weren't certain whether to report it or not.

CAPCOM: Is there a problem with the capsule? Like I said, we're showing all green down here.

Evans: No, not that, Houston. I was looking out the port side window, at the moon below. And, well, I think I saw something on the surface. Something that creeped the hell out of us.

(A pause of several seconds)

CAPCOM: Roger. What was it you saw?

Schmitt: It wasn't only him, Houston. We each saw it too. What looked at first like a reflection from inside the Tsiolkovskiy crater. Eugene was worried that making any mention of it might jeopardize the mission. And maybe he's right, but Ron and I felt it was too important to keep to ourselves.

CAPCOM: Roger, copy that, Harry. Eugene, as commander, is there anything you'd like to add?

Evans: No, Houston. Not in way of contradiction. Ron and Harry are telling the truth.

CAPCOM: I copy you. Can you provide any further description about what you saw? Was it only a light?

(Another pause)

Evans: Negative, Houston. As we came around, we each took turns and got a real good look at it. The size... it was really something else. Made me wonder if the Russians had somehow beaten us to the punch.

CAPCOM: Beaten us? Please explain, Ron. What was it you saw?

Evans: I feel downright peculiar saying it, Houston, but it was a cluster of buildings. A habitat camouflaged to blend in with the moonscape. And it was huge. And if I had to guess, I'd say it had been there an awfully long time.

Chapter 41

Site 17
Xinjiang, China

"None of this makes any sense," Karen shouted, her mask fogging up from her elevated breathing rate.

Her heart wasn't the only one pounding. Sienna had only been here a short time and yet she was getting hit with one bomb after another. They were still standing in front of the red steel door with the image of what looked like a space elevator. The problem was, not everyone knew what they were talking about.

"It's a theoretical solution to moving cargo into Earth's orbit," Zhou tried to explain. "Using rockets is expensive, not only since they cost a fortune to build, but also because the boosters aren't always recoverable. Which makes it as foolish as buying a new car every time you wanna run to the grocery store."

"All of this sounds insane," Devon said. His bulging eyes hadn't come off the image on the door since they found it.

"Dr. Zhou is right," Sienna said. "Rockets are launched in stages. As the first and second expend their fuel, they fall away, normally back to Earth, touching down in the ocean via parachute."

"Which is why some madman or genius," Zhou said, "thought it might be a better idea to make the journey in an elevator."

Karen was still shaking her head. "Devon's right. This does sound rather preposterous. Most of the elevators I'm familiar with have a building holding them up. What exactly keeps this space elevator of yours upright?"

"A little something called centrifugal force," Zhou said with a smile. "I suppose the easiest way to picture it is a two-pound weight at the end of a rope. Now imagine holding your arms out and spinning in circles. What do you think will happen?"

"The force of the rotation will keep the rope taut," Karen said, understanding hitting her all at once. "Like an Olympic hammer thrower."

"Correct," Zhou said. "They spin around with a ball on a chain. In our example, the Earth is our thrower, spinning in circles. All you need is an anchor to keep it tethered to the ground, an exceptionally strong cable and a counterweight at the other end. That's the bit that remains in orbit."

"And that's where we are now," Sienna said, digesting the significance of what they had just discovered. "This structure was the anchor."

"It looks that way," Zhou said.

"There is a potential problem with that hypothesis," Devon was quick to point out. "For a space elevator to work, it would need to be placed along the planet's equator, since that's where vertical centrifugal forces would be strongest."

"I've seen the simulations," Sienna jumped in. "Over time, the equator has moved. And it isn't necessarily a question of the Earth tilting on its axis. Don't forget, the planet's crust sits atop a layer of magma and is constantly in motion."

"She's right. The equator once ran along this spot," Zhou said, confirming what Sienna was telling them.

She nodded. "Thirty million years ago, I believe."

Devon lifted a hand, motioning to the structure. "Well, even if that is so, we still have a much bigger challenge on our hands."

"Yeah, understanding who built this place," Karen said.

"It sure as hell wasn't us," Sienna told them. "*Homo sapiens* only really showed up on the scene some two hundred thousand years ago."

Shifting his weight to his other leg, Zhou was considering Sienna's statement. "I've been pondering this very question since we first dated the site. How could it be that a past civilization this advanced would leave so little trace of its existence? The conundrum knocked around my head for a while before I began to consider another, far more radical possibility. What if Earth was merely a colony for an entirely different race of beings? Colonies like we hope to have one day on the Moon and Mars."

It made a certain amount of sense. Although Sienna could see the idea made the group rather uneasy.

"Head to places like India and you'll see what I mean," Zhou went on, seeing he needed to elaborate further to clarify his hypothesis. "There are innumerable structures still standing that were built by the British back when it used to be a colony."

269

"You're talking about ancient aliens," Devon said, noting the discussion had departed into unknown territory. "The guy with the crazy hair on TV. I think what's more likely is we simply made a colossal mistake in dating the site. This is probably some high-tech Japanese bunker left over from World War 2."

"I like Devon's idea," Karen said. "Maybe we should go back to square one and reexamine our dating protocol."

Zhou cleared his throat. "A smart man once said that 'Two possibilities exist: either we are alone in the universe or we are not. Both are equally terrifying.'"

The truth of those words seared a hole in Sienna's soul. Either way you sliced it, this was going to be a discovery of monumental and frightening proportions. Going back to retest the date was a safe bet, but one she felt would only reinforce the earlier findings. This place was old, about as old as they came. And dealing with that head-on was proving to be a scarier prospect than any of them had probably ever considered. Fear and emotion, however, collided with cold hard facts the way ocean waves collided with cliff walls. That was to say, it shattered them.

John chimed in from the control room. "The heat source we detected is on the other side of that door. Is there any chance you can make it in there?"

"I'm going back," Karen said, her features pallid and sickly. She had the look of someone who'd just had her entire worldview slashed and burned before her eyes.

"I'll go with her," Devon said, guiding one of her arms around the back of his neck and over his shoulders.

Sienna shot Zhou a nervous glance. "And then there were two."

•••

They studied the door for latches or handles and found none.

"I'm open for ideas on how to move this door if you have any," Sienna offered.

Zhou made a growling sound at the back of his throat. "When in doubt, push."

Together, they set their gloved hands against the smooth metal surface and did as Zhou had suggested. Sienna's boots slid on the dusty floor as she gave it everything she had.

The other team was off exploring the northern wing of the structure. Zhou was just about to call them in for help when the heavy steel door began to give. Both of them strained under the effort. Once they'd created an opening wide enough to pass through, they eased up.

Sienna was the first to enter.

"What do you see?" Zhou asked, following closely behind.

"I'm not sure," she replied, a hesitant quality to her voice.

They entered what appeared to be an empty chamber. Zhou studied his footprints in the virgin powder around his boots, and suddenly knew what it must have been like for the early astronauts on the moon.

The room was circular with a high ceiling. To their left, another metal tablet hung on the wall. Like the one before it, the lettering resembled hieroglyphs, many of them rounded. Not much of a surprise there, assuming Zhou's space elevator theory was correct, and he believed strongly that it was.

"Hey, John," Zhou called to the control room. "Do you read me? We're inside the central chamber."

"Reading you loud and clear, Dr. Zhou," John replied.

Zhou spun in a slow circle. "Whatever that power source was we saw in the read-out, it isn't coming from here."

They heard a surprised murmur and the shuffling of papers. "Hold tight, Dr. Zhou, we're rechecking the data on that."

"Look for a lower level while you're at it," Zhou suggested, confirming again the room was empty. He exchanged a look with Sienna, who shrugged.

"False alarm maybe," she offered, standing beneath the stone tablet and struggling to make sense of it.

"All right, Dr. Zhou, we've gone over the images twice now and each time we find a dim energy signature coming from inside. And the level you're on is the only one there is."

"No basement, eh?" Zhou asked, disappointed.

"Sorry to let you down."

Sienna spun on her heels, surveying the ceiling.

A gasp escaped Zhou's lips. "Don't move," he told her.

Her eyes widened. "What do you mean, don't move?" she said, fear gripping her stiffening body to the point where even her normally supple lips hardly budged.

"Look down at your feet."

Slowly, she did as he asked and saw a section of the floor where her feet had disturbed the powdery accumulation on the ground. Streaming up from one of the spots she had cleared away was a shaft of light. It illuminated the inside of her mask and the expression of fear currently plastered over her face. "Uh, any suggestions?"

"Yeah," Zhou said. "Carefully take three steps to your right."

Sienna did and when she looked down, she let out a tiny yelp of terror.

Staring back at her from the glowing light in the floor was a face.

Chapter 42

Apollo 18, 1973
Lunar approach

Knight: Houston, Commander Joe Knight here. We are at 10,000 feet on approach for lunar landing.

CAPCOM: Roger that. We got you at 75 feet per second, down 35.

Knight: Copy. All right, Harry, bring us in.

Schmitt: Yeah, no pressure.

CAPCOM: Joe, you're gonna make the kid soil his diapers.

Knight: (laughter) Naw, his suit's equipped for it.

CAPCOM: Fuel reads 60 seconds. Your Delta-H looks good.

Schmitt: Roger that.

Knight: Status on the AGS?

CAPCOM: The abort guidance looks good to us.

Knight: There's the Earth. Still too far to see much of the surface. But we just passed the first hump. Yaw to zero. 2500 feet, 52 degrees.

CAPCOM: The H-dot still looks good.

Knight: Fuel at 30 seconds. Pitch warning light. Harry, straighten her out.

Schmitt: Roger that.

CAPCOM: Reduce your speed by at least 20. We got you at 30 feet per second.

Schmitt: On it.

Knight: I have a visual on Tsiolkovskiy Crater. The target's directly in the center. See if you can't set us down about a hundred yards away, Harry. Get us on the green.

CAPCOM: Save the golf analogies for after you touch down.

Knight: Roger that, Houston.

Knight: Okay, 9 feet per second. 115 feet. Fuel 10 seconds. We're getting some dust. Harry, move her forward a touch, will you?

Schmitt: No problem.

Knight: Okay, get ready for touchdown. More dust now. 10 feet. 5 feet. 2 feet.

Schmitt: And contact.

Knight: Engine stop command override, off. Mode control, hold. Guidance and navigation, auto. Hell of a job, Harry. Glad to see we're still in one piece.

Schmitt: We get you there in one piece. That's my motto.

Evans (from orbiter): Great job, gentlemen. I'll buy each of you a nice cold one when we get home.

CAPCOM: As long as you're buying, we got a lot of thirsty engineers over here too.

Knight: Houston, do me a favor. Would you find Lou-Ellen and tell her we made it down safely? Oh, and tell her I won't be home for dinner tonight.

CAPCOM: (general laughter from Mission Control) It'll be my pleasure.

•••

Joe looked at Harry Schmitt sitting next to him and grit his teeth. The friendly banter with CAPCOM was about all either of them could do to settle their nerves. They'd been chosen for this mission for their coolness under fire. A quality Commander Cernan had also possessed, but something about seeing a building on the moon that had no business being there—well, that had a habit of forcing a man to take a long hard look inside. When that moment came, some men blinked. Didn't make them any less worthy of respect. Some just felt things more strongly than others. And others still felt strongly and pushed that gnawing unease into a corner where it couldn't lash out.

If anything, Cernan bowing out from Apollo 18 was exactly what Joe had wanted. Maybe even what he'd needed. A shot at finally ditching the bridesmaid's outfit. Ron Evans and Harry Schmitt, both from Apollo 17, had opted to stay on for 18. Professional as they were, his fellow astronauts could not be more different. Ron was short, rather stocky and even at the ripe young age of thirty was in the final stages of baldness. He was also pure gut. Sure, his brain worked just fine—in fact, he was one of the smartest men Joe knew—but the filter through which he measured all stimuli always came down to how he felt in a given situation. He was a geologist. He'd even bumped a rather sour former X-15 pilot off the roster for Apollo 17 because studying moon

275

rocks and teasing out what they might tell us about the Earth was the main purpose of the mission.

Harry on the other hand was far more handsome, with a darker complexion. He also came from an electrical and aeronautical engineering background, which made him twice as methodical, a trait that also opened him up to the insidious pressure trap. "Show me a man who seeks perfection and I'll show you someone languishing in disappointment and self-flagellation." That was what Joe's father used to tell him on a daily basis. But give Harry a mission with clear parameters and you could bet your bottom dollar it would get done and get done well.

As proof, Harry had suggested a series of lunar satellites designed to enable constant communication with mission control back on Earth. Without them, the mission they had come to perform would have been infinitely more difficult, if not downright impossible.

So where did Joe fit on that spectrum? Thankfully, the personality tests the wise folks at NASA had subjected him to put him squarely between them. One part gut and one part brain. At their best, they became a single entity, operating on an almost automatic level. At their worst, well, Joe was happy to report the NASA nerds didn't think that would be a problem either.

Green lights from the command console blinked in Joe's eyes, but he wasn't seeing that right now. Because both men were staring out the lunar lander's two tiny windows at the target they had travelled nearly four hundred thousand miles to investigate. It was a collection of ashen-colored buildings made to resemble an outcropping of dormant volcanic rock.

The lander had set down the equivalent of two football fields away. That meant, dressed in their A7LB pressure suits, they would travel there by buggy. The official designation was the Extravehicular Mobility Unit or EMU. NASA, if nothing else, was an acronym factory. And that was precisely why Joe would call it a buggy.

He took one final look outside and understood why Harry's eyes were glued to the alien buildings like a kid's tongue on a flagpole in January. It appeared that the lunar module wasn't the only object in Tsiolkovskiy Crater with windows. But it wasn't so much the windows that had them a touch spooked. It was the light they saw shining out of them.

Chapter 43

Site 17
Xinjiang, China

Both teams were now assembled in the chamber, along with Li, who had been outfitted with a protective suit and mask. Had a picture been taken, it would have shown a rather stunned group of scientists staring down in awe. Flush against the floor was a smooth, oval slab of glass. And beneath that lay the body of what could only be described as an alien being. These men and woman of science formed a semi-circle around the encased figure, like mourners at a burial—an impression only reinforced by the soft indirect lighting that bathed the body in an otherworldly glow. For all they could tell looking at the impeccable state of preservation, it might very well have been placed there yesterday, rather than millions of years ago.

But feelings of reverence and amazement said nothing about the shape of the creature they were observing. And make no mistake about it, each set of eyeballs present was scrutinizing the being in utter disbelief, searing every feature of its form into their mind's eye. The surreal quality of such a moment was beyond what any of them could ever have imagined.

Staring long enough with squinted eyes, one might almost think it was human. It bore two short, squat arms along with a thick pair of matching legs. The being also possessed a wide, powerful neck that resolved itself into a large, bulbous head. Its features were delicate and also comparable to that of a human: small narrow mouth, a tiny set of ears and, though closed, two generous-looking eyes. The flesh was pallid with the slightest hint of sage, which, for some present, immediately served to invoke thoughts of little green men. For many, that fact alone provided the greatest epistemological challenge, since it forced them to do battle with every derisive comment uttered by skeptics in the media and elsewhere over many decades. This had provided the mechanism by which sightings were ruthlessly brushed aside. Little green men from outer space. Over time it had become something of a punchline. Now, they were standing in a room filled with more PhD's than people and not one of them was entirely sure what to think.

"What are the chances it's still alive?" Sienna whispered, breaking the long, uneasy silence.

"Well, one thing's for certain," Zhou said. "We won't find out standing around with our jaws on the floor."

Li was next to him, the palms of her hands clamped together as if in prayer. Zhou's eyes jumped between his Communist minder and the alien under the glass.

"This doesn't get out," Zhou told her. "Not until we know what we have here, right?"

She nodded in a distant, dreamy kind of way.

"Everybody out," Zhou ordered, a command he needed to repeat more than once before people began to obey.

"What's your plan?" Sienna asked.

"Simple," Zhou replied. "We're gonna open it."

"Wait a minute," she protested. "Are you sure that's such a good idea?"

"Let's be honest with ourselves. At some point, this being, wherever it's from, is going to get confiscated and disappear into some government warehouse. This may be our greatest—no, make that our only—opportunity to learn anything about who they were and why they were here on Earth."

"And what if it wakes up? Are you going to sit down and have a conversation with it? Hell, you don't even know what they eat."

"Dr. Panov," Zhou growled. "Please don't forget that you're here as my guest."

"I haven't. I just want to make sure you've thought this through. The laws of unforeseen consequences can be harsh and unforgiving."

His face softened. "I'm sorry, but the decision's been made."

•••

It was another few hours before Li was able to use her connections with the Xinjian governor's office to procure two biocontainment suits. Even if Zhou wasn't interested in addressing Sienna's objections, he understood that alive or dead, alien biology could pose a grave threat to the planet—a threat that had played out many times in humanity's own past whenever one distant group encountered another.

The circular chamber with the alien figure had been cleared except for Zhou and Karen, who were both decked out in the biosuits Li had procured. Zhou was pushing a stainless-steel cart that had two levels. On the top was a defibrillator and first-aid equipment, a comical sight for several reasons. The first was that it indicated Zhou's optimism that cracking the lid would awaken the being inside the same way the prince's kiss had woken Sleeping Beauty in the children's fairy-tale. It also said something about their confidence that if the being did open its eyes, a handful of Band-Aids and cotton swabs would get it up on its feet.

In contrast, the cart's bottom shelf housed chisels, pickaxes and two crowbars, a reminder of the far less elegant truth of what they were about to do. Sienna had little knowledge of archeology and the norms of the discipline, except for an article she had read about the eighteenth-century fad among European noblemen of pillaging sacred Ancient Egyptian sites. The main part of the article had been to highlight that while the pickaxe had once been the favored tool among amateur archaeologists, the soft brush had long ago taken its place.

Sienna stood in the rather crowded confines of the control room. All eyes were glued to the monitor as Zhou and Karen approached the glass coffin and set to work. Zhou's first few strikes with the pickaxe directly to the glass appeared to have little to no effect, other than sending a painful jolt up his arms.

"I suggest you concentrate on the concrete floor instead," John said.

"No kidding," Zhou replied, swearing under his breath.

He and Karen grunted and groaned like a pair of pro tennis players as they made slow, steady progress. And slow was the operative word. Every strike caused the tip of the pickaxe to bend a little bit more, rendering it useless, until Zhou finally had one of the workers leave every pickaxe they could find by the red metal door that sealed the chamber.

Perhaps half the control room had either left or was nodding off by the time Zhou radioed back to let them know they were deep enough. The video feed from their helmet cams showed a hole about a foot deep along the edge of the metallic container. Near the top was an inch-thick layer of glass, or at least something that resembled glass.

Zhou and Karen transitioned to the crowbars.

Karen hesitated and rubbed her gloved hands together.

"Everything all right?" John asked.

"Fine," she replied. "Apart from the eight thousand blisters covering my hands."

"I promise," he replied, "when this is all done, I'll personally get you a full manicure."

"How about a new pair of hands instead?" Zhou interjected. "She's not the only one suffering here."

The radio on the table in front of John crackled to life. "Security checkpoint to home base."

Sienna glanced at the monitor showing the checkpoint leading into the dig site and saw a line of Chinese military vehicles.

"Oh, crap," she blurted out. Then to John—"You better tell them to hurry. Looks like someone spilled the beans about our little friend down there." She glanced over to Li, who looked sick with fear. Or was that a look of guilt?

John's eyes were frozen on the monitor, watching as their skinny guard was pushed aside.

"John," Sienna shouted. "Aren't you going to warn them?"

He turned and looked at her, his eyes wide and vacant.

She plucked his headset off, put it on herself and pressed the button to speak. "Dr. Zhou, Karen. We've got company and not the good kind. So I suggest you hurry it up."

"Company?" Zhou repeated, not getting it.

"The Chinese military," Sienna shot back. She turned to Li. "You're the government liaison, right?"

Li stayed quiet, working the same mime routine John was practicing.

"Someone needs to get out there and stall them," Sienna called out to anyone in the room who would listen.

Devon rolled up his sleeves. "I guess we'll see if those Mandarin classes are about to pay off." He ran from the control room and up the dirt path which led from the site. Once the column of military trucks cleared the checkpoint, they would pass directly by him.

Sienna felt beads of sweat rolling down the sides of her face. In the chamber, Zhou and Karen were struggling with the crowbars. "How's it going in there?"

"As badly as it looks," Zhou said through grit teeth. "This thing isn't budging."

Sienna watched from Zhou's point of view as he dug the crowbar's teeth between the metal frame and the glass lid and struggled to separate the two. A little deeper in the hole, still partly covered with dirt, was a red light.

"John, zoom in there, will you?" she asked, pointing to the anomalous feature on the screen.

Still dazed, the normally self-assured John did as he was told. But the image kept moving out of frame. "Zhou's moving too much."

"Then freeze it when the camera's looking back in the hole." She didn't want to distract Zhou from his efforts for something that might not get them anywhere. "Okay, freeze it right there. Good. Now zoom in." Sienna took a step closer to the screen and ran her finger along what looked like a red light.

A quick glance at the front gate camera revealed the convoy was no longer there. Other cameras picked them up coming down the road that led directly to the dig site. Time was ticking away and fast.

"Zhou," Sienna called out. "I need you to stop what you're doing and clear some of the debris from the hole you dug. Once you do, check inside of it for a red light."

"I'll do it," Karen said, getting down on her hands and knees and poking her arm under where Zhou was working rather unsuccessfully with the crowbar.

One of the cameras showed Devon crest the small hill and stand in the middle of the dirt road, waving his arms as the convoy approached.

"Try to run your finger over it," Sienna said. "See if it's a button or something else."

Karen did so. They watched the halo of light inside the container switch off. She pressed it again and the light came back on.

"Forget the crowbars and keep digging," Sienna told them. "If there's another button in there, it might just pop the lid."

In the other monitor, the convoy was stopped before Devon. A lone Chinese figure in the lead vehicle was visible from the waist up as the two men shouted at one another. Devon was waving them away, as if telling them they had no right to be here. So far the delaying tactic seemed to be working.

"I think I found something," Karen said. She pressed a new glowing red button she had found and the side of the glass lid closest to them jumped a few inches. A heavy stream of compressed air hissed out at them. Zhou raised himself onto one knee and lifted the lid. He then straddled the container, staring down into a cloud of white vapor, obscuring the figure inside. Zhou waved it away with his gloved hand.

A gasp next to her drew Sienna's attention. The grad student's hands were clamped over her mouth, her face a mask of horror. The lead Chinese vehicle pushed forward, driving over Devon, killing him instantly.

That was when Sienna knew the situation was no longer just serious. It had become deadly.

Chapter 44

Apollo 18, 1973
Tsiolkovskiy Crater

The buggy bounced along the lunar surface at a steady sixteen miles an hour. Joe was driving while Harry sat in the passenger seat. What most people didn't realize was that the A7LB EV space suit was like wearing Earth's atmosphere around their body. While it allowed them to breathe and maneuver around in the unforgiving vacuum surrounding them, it also made articulating limbs a royal pain in the ass. The gloves also had a nasty habit of driving you crazy, especially whenever you needed to pick something up off the ground. Joe gripped the buggy's steering as the vehicle's wheels cut through undisturbed lunar dust. He glanced back, tracing the tracks that led to the lander.

Ahead, what could only be described as a moon base began coming into clearer focus. Satellite photos from the air revealed the overall shape of it. Most of the habitat had been built into the mountain itself, apart from the few odd shapes jutting out near the top and the windows they'd spotted earlier. But that wasn't all. Five curved structures snaked out from the central mountain core. From orbit it looked something like a five-bladed throwing glaive laid on its side with the peaks of jagged rock perched in the center. It made for quite an impressive sight.

Recording and transmitting the images were cameras that had been built into the buggy as well as those they were wearing on chest rigs. Thanks to Harry's moon satellite brainchild, the images were being sent directly to CAPCOM. The distance of over four hundred thousand kilometers between the Earth and the moon meant the image was delayed by little more than one point two five seconds.

"Throttle back a bit, Joe," CAPCOM said. "See if you can't steady out the cameras. We're all getting carsick down here."

Joe let out the kind of easy laugh that would remain a trademark of his tough but fair personality until Lou-Ellen's accident all those years later. "Roger that, Houston. That any better?"

"Much."

"What do you make of it?" Joe asked, hoping for a little something extra before they went and knocked on the door. You show up at someone's house unannounced and there was no telling what might happen.

"Still no acknowledgement from the Russians on whether or not it's theirs," Capcom replied. "Letting you know, Evans in the orbiter should be over your position any second now."

"Copy that," Joe acknowledged. If they needed to beat a hasty retreat, Evans would be the one they'd need to rendezvous with after they blasted off the surface in the lander.

Harry piped in. "Hard to imagine if it was the Russkies they wouldn't have planted a Soviet flag somewhere."

"Right," Joe added. "Or carved Lenin's face into the bedrock façade."

They were drawing closer and already Joe could see the base had suffered some damage. It appeared a chunk the size of a 1970 Oldsmobile station wagon had been sheared off the mountain's side and sent crashing into one of the spiral arms. A smaller crater was visible to their left along Tsiolkovskiy's edge.

"A crater within a crater," Evans said. "There's something poetic about that."

"Or frightening," Joe countered. "Looks like it came in at a shallow angle and clipped the structure before impacting the crater wall. Any thoughts, Houston?"

"Yes. It goes to show, when you're in a shooting gallery, sooner or later you're going to get hit."

CAPCOM had a point. A simple look at the moon through a pair of binoculars revealed craters within craters. Unlike the Earth, the moon had no tectonic plates or weather to buff and sometimes entirely erase the consequence of such meteor impacts. But time was perhaps the most important part of CAPCOM's point. In a place like this, there was no telling when the damage had actually been done.

"Houston, I'm heading for the damaged spiral arm."

"We copy you. Harry, see if you can't get a sample from the fallen rock face."

"Will do, Houston."

They were maybe a hundred yards away, still plowing through virgin moon landscape, a sensation both terrifying and reassuring at the same time. Secretly, Joe couldn't fathom the thought of encountering another life form here, human or otherwise. Equally unnerving was the prospect the site had sat abandoned for hundreds, thousands or perhaps millions of years.

Joe pulled the buggy up alongside the spiral arm, maneuvering the vehicle so the fixed camera was facing the gaping hole torn in the side. The two men disembarked, and Harry went straight for the rock, while Joe bounced along toward the opening. The chance of not looking like a fool while walking on the moon in such low gravity was nil. At seventeen percent of Earth's gravity, regular steps simply didn't work, just as regular steps wouldn't work were one attempting to walk along the bottom of a lake. The single form of human-powered locomotion Armstrong and Aldrin had discovered back in 69 was still in use four years later. Joe called it the bunny hop, because that was essentially what you did. You kept your feet slightly apart and hopped around, trying your best not to over-rotate and end up on your face. Moon dust was a pain to clean off your suit. The whiter the suit, the better hopper, hence the term bunny.

Try as Joe might, distracting his mind with trivia wasn't doing a damn thing to calm that tingly feeling creeping up the pressurized flesh of his legs.

The walls of the habitat were white and thin. Translucent spaghetti strands of what looked like fiberoptic cable reached out from the wall lining. Joe had a light on his helmet. He switched it on, peering into the dimly lit space. The glow speared loads of debris he didn't recognize. They appeared to be crates, many of them empty.

"Harry, I'm heading inside," Joe told his partner. "You coming?"

"Be right there, Joe. Just collecting a quick sample."

"I know you're a geologist, but go easy on the rocks, will you? We go over our weight allowance and we'll never make it back to the orbiter."

"Look, I'll take them for now and throw them overboard if need be."

"Okay, we agree," Joe said stepping inside the opening sheered by the falling rock. His eyes traced up automatically at the thought of some fresh boulder falling on his head. Above him he could just make out two of the mountain peaks, both of them brimming with more darkened windows he hadn't noticed while driving up. Before him was a white door with a silver metal bar running horizontally across the center. But it was only when he approached that he realized the metal door towered over him, measuring some ten feet in height. What was left of the shattered ceiling here was taller, at least fifteen feet and perhaps even higher than that.

Joe walked up to the door, laid his gloved hands on the silver bar as far apart as he could and began applying pressure in a clockwise motion. When that didn't work he tried it the other way. A moment later, Harry appeared at his side and proceeded to help.

The bar was being stubborn, but Joe could feel it slowly giving way. He grit his teeth and really put his back into it. Without warning, the bar gave way, spinning like the prop on a World War Two fighter before locking into place. Compressed air hissed out from around the edges. Joe and Harry pulled it open, kicking aside dust and debris from the path of the bottom rail. Inside was another door just like it.

"Houston, it looks like an airlock," Joe said.

Harry agreed with the assessment.

"Close the door behind you then," CAPCOM instructed them. "Just on the off chance the interior is pressurized."

Joe and Harry did as they were told, sealing the outer door before struggling and finally opening the inner one. More compressed air escaped. When it cleared, both men stepped inside.

Chapter 45

Joe and Harry found themselves in a gunmetal-gray corridor. Rows of struts, spaced ten feet apart, ran up from the floor across the ceiling and down the other side. A dim ribbon of light glowed at their feet and ran the length of the hallway, disappearing around a curve. Vertical slits of soft lighting appeared at eye level on the struts closest to them. Joe could hear the quickening hiss of his breath going in and out, the thump of his heartbeat pounding in his ears. But it wasn't only from the wonderment before them. Joe was also feeling an incredible weight pressing down on him.

Their space suits clocked in at an astonishing hundred and eighty pounds, including the backpack. While outside the moon's gravity amounted to seventeen percent of what it was on Earth. In here, it felt somewhere closer to fifty. That meant each man was effectively carrying around ninety pounds of gear. Hence the rushing blood and the beads of sweat collecting on both men's faces.

"Houston, tell me to God you're receiving this," Joe said, breathing hard.

There was no response.

Joe turned to Harry, who seemed to be having a moment of his own. "Have you been able to get through to Mission Control?"

Harry moved over to the wall or bulkhead or whatever the hell it was and pressed his gloved hand against the smooth darkened surface.

"Harry, don't flake out on me, man."

"Huh?" Harry took a few steps forward and a new set of vertical lights flickered on. It reminded Joe of the lander and how it would remain in standby until one of them woke it up. Maybe the same thing was happening here. The installation, one not likely built by human hands, was stirring awake.

His gaze dropped back to the corridor. A rough measurement put it at twenty feet across. The distance between the floor and ceiling was also twenty feet. Continuing his rough estimates, Joe counted ten feet as the length between each of the struts. Multiples of ten. He was seeing it again and again.

"They've been fixing it," Harry said, looking around.

"Houston, are you there?" Joe called out again.

"Did you hear what I said?" Harry's voice was strained, emphatic.

"Fixing it how?" Joe asked, convinced that if they returned to the vacuum, Houston would be there. And yet Joe was also thoroughly hesitant to leave in case they somehow got locked out and never made it back inside.

The glare from the lights on the struts made Harry's olive skin look even darker. "If you bend over and study the floor, you can see where it's been patched. The materials are close, but not identical. Same thing goes for the walls. I'm sure it's the same up and down the corridor and into any room we're likely to find."

"Okay, fine," Joe nearly snapped, but bit his tongue. "What are you trying to say?"

"I've seen patch jobs before," Harry said, running a hand along a wall joint. "I've also seen full-on renovations and this strikes me as the latter."

While Joe had an engineering background, Harry's was far more extensive and impressive. "Okay, I'm listening."

"If I had to guess, I'd say this place has been here a long time and the current occupants had to work with what they had." He stopped down the corridor in his heavy boots, pointing at all the places where someone with knowledge of such things might notice asymmetries. Obsessing over tiny flaws was normally a personality trait that got regular folks on Earth into trouble. In this place, however, Harry's obsessive tendencies were having the opposite effect. He grew quiet for a moment, deep in thought. Then finally—"If you ask me, I'd say we're dealing with a Scott's hut situation."

Joe felt his neck straighten. "A what?"

"In 1911, the Antarctic explorer Robert Falcon Scott built a hut on the shore of Cape Evans on Ross Island. In the years that followed, the hut was used by other explorers who were passing through. In many cases they supplemented its stores and repaired whatever needed fixing. It resulted in a patchwork of renovations and a rather eclectic look."

"You're saying whoever made these repairs wasn't the same group that built it?"

Harry nodded. "The geology of the rock formation outside supports that. If I had to guess, the original work was done…"

"Go on," Joe urged him.

294

"Well, I almost said thousands of years ago. But that isn't right. You see, the moon is made up of four distinct geological layers: core, mantle, crust and finely crushed rocks on the surface."

"No kidding," Joe snapped, eyeing his dusty boots. "So what'd you find?"

"It's the dust layer that provides the best chances of finding a date," Harry told him. "Which is why I compared the layers of dust near the newer sections to the ones near the older parts. By my estimates, the place was built around twenty-five to thirty million years ago."

Joe's hands cupped his visor.

"And who knows what state it was in when the latest tenants found it."

"I'm just trying to wrap my head around what you're saying."

Harry nodded. "It's far out, I know. But that's what I'm seeing."

"But if the original inhabitants are long gone," Joe said, taking Harry's observations to their logical conclusion, "then where are the folks who live here now?"

Harry didn't have an answer to that one. For Joe, that only served to elevate the fear that was fighting to take over. A beep in his ear indicated their oxygen levels were down to twenty percent.

"All this extra weight has gobbled up our air," Joe said, wishing, at the same time, they could both leave and stay.

"You're right, we should head back," Harry suggested, ever the cautious and calculated one.

"What about the extra backpacks in the lander?"

Backpack was slang for the portable life support system (PLSS), a forty-pound device that enabled extra-vehicular activity such as this.

"Houston's not going to like that, Joe. We might need every last drop during our rendezvous with the orbiter."

"I don't wanna head back," Joe said. "Not yet. I mean, hell, we're barely in the door and already we gotta leave?"

"There'll be other missions," Harry said, a pleading quality in his eyes.

"Yes, but we don't know that, not for sure. And it may not be us again. I say we leave when we're down to thirteen percent."

"That's cutting it a little close, don't you think, Joe?"

Joe was growing more impatient. "It will be if we keep wasting all our air arguing. We gotta find something to take back with us. Otherwise, we'll both be left to wonder what all this was about."

"Fine," Harry relented, although clearly strained. Breaking protocol wasn't easy for a guy who liked to make sure the items on his nightstand were always laid out in symmetrical patterns.

The two men pushed forward, the corridor illuminating their path with every laborious step. They came to a large and brightly lit room filled with what might have passed for a med lab. An eight-foot-long metallic operating table stood in the center of the room. Next to it sat a tray that contained tiny metal pellets in sizes ranging from the tip of a ballpoint pen down to what looked like flecks of metallic dust. Joe stared at them, mesmerized. They seemed to be shimmering in the soft light.

"Whatcha got there?" Harry asked, intrigued by discoveries of his own.

"I'm not sure. But tell me you got a big enough sample bag to fit everything here."

Harry fumbled through a pouch at this waist and produced one. "Will this do?"

Joe took it. "It'll have to," he said, carefully lifting the metal tray with his thick gloves and dumping the contents along with the tray into the plastic bag and sealing it. Joe lifted the transparent bag and examined the prize they'd taken from an alien medical facility. It looked to him like a range of the world's smallest ball bearings. It was hard to tell what, if anything, was inside or what they would be doing in an area like this. What could possibly be the point of a medical device small enough to fit on the head of a pin?

Chapter 46

Site 17
Xinjiang, China

Dr. Zhou watched with acute impatience as the tendrils of smoke lifted from the alien figure lying before him.

From a million miles away, a voice he vaguely recognized as Karen's was asking him a question. "Is it still alive?"

For what felt like an infinity, Zhou didn't have an answer to her question until at last the smoke had cleared enough for him to get a better look. He reached out one of his gloved hands and touched part of the creature's chest not covered by the metallic mesh shirt it was wearing. Although its flesh was a different color from human skin, he could see it was supple. He studied the chest, watching for signs of movement. But who was to say the rules that governed human biology would also be at work here? Exo-biologists, a fancy term for folks who imagined how life forms from other planets might look, were often critical of Hollywood depictions showing humanoid figures. That wasn't the way it would be, these scientists often lamented. Human beings had a fairly unique physiology, even on our own planet. The chances we would encounter another intelligent species that resembled us in any way, shape or form was ludicrous. Well, if he ever got the chance, Zhou was eager to tell them how wrong they had been.

"Dr. Zhou." This time the voice belonged to Sienna. "They're going to be here any minute."

Zhou nodded, painfully transfixed. Seeing the figure before through the glass had been like looking at a two-dimensional picture. This was something else. Tactile and real in a way he hadn't anticipated.

Even from an initial inspection, there was no clear sign of the being's sex. He hadn't noted breasts nor a bulge between its legs. But he also knew from Sienna's frantic update that there wouldn't be time for any of that.

"It's changing," Karen said, still beside him. She was looking at the face.

Zhou followed her gaze. The creature's eyelids, larger than our own, but recognizable as lids nevertheless, were still firmly shut. But that wasn't what Karen had been drawing his attention to. Its skin was no longer the color of sage. Dark circles had formed around the eyes. The flesh on the cheeks was turning purple and, in some places, black.

"It's decomposing," Karen said.

If Zhou was going to get a sample, he needed to grab one soon before it rotted down to the bone. He placed his gloved index and thumb on either side of its mouth and squeezed. The opening itself was rather small and yet he watched a pair of thin lips slightly part. He held out his hand and called for the scalpel. Karen obliged and waited with the small sample tubes. Zhou made several incisions in various parts of its body, sealing each into a properly labeled plastic container.

That was when the Chinese soldiers began pounding on the red steel door that separated them, ordering them to open up. Zhou and Karen shared a look. There was no question they would need to surrender. Zhou used the scalpel to cut a hole near the ankle of his biosuit seconds before Chinese troops burst into the chamber and arrested them.

•••

Every member of Site 17 was brought to a local Chinese army base and locked ten apiece into a mirrored row of jail cells.

Sienna was still reeling from Devon's death. He had stood there defiantly, like the Tiananmen Square Tank Man decades earlier. Back then, a lone, defiant protester had held up a column of tanks until friends or sympathizers had whisked him away. Devon hadn't been so lucky. The Chinese had apparently also learned a thing or two since 1989, namely that the penalty for making them look weak was death.

She couldn't help but wonder whether the same fate awaited each of them. In spite of being indoors, Sienna felt herself struggling for air. Hard as it was to believe, the planet seemed to be turning on them more and more with every passing day. She wondered what future generations, if there were any, might look back and think about the present. Who was she kidding? There was no denying the world had come together, as much as a thoroughly dysfunctional planet could be expected to, and yet that had still not been enough to save humanity. She'd spent her life reading ice cores and studying glaciers. They were in retreat. That was not in debate. The question that remained, the only one worth answering, was whether *Homo sapiens* would survive the Earth's most recent attempts to wipe them out.

300

Unless, all along, you've been wrong about this, a nagging voice whispered into her ear.

Zhou and Karen were sitting across from her, one looking more despondent than the other. Hard to fathom being at the head of a world-changing discovery, only to have the carpet ripped out from under you at the last minute. That was how her father must have felt when he'd come upon something deep in the Pacific that had not only challenged his understanding of the world but also left him frightened and uncertain. Much the way Sienna was feeling now.

And what could that have been? she wondered. Her gut was telling her there was a link between Neural-Sync's use of metallic hydrogen, her father's mysterious discovery in the Pacific and the discoveries at Site 17, some thirty million years old.

"You got smoke coming out your ears," Zhou said, as he watched Sienna wrestle with her thoughts. "I suggest you save your energy."

"Not an easy thing to do, under the circumstances," she replied, crossing her arms and pressing her back against the cool stone wall.

"I wanted to thank you," he said enigmatically.

"For what?"

"When John froze, you jumped in to take his place. Not only that, but we would never have gotten that lid open if it wasn't for you."

Sienna nodded. "Not that it did us much good. The Chinese confiscated the samples, locked down the site and have thrown us all in the clink."

A grin spread over Zhou's tired face. "Anyone ever tell you you're a glass-half-empty kinda gal?"

She returned the gesture. "If you only knew."

Sienna was about to ask him what it was like seeing the alien figure up close when Li appeared before their cell. She pointed to the three of them and ordered the guard to open up. She had done something to avoid arrest herself for failing to disclose the true nature of the discovery at Site 17, which did not bode well for them.

Sienna, Zhou and Karen stood and exited the cell while the others stayed behind. A handful of voices called out, asking what was going on.

Consider yourselves the lucky ones, Sienna thought, but didn't have the heart to say.

Li brought them up three flights of stairs. Their next stop was an interrogation room and copious amounts of torture, Sienna was positive of that. Which was why she was shocked when Li led them outside and toward a black civilian van.

"What's going on?" Zhou asked.

"I know what you did back at the site," Li told him. "Once the base commander finds out, he'll have you executed at once."

An ashen look came over Zhou's normally stoic features.

"What about the others?" Sienna asked.

"As soon as the commander realizes the futility of holding them, they will be released. The site and all proof of it is what my military is interested in protecting." She turned to Zhou again. "Which is why you must leave immediately. But only on one condition."

Zhou regarded her knowingly.

"You must honor your promise to me and my family."

He took her hands. "I will."

The sparkle of hope in her eye said she believed him. "You are a man of your word and I thank you. I've

302

already instructed the driver to bring you across the border into Mongolia. There you will reach the airport in Golvi-Altay and head for home. Now go."

Zhou took her hands and kissed them. Then the three climbed on board before the van pulled away.

It wasn't until they had left the base and crossed the Mongolia border that Sienna's mind returned to something Li had said. "Why was she so certain you would have been executed?"

Karen was shaking her head in a disapproving way.

Zhou reached down and removed an object he'd stashed in his shoe. But Sienna knew what it was before he brought it into the light. Zhou had kept one of the biological samples he'd taken from the alien body. Now, no matter how the Chinese military attempted to cover up the truth, tangible proof existed of what they had found at Site 17.

Chapter 47

Apollo 20, 1975
Tsiolkovskiy Crater

Joe Knight stood on the lunar surface for the second time in his life, eyeing with anticipation and no small amount of dread the torn wing of the alien facility they had found during Apollo 18. Hard to imagine that had been nearly two years ago.

1974 had brought with it Apollo 19, where the three of them had been tasked with playing backup once again. But Joe, Harry and Ron hadn't been completely out of the loop. Far from it—during Apollo 19, they'd filled the CAPCOM role, helping to direct the action from Mission Control as a fresh crew explored the alien installation. NASA had dubbed it Icarus One and its missing inhabitants Icarians.

Apollo 18 had proven to be something of a mixed blessing for Joe. It had been difficult returning home from perhaps the most important space mission of all time only to be threatened with life imprisonment or execution if he ever breathed a word of what they had discovered on the far side of the moon. He wasn't a man driven by ego or adulation. That was one of the character traits that had won him a seat in the first place. But returning home as regular old Joe, rather than Joe the astronaut who'd walked on the moon… well, that had proved a different kind of challenge.

As soon as he had arrived, he'd handed over the sample bag they had filled with those twinkling metal spheres. His engineering mind had struggled to make sense of what he was looking at and what, if anything, these tiny objects might have been used for. The folks at NASA were also at a loss. On more than one occasion, Joe would swing by the lab, inquiring as to whether they'd finally figured out what the exotic-looking metal was made of. For the first few months, the only answer he got was, "We haven't tested them yet." Or, "We don't know." Soon enough, he started hearing a different kind of answer.

"I'm sorry, Joe," the lead scientist told him. "We don't know what you're talking about."

"What do you mean, you don't know?"

"We don't have any record of samples like that ever arriving."

This had only served to strain Joe's already tenuous grip on his temper, that shadowy mark on his personality he had struggled to control his entire life. "Wait a sec, Mac, you did get Harry's rock samples and those bits of broken debris we collected in the shattered part of the corridor, right?"

"Yes, we got all that."

"But not the twinkling metal spheres?"

"There wasn't anything in the bag you handed over except a metal tray and we haven't gotten to that yet."

"But the chest cameras we were wearing," Joe protested. "Surely, you can see Harry and I putting them into the bag."

"Sorry, Joe. Archives isn't my department. Besides, those films were black and white and grainy as all hell."

Something stank and stank bad. Despite opting to bite his tongue in that moment, that was exactly what Joe remembered thinking. He knew from experience there wasn't anything that could be gained from angering the head technician, even if the man was lying or had been told to lie.

That had only strengthened Joe's resolve to make it back to the moon. And if he did, he'd vowed the next time he would keep something for himself.

"Joe," a voice called over the radio in his space suit.
"Huh?"

"I been asking if you're ready to head inside," Evans said. "Time's a-wasting."

NASA, in their infinite wisdom, had seen fit to shuffle the crew responsibilities on Apollo 20. They'd decided this time that Harry Schmitt would stay with the orbiter and that Ron Evans would join Joe down on the surface. The two men got along great. That wasn't the issue. Joe just knew entering the labyrinth of corridors inside was an experience that tested a person in ways they couldn't imagine. Two years ago, it had rooted him and Harry in place for precious minutes as they'd marveled at their surroundings, their minds abuzz with questions about the people who had built the place and their intentions for Earth.

"Okay, let's move," Joe said. "Houston, we're about to enter Icarus One."

"Copy that, Joe," CAPCOM replied. "Good luck and Godspeed."

•••

Joe and Ron Evans made their way through the airlock and inside the complex. Several of the corridors and rooms closest to the entrance had already been explored and documented. The goal for this particular excursion was to push into a large dark spot on their map and see what, if anything, was there. It was an objective they knew might require more air than the standard backpacks would allow, which was why Joe and Ron were each carrying a backup. Except each pack weighed forty pounds. Not such a big deal in zero-G. But a far bigger and heavier deal in here at fifty percent of Earth's gravity.

They set the packs down by the airlock entrance. This way, if they started running low on air, they could always double back, swap out the old units and continue the mission—a hard lesson they had learned during Apollo 18.

Dusty footprints on the floor spoke of the last Apollo crew to walk these halls and the roughly hundred and forty pounds of tech the Pentagon had instructed them to bring back. Now it was Joe and Ron's turn again and they were doing all they could to make up for lost time.

Red smiley stickers on doors and along hallways indicated areas already explored. The streak of soft lighting along the floor veered left and right as they pressed on.

Eventually, they left the red stickers behind them. Beyond this point were places never before seen by human eyes.

Joe could hear Ron's heavy breathing.

"Keep yourself steady," Joe advised him. "Get your breathing under control or you're gonna chew through all your oxygen before we get there."

"Roger that," Ron replied. "I just don't like being cut off from Houston like this."

"Houston's a quarter of a million miles away. If we run into any problems, there isn't a whole heck of a lot they can do to help."

"I get that," Ron said. "But they sure helped Apollo 13 out of a bind."

Ron did have a point, although there wasn't anything that could be done about establishing contact, short of blasting the roof off this place. Their radio signals weren't able to penetrate the walls of this place and there was nothing either of them could do about that.

Please, God, Joe thought ironically. *Grant us the serenity to accept the things I cannot change, the courage to change the things I can, and the wisdom to know the difference.*

They followed the corridor to the right. As they approached, vertical lights on the walls blinked on, pushing away the immediate darkness before them.

They passed two sealed rooms on their right.

Ron poked a thumb over his shoulder. "Shouldn't we take a peek inside?"

"Maybe afterward," Joe said, continuing on.

"Haven't you considered that every door we find could be hiding a cure for cancer or an end to hunger?"

"This isn't *Let's Make a Deal*," Joe scolded him. "We didn't come here to guess which room holds the biggest breakthrough. We'll get to them—if not us, the next group."

Ron didn't seem all that satisfied with Joe's answer.

"Look," Joe said, after stopping and turning around. "Our mission is to explore this dark patch on the map and that's exactly what I intend to do." What Joe didn't bother to tell Ron was that he expected this area might just hold the greatest breakthroughs of all. Why? The main reason was the layout of Icarus One. A central structure with spiraling arms, very much like the galaxy itself. And it stood to reason this was where they kept their most prized possessions.

"There's nothing to say we can't split up," Ron said, thinking outside the box, as always.

Joe nodded. "No, there isn't. If you do, just be careful with what you touch and be sure to keep in close radio contact."

"Roger that," Ron said and peeled away, retracing his steps to the first sealed door they had passed.

Joe carried on, following the hallway as it slowly bent to the left. Twenty feet on, he came to a break in the wall. He swiveled his helmet as well as the light connected to it, revealing what looked like an arched doorway. His pulse quickened.

Easy, Joe, that old familiar voice said.

He had closed the distance by half when he saw the arch come into view and he suddenly realized there was no door. Upon reaching the entrance, Joe peered into the darkness, the tiny light from his helmet swallowed by the immense size of the chamber.

He took a single step inside and watched the room explode with dozens of horizontal rings of orange and red light. The illumination climbed the walls around him, quickening as it reached the domed ceiling, ending as a single bright glowing ring above. The residual flashes of orange and red gradually faded, leaving only the sun-like ring of light above him. Joe stared at it in wonder, lowering his sun visor to protect his retinas from the intense brightness. But Joe's comparison to the sun wasn't entirely accurate, was it? Now that he thought of it, the blissful glow trickling down on him from above looked far less like the sun than it did light from heaven

309

itself. The thought was a strange one, even for a guy like Joe who had been raised Catholic, but hadn't sat in a pew since his first Communion.

"Joe," Ron's voice said, intruding on the moment. "You there?"

"Not now, Ron," he snapped. "I'm busy."

"Well, don't get so caught up you run out of oxygen. I'm already down to fifteen percent. I'm gonna swap backpacks."

"Sounds good," Joe said, slowly spinning around with his arms outstretched. He was basking in the light, soaking in the calming, Zen vibe fluttering through every nerve fiber in his being.

"I suggest you do the same."

Joe nodded, even though Ron wasn't there to see it. "Sure thing, Ron."

But Joe wasn't on the moon at all, was he? No, he was back home in Texas with his sweet Lou-Ellen, cradled in the nook of his arm, staring up at him adoringly. He was nestled in a cocoon of love and total acceptance and a big part of him never wanted to leave this place.

He'd been spinning for several minutes when he suddenly blinked and shuddered. The effect was jarring, like being woken from a wonderful dream only to find yourself in a cold and desolate landscape.

That was when he looked down at his feet and noticed the metal plaque. Joe squinted, trying to make out the strange symbols etched into the titanium faceplate. They resembled artifacts he'd seen in books from Ancient Egypt. But these shapes were far more geometric. Triangles, circles, squares, all in varying sizes and configurations.

Joe's eyes left the plaque and settled on his boots, powdered gray from the moon's dusty surface. A new source of light shone beneath them. Joe took a step back and gasped when he saw the face beneath a thick pane of glass. Whether they were male or female, he couldn't say, but they were rail-thin, like taffy stretched out on a hot summer's day. And although they didn't look to Joe like any person he'd ever seen, they did have two distinct arms and legs. The figure was dressed in a tight-fitting mesh body suit.

A call from Ron startled him. "Joe, I was just outside, about to give Houston an update when Harry came on the line from the orbiter. He said he saw a large glowing craft hovering above Icarus One. Said he suddenly lost sight of it."

Ron's words weren't making any sense. "That can't be right, Ron, we're the only ones out here."

"Apparently not. I suggest you start headi—"

A burst of static rattled Joe's ears.

"Ron, do you copy me?"

He called again, but the only reply was the soft hiss of static.

Chapter 48

The vein that ran down over Joe's temple was engorged now and thumping wildly. "Okay, stay put, Ron, I'm heading your way." Joe checked his oxygen tank and saw he was down to nine percent. He swore, fighting like mad to put one leg in front of the other. The sense of being in a nightmare was strong now. Any moment he would wake up sitting in the lander, waiting for separation and entry onto the moon's surface. He was sure of it.

"Come on, dammit," he shouted, when that didn't happen. The lactic acid torturing his thighs was also burning much-needed oxygen.

A stream of static continued from Ron's radio.

Joe was about ten feet from the arched doorway when he caught movement in the darkened corridor. He stopped abruptly. "Ron?"

Something tall and thin came striding into the domed room with the labored gait of a giraffe and the body of a humanoid. It was dressed in a dark, tight-fitting mesh suit just like the elongated body he had seen lying beneath the glass case like a Virginia slim cigarette.

In case of emergency, break glass, he thought and almost cackled with hysterical and terrified laughter.

Keep your head on your shoulders, young man, he scolded himself, the way his father used to whenever Joe stepped out of line, which in those early days was more often than not.

Joe's eyes traced up the figure's lean body, distinctly aware that its height measured at least eight feet tall. Between what he took for shoulders sat an octagonal helmet with a shaded visor. It turned its body, as though in slow motion, watching as another just like him entered. Then came Ron, shuffling forward, followed by a third being.

Joe would have marveled at how majestic they looked had he not been two seconds away from crapping himself.

The equally terrified expression on Ron's face did nothing to ease Joe's certainty the Three Bears had just come home and found Goldilocks in one of their beds.

"Ron, do you read me?" Joe called out over the radio, his tongue dry and fighting him on every word.

His fellow astronaut must have seen his lips move and shook his head.

The group began heading toward Joe, who felt himself backing up, almost involuntarily. For a split second, an image crossed his mind of running at full speed and taking the lead guy out at the knees. He glanced down at his air and saw it was at five percent.

I'll probably suffocate before I even get there, he thought, resigning himself to his fate. Besides, killed by an advanced alien species wasn't the worst way to go out.

The lead being stopped ten feet from where Joe stood. Lifting an arm, it tapped something on its wrist. Joe wondered if this was where the floor dropped out from under him. Or better yet, whether they were

313

waking up their friend, who looked to Joe like he could very well be sleeping.

Instead, plumes of condensed air began shooting out from vents in the walls and even the ceiling, filling the chamber with a rather dense cloud. Before Joe could make a run for it, the cloud quickly grew thicker.

The lead creature studied its wrist again and then lifted both arms to remove its helmet. The other two followed suit.

That was great for them, but Joe's air was down to three percent and the alarms were blaring in his ears like mad.

Each breath was getting harder and harder, but Joe still couldn't take his eyes off the three alien faces staring back at him. Their skin was mostly pale with a slight hint of gray, or was it green? Joe couldn't say which. They had eyes and ears and noses, even chins. Except their features were small, one might say tiny. For the first time in his life, Joe felt like little more than an ape next to these otherworldly and graceful beings.

The one in the middle approached him with his hand out. Joe counted the fingers and saw that there were five. Hanging from the palm was a cup. The creature held it up to his face, showing him how to use it.

Joe removed his helmet and accepted the mask. Across the room, Ron was doing the same. He pressed it to his lips and drew in a breath. Cool air filled his lungs and a sense of relief washed over him. The rim of the device somehow sealed to his face, freeing up his hands.

"Thank you," Joe said.

The being who had handed him the mask watched him, tilted his head inquisitively and then looked back at the others. The leader tapped his wrist again. As soon as he was done, the alien began speaking in a beautiful, melodic voice, one that sounded to Joe's ear like the melancholy song from a humpback whale. Of course, neither Joe nor Ron understood a word of it.

From twenty feet away, Ron, now wearing a breather, had his shoulders arched in a shrug.

"Do you speak English?" Joe asked, feeling like an idiot tourist trekking through Europe.

His question was no sooner out when he heard their singsong language echoing back at them from every direction. It was as though the walls were one giant speaker.

The lead being spoke and a split-second later Joe received the shock of his life.

"Yes, the language you call English is one of many we know."

"You have got to be shitting me," Joe replied without thinking.

The translator went to work, producing what Joe could only assume was a look of confusion on their faces.

"My name is Joe," he said, patting his chest. "What do they call you?"

The lead being bowed. "There is no known translation for my name. I am known as the crosser of great distances."

"Strider," Ron said. "That's what we'll call you."

"That sounds agreeable."

"Let me start with the obvious," Joe began. "Why have you come here?"

"We are in search of new species and new opportunities."

Joe's brow scrunched up. "Opportunities?"

"Opportunities of exchange," Strider clarified.

"Oh, you mean trade," Joe said, relieved. "You would like to trade with the people of Earth?"

"That is correct."

"But why us? I mean, what do we have you can't find anywhere else?"

"What you call a rare Earth mineral that only exists in the deepest parts of your oceans, one that is very precious to us. We have collected it from many surrounding worlds. Yours is the last within our reach."

"You mean you can't just find it on another planet in some other solar system?"

"That is correct. Even our advanced ships have their limits."

Joe was suddenly struck with the bizarre realization that an interplanetary trade deal was taking place and he was the lead negotiator.

"But with all your advanced technology, why not just go and take it?"

Ron threw him a look, but frankly, if these guys were smart enough to get here, there was no way they hadn't already thought of that.

"It may surprise you to learn," Strider replied, "but both of our species stand to benefit a great deal from contact. My people gain access to the mineral we require. In exchange, your people will receive new technologies that will greatly help your world."

"What kind of technologies?" Joe asked, his mind giddy with the possibilities.

"There are many. We can show you how to shrink the size of your current computing machines. Make them infinitely more powerful and portable."

"And that translation business," Joe said. "We could really use that on Earth too."

"One day you will have it. Once every ten years we will return to ensure that our deep-sea machinery continues to function properly. And it will be at such time that we will provide your people with one new technology."

Joe was nodding. "New tech every ten years."

"That is correct."

"Wow, that sounds like a great deal, Joe," Ron said, a grin running from one side of his face to the other. "Go ahead and accept, before they change their minds."

Joe held up his hands. "I should tell you up front, as great as it sounds, neither Ron nor I are really in a position to say yes. I hope you understand."

"Uh, Joe," Ron said sternly.

"With whom shall we speak then?"

Joe frowned. "Well, that's a tough one. It's hard to say who speaks on behalf of all of humanity."

"We are quite familiar with the tribal nature of your species," Strider told him.

"Great, so then you understand."

"Yes, we understand that at this moment there are two dominant tribal units on your planet. The Americans and the Soviet Union."

"That's one way to sum it up," Joe said, surprised by how well versed they seemed to be about Earth's politics.

"Do you suppose the Soviet Union would be more receptive to our deal?"

The muscles on Joe's face went slack. Twenty feet away, Ron didn't look much better. If these tall stick men started funneling new technology to the USSR, the whole world would soon be speaking Russian. That wasn't a risk Joe or any red-blooded American was willing to take. Sure, it might turn out these aliens were

317

getting the better deal, but what were a few minerals compared to being ruled by a Communist dictatorship? Besides, it was hard to miss something you didn't even know you had.

"Okay, okay, we accept," Joe said, panting. "But you'll need to work out the details with our people back home."

"That is acceptable," Strider said, the English translation echoing around them.

Joe thought of the metal beads he'd found in the med lab during his last mission. He asked Strider about them.

"They are the casings for enhancements," Strider said, reaching into a pouch on his belt and dropping one in Joe's palm. Joe looked down and saw the tiny speck shimmering back at him. "It is made from a precious metal. One only we can make. For now, we can provide it for you. In time, you will learn to make it on your own."

Strider excused himself after that and asked the other two to escort them back to the airlock. Joe and Ron were both walking on air the entire journey home. The dream had turned into a nightmare only to turn back into a dream. His head was spinning. But there was one thing he was sure of. Joe Knight had just saved the world from a Communist takeover and no one was ever going to know about it.

Chapter 49

...*Over to Japan now, where fishermen from the Ryukyu Islands have been reporting strange lights out at sea. Footage captured by the captain of one ship purports to show a large craft descending from the sky before splashing into the ocean. Other witnesses claim to have seen similar objects rising out of the water and darting away at impossible speeds. While accounts differ, one thing they all seem to agree on. Whatever they were, they were silver, emitted an eerie glow and didn't make a sound.*

The astronomers and scientists we spoke to attribute the sightings to a wide range of natural phenomena, a list that includes meteors, bright stars and hallucinations, but sadly, not otherworldly beings. Or in this case, perhaps a little too much sake.

In other news, air quality around the world continues to deteriorate as the death toll from lung-related illnesses rises for the seventh year in a row...

Chapter 50

New Everglades, Florida

Ben scratched the side of his head, struggling to come to terms with everything Joe had just told him. It was dark outside, the rhythmic sound of cricket chirps filling the night air.

"So that's how it's gone down these last fifty years," Joe said, wrapping up his story. "The Icarians show up every ten to twelve years, they meet with a committee of scientists, politicians and military personnel, hand over a new piece of tech and then reaffirm the treaty for the following ten years. Wasn't long before I was shut out of the process with nothing more than a pat on the head. Looking back, I should never have agreed."

"What's made you change your mind?" Ben asked him.

"Isn't it obvious?" Joe snapped. "Look what they've turned us into. A nation of crack addicts. And I don't mean the stuff you find on the street. I'm talking about techno-crack. Without a doubt, the government's the worst of them all. It's part of the reason they cut me out of the loop. When the Icarians were dangling advances in things like miniaturization, nanotech, fusion power, the last thing the bureaucrats wanted to hear was someone telling them to slow down and think things over. After the first delivery, a microchip hundreds of times smaller and faster than anything we had, it became clear to me what the Icarians were up to. They weren't giving us their top-tier tech, but stuff just far enough ahead to keep us coming back for more. And we did, over and over, to the point now that technological innovation in our country's at an all-time low. I'm sure you didn't know that. And why would you? In one way or another, most of what's out there is thanks to them."

Ben grew quiet, wondering what that said about Neural-Sync. He thought about the sample Joe had sent in to Tatiana, the one Strider had handed him back on Icarus One. Clearly, tests showed both of them were metallic hydrogen. Was alien technology his company's secret sauce and could his discovery of that fact have precipitated his attack? It seemed hard to imagine he wouldn't know the source of his company's solitary invention.

Joe was watching him with a certain look of amusement. "Heavy shit, isn't it? Now you see why I wish I'd told those aliens to take a hike."

"And if you had," Ben reminded him, "what was stopping them from approaching the Russians?"

"Nothing," Joe said grimly. "A classic damned if you do, damned if you don't, if ever I've seen one."

Ben glanced down and remembered the date and GPS location written on his arm in blue pen. He told Joe about it. "Could that have anything to do with the next arrival?"

"It likely has everything to do with it," Joe said, steely-eyed.

Ben had also come up with a location in Arizona. Barringer Crater. Something that hadn't made sense to him at first, but after listening to Joe tell his tale, it was starting to take on new meaning. He told Joe about it.

"Far as I know, the Icarians pick a different location every time they visit," Joe explained, heading back to brew a fresh pot. "The first year they did it inside a secret chamber behind Mount Rushmore."

"Secret chamber? I didn't know there was one."

"Few do, and that's the point. They like to meet in out-of-the-way places. The notion of getting them in front of the United Nations or the White House is preposterous. But that implant company of yours is only the tip of a much deeper iceberg than most folks are willing to accept. Imagine waking up one morning to learn everything you'd been told was a lie. Imagine other nations catching wind that the United States was receiving advanced technology from an alien race. It's more than they're willing to accept. That's why it has stayed a secret for so long. Every once in a while, someone gets a hold of the truth and tries to go public. Soon enough their life, assuming they still have one, is in tatters. Rumors of pedophilia are leaked to their employer. Bam, they're fired. Private photos of the person's spouse are hacked off a phone. Bam, they're divorced. Isn't long before they're either leaping off the end of a bridge or running around talking like a nutjob."

Ben felt a pain in his belly as though he'd been struck. What Joe had just said described perfectly what Ben had gone through over the last few days. Here he was, in the New Everglades, trying to track down a man he'd never met to discuss an event in American history that most would say had never happened. By all appearances, Ben was the walking definition of a nut.

Had he been about to leak proof of the biggest conspiracy in the country's history? Had Amanda's death been an attempt to strip him of any credibility? And when that hadn't worked, was that why the plan had been shifted to neutralize him entirely?

The next question was much harder to answer. How could any of this be stopped?

•••

"So are there any signs before the Icarians' actual arrival?" Ben asked, pacing back and forth. "A blood moon, a total eclipse or dogs and cats suddenly getting along?"

Joe returned with more coffee, grinning. "That's an easy one. Their return usually starts with a flap of unexplained sightings. You know how it goes. Advanced craft of unknown origin whizzing through our skies, plunking in and out of the world's oceans."

"Sounds like a typical UFO sighting to me."

Joe nodded. "I suppose it does. That's what they are, after all. Extraterrestrials."

"Yeah, but something isn't adding up," Ben said. "You told me the agreement with the Icarians began in 1975 after Apollo 20."

"That's right."

Ben did a simple search and pulled up a website on his phone. "UFO sightings like the one you described do tend to come in groups and often tend to be years apart. That much is true. But the phenomenon as we understand it pre-dates the Apollo 20 mission by thirty years."

Ben was referring to sightings by pilots during World War Two who claimed to have witnessed glowing balls of light following their planes, craft they nicknamed 'foo fighters.' Or Kenneth Arnold's sighting from 1947.

There were plenty more, and Ben was in no mood to list them all.

"You're absolutely right," Joe admitted. "I never did ask Strider directly, but I suspect their people have been coming here for many years."

"Strider also suggested they would never take resources from another planet without first entering into an agreement with its inhabitants."

"He did," Joe confirmed, growing impatient. "But where are you going with all of this?"

"If Strider was telling you the truth, then what have they been doing here all this time?"

Joe shook his head. He was staring down at his feet. "I'm not sure. Perhaps they were studying us?"

"That's what I thought. But for what purpose?"

Joe didn't have an answer to this one either.

Ben's mind was busy comparing what Joe had told him to everything else he'd learned when something clicked. He told Joe about Dr. Lang's discovery that an unusual signal on the radio band was sending instructions for NEDs to release opiorphin into people's systems, effectively feeding them low doses of anesthetic. "But Lang couldn't tell where the signal was coming from."

Joe swallowed hard. "Is it somewhere between the microwave and radio wave range?"

"Exactly. You know the one?"

The radio equipment Ben had seen when he first arrived was in the far corner of the room. Joe headed there now, switching on the power, drumming a beat with his foot while he waited. "I became something of a ham radio enthusiast after I left NASA," he explained. "I used to chat with some of the locals. The few truck drivers left on the roads, hauling goods up and down the state. And sometimes I'd just scan the dial, looking for someone to talk to. So one day I came across what sounded to me like what astronomers call a fast radio burst. I didn't think it was possible since FRBs, as they're called, are extremely powerful and originate from deep in outer space. Not to mention I should never have been able to pick it up on my little ham. Well, it took me weeks to triangulate where that signal was coming from and when I finally did, the answer didn't surprise me one bit."

"The moon?" Ben said, fear clawing at his every breath. Joe didn't need to tell him he was right, Ben could see it written all over his face. "But it doesn't make sense."

"How so?" Joe said, not catching the full measure of what it meant.

"If you're right and the radio bursts as you say are being sent from the moon's surface, the only logical culprits are the Icarians. Which begs the question. Why would they be sending a signal designed to anesthetize people with NEDs, a number that's skyrocketing by the day?"

The placid look on Joe's face was gone now. "Maybe to keep them docile. Stop them from asking too many questions."

That was what Ben had also been thinking. "Which leads me to the most disturbing question of all: what is it the Icarians are trying to hide?"

The spell was broken by the sound of an incoming text. Ben checked and saw it was Lori.

Ben, get out of there right away!

Outside, the dog began barking. The look of concern on Joe's face mirrored his own. "I think we got company."

Chapter 51

"Any chance you have an extra shotgun to spare?" Ben asked, quickly peering into the darkness before he drew the curtains.

Joe stalked over to the desk with the radio and punched a red button.

"What's that for?"

"You've heard of releasing the kraken," Joe said with delight. "Well, that button releases the gators. Forgot to feed them this morning, so they should be real hungry."

Ben wanted to laugh, but all he could feel was the tightening knot in his belly and the steady drumbeat of blood in his ears. "How about that shotgun?"

Joe threw him a stern look. "Keep your pants on, will ya?" he grumbled as he bent down, reached under the easy chair and drew up a Remington pump-action shotgun.

Now Ben couldn't help himself and let out a dry, nervous laugh. "You keep a loaded gun under your reading chair?"

"Son, I keep a loaded gun under everything I can. You would too if you lived ten miles from your nearest neighbor and thirty from the police." He tossed over the weapon.

Ben caught it and racked a shell into the chamber. Outside, they heard a shriek of pain followed by a volley of shots. Then silence.

"Gators one, bad guys zero," Joe said, hunkering down next to the sliding glass door at the back of the house. Staying low, Joe winked as he made his way to the front.

A gas canister smashed through a side window five feet from Ben's position. It skittered onto the ground, kicking up a plume of ashen white smoke. Ben rolled over the ground, snatched it in one quick motion and tossed it back outside. Another crashed into the kitchen and Joe did the same.

Then came the sound of more shots being fired followed by screams. It seemed the gators were eating well after all.

Shattering glass from one of the bedrooms drew Ben's attention at once. He kicked open the door and leveled the Remington. A propane tank from Joe's back deck had been tossed through the sliding glass door. Crunching over the broken glass was a spec ops type in black camo. Ben swiveled the barrel over his chest and fired. The concussion jerked the weapon back against his shoulder as a slug caught the man square in the chest, dropping him on the spot.

Shots from outside filled the bedroom, splintering the wood paneling next to his head and the door frame behind him. Ben dove, rolling over the bed and onto the other side as more bullets tore up the spot he had just been standing in. If he stayed here a second longer, he risked getting pinned down. He bobbed his head and saw another spec ops soldier heading for the hole in the glass door.

Three... two... one.

327

Ben sprang up, ready to make it two for two, when a kick from his left sent the shotgun flying out of his hands.

Spec ops saw this and lifted his weapon. Operating on pure instinct, Ben leapt at the soldier in black, curling his torso in mid-air and sending his shoulder into the man's rib cage. The force of it knocked the man clean off his feet and back out onto the deck where he landed with a loud thud.

Ben hit the floor in a pile of glass that cut through his clothing. He was only about halfway up when a pair of rough, powerful hands grabbed him and threw him out of the bedroom and into the hallway. Ben's back hit the drywall, causing an indentation in the wall and a jolt of electricity up his spine. The man who threw him with such ease spun and that was when Ben recognized him as the one from the roof. The one he'd called Wiry on account of his slight stature.

Mustering his strength, Ben willed himself to his feet right in time to spot an overhand punch sailing towards his jaw. He ducked that, along with another fist that poked a clean hole right through the gyprock. Bending forward in the act of dodging, Ben twisted his shoulders, unleashing an uppercut which caught Wiry under the chin, rocking his head back. Lunging forward, Ben followed up with a left hook and then a right, the power of his blows landing into his opponent with unrestrained force. A normal man would have been killed. But not a person whose brain was as boosted as that of his opponent.

Blood ran down Wiry's chin and his left eye was already swollen shut. A couple more shots and it would all be over.

Wiry jerked his head forward, head-butting Ben on the nose, sending him reeling backwards over the coffee table and onto the couch.

Ben felt his vision bobbing and weaving in and out of focus. Wiry was coming forward now to finish him off. Ben pulled in his legs and kicked out, striking Wiry in the chest. The blow launched Wiry back against the glass door, shattering it as he fell through.

Ben staggered to his feet, ordering his legs to move forward and finish this.

"Get down," Joe shouted. Without needing to be told twice, Ben dove to the floor. He was down in a push-up position when he heard the shotgun blast and felt the wind from the pellets sail over his back and into their intended target. It was the spec ops guy he'd shoulder-checked onto the back deck and now he lay dead.

Rising to his feet, Ben caught sight of Wiry, charging at Joe.

The old man lowered his shotgun and opened up, shredding both of Wiry's legs. The assassin fell into a heap, clutching at the little that remained below his knees.

Ben and Joe made a quick search of the grounds to make sure none of them were left. From the living room came Wiry's cries of agony.

"You have anything to give him?" Ben asked, not relishing seeing anyone in a state like that, even someone who had tried to kill him.

"I might have a bit of morphine left from when my prostate tried to kill me."

Ben smiled weakly. "I wish I had your powers of invisibility." He noticed a five-inch red spot on the back of Joe's shirt. He stopped. "Hey, you got hit."

329

Joe looked down with surprise and raised his shirt. "Oh, crap. I got shot in the love handle." He inspected it some more. "Looks like it went clean through. You go take care of your friend by the sofa and I'll get the morphine."

Ben did just that, grabbing a couple of dish towels and using them to tie tourniquets around Wiry's legs. Joe showed up a minute later with two white tablets. "He gets one now and if he plays nice, one on the way to the hospital."

Wiry didn't seem to have a drop of fight left in him. He took the pill eagerly and swallowed it down without water. Then he leaned back on the living room floor, grimacing.

Joe surveyed the damage done to his home and shook his head in annoyance. "I don't think the insurance is gonna cover this, do you?"

"Depends," Ben replied. "Did you get the home invasion policy or the regular one?"

"Regular," Joe said, finding his coffee cup on the ground and inspecting the contents to see if it was still drinkable. He flicked his wrist, tossing it on the floor. Joe fished the phone out of his pocket.

"Wait a minute before you call that ambulance," Ben said. "Looks like the morphine's already kicking in."

"You wanna ask him some questions?"

Ben nodded. "One or two, yeah, but I don't think I should be here when the cops arrive."

A light shone in Joe's eyes. "Sheriff Sims will think I'm a regular Dirty Harry."

"You are, Joe," Ben assured him. "I probably wouldn't be here if it wasn't for you and your gators."

Joe rose to his feet. "Speaking of which, I gotta corral them back into the pen. Be right back."

Ben watched the old man limp out of the room and then turned back to Wiry. "How about we start with your name?" Ben said, grabbing him by the shirt and pulling him into a seated position.

Wiry moaned.

"You want me to keep the pain away? There's no one to boost your equilibrium here. Now start talking or you're gonna wish I'd left you to bleed out."

"M," the man said in a hoarse voice.

"M? What kind of a name is that?"

"The only kind that has any meaning."

"Who sent you here?"

A dribble of blood ran down the corner of M's swollen lower lip. "Isn't it obvious?"

Ben raised a fist to strike him.

"Granger." Blood was still pouring down M's legs, in spite of the tourniquets.

"Was he the one who ordered you to kill Amanda?"

"You don't have a clue, do you?" M said, a look approaching amusement forming on his battered face.

"Clue about what?"

"Of course it was me. But Granger wasn't the one who sent me. That was Lori's doing."

Ben felt his aching body stiffen with a jolt of astonishment and betrayal. "Lori? I don't believe it."

"What reason would I have to lie? Look at me. You can talk about hospitals all you want, but you know I'm not gonna make it."

"What about Michelle?"

M's face drew a blank.

"The agent they call Mirage. What can you tell me about her?"

"I haven't got the foggiest idea what you're talking about. If she's real, she's better at the game than I ever was." M's words were coming slower. His flesh was ashen, and his eyes lolled around lazily in his skull. The man was dying. "Oh," M said, drawing out the word like a drunken sailor. "I know who you're talking about."

Ben leaned over him. "You know her? Where is she?" Michelle or Mirage or whatever the hell her name was, she apparently was holding a copy of everything Ben had found. Everything that had gotten Amanda killed and thrown his life onto a knife's edge.

"Her name's not Michelle," M said, his slow grin becoming a look of surprise and then sadness. "You know the light you see when you die? It's a lie. There's nothing here but blackne—"

M went quiet and Ben shook him. "What's her name? Come on, finish what you were saying."

A hand pressed down on his shoulder. "He's gone, Ben." It was Joe.

Ben looked up at him, still reeling. His phone started to ring. It was Sienna.

"Where are you? I've been trying to call." She sounded frantic.

"Reception here is spotty. Besides, I kinda had my hands full." Ben pulled the phone away from his ear and saw that the glass was cracked.

"Is everything all right?"

"I'm alive and so is Joe. Let's just leave it at that for now."

"Hmm, that doesn't sound good. Well, I'm glad to hear you're okay. We had a few run-ins of our own in Xinjiang. You won't believe what I discovered."

"Where are you now?" he asked and then caught himself. "Wait, don't tell me. Not over the phone. Go and download Zoomis Chat, it's an app with encrypted messaging. I'll send you a location where we can meet."

332

"Okay, Ben," Sienna said. "I'll do that right away." They hung up.

The sound of Sienna's voice was like a breath of fresh air. He wanted to hear all about her visit with Dr. Zhou and what she'd learned there. But try as he might, Ben's mind kept circling back to what M had told him about Lori. Had that simply been a final act of vengeance from a foe who'd repeatedly tried to kill him? Or could it possibly be true? And how did any of that relate to M's cryptic answer about the agent's name? There was only one way to find out. Ben checked the countdown timer on his phone. The Icarian delegation was set to arrive in seventy-two hours. He would have to move fast.

Chapter 52

Joe brought Ben back to Rusty's via fan boat and they said their goodbyes. Ben assured him he would soon return to help set right whatever damage had been done to his home. Joe told him he was welcome back anytime, but that he shouldn't even consider trying to pay for the damages.

"We'll go out for dinner and a few drinks and call it even."

They shook on that with Joe promising he'd get the gunshot wound on his left flank checked out and call the police to report the attack.

From there, Ben's trusty sedan, waiting patiently for him in the parking lot by Rusty's, brought him back to the airport where a flight to Seattle would do the rest.

Six and a half hours later, Ben was in a taxi driving through punishing sheets of rain on his way to Lori's house. He sent her a text.

Ben: I need to speak with you urgently.

Five minutes later she replied.

Lori: Now? It's not a good time. Are you safe?

The cab pulled up to her house, ultra-modern with large windows that looked onto Laurelhurst Park. The wipers were on full, each pass wiping the windshield clean just long enough to catch a glimpse. But a glimpse was all he needed to see that the lights were on and someone was inside walking around.

Ben: Yes, I am. Thank you for the heads up. I need to know where you are.

It was a test of sorts. Mainly to see if he could trust her.

Lori: Out of the country, I'm afraid.

"Out of the country, my ass," Ben said. He paid the meter, got out and crossed the street, the rain drumming down around him.

Ben spotted a small terrace on the second story. The chances were good that once Lori had returned home, she had locked the front door. But terraces were often left unlocked, usually because people assumed there was no way anyone could get up there.

A recycling bin gave him a boost up to the edge of the wood planking from the deck. From there a power chin-up got him high enough to reach the railing. Ben hopped over and checked the terrace door, turning the handle and finding it unlocked. He should have been a jewel thief.

Carefully he worked his way out of the bedroom and down to the main floor. The odor of spaghetti sauce wafted up at him. The only thing he'd eaten recently was airplane food. The smell of a home-cooked meal was causing his stomach to cramp. He heard movement in the kitchen and turned the corner to see Lori about to fill a pot with noodles. She paused in the act and then grabbed the pot of boiling water, turned and flung it at him in one swift motion. Ben rolled out of the way and closed the distance before she got any other stupid ideas.

"Oh, Ben, you scared me. I didn't know it was you."

Sure you didn't, he thought, but kept to himself. "Who'd you think it was, M?"

Her face blanched.

"Yeah, don't worry. I took care of him. I do appreciate the heads up, although I'm still wondering how it was you knew of the attack if you had nothing to do with it."

"You killed M?" she asked, ignoring the second part of his statement.

Ben nodded. "Along with anyone else you send to kill me or anyone I love."

Lori feigned ignorance and did a darn good job of it. "What you're saying makes no sense. Why would I warn you, if I was trying to kill you? A few days ago, I sent M to locate you and bring you back so I could talk some sense into you. Protect you, not kill you." She fell back onto the sofa with a hard thud. It was a right-angle thing, hard as hell and probably cost a fortune. The same was true about most of the stuff in his adoptive sister's place. Joe's home in the New Everglades might have been a touch dated, but at least you didn't need a chiropractor after taking a seat.

"I didn't set out to hurt him. He came to me with a half-dozen of his friends."

Lori only shook her head.

"You must have missed the part where I told you he tried to kill me."

"I wish you'd only stopped before things got so out of hand."

"Stopped," Ben said, incredulous. "Don't you know where the NED technology came from? It sure as hell wasn't me."

Lori nodded. "I know, Ben. It comes from China."

The burst of laughter shot out of Ben's mouth and echoed around the sparsely furnished room. "Are you playing dumb or do you really not know?"

She stared up at him, defiantly. "Russia?"

"Let me guess, you were told it was tech stolen from a foreign nation we managed to back-engineer."

"Operation THOTH," she said, knitting her brow, her hands folded like a nun about to do penitence. "It's Neural-Sync's deep dark secret. We knew it didn't come from us, our role was merely to introduce it to the general population. It was part of a USA-first program. The Chinese were doing the same to us. Besides, as patriots, we all have our role to play and this was ours."

"Not mine," Ben said. "Not anymore. But you're wrong about the origin. Didn't you wonder why the stuff was so advanced? We're talking light years ahead of anything else on the market. Heck, our competition couldn't even rip us off because there was literally no way on Earth they could have duplicated the metallic hydrogen casings we were using."

"The government sent us massive shipments once every few years."

"Ten, to be exact, isn't it?"

Lori nodded.

"I'm sure you're wondering how a guy with amnesia could know such a thing. We didn't make the casings, nor were humans responsible for the microscopic circuitry they were housing."

"What are you saying? That it was…" Her eyes slowly traced their way to the ceiling.

Ben was nodding, his deep blue eyes burning into her.

"…extraterrestrial technology?" She spoke the words in short, deliberate chunks.

337

"If only you knew what I've seen these last few days."

"I wish you'd have come to me," Lori said, a pleading quality in her voice.

"Come to you? M told me you were the one who ordered him to kill Amanda."

Lori raised her arms defensively. "I did, I admit it. I ordered him to break into your house and kill your girlfriend."

"In order to frame me," Ben shouted, filling in the blanks of her sick plan. "You wanted to discredit me, so no one would believe the bombshell I was about to reveal."

"That's right," Lori said. "But please, let me explain. I was told you were about to blow the lid off of Neural-Sync and expose that our flagship product…" She drew short. "Well, let's be honest, that our *only* product came from the theft of military secrets from a foreign country. You were about to sink us, Ben, but I swear I knew nothing about any aliens."

His eyes narrowed. "You still told M to kill Amanda."

"Granger wanted both of you dead. He was enraged that you were snooping around and not heeding his warnings. He passed the order down to me and I refused to carry it out. Instead, I convinced him that killing you would draw too much attention. But framing you for Amanda's murder would save the company and your life."

"Who the hell is Granger in all of this? He's on our board of directors, that's all."

Lori shook her head fearfully. "He's a very powerful man. You don't want to cross him, trust me."

"Well, he's crossed me, so it's a little late for that."

"Granger never went into detail about what he said you had on us," she told him. "Only that you were in touch with a reporter named Elizabeth Howard and had given her a USB. But even after they got Howard, Granger knew you'd hidden the proof of what was going on somewhere else, somewhere only you knew. M attacking you as he did and causing the amnesia, well, that was just a stroke of good luck." Her face changed. "Or in your case, bad luck."

Ben rolled up his sleeves and buried his head in his hands. "But how could you? You were my sister, even if not of flesh and blood."

Lori's eyes began to tear up and she rubbed at her lids, wiping them away. "What's that written on your arm?" she asked.

"A timer," he explained. "A countdown until the aliens return to Earth in order keep the human race a bunch of tech addicts." At this point, he planned to expose what he'd learned to the world. Why not start with her? He ran through the highlights of Joe's time on the moon at Icarus One and the trade relationship that had flourished over the decades between our two races.

"And the other one?" she asked, looking more than a little overwhelmed by the magnitude of what Ben had just been recounting.

"4043191165708," Ben recited from memory. "I thought it was part of a phone number or a GPS location. I have no idea what it's for." What he was really doing was trying to figure out what he would do about Lori. She was his adopted sister. There was no excuse for her actions, however well intentioned. But should he call the cops? And if he did, what would he tell them? At this point, they had a single suspect in mind and it was him.

"Those numbers are from a Neural-Sync serial number," she said, sitting up now.

"A serial number?"

"Yes, to an NED. I deal in this stuff all day long. It indicates what production batch they're from, along with the year of delivery. This is one of the earliest models." Their eyes met. "Mine is the second oldest." She read him a string of numbers that were nearly identical except for the last digit.

There was only one reason Ben would have written down the serial number of his own NED. Because that was where he had hidden the files. Proof of everything he had discovered, in this case twice. Once before M had come to his home and framed him for murder. And again in the handful of days that had followed.

Lori sat staring up at him, a weird mix of emotion on her smooth face. "So what now?"

"You're gonna tell me how to find Granger."

Just then a message from Sienna came through on Zoomis Chat.

Sienna: I'm here.

Ben: Change of plans. Meet me at Knut's

Ben turned back to Lori. "Now, about that DVR recorder M stole from my place. I need it."

Chapter 53

Ben arrived at Knut's to find Sienna already there about to start snacking on a sandwich. They embraced and she pulled away, concerned.

"What happened to your nose? Every time I leave you, you show up with a fresh injury."

Ben smiled coyly. "I ran in to our wiry friend from St. Petersburg."

"Oh, goodness," she said, her face scrunched up.

"No need to worry," Ben assured her. "My wounds will heal. Although I can't say the same for the other guy." He turned to Knut and patted him on the shoulder with his numb hand, shaking the big guy's monocle in the process. "I may be bruised, but Knut looks like he's still asleep."

The techie's eyes were puffy and red. "I go to bed early," he said, sounding as crabby as he looked. "It might do you some good too."

Ben laughed. "I plan to sleep for a week when this is over." He set down the DVR recorder.

Knut's eyes went wide. "You found it?"

"I sure hope so," Ben replied.

Sienna ran a hand over it. "Where was it?"

"Where do I start?"

"How about from the beginning," Knut suggested, flipping up his monocle and lowering himself into a chair.

Ben did just that, telling them what he'd learned from Joe Knight about Apollo 17's discovery on the far side of the moon and the secret NASA missions that had followed. He described in detail Joe's recounting of events—the chamber with the light and the body and the unforeseen arrival of the Icarians. He told them the reason they'd said they were here, to mine a rare Earth mineral only found in the depths of the world's oceans, and their promise to offer advanced technology for the right to do so.

Knut's eyes were wide with fascination while Sienna's face registered a much more complex range of emotions.

"So these Icarians killed my father when he got too close to one of their machines," Sienna said, angry.

"It looks that way," Ben replied. "Joe spoke about Icarian maintenance ships inspecting the machinery along the ocean floor. If I had to guess, I'd say the *Archipelago* was simply in the wrong place at the wrong time. Joe also suggested the Icarians have been coming to Earth since sometime in the 1940s."

Sienna shook her head vigorously. "They've been coming for a lot longer than that."

"How can you be so sure?" he asked.

Sienna then revealed everything she had seen at Site 17 in Xinjiang, from the concrete structure millions of years old, to the realization it was the base to an ancient space elevator. But her description of the plaque and the body sent shivers up the back of Ben's neck. It was exactly the same thing Joe had seen on the moon base. But there was one notable difference that neither of them quite understood. Sienna described the alien under the glass in China as short and rather stout while the being on the moon base had been stick-like and over eight feet tall. It was a discrepancy they didn't understand.

"There's got to be an explanation," Sienna insisted.

"I think I know where to find it," Ben said. He pointed at his head. "I met with Lori just now and had a conversation I won't soon forget. When M, the assassin who attacked us in St. Petersburg, lay dying in Joe's living room, he told me he was the one who had killed Amanda."

Sienna's hand covered her mouth. "We should have known."

"That was hard enough to hear. But not nearly as hard as when he told me who had ordered him to do it."

"Your sister?" Knut said, sitting up, looking shocked and disgusted.

Ben nodded.

"That's crazy," Sienna burst out. "But why?"

He recounted his sister's explanation, that she was only saving him from a worse fate imposed by Granger.

"The guy you had lunch with?" Sienna asked, confused. "But why is he so powerful?"

"First of all, it wasn't much of a lunch," Ben admitted. "Secondly, Lori claims he really works for some shadowy government agency that hands certain bits of alien tech to US industry. Apparently, they've been doing it for years. Neural-Sync was one of their beneficiaries."

Knut exploded into a sick gale of laughter. "No wonder your implant was so much more advanced than everyone else's. The government was playing favorites."

Ben wasn't proud of that. "Seems that way. But you see, they claimed the stuff was reverse-engineered from China, which is bad enough. When Dr. Lang originally approached me with his concerns about the health risks involved, it must have made me look into things a little deeper."

"So you pulled a thread and before you knew it, the whole sweater was unraveling in your hands," Sienna said.

Mentioning Dr. Lang only reminded Ben of the numbness he noticed creeping up his arm. "There's more," he told them. "And this part is maybe the most serious of all. For some reason, the metallic hydrogen in the implant turns the human body into a kind of receiver."

Sienna's brow scrunched. "A receiver for what?"

"Instructions they're sending directly to the device."

Now Sienna was really freaked out. "To do what?"

"The signal tells the NED to stimulate the release of opiorphin, a type of anesthetic produced naturally by the body."

"Anesthetic?" Knut said. "I don't get it."

"Neither did I, at first," Ben told them. "Until it became clear. The Icarians are trying to cloud our minds, distract us, and most importantly of all, numb us."

"To what?" Sienna asked, afraid.

"Something very bad."

"Are we talking invasion here?" Knut asked, almost on a lark.

"We might," Ben said. "Maybe this is stage one. I don't know. The truth is I'm only guessing. But I think the key might be hidden in my NED. After Lori confessed her part in this, she also helped me figure out where I'd hidden the proof." He turned to Knut. "And that's why we're here."

Knut looked disappointed. "That's too bad. I thought you two just missed me."

The weak smile on Sienna's face made her position perfectly clear. She wanted to laugh, probably wanted it more than anything, but the direction the conversation had taken was freaking her out.

They moved over to Knut's workshop where the big guy flipped his monocle back and sank into his well-worn computer chair.

Ben pulled out his phone and started the Neural-Sync app as Knut opened the company's webpage on the computer.

"Tap it to the back of your neck like last time and then stare at the images you see on our phone," Knut told him.

Ben did so.

Authentication Confirmed.

"Okay, we're in." Knut said, going to the device's storage. "Yeah, see this is what confused me last time. You've got five extra gigabytes on here."

"That must be it," Ben said. "Can you extract it?"

"Who do you think you're talking to?" Knut asked him, winking. "Bring me that recorder and I'll have a look at that too."

Sienna grabbed the black box and set it on a pile of papers next to him.

"Forgive the mess, by the way, the maid is off this week," Knut said, feigning embarrassment.

"I think she's been off for a while," Sienna said, grinning. She went back to where Ben was standing.

"There's something you're hoping to find, isn't there?" she asked him.

345

"Besides proof that the government has been engaged in the most heinous coverup in US history? I suppose there is. The deeper I've gone into this, Apollo 20 and Operation THOTH, all of it, a granule of suspicion has been growing bigger and bigger."

Sienna looked at him, her green eyes warm and inquisitive. "And what's that?"

"That as clever as the government thinks they are being with all of this, the Icarians are up to something. For me, these past few days haven't been a journey of discovery, but rather a journey of rediscovery. I had already been to many of the places, spoken to many of the same people. But the one thing I couldn't find was where exactly in the Pacific I sent your father on that fateful expedition. I'm afraid whatever it was he saw went down with him and his ship."

She seemed to consider this. "You think seeing that will reveal the Icarian plan?"

"I'm hoping it will. Otherwise, we'll only grow more and more dependent on these handouts they're giving us and who knows where that will end."

"The master has delivered," Knut shouted from the other room.

Sienna shook her head. "He's good at what he does, but that doesn't change the fact that he's a weirdo."

"The best ones are." They stepped back into the workshop. "So show us what you found."

"A veritable treasure trove," Knut said. He ran his finger down the list of PDF files, clicking on a few as he went. "Top-secret files on Operation THOTH, details about Apollo 18, 19 and 20. A copy of the trade agreement between the United States and the Icarians."

"Oh, how our allies are going to love learning how they'd been shut out of the most consequential event in human history," Sienna said.

And she was right. This wasn't only going to blow up domestically. It was bound to have a colossal impact worldwide.

Then one of the folders named *Panov* caught his eye. "Click on that one," he told Knut. Inside was a recorded phone conversation. Knut played it.

In it, Ben and Nicholay were discussing the final details of the expedition. Ben glanced at Sienna beside him and saw tears streaming down her face. He put an arm around her. "It's just so hard to hear his voice. Somehow, I don't have a recording of him anywhere."

"Go back a bit, will you?" Ben asked.

Knut did.

Ben: "That's where I want you to start. There are other targets. I'll send you those when you're en route, but start there."

Nicholay: "How deep are we going?"

Ben: "Right to the bottom, Nic. The target's sitting on the ocean floor. Snap some pictures and get some clear video. We need to figure out what the damn thing is."

Nicholay: "Not a problem."

Sienna's shoulders slumped, but it wasn't only from the sound of her father's voice. It was obvious the recording didn't contain much useful information.

Ben was running through the events of the past few days at high speed when something occurred to him. He whipped out his phone and pulled up his email.

"What is it?" she asked him.

"Following your father's first descent, he sent me an image he'd taken from the sub." Ben found it and forwarded it to Knut. It was the same one Ben had stared at falling to sleep that first night.

They watched it populate in the big man's email.

"What are we looking at?" Knut asked, opening it.

"I think I see the opening of a deep-sea vent?" Sienna said, moving closer.

"Perhaps," Ben replied. "But that isn't what I'm most interested in. Make it larger, will you?"

Knut did, revealing additional information at the bottom of the picture. Shots taken from a sub normally contained readings on the name of the ship, the depth and...

"There it is," Sienna said, pointing.

GPS coordinates.

"Punch them in," Ben suggested.

Knut did so using a map program and at once a marker popped up halfway between Hawaii and San Francisco.

Tapping the screen, Ben said. "We need to see what's there."

Sienna's eyes widened. "Is that safe?"

"Hell, no," Ben replied. "But staying home is far more dangerous. This is the last bit of proof we need before the truth can come out." Ben bent down and whispered into Knut's ear.

The big man nodded. "I can do that."

Then Ben turned to Sienna. "What are the chances your dad has a colleague with a ship anywhere near that point on the map?"

Sienna wavered. "Maybe Dr. Lisowski. She's been studying the migratory pattern of bluefin tuna. It normally puts her right in that area."

"Does she have a ship big enough to land a helicopter?"

Sienna threw him a look. "She works for NOAA, so yes."

He turned to Knut, suddenly aware the numbness in his right arm was crawling up his shoulder. As soon as it reached his chest, it could seize up his lungs and kill him instantly. There wasn't any time to lose. "Don't forget."

Knut winked. "I'm on it."

Sienna gave him another disapproving look. "It's not very polite to keep secrets."

"I'll tell you along the way."

"Along the way?"

Ben grinned. "Get a hold of Dr. Lisowski and let her know we're coming."

Chapter 54

The Sikorsky S76 sped east from Honolulu, travelling at over one hundred and forty knots. Ben and Sienna would soon rendezvous with Dr. Lisowski on the NOAA ship *David Starr Jordan*.

"Ten minutes," the pilot called out over the onboard radio.

There was nothing on the horizon except for the white foam from deep ocean swells. A six-hour flight from Seattle had gotten them to Honolulu. Now the helicopter was aiming to complete the journey, assuming, that was, they could find the *Starr Jordan* in all this open space.

Sienna's normal habit of twisting her hair in ringlets wasn't possible while wearing a helmet, so she had resorted to squeezing her hands into tight balls. Ben saw this and laid his own hand on hers. She glanced over, offering him an appreciative grin, and kept on kneading.

Ben didn't want to make matters any worse, but Sienna had every reason to worry. Assuming Lisowski was willing to co-operate, she could be jeopardizing her life and that of her crew by agreeing to investigate the ocean floor. It was a risk, but one Ben felt was well worth taking.

Soon, a white dot appeared on the horizon. At first it looked like a cresting wave before it grew larger.

"There she is," the pilot called out, pointing.

The ship was white, which explained Ben mistaking it for the top of a giant ocean wave. She was nearly two hundred feet in length with a helipad at her stern.

The chopper touched down and Sienna let out a deep sigh. Ben smiled. If they made it out of this in one piece, they'd need to fly back the same way they came.

The stifling heat wasn't the only thing to greet them aboard. So was Dr. Lisowski, with outstretched arms that she quickly wrapped around Sienna.

"I can't tell you how sorry I am to hear about your poor father." Although a full-fledged American for many years now, her Polish accent had never completely left her. The scientist's gaze shifted to Ben. "And you must be Mr. Fisher."

Sienna hadn't bothered to use an alias, he realized. Perhaps this far out to sea it didn't matter. Ben greeted her.

"Are you hungry?" Dr. Lisowski asked. She was a tall wispy woman with straw-colored hair and a gangly frame. "Let us begin by filling your bellies. We aren't far from the point on the map you indicated."

"Thank you for doing this," Sienna said. "You have no idea how important it is."

Dr. Lisowski shrugged. "You didn't tell me what we're going to see, but that's okay. Your father was a great man and he raised a wonderful daughter. It's the least I can do. If the people at NOAA raise any objections, I'll send them an email with detailed instructions on how to bite me." She smiled broadly, revealing a wide gap between her two front teeth. "But come, first we eat."

351

Ben and Sienna followed her below. The *Starr Jordan* had a crew of fourteen and could accommodate another thirteen scientists. She brought them to a small galley and sat them down. "François, bring us each a roast beef sandwich." She turned to them. "You eat beef, don't you?"

"And nothing else," Ben said, grinning.

"Good, good. Now, our deep-sea AUV can dive up to six thousand meters."

Ben nodded. "That should be plenty."

Dr. Lisowski folded her hands together. "Great, so what exactly are you looking for at such a depth? If it's your father's ship, I heard that was found near Antarctica." Visible goosebumps formed on her bare arms from the mere thought.

"What may lie below is one of the targets he was looking for," Ben explained.

"A target you sent him to investigate?" Like the woman's features, her questions were pointed.

"That's right," Ben said, trying not to stammer. He hadn't anticipated her knowing about that.

"Mr. Fisher, I also hear rumors the police are looking to talk to you about a murder."

"He didn't do it," Sienna blurted out with perhaps a little too much force.

Dr. Lisowski was bobbing her head, weighing the situation.

Sienna took her hands. "I know this is going to sound crazy, but we believe there may be something down there not put there by humans."

Ben cringed.

"Put there by who then?" Dr. Lisowski asked. A logical question given what had just been thrown her way.

352

"A civilization more advanced than our own," Sienna went on. "A civilization that may not have our best interests at heart."

"That's one way to put it," Ben said. He had felt avoiding the true reason for their visit here was the best strategy for gaining Lisowski's trust and cooperation. If she thought they were crazy, they'd be done for.

"Let me tell you something," Dr. Lisowski said. "Ten years ago, after my team first got our hands on the *Starr Jordan*, we were so excited that we pushed out of San Francisco Bay and into the Pacific the same morning. The ship was less than two hundred nautical miles off the coast when the captain called me to the bridge. He sounded a bit weird, which made me think there was a problem with the ship. But I was wrong. One of the deck hands had seen a bright light low on the horizon. You see, the crew is trained to spot the difference between a star and a plane. They wouldn't be much good at their job if they couldn't. Eager for a better look, the captain and I shuffled out onto the bridge deck, each of us peering through a giant pair of marine binoculars. Without a word of a lie, what I saw that day took my breath away. A ship at least two soccer pitches long was just sitting there, sparkling like a jewel in the sky. But looking through the glasses you could see it wasn't just lights, it had a shiny metal shape and it was carrying something big beneath it. Together they descended toward the water and disappeared. I looked for a long time after that and never saw it again. Since that day, I've always wondered if it was one of ours."

Ben's eyes fell. "I'm afraid not."

"But you can't say they mean us any harm," Dr. Lisowski said, a touch of eagerness in her voice.

"That's what we're here to find out," he replied, as evenly as he could.

A voice came over Dr. Lisowski's radio. "We've arrived at the location."

"Copy that, John." She looked at them. "Let's get that answer then, shall we?"

•••

Deckhands lowered the unmanned sub into the water while Ben, Sienna and Dr. Lisowski convened in the control room. Before a wall of nine monitors sat the sub driver. A joystick rested by his right hand. Bubbles fluttered by the three sets of cameras as the sub made its descent to the bottom. The driver called out the depth every one thousand meters. Several tense minutes passed as the view through its cameras got darker and darker.

"Switching on LEDs," he said.

"How long until we reach the bottom?" Sienna asked.

"Nine hundred meters."

Dr. Lisowski began to look doubtful.

Sienna noticed the change. "Is something wrong?"

"Only that we've swept the area with radar already and haven't detected a thing," she said. "I'm starting to worry we may be wasting our time."

Sienna was just about to tell her to be patient when the vague shape of something large loomed out at them from the silty depths.

"You recording this?" Ben asked.

"Damn right I am," the driver replied.

"Get in closer, would you?" Dr. Lisowski ordered him, pushing herself right next to the screen for a better look.

The AUV continued to descend, bringing the edges of something immense into view. A moment of breathless silence passed as each of them attempted to ascertain what exactly they were seeing. Not only huge, but growing larger by the second. It looked as though an enormous dart, two hundred meters high, had been driven into the ocean floor. Surrounding the dart was a metallic-looking skin that was inflating.

"What the hell is that thing?" Ben asked, pinpricks of fear dancing up his arms. "And what on Earth is it doing?"

Dr. Lisowski lowered her glasses in utter astonishment. "It appears to be filling with ocean water."

Sienna tapped the AUV operator on the shoulder. "Can you zoom in a little near the top?"

Slowly the image narrowed as it drew closer, revealing a nozzle fifty feet wide.

"But look," she said, pointing at the screen. "There isn't any disturbance at the opening. If this thing was sucking in water, surely the signs of it would be obvious."

"What then?" Ben asked.

"What's beneath that spot?" Sienna wondered. "A metallic bladder able to withstand the crushing forces at this depth. Whatever this is, it wasn't put here by us."

With every second that passed, the object grew larger.

"Well, it's gorging on something," Ben said, stating what was already fairly blatant. "The question is what? And how full will that bladder get before it bursts?"

"Is there anything special about this spot?" Sienna asked Dr. Lisowski again, whose gaze was still fixed on the screen.

"Special?"

"Yes, deposits of anything important," she clarified. "We were told the aliens were mining for rare earth minerals beneath the ocean floor."

Dr. Lisowski shook her head. "No, the only thing in this area is a large methane hydrate deposit, but I don't see why…"

Fear lanced through Ben's heart. "Is the *Starr Jordan* directly over this thing?"

Dr. Lisowski's eyes went to the radar. "Yes, why?"

"Tell the captain to move the ship as fast as he can."

"Not until you tell me why," she shot back.

"That bladder isn't filling with water," he shouted. "It's filling with methane and once it gets released it's going to create a massive air pocket that will swallow the entire ship. Now tell the captain to get us out of here before it's too late."

"What about the NAV?" the driver said. "If we lose connection, we may lose it forever."

"The NAV or your life?" Ben cried. "Which would you rather have?"

The bladder's expansion was starting to slow.

"Hurry, dammit!" Ben said, more than happy to risk hurt feelings if it might get them to safety.

Dr. Lisowski picked up the radio and called the captain.

"Yes?"

"Don't ask questions, just move the ship at least a mile off our present plot point and do it quickly."

"What about—"

"No questions, I said. Now do it."

"Yes, ma'am."

Already tiny bubbles were trickling up from the opening at the top of the alien structure.

The ship began to vibrate as the engine throttle was set to full. The force of the forward movement pushed them all back. Ben caught the back of the driver's chair with one hand and Sienna with the other.

The NAV wasn't connected by a cable, so the image was still coming in and would until they went out of range. The bubbles were growing more numerous. Watching it in mute horror, Ben and Sienna could only pray they had enough of a head start to escape the worst of it.

Suddenly, the image from the NAV shook as the bladder's walls contracted, releasing a massive bubble.

"Here it comes," Ben said. "How long before it reaches the surface?"

The driver sat frozen in place, white-knuckling the joystick.

Ben repeated the question, this time more forcefully.

"I don't know," the man stammered. "A minute. Maybe less."

They were all silently counting in their heads. Was this how the *Archipelago* had gone down before it had been crushed into a ball and somehow deposited thousands of miles from the scene of the crime? If an Icarian craft did happen upon the sunken ship, it would have made sense for them to move it or risk their machine being discovered.

Thirty seconds.

Ben pulled Sienna in close. Her arms were wrapped around him almost tight enough to cinch the air from his lungs. They looked into each other's eyes and Ben felt that if he had to go, there was no one else he'd rather have by his side when it happened.

The ship began to shudder and list, first starboard then to port. Then the bow rose in the air, as though they were cresting a giant wave, when in reality, part of the ocean had likely disappeared beneath them.

"Hold on tight," Ben shouted.

Like a swinging mallet, the ship came back down, kicking up sea spray on either side of her, throwing everyone forward violently.

There was a terrible smell in the air as they rose to their feet. Sienna was the first one up and helped Dr. Lisowski and then Ben.

Shaking his head, Ben said. "Is this heaven?"

Sienna punched him in the left pec. "You nearly got us killed coming out here," she said.

"And managed to save us," Dr. Lisowski said, rubbing the side of her head where it hit the floor. "It's been quite a trip for you, hasn't it?"

Ben smiled and stepped out into the blinding sunlight and oppressive Pacific heat. Behind the ship the water was still roiling. Luckily, the deck chains had secured the chopper to the helipad or they might have lost their ride home. He was thinking about the methane bubble, wondering what it all meant. The odor out here was terrible. Like a giant rotten egg sandwich. It meant the methane had been mixed with sulfur, probably from decaying plant matter, since the former was generally odorless.

"Have you thought of changing your name to Ben 'Close Calls' Fisher?" Sienna asked, appearing next to him.

He laughed. "I might not have any other choice. How much time before the Icarian delegation arrives?" he asked her, still watching the turbulent water behind them.

Sienna pulled out her phone. "Twenty-one hours."

"A helicopter ride back to Hawaii and then on to Arizona," Ben said. "We might not make it."

"Well, that's weird," Sienna said, still staring down at her display. "I got a text message all the way out here."

Ben smiled. "There's a sign in the mess hall for CellSea, an at-sea provider the NOAA uses. Who's it from?"

Her face scrunched up, Sienna said, "Dr. Zhou." She dialed his number and flipped her hair as she pressed the phone to her ear.

Ben was pointing to the palm of his hand. Understanding flashed on her face and she put the call onto speakerphone.

"Dr. Zhou, it's Sienna, how are you?"

"I'm as good as can be expected," he replied. "It's great to hear your voice. Listen, I wanted to let you know about the testing we did on that biological sample from Site 17."

"The alien body?" she said.

Ben was listening with great interest.

"Well, that's the thing," he replied. "You see, my background is with the ancient Denisovans."

"Yes, I'm familiar with them," she said. "An ancient cousin to *Homo sapiens*, like the Neanderthal."

"That's right, I've spent a long time tracing back our hominid family tree and there's always been a distant branch that's been missing. You can plot each point along the journey as the tree branches out from furry mammals to an assortment of different species. My point is, the alien being we uncovered in China isn't an alien at all. He was a distant human ancestor who appears to have lived around thirty million years ago."

The news hit her like a strong wind. She took a second to catch her breath, one filled with the rotten smell of methane. "The dates match with the findings around Site 17. Okay, Dr. Zhou. Thank you for telling me."

"Don't hang up," Ben said.

Sienna looked at him. "What is it?"

"Ask him what the air was like back then."

"Thirty million years ago?"

"Yes, ask him."

Sienna did.

"Well, back then the planet was much warmer," Zhou said. "CO_2 and methane levels were considerably higher, but it appears we're well on our way."

Ben was staring at her, watching the light begin to shine behind her eyes.

"The Icarians and the people who built that space elevator at Site 17 were one and the same," Ben started to explain.

"But the physical differences," Sienna said, perhaps not wanting it to be true.

"Joe told me how the moon base was a patchwork of old and new. Parts of it had been damaged by meteors, but there was no telling how long ago that had happened. The Icarians used the moon as a springboard to leave our solar system. Either they all left or the ones who stayed behind didn't make it."

"Those who left," Sienna continued, "likely went to a planet with an atmosphere similar to that of Earth thirty million years ago, but with slightly less gravity."

"That's right, and over time it must have had the effect of elongating what was once a stout species."

"But why didn't they just keep coming back?"

Ben shook his head. "Who knows, maybe at some point after arriving, they also went through something like a dark age. It's happened many times with us on

360

Earth. Much of the Enlightenment was humanity rediscovering scientific principles known to the ancient world centuries earlier."

"On Earth," Sienna said, pushing the ball along, "we knew about that past through myth and legend and in some cases written histories."

"Perhaps that was what Earth was to the Icarians, a myth of their home world," Ben said, a certain sadness in his voice. "And as soon as they had the means, they sought to see if it was real."

"How many expeditions have been launched searching for Atlantis?" Sienna wondered.

"The drive to find a person's roots," he added. "The home they once knew. Perhaps that's a drive common to all intelligent species."

Sienna shivered in spite of the heat. "The machine might explain why methane levels have been rising so rapidly. But what about CO_2?"

"What we saw today is likely only the tip of the iceberg. There are probably hundreds, maybe even thousands of these things beneath every sea and ocean, all of them in places too deep for us to venture."

"Except when we stumble onto them by accident," she said, clearly thinking of her father. She went back to what Ben had been saying. "As a greenhouse gas, methane is about thirty times more potent. I'm afraid to ask why they would do such a thing even though the answer is staring us right in the face."

"It is," Ben agreed. "But we need to say it anyway and get used to hearing it. The Icarians are trying to terraform Earth back to the way it was millions of years ago."

"So they'll be able to breathe again," Sienna said, starting the thought.

"And we won't," Ben went on to finish it.

Sienna grew quiet. "But they left the Earth a long time ago and now it's ours."

Ben's eyes flashed. "I'm not sure they see it that way. I mean, determining ownership over land has always been a problem, even for humans. Just ask the Native Indians in the Americas or the Palestinians. From the Icarian point of view, they were the original inhabitants and the planet's rightful heirs."

Looking down, Sienna said, "Well, one thing's for sure. This was not the alien invasion anyone was expecting. It certainly eliminated the logistical problems of transporting millions of troops across the vastness of interstellar space."

"Millions of troops they may not have," Ben interjected. "And why bother when you can appeal to humanity's greatest strength and their most glaring weakness? Greed. An insatiable hunger for anything and everything. It has made us strong and is now being used in the most twisted of ways to destroy us."

Chapter 55

By the time Ben and Sienna landed in Flagstaff, Arizona, the sun was already arcing on its final descent, turning the sky into a breathtaking work of impressionistic beauty. But the gorgeous view only distracted from the more pressing reality. In less than two hours the Icarian delegation would land.

"Is everything in place?" Ben asked Sienna after she got off the phone.

"Looks that way. What about on your end? Do you think she'll be there?" Sienna was talking about Lori.

After he had paid her a visit, Lori had apparently confronted Granger and gotten him to 'fess up regarding the true origin of the NED technology. She had also pressured him into inviting her to what was ostensibly a diplomatic mission. All of which worked in their favor because with the high level of security around the Barringer Crater landing zone, they were going to need someone to get them inside.

"Don't worry," Ben assured her, waiting for the fasten seatbelt sign to go out. "She'll be there."

"Although after what she's already done," Sienna hit back, "I don't see how you can trust her."

"I'll never forgive her," Ben admitted. "But when she had the opportunity to have me killed, she didn't take it. When I met with her in Seattle, I could see she was looking for something I couldn't give her."

"Forgiveness?"

Ben shook his head. "Absolution."

They disembarked and made their way through the terminal.

Waiting for them by the front door was Lori, a tense look on her face. She was holding two garment bags.

"What's wrong?" Ben said, suddenly concerned.

"We need to hurry," Lori told them. "Granger says they might be coming early."

"The Icarians?"

Lori nodded emphatically. "Yes, and it's nearly an hour's drive from here." She motioned to the bags. "I brought what you asked for."

Sienna looked puzzled.

Inside each bag was formal clothing.

"It's a diplomatic mission, after all," Ben reminded her. "We might stick out a wee bit showing up in jeans."

Ten minutes later they were heading to Lori's SUV in the terminal parking lot. Sienna was fixing her hair. The low-cut navy-colored dress she was wearing made her look stunning.

Ben tried not to stare, instead tugging the cuffs of his shirt out from under his black suit jacket.

"You look exquisite," he told her, unable to hide his admiration any longer.

"Huh?" she said, preoccupied. "Oh, yeah, you don't look half bad yourself."

He laughed. "Gee, thanks."

A brief and much-needed moment of levity in what might be the most consequential moment in human history. It was no exaggeration to say that the fate of the human race truly was dangling by a single, tenuous thread.

Moments later, they reached Lori's SUV in the terminal parking lot and started to get in.

"Maybe I should drive," Ben suggested.

"Sienna should be the one," Lori countered.

She and Ben exchanged a look.

"That actually makes a lot of sense," Ben said. "If we were going to any other function, the CEO and COO of Neural-Sync would be in the back. In which case, you'd be our driver."

Ben wished he had a camera to snap a picture of the daggers in Sienna's eyes.

"But are you a good driver?" Lori wondered, probably against her better judgment.

Sienna got in the front seat and grinned. "Just watch me." She started the SUV's electric motor and swung out of the parking spot in record speed, her tires screeching to a halt as the nose of the vehicle evened out. "Buckle up," she said and floored it.

•••

It was hardly an exaggeration to say that Lori's crushing grip on his hand lasted the duration of the ride to Barringer Crater. The landmark was just off the famed Route 66, having formed fifty thousand years ago when a hundred-and-sixty-foot chunk of nickel-iron slammed into the Earth's crust, leaving a hole in the ground a thousand meters wide and nearly two hundred deep. NASA was said to have used the crater as a training ground for the Apollo missions in the 60s and 70s, which lent the location a special sort of irony not lost on any of them.

Sienna pulled off Route 66 and eventually up to a checkpoint right outside the visitor's center, a collection of flat-roofed red brick buildings that hugged the crater's edge.

The guard stepped forward. He was military, dressed in desert cammies.

"Mr. and Ms. Fisher from Neural-Sync," Sienna said in as stoic a voice as she could muster.

The guard motioned for Lori to roll down the window.

"I'm sorry, ma'am, but I don't see Mr. Fisher on the list."

"That's impossible!" Lori snapped. "He's the head of our company. Get Mr. Granger on the phone."

"Granger?" the guard said with noted anxiety.

"He's heading this delegation," she continued. "And I'm sure he won't appreciate having his time wasted over a simple clerical error."

The guard glanced down at his list and back at Lori, who stared back at him unflinching.

"All right then, go ahead."

She nodded and Sienna drove through.

They arrived at the reception and Sienna programmed the car to go park itself. All three of them got out and entered to find the place mostly empty. A handful of men and women in suits stood around mingling, many of them titans of tech industries like their own, each and every one of them perhaps beholden over the years to the same Icarian handouts that had put Neural-Sync on the map.

A woman in the main reception was handing out air filters.

"Why do we need this?" Lori asked. "Isn't the event being held in here?"

366

"I'm afraid not," the hostess said, pointing to the long glass catwalk. At the end of it was an elevator that would bring them down to the crater floor.

The three of them headed toward the elevator. It was dark outside and the lights in the crater illuminated a group of about fifty people gathered before a screen twenty feet wide. A master of ceremonies was explaining the origin of the crater and the importance of the decennial event about to take place.

Ben, Sienna and Lori each equipped their transparent air filters as the elevator doors let them out at the crater floor.

Ben spotted Granger mingling with the crowd and his fist instinctively closed around the USB in his pocket, the one that contained all of the evidence downloaded from his NED, along with the video of M framing him for murder. While that might help clear his name, it was only the appetizer for the main course—the video of the Icarian device they had taken in the Pacific. An image was worth a thousand words, as they say, and Ben was certain this would expose the Icarian deceit and their plan to terraform the planet right out from under our noses.

A blonde woman wearing a tuxedo and holding a silver platter asked if they'd like an hors d'oeuvre. Ben shook his head, his gaze still locked on Granger.

"We'd love one," Sienna said, elbowing Ben in the ribs.

He took one and as he did let the USB slip onto the tray. The waitress smiled and walked away.

"How was I supposed to know what Willow looked like?"

Ben and Sienna had only just found out that Willow and her overzealous eco-warrior friends had been

367

working to infiltrate this most recent Icarian delegation for several years.

Sienna shrugged. "Well, now you know. I can't wait to see everyone's faces when they feed the videos onto the big screen."

For Ben, there was only one person whose expression he wanted to see and that man was less than twenty feet away. Granger was being pushed around in a wheelchair replete with two oxygen tanks. The smug bastard wouldn't know what hit him.

The plan called for Willow to hand the USB to Birch, who would then make his way into the broadcast booth and put it up.

Ben started heading for Granger when Sienna grabbed his arm to stop him. "What are you doing? You're going to blow our cover."

Lori also begged him to stop. "At least wait until you've exposed the truth."

"I don't want to give him a chance to tuck tail and run away when everything turns sour."

A digital clock above the giant screen was reading five after nine. Cameras set up on the roof of the visitors' center were scanning the skies for signs of the approaching Icarian craft. Soon, the image on the screen changed to a glowing ball of light. The Icarians were coming. The crowd began to cheer. Ben pushed through clumps of people, many of them pointing and smiling with feverish anticipation—men and women at the top of their professional and social game all reduced to giddy children at Christmas.

"What do you think they're bringing us this time?" one woman asked.

"I heard from a reliable source it would be fusion power," someone else replied.

"Is that so?" said another. "A friend in the Pentagon told me under the strictest of confidence anti-gravity was definitely next."

Ben reached Granger and stood before a man who seemed to have aged since the last time they met.

The old man drew in a deep gulp of oxygen, the edges of his lips curled into a sick-looking expression that might have passed for a grin. "I didn't think you had the balls to show your face around here."

Ben's eyes flicked up to the screen. It was still showing the incoming craft, making a slow, dramatic descent. A large X on the crater floor marked the proposed landing site.

"Enjoying the show, I hope." Granger said, after he'd decided Ben wasn't going to dignify his first question.

"Not as much as you're about to."

The old man's expression changed. "I hope you haven't done something stupid. I'm sure even you wouldn't deny humanity a technology that could help save us."

"Or enslave us," Ben shot back.

"Oh, you're not on about that again, are you? Listen to me very carefully," Granger said, his voice thick and gravelly. "Lori disobeyed a direct order and could be court-martialed and shot."

"Court-martialed?" Ben wondered if the old man was losing his mind. "That's a military punishment."

Granger nodded. "That's right. Who do you think you work for?"

Ben remained quiet, not sure where this was heading.

"You've lost more of your memory than I thought. You don't actually think your real name is Ben Fisher, do you? Some know you by your codename instead. Mirage.

Frankly, I always thought that sounded a little pretentious." That smug look was back and stronger than ever. "That's right, your real name is Michael Mackay and you work for the Defense Intelligence Agency. You and the woman you thought was your sister were slotted into Neural-Sync as a means of disseminating the technology to the general public. Both of you agents lying to the world. By far the biggest irony has to be that the specter you've been chasing this whole time was you."

Ben felt the world spinning away from him. He brought his hands to his temples to ease the throbbing pain. The numbness that had been plaguing him for days had moved past his shoulder into his chest. It had also crept into his feet and left hand.

Two guards appeared with Lori and Sienna in handcuffs.

"Place him under arrest," Granger said.

"Can't you see he needs a doctor instead of shackles?" Sienna shouted.

"I'll be the judge of that, darling," Granger snapped, a rare break in his otherwise cool demeanor.

More security moved in from behind Granger, holding Willow and her two accomplices. One of the guards handed Granger the USB.

"They were attempting to upload this to the screen," the guard informed him.

No one around them noticed the drama unfolding because they were mesmerized by the Icarian craft, hovering a hundred feet above the crater's edge.

Granger crushed the USB as he had the previous batch of evidence. "Seeing your little videos is the last thing the world needs."

Ben shook his head. Although uncertain who he was, he knew one thing for sure. "All of you have been blinded. They aren't here to save us. They're here to watch us slowly suffocate."

One of the guard's radios came to life. A second passed before all of them were filled with frantic voices.

Granger turned to face the hovering Icarian craft. He waved at it with his yellowed hands. "Are they going to land or what? What's keeping them?"

"Sir, I'm afraid we have a problem," a guard said.

"Problem? What are you talking about?"

The giant screen flickered off the craft and switched to the drone circling the crater. News vans were streaming into the visitors' center along the crater's edge. Behind them a solid line of headlights stretched back in all directions.

A withering smile crept over Ben's features. True to his word, Knut had forwarded the files to every news station in the western world. Now there was no place left to hide.

The skittish Icarian craft blinked and then darted away, until it became just another star in the sky.

"What on Earth have you done?" Granger shouted, wheezing for air and descending into a fit of violent coughing.

"The world's been asleep for far too long," Ben said, his legs feeling weak. "It's about time they woke up." The last word had barely escaped his lips before Ben stopped breathing altogether and collapsed.

Chapter 56

Ben Fisher or Michael Mackay—he wasn't quite sure who he was anymore—woke up in the hospital. Sienna was sitting by his bed dozing off with a book in her lap.

"Hey, you're awake," she said, sitting up, her eyes twinkling.

He became aware that the numbness in his body had retreated to his fingers and toes. He held up his right hand and made a fist, examining it.

"The doctor said your extremities might take a little longer," she told him.

He tilted his head and winced from the pain at the back of his neck.

"Okay, Nurse Panov orders you to take it easy," she said. "To save your life they had to remove the NED from your brain. It wasn't exactly smooth sailing. Seems it's easier to get that darn thing in than it is to take it out. You've been out for a week."

Ben tried to smile. "I guess I got my wish, after all. What happened after I passed out?"

"Well, everyone tried to flee, but the road was blocked with pesky news vans." She laughed. "The story's been running all day and night for a week straight. The news outlets that didn't believe it at first are now playing catch-up, especially after the early birds caught clear footage of the Icarian craft hovering over the crater before it darted away. I also heard from Dr. Zhou again. He's helping Li and her family move to America."

Ben nodded with approval. "He stayed true to his word."

"I knew he would."

He eyed her. "Do my ears deceive me or are you starting to sound like an optimist?"

She slapped his arm playfully. "I'm trying it on."

"Well, it suits you," he said, winking.

Sienna filled him in on everything that had come to light over the last week. How Neural-Sync had been established by the DIA as little more than a front to inject alien tech into the civilian world. True to its compartmentalized nature, Ben and Lori had been lied to by Granger and the other heads of that secretive department they had worked for so faithfully. Granger had led them to believe the tech was stolen from the Russians or the Chinese. It was only after Dr. Lang reached out to Ben over the NED's inherent dangers that Granger's lies had slowly begun to unravel. And once the full, sordid picture had come to light, silencing Ben had become their main priority.

It had also come to light that the Icarians had been helping to tip the climate scale since the mid-1940s, about the same time UFOs had begun to take shape in the popular consciousness. Humanity's rising CO_2 emissions had provided the perfect cover for their plan to terraform the planet back to the way it had been all those millions of years ago. The promise of technology in exchange for mining rights had only been designed to enlist power-hungry governments on Earth to keep their activity a secret. Of course, not even Granger and the

DIA had known what was really going on until Dr. Panov's fateful trip to the Pacific.

Sienna watched him, smiling as she unfolded a sheaf of papers for him to read. "These came for you."

"What are they?" he asked, squinting.

"Bills. Lots of them. Mostly for plane tickets and cab rides." She flipped through them. "There is one here for one helicopter rental, and thirty grand for the taxi you trashed outside Seattle."

Ben cackled with laughter. "Listen, all I wanna know is whether we're still under arrest."

"Of course not. Especially after the surveillance video from your house proved your innocence. The world owes you. Although there is one slight problem."

He grimaced. "What now?"

"Well, no one knows what to call you. Ben or Michael." She reached behind her and came out with a folder.

"What's this?" he asked, still groggy.

"Your past," she answered, the words hanging in the air like a choking mist. "Everything from your childhood to your work as an agent in the DIA."

He thought about that for less than a second. "Michael Mackay died that day on the floor of his Seattle mansion. Take that folder and burn it. And if anyone asks, tell them my name is Ben Fisher."

"Well, if it's not too soon, Ben, I wanted to know what your plans are for the next few months. Every channel on the planet is itching for an interview, not to mention the lecture circuit."

"Geez, that's a lot to think about. What have you told them?"

"They don't want me, they want you."

"Bull, you're just as much a part of this as I am." Ben reached his hand out and Sienna took it. He squeezed it gently, staring into her eyes. "Tell them I won't go unless it's the two of us. Afterward we'll go on a long vacation somewhere."

Sienna smiled. "Just promise me one thing, Ben."

"Anything."

"No more boats."

Chapter 57

One week later…

Heads continue to roll in the aftermath of what some are calling the Icarian scandal. Oversight committees in Congress have vowed to punish high-ranking members of the intelligence community who withheld vital national security information from Congress as well as from the people of the world.

DIA senior agent Nathaniel Granger, seen by many as the mastermind behind the black project, was arrested earlier this week by military police. Bail was denied despite his pleas for leniency on account of his failing health. Inside the tribunal yesterday, Judge Williams was quoted as saying, "If the charges prove true, Mr. Granger, you didn't only sell out your country. You sold out the entire planet."

Now on to the Pentagon, where the Chairman of the Joint Chiefs is remaining tight-lipped about retaliation against the Icarians. He was able to confirm that military operations were underway to destroy the alien structures in order to prevent any further warming of the Earth's climate.

The Pentagon has also denied reports of nuclear detonations detected on the far side of the moon, although recent satellite imagery reveals signs of such an attack in the center of Tsiolkovskiy Crater.

And finally, an emergency recall is being issued by Neural-Sync, the makers of the brain implant technology that swept the globe less than a decade ago. After news of their role in the controversy broke, the stock price of the publicly traded company has plummeted. When asked to comment, the enigmatic CEO Ben Fisher had this to say: "Let it rot."

Real life versus fiction

While *Augmented* is a work of fiction, several of the elements that went into building the story were drawn directly from newspaper headlines and magazine articles as well as from medical and scientific journals. Here are just a few.

Metallic Hydrogen:

Most of us who learned about hydrogen back in school know it as one of the most abundant elements in the universe. The famous chemical formulation H_2O consists of two atoms of hydrogen and one atom of oxygen. But the form it takes when it's by itself changes greatly depending on the environment it's in. For instance, at room temperature it's a gas. Supercooled to minus four hundred and fifty Fahrenheit and beyond, it becomes a liquid. And in even more extreme environments, like the core of a gas giant, scientists believe hydrogen can be compressed into a metal. For many researchers, metallic hydrogen's unique properties could open up a realm of as yet unimagined possibilities. It's considered the holy grail of physics. Scientists recently claimed to have produced a microscopic quantity by compressing a sample of hydrogen in a diamond vice, although their results are hotly contested.

Neural Implants:

Expect to hear a lot more about neural implants over the next decade or two. As discussed in the novel, the majority of devices presently on the market are large and rather awkward. Not only that, but inserting them into the brain often requires holes drilled through the skull. If that weren't bad enough, keeping the device powered means wires going from the device to an external battery pack. Despite these challenges, the benefits to patients with a wide range of diseases and impairments is extraordinary. More surprising, hundreds of thousands of people are already using some form of neural implant. The majority help with loss of sight or hearing. Some devices can help amputees control robotic limbs. Others allow paraplegics to surf the internet. And that's only scratching the surface.

Although the depiction in the novel might seem fantastical, scientists do one day hope to insert neural implants via the bloodstream where they could be guided to critical parts of the brain. Moreover, they hope to solve the problem of bulky battery packs with nano-sized power plants that park in a vein and use the body's blood flow to generate electricity.

Neuros:

This one was loosely inspired by the Pokeman Go! craze a few years back. If you remember from the story, Neuros are the currency used by Neural-Sync implantees to upgrade various cognitive, emotional and physical abilities. The majority of brain implant stories you come across tend to treat the device's enhancement as either on or off. Flip a switch and you're brilliant. Turn it off and you're back to being a doofus. From a business point of view, incrementalizing the process would make the most financial sense. Already, it's a model becoming more and more common.

For me, the gradual improvement theme also struck at the very core of who we are. Love it or hate it, most folks are hard-wired to seek out some kind of competitive advantage. It's everywhere around us, from plastic surgery, to paying bribes to get your kids into college, to standing in line for hours to buy the latest technology. But rest assured, there was no judgment on my part in highlighting this tendency. I tend to approach my stories as something of an anthropologist, studying the bizarre habits and rituals of Western culture the way we once did to those we labeled inferior and uncivilized.

Space elevator:

First conceptualized by a Russian scientist in the late nineteenth century, space elevators may one day provide a safe and economical means of pushing humanity out into the solar system and beyond. The principle relies mostly on centrifugal force and consists of a tether with one end anchored to the Earth (somewhere along the equator) and the other end to a counterweight positioned in geostationary orbit. Of course, theories are well and fine, but we have yet to produce a cable strong enough to withstand the immense forces it would need to endure. One popular proposal has suggested carbon nanotubes, but recent findings suggest they aren't nearly as strong as we thought. Alas, the search goes on.

While a suitable tether remains to be worked out, there is still hope that to future generations, riding the elevator may take on an entirely new meaning.

Climate Change:

I won't lie, this was a tricky topic to cover, mainly because it seems these days everyone holds strong views on the subject. As I understand it, there are three main camps. The first holds that the Earth's climate is changing and humans are to a greater or lesser degree responsible. The second agrees that the climate is changing, but suggests it's simply part of the planet's natural cycles and humans aren't really to blame. The third group suggests there is no change, and that we only think there is because of fears ginned up by the media, which thrives on scaring the hell out of us.

Here's the thing, what I really wanted was to write a story about a sneaky alien race that comes to reclaim their old planet. And a big part of that plan involved terraforming Earth back to the way it was thirty million years ago. It was a story I wanted to tell because it sounded fun, and also raised a number of interesting moral issues. For example, do we own the Earth simply because we're living here at the moment? If we left and returned, would we view the current inhabitants as squatters or unworthy if they happened to be weaker than we are? A quick look back to the Indian Wars of the nineteenth century and more pointedly to the ongoing conflict between Israel and Palestine casts these questions in a new light.

I hope the path I chose leaves enough room for all sides to feel slighted, which would be a good thing. My job isn't to tell anyone what to think. My job is to tell a fun story that, for a brief moment, chases away the insanity of your everyday lives. If it leaves you pondering questions, great. If it doesn't, that's okay too. If you made it this far, it means you agreed to come along for the ride. I hope you'll find it was well worth the price of admission.

Harrison H. Schmitt & The Tsiolkovskiy Crater:

Harry's character featured in Joe Knight's recollection of the Apollo missions was based on a real astronaut. Although in real life he goes by Jack, I decided to make it Harry since juggling between 'Jack and 'Joe' could get confusing. Like his counterpart in the novel, Schmitt was a geologist who was a member of Apollo 17. The reason I'm including him here is because Schmitt originally lobbied to have Apollo 17 land on the far side of the moon, even suggesting Tsiolkovskiy Crater as a landing site. As part of his proposal, he envisioned a series of specialized satellites positioned around the moon so the astronauts could communicate with Mission Control. With budgetary and safety concerns looming, the plan was abandoned. I thought it only fitting that I did what I could to honor his wish.

Thank you for reading
Augmented!

I really hope you enjoyed the ride!
As many of you already know, reviews on Amazon
are one of the best ways
to get the word out and allow me to keep producing
the kinds of books you enjoy reading.

Want another thought-provoking sci-fi adventure?

Try the
Extinction Series!
or
The Genesis Conspiracy!

Phone #
U.A.
1-888-204-5506.

Made in the USA
San Bernardino, CA
21 July 2019